Turning on the Tide

JENNA RAE

Bella
BOOKS

2013

Bella Books, Inc.
P.O. Box 10543
Tallahassee, FL 32302

First Bella Books Edition 2013

Editor: Medora MacDougall
Cover Designed by: Sandy Knowles

ISBN: 978-1-59493-392-9

Other Books by Jenna Rae

The Writing on the Wall

Acknowledgments

Thank you seems like a small phrase for the love, support, and encouragement I have been offered by my family and friends. I especially want to thank Ben, Josh, Lee, Morgan, Dan, Gracie, and Pumpkin.

I have been the fortunate recipient of help, guidance, and insight offered by the brilliant Kathalina Chandler, Morgan Curtis, Karin Kallmaker, and Katherine V. Forrest. Many thanks, also, to the dedicated staff at Bella Books for all that you do.

About the Author

Jenna Rae is a California native who grew up in and around San Francisco and lives in northern California. She teaches English, mostly as an excuse to talk about books and writing and reading. When she's not writing, teaching, or reading, Jenna likes to garden, crochet, and try out new vegetarian recipes. She is the devoted servant of two occasionally affectionate and frequently sleepy cats.

CHAPTER ONE

She's young and maybe that's what has clouded my thinking. The rest have been at least a decade older, a thing I had not considered until just this moment. I stand over her for several long minutes, shaken by my failure to anticipate how her youth would affect me.

I try to shake it off. I was right to bring her here. I gave her all three tests and she failed each one. I take a deep breath and collect myself, the way my friend showed me. I scrub sweat from my face and neck.

The lost girl sees my hesitation and hope flickers in her eyes. It's cruel to let her think she might survive. Time to get it over with. Changing procedure is dangerous for both of us, and I don't like the recklessness of improvising. I developed the ritual carefully, and it works. I would be happier doing things the usual way, but it's her needs that matter, not my own. Besides, my therapist has been encouraging me to get more comfortable with spontaneity.

The lost girl stares at me, puppylike, and I turn away. Breaking eye contact is a breach of protocol but a necessary one. I fight the impulse to end it all quickly and abruptly, without even the skeleton of the ritual. It wouldn't be so bad for her—a second, maybe two, of pain and fear. But it would leave her confused and she would fail to achieve the joy of rest followed by the sweetness of oblivion. It is important that she knows her deliverance is a gift born of love.

"You're very special to me," I assure her when she whimpers in panic. Her eyes widen and I shake my head. "No, no, please don't be scared. I am going to help you."

Her eyes are black with fear.

"I love you," I whisper, smiling gently. She thinks then that I'm going to use her sexually and she retreats inside herself. This is good. Step one in the final stage, it saves her the sharpest edge of fear. She relaxes against the bulkhead and stops fussing with the restraints. The usual procedure would now take about twenty, twenty-five minutes, but the change—the result of my unexpected weakness—means we have only moments.

"I want you to understand that you are a good person, sweetheart."

Her glassy eyes reflect exactly nothing back. This too is good. It means she is inside herself, only vaguely aware of me.

"You deserve to be happy and safe, to know that you are loved. Do you know you are loved?"

No response.

"You are a bright and shining light, an innocent babe of the universe. I offer you the gift of peace."

I give her the first injection and watch her eyes ease closed. I shift her down to lie more comfortably on the bunk and check my watch. I count the minutes, eying a small drop of blood, bright in the crook of her inner arm. I blot the golden-pink skin with a tissue and fold it, tucking it into her jacket pocket. She looks like a true angel, her face soft, her hair a shining cloud. After the second injection, I watch the color fade from her cheeks and the softness turn to laxness. It's both subtle and distinct, the way life drains from the body. I mouth the words to the old prayer and let myself grieve for the child she once was and woman she should have been.

I complete the task, cradling her gently and carrying her up the narrow galley stairs. I have timed this precisely so that the moon is a faltering crescent in the somber sky and the current will pull her into the womb of the central Pacific. The splash is, as always, louder than I expect, and I watch the last inches of her drop into the ink with a pang of disappointment. Cutting out so much of the ritual made it empty and I feel the pull of defeat. I could give myself the shots, I think, and I would have peace too. I could be saved and never have to feel a moment's pain or grief or anger. My suffering could end, the way it has for so many others. I rub the pocket of my jeans, feeling the bulge of the used syringes before easing them out and tossing them in behind tonight's precious cargo.

"Her name was Paula. She is washed clean and will never suffer again."

As I hear my own words, I know I cannot follow Paula into the drink. How can I? There are others out there, thousands of them, and no one else is going to save them.

"I'm so tired!" I pull anchor and start up the motor. The sound drowns out my self-pity and I grin. The worst thing in the world is to be worthless, and I have spent much of my life a useless blob of cells, a soulless animal. Only for the last year or so have I known of my true calling. My friend has given me many gifts, but this is the one that has shaped me. I lean into the biting wind, feeling the current's tug for a moment. I drifted before my friend pointed me in the right direction. I let myself be taken along the current like a useless thing. But I have purpose now. I have a mission and will never falter until it is fulfilled. I take the wheel again and steer toward Marin County and the charade I must enact to fulfill my life's work. It is wearying, this playacting, and I used to chafe at the dishonesty of it. But my greater purpose subsumes any other considerations, as my friend so carefully explained. She was right, as she usually is.

I watch myself as if from afar and feel a rush of pleasure. My eyes are not mere orbs of seeing but cameras that show the reality behind the lies. My mouth is not simply an eating, talking mechanism but an instrument of the truth. My hands are not mere bundles of nerves, bones and flesh but perfectly formed tools of mercy. My body, my soul, my mind and my whole self exist for a single noble purpose, and I know I am one with all that is good and right in this world. I laugh as the defeat that has been sucking at my feet falls away. Alight with purpose, I fly across the bay toward the dark, fertile shore.

CHAPTER TWO

"How come you never listen to the radio?" Del had asked a few days back, and Lola had shrugged away the question, dismissed it with some blithe response about how she'd never actually owned a radio. Del had two stereos and a radio in nearly every room, and she even wanted to get some special thing on her new motorcycle to listen to music on that. Del wasn't even aware of it, but she sang along with the radio all the time. She had a surprisingly sweet, clear voice, a little low, a little husky sometimes. It was incredibly sexy, the way her voice danced along a melody and her body bounced with the rhythm. Lola had more than once stared rapt at Del's shaking head and curved lips, letting the sound of Del's melodious voice hypnotize her into sudden sensual pleasure and anticipation. Del was an attentive, sensuous, confident lover, a reality that seemed to correlate with her easy entry in melody and tempo. Lola was a terrible lover, she knew, and maybe letting herself ride some music would help her get in touch with her body and its rhythms. Now, glaring at the white screen of her computer, trying to ignore the silent metronome of the cursor, Lola thought about this.

"Maybe I live too far inside my own head," she murmured, sitting back. "Maybe I—"

The doorbell startled Lola, and she hurried to peer through the peephole.

"Janet?" Lola had seen Del's ex-girlfriend only once, in a crumpled half of a torn photograph. The woman before her was a shadow of the glamorous beauty from the picture. She looked gray, shrunken. Her long, somber hair hung in lank strips. Dark hollows ringed her beautiful almond-shaped eyes, and her full, wide mouth was drawn tight and colorless. Lola yanked open the door.

"Help me, please!" Janet clawed at Lola's arms, her chest.

"Ow! You shouldn't be here."

"Please, they're going to kill me. Please, please, please." Janet's eyes were fixed somewhere off planet, and Lola relented, pulling Janet in and leading the way to the living room. Janet huddled against her, shaking, though the day was warm and bright. Lola fought for calm.

"Come on, settle down. Tell me what's going on."

"If only it were that easy," Janet whispered.

"Should I call nine-one-one? Is there someone coming here now?"

Janet shook her head and stood gazing around the room. "You changed everything."

Lola frowned. "I'm calling Del."

Janet nodded and took a deep breath. "Yes. Please do."

"She may be pretty angry."

Janet made a face. "I know."

Lola watched Janet stride on suddenly surer feet toward Del's kitchen. She knew the way, certainly. She'd lived here with Del for, what, five or six months? Longer than Lola had, so far.

"Mind if I help myself?" Janet called the question over her shoulder, snagging a mug from the cupboard over the sink and pouring coffee. "I'm freezing."

Lola shook her head and watched Janet settle into a chair. "Someone's after you? You seemed pretty freaked a minute ago."

Janet met Lola's gaze, offering a half smile. "You think I was shamming?" Her eyes dropped, and her mouth settled into a grim line. "Trust me, I'm dead serious."

"So, you're in some mysterious, unspecified danger, and you expect Del to drop everything and help you."

It wasn't a question, and Janet's response was a shrug. The message was clear. No matter how hurt and angry Del might be, Janet's confidence was absolute—Del would help her. Was that confidence real, or was this all a show?

"Are you even in trouble, or is this all a big game to you?"

Janet laughed hard enough to spill some coffee on the table. "Don't you know? Everything is a game."

"Get out."

"Last time I checked, this wasn't your house. If Del wants me out, she can kick me out herself."

"She's going to, Janet. I guarantee it. Why put her through this?"

"Because I have to." Janet rubbed her eyes.

Maybe that was true. If she and Del ever broke up, would Lola be able to walk away? Or would she find herself desperate enough to play games like this? Of course, there was another possibility, wasn't there? Maybe Janet really was in danger. Maybe Janet really was afraid and desperate and in need of help. Lola tapped out her text to Del while watching Janet warm her hands on her mug. She felt a chill of her own and wished she'd decided to take Marco up on his offer of an outing. If she'd been at the movies with her friend, she wouldn't have answered the door. Janet would not be sitting here, looking like she belonged in Del's life more than Lola did.

"Janet, please think about this. You hurt her a lot. Now you're expecting her to help you, or to go along with whatever you want. What's going to happen?"

Janet blinked slowly. "All I can do is wait for Del and see what she does."

"But you think she'll help you?"

Janet shrugged. "How did you two meet?"

It was Lola's turn to blink. "She saved me from a creep."

"Ah."

CHAPTER THREE

"Wish they were all this easy," San Francisco Police Inspector Tom Phan commented, as he and his partner, Del Mason, walked out of the station together.

"Watch out," Del warned, only half joking. "You'll jinx us. The next one'll be impossible."

"Okay, ignorant peasant, what else should we do? Throw salt over our shoulders? Sacrifice a chicken?"

Del crossed her fingers. "Got it. Now we're covered."

Phan rolled his eyes and sketched a wave, and she watched him trudge over to his battered Toyota pickup. Their work on the latest homicide was finished, but the victim was still dead. Yeah, she'd been cheating on her husband, but he could have divorced her instead of murdering her. What, Del wondered for the hundredth time, was wrong with people?

Del shook off the question as she gunned the bike's engine, glad again she'd traded in her old Honda for the larger Suzuki.

Her neighbor, Phil had warned her, back when she'd bought the Rebel a few years before, "It's a gateway bike."

Del grinned, weaving through the snarled evening traffic. Phil looked like an egghead, but he knew his bikes. He was the one who'd recommended the newer Boulevard, and he'd been right. It sat higher and was more powerful, and it was definitely more comfortable, especially with a passenger.

There was a vibration in her back pocket, and Del used the break of a stoplight to read a text message from Lola: *Janet is here, says someone is after her. Come home, plz?*

Del shook her head, too nonplussed to respond to the text.

"I should answer that." But she wasn't sure what to say. She put away the phone. Lola would understand. She always understood, unlike Janet.

A few months into their relationship, Del stood Janet up. They'd planned to meet at Fisherman's Wharf and "do the whole tourist thing," as Janet put it. But Del got stuck waiting for an interview with an important witness. She should have called or texted, she knew, but she wasn't in the mood to listen to Janet's complaints. It wasn't the first time she'd stood up a girlfriend, and it didn't seem like a big deal.

At first it looked like Janet would be like Del's previous lovers. She said they could just go again the next night but warned that she didn't enjoy being stood up. But Del was delayed at work again, and she again forgot to call or text.

"It happens," Janet said with a funny little smile. Del knew what that smile meant, she'd gotten it from a dozen other girlfriends. It meant she was trying not to cry. Del had decided long before that this little smile was designed to elicit guilt and affection. Women were trained to manipulate people from the cradle on, and many weren't even aware they were doing it. Janet would, Del told herself, learn to get over her little hurt feelings and figure out soon enough that being with a cop meant being stood up, waiting for late dinners and not getting away with mind games.

Instead of a second rain check, Janet suggested Del call her when she got home from work the next night. Janet would come over and bring takeout, and they would relax in front of a fire. This sounded great to Del, who hadn't been all that thrilled to go to Fisherman's Wharf anyway.

The next night at six she called Janet, who said she'd be there in less than an hour. Del opened a good bottle of wine, took a shower, straightened up, and checked the clock. Janet wasn't there by seven, and Del was a little peeved. She'd worked late every night for a week, and all she wanted to do was eat and talk and relax. She tried to read, but the ticking of the clock seemed to get louder and louder. Del again called Janet and got no answer. She texted, no answer. Now she was getting worried.

Del called in to see if there had been any traffic incidents reported in the area between their homes. Janet rented a tiny flat in the Western Addition, which she for some reason persisted in calling the NoPa, as in North of the Panhandle—just the kind of gentrification-oriented bullshit she *would* swallow. Del was waiting for Janet to ask if she could move in and was getting tired of waiting for it. It was a hell of a lot more convenient to have the girlfriend live in than to have to deal with the back and forth of two places. Every woman before Janet had started making noises about moving in by the end of the first month.

"This is stupid." By the time Del had hopped on the bike and cruised up and down the dozens of routes between the Western Addition and the Castro, Janet was three hours late. Del called again, again got no answer, and went to Janet's apartment.

When no one answered her knock, Del picked the pathetic excuse for a lock. The apartment not only was deserted, it barely looked like anyone lived there. Del would wonder later why she wasn't more curious about that, but that night she just cleared both sparsely decorated rooms and zipped back home.

She paced by the front window, willing Janet to show up. She'd only been home a few minutes when Janet did just that. Del froze in place when the familiar little Fiat pulled up. Was she okay? Janet snagged a paper bag—food from their favorite Vietnamese place, locked her car and sauntered up the stairs while Del watched her from the front window. She didn't seem to be injured or in shock or disoriented. She didn't seem drunk or drugged, either. She certainly wasn't rushing to get to Del, who yanked the door open.

"Where the hell have you been?"

Janet just stood there, her mouth drawn in. There were tears in her eyes.

"It's awful, isn't it?"

Then Del understood. Finally. This was punishment for standing her up the two previous nights. Del slammed her palm against the doorframe and let her hand slide down. She went from fired up to deflated. She turned around without a word and walked into the kitchen.

She poured a double slug of vodka into a coffee cup and chugged it down, then did the same thing again. Janet stood next to her for a long time, saying nothing. Finally, Del nodded and pulled Janet in for a hug. They didn't talk or make love or fight. They went to sleep on the couch, huddled together, and they never brought it up again. The next time Del knew she would be late to meet Janet, she sent a text.

Shaking off the recollection, Del took a detour on the way home. Wanting to cool off, she went zipping across the Golden Gate Bridge and along the gorgeous Marin headlands. She opened up the bike and let the cold air and freedom push away the garbage in her head. Reluctantly, she headed back into the city and wandered toward Lola and Janet. On the last turn home, she spied a gleaming red Aston Martin parked in front of her house. She slowed and almost bobbled the bike. That car! She'd seen one in an ad and thought it was cool, mentioned it to Janet once, months before, during one of those silly conversations, lolling in bed and talking about nothing. One of those moments when it had felt like Janet really loved her.

Del grunted and slowed to check out the showy vehicle—it was exactly the car she'd pointed out, the DB9 Volante, and it was the kind of showpiece only a drug dealer or a movie star would drive. Or an heiress pretending to be a substitute teacher so she could use Del to dig up dirt on the police department. A job well done, including good details like renting a shithole of a flat in the Western Addition and driving a rusty old Fiat.

Props for an actress in a crappy play about a stupid, lovesick dyke cop. Del's breath turned sour and she grunted to herself.

She parked the Boulevard in the garage, knowing Lola would hear the automatic door, and took her time going upstairs. Lola was kind, compassionate, tenderhearted. She could be manipulated all too easily. Taking a deep breath and easing it out, Del made sure her expression was neutral before she went in. Lola can't help being a softie, she reminded herself, and Janet is the queen of manipulative bitches. *She sure fooled me and I'm supposed to know better.*

She looked around and saw no sign of anyone. She tensed and let her hand hover by her duty weapon. Then Lola was at the top of the stairs, wearing a white shirt and jeans, and Del remembered the first time she saw Lola at the top of those stairs. The first night they were together. She wore white then too. Del had thought of it as bridal then. Or was it a protestation of innocence? Janet wore white a lot, and she was no innocent. The two women were polar opposites. For the first time, Del realized there were things about Janet that reminded her of Momma—the desire for glamour, the impatience, the selfishness, the short temper. How had she never seen that before? What did Lola have in common with Momma and Janet? Del had to smile, thinking about it.

"Pretty much nothing. Two legs, breathing air, that's about it."

Lola frowned, clearly nonplussed by the mumbled nonsense, and Del shook her head. She took the stairs two at a time to pull Lola into her arms.

"Careful," she warned herself, unaware that she spoke aloud. "Don't crush her." But her arms tightened.

Lola squirmed and laughed, a nervous sound, and Del released her.

"Are you mad?"

Del heard the tremor in Lola's voice and forced a tight smile.

"Yes."

"I'm sorry." Lola shrank away.

Does she realize she's doing that?

"No—"

"I'm sorry, Del."

"At her. She shouldn't have put you in this position."

Lola shook her head. "She seems—"

"Okay." Del cut in, working to keep her voice and face neutral. "But notice, she came when I was at work."

"Ye-es. Uh, let's eat before we—is that okay?"

Del nodded, unsure what else to do. Where was Janet? Well, she decided, Lola would let that cat out of the bag when she was ready. Sometimes it was better to let people take control of a situation and see what they did.

Lola gestured at Del to sit down at the kitchen table and started serving dinner—chicken cacciatore, one of Del's favorite meals. There was a peach pie cooling on the counter, another favorite. Something smelled sweet and flowery. Was Lola wearing perfume? That was a first. Del preferred the way Lola smelled without perfume. She was wearing makeup too, a lot of it. Del's mouth tightened.

Lola started telling a long story about nothing, making it funny and light. Del nodded, smiled, pretended to listen, but her head was filled with a smoke-tainted wind. This wasn't Lola being sweet; it was a strategy. She'd tucked Janet away somewhere out of sight so she could soften Del up with dinner and kisses and sweet talk.

Am I really that scary? What does she think I'm gonna do? The chicken turned to mud in Del's mouth. After all this time, Lola was still paralyzed by her fears. She wouldn't talk about the violence that had colored most of her life, but Del saw its scars.

She hated the way Lola shied away from confrontation. She hated the fear in her eyes when Del seemed angry. She hated the way Lola still had to be reassured in bed, the way her first instinct was to shy away when touched. The anxiety, the nightmares, the little manipulations she wasn't even aware of—Lola's fear had become the third person in their relationship. There were times when Lola looked at her and Del knew she was seeing Beckett. Fearing Beckett. Anticipating angry words or a punch or a kick or a shove. Del pushed her plate away, ignoring Lola's intake of breath. She was exhausted from pretending to eat and was careful, easing out of her chair around the table to pull Lola up and toward her.

"I think we've avoided things long enough, don't you?"

Lola nodded but refused to meet Del's eyes.

"I would never get mad at you for being nice. You know that, right?"

An audible swallow accompanied Lola's second nod, and Del's stomach flipped when she heard it.

There was silence. Del resisted the impulse to crush Lola to her. How long would it take before Lola really trusted her? Would Lola ever really trust her?

"I love you."

"I love you too." Lola pulled away, straightening the chairs, and stood on the other side of the table.

Like she needs protection. Del fought resentment.

"Can we talk about it?"

"Yes, of course. Sorry." Lola busied herself, clearing the table. "I didn't mean to upset you. I'm sorry. Janet showed up this afternoon. Obviously. You saw that car."

Del nodded, her face blank.

"So," Lola continued, after a pause. "I know you don't want her here. I don't either. I know she hurt you. I hate her for hurting you."

Why does it feel so strange? I hate Beckett for hurting her, so why does it seem strange that she hates Janet for hurting me?

"I don't want to feel sorry for her." Lola's voice quavered. "She's the enemy. She's a terrible person, but—" Lola stopped, pursing her lips. "She's scared."

And that reminded Lola of when she was scared. That, Del knew, was what Lola meant. She was helpless and afraid, and no one helped her. Not when she was a kid and not with Beckett. Del's resentment seeped away.

"All right."

The surprise on Lola's face would have been comical under other circumstances. It made Del's stomach churn. She forced a smile onto her face, and Lola tried to match it but ended up grimacing. It looked like someone had put big pliers in the corners of Lola's mouth and forced them up and out. It was gruesome. Del looked away.

"All right," she repeated.

"You're not too mad?"

"I'll talk to her, is that what you want?" Del felt like she was luring a frightened deer back from the edge of a cliff. One wrong move, and the doe would leap blindly into the abyss. Didn't she always feel like that?

She was tired of luring the doe away from the cliff. She hadn't felt how exhausting it was until this moment. Not that it was Lola's fault, of course.

It's not my fault either. Del pushed away the thought and focused on Janet.

"Odds are, she's just exaggerating. She's a manipulator, Lola. I told you that, I know I did." She heard the bitterness in her words and took a second to temper her tone again. "But I trust your judgment. Okay?"

Lola nodded and Del let her breath out in a slow exhale. The doe was veering closer to her and further from the cliff. Again she felt resentful and then immediately guilty.

I'm pissed at her because my ex showed up? Nice.

"Where'd you hide her?"

Lola's nervous laugh bubbled up and Del made herself smile.

"The—my house."

"Oh." Del had been wondering for months when Lola would bring up the fact that her house was sitting empty down the street. Del had gotten in the habit, back in the first week, of picking up the mail there and bringing it home with her. She hadn't imagined she'd still be doing that come September.

"I just wasn't sure where else. I know you don't want her here."

The doe was edging away again and Del nodded with feigned enthusiasm.

"No, yeah, that was a good idea."

Lola offered an echo of the awful smile, and Del looked away for a second to erase the picture from her mind. She would love to never see that smile again. She pasted on a professional look and crinkled her eyes at Lola.

"You want to go over there, talk to her?"

"If that's okay." Lola got up and pulled out a plate of leftovers she'd wrapped up, adding a glass container of homemade chocolate chip oatmeal cookies.

"Are those just for her?" Del tried to keep her tone light, but Lola held out the cookies as if to ward off outrage.

"No, no. Of course not. I thought we'd sit down, have some coffee. Keep it friendly." She was nervous all over again, still holding out the jar of cookies like a talisman.

Del waved the cookies away and forced another fake smile.

"Sure, yeah. Why not? As long as I get some of those!"

Lola rewarded her efforts with an even worse phony grin. It was ghastly, and again Del had to look away. She gestured Lola ahead of her and took a deep breath to clear away her frustration and annoyance. Dealing with Janet was going to be frustrating and annoying enough all on its own.

"Did you go in?" Del asked this while they were crossing the street.

"What? Oh. Yes."

"Was it hard?"

Lola exhaled loudly. For the first time since she'd gotten home, Del felt like she was hearing and seeing the real Lola.

"I should have done it months ago. I've been self-indulgent, just pretending the house wasn't right there." She slowed and Del half-turned to see her face. "I'm ashamed of being such a coward."

"You aren't a coward. It was traumatic. Anyone would have been scared."

"Maybe," Lola conceded. "But a normal person would have gone home and dealt with it. I should have been stronger."

Lola's face twisted with self-loathing and Del looked away. She hated that look almost as much as she hated the kicked-dog look, sometimes maybe more. Was either of them worse than the horrible fake smile? Del shook her head.

"I've handled everything wrong. The way things started between us, I wish I could go back and do things right." Lola shrugged. "Ah, it's not important right now."

"Tell me, please?"

Lola shook her head. "Let's deal with Janet first. I just wanted to say that I'm done being a weakling." She fished out her keys to open the door, and Del followed her, wondering what exactly that meant.

CHAPTER FOUR

Lola had apologized earlier, holding out the bundle of clothes and averting her eyes.

"Sorry I didn't bring you any underwear."

Janet, standing naked and still shower-damp in the living room, had shrugged.

"No biggie. I don't wear any."

Lola had just nodded, unable to think of a reply. She'd left then, relieved both to get away from Janet and to escape the house she'd once loved. Now she was back again, and again she felt like a big, stupid, awkward lump. Janet was curled up on the big beanbag chair Lola had lugged over, and she looked comfortable and relaxed. The borrowed yoga pants and sweatshirt hung off of Janet's tiny frame. Even Lola's socks were too big on Janet. She was impossibly, inhumanly beautiful.

It would be easy to hate her, wouldn't it? Lola shook off the thought. She'd never had such a jealous, mean-spirited reaction to another woman, and it startled her.

"You." Del's voice was flat, and Lola followed her into the kitchen like a puppy forced to look at the puddle it had left on the carpet. Janet trailed after them, sighing heavily as though annoyed by the inconvenience of moving. She waited until Del sat, then sank into the chair across from her.

Lola unwrapped the food while Del played server, putting extra cream and sugar in Lola's mug, plunking down her own and Janet's unadorned. Janet pushed around the food Lola had brought, watching Del and ignoring Lola. Lola's gaze darted between the two women and she tried to feign calm.

Del was bristling with tension she tried to cover with obvious effort. She rubbed Lola's back as she sat next to her. She was vibrating with rage, and Lola had to force herself not to cringe away from that seemingly casual, too-heavy hand on her back.

Janet waited a moment, then pushed away the plate of food. Lola watched her carefully. Even drawn and tired, Janet was beautiful. Was she wearing makeup? It was hard to tell. She looked like a supermodel, with her huge, dark eyes, her perfect cheekbones. Add her full mouth, her delicate limbs and smooth, dewy skin, and you had an exotic beauty worthy of any magazine cover. It was, Lola thought, easy to see why Del had found her attractive.

Oh, Lola recalled, and she doesn't wear underwear. And she stands around naked in front of people without being shy or ashamed.

Why did I let her in?

It had been easier when Lola had imagined Janet as a club-footed, humpbacked Cyclops with bad hair and a disfiguring skin condition. She reminded herself again that jealousy was ugly, that beauty was only skin deep. It didn't do any good. If she were Del, she would choose Janet. Who wouldn't?

"Del. I'm sorry to show up uninvited. I know you're upset."

Janet's voice was low and Lola had to lean forward to hear her. Del, she noticed, sat back.

Janet's voice rose fractionally. "I had no right to come to you."

There was a long pause.

"Lisa has been very sweet," Janet continued. Lola could have sworn that her beautiful eyes, framed by suspiciously dark, generous lashes, were guileless.

"Lola," Del corrected, her voice too loud. Janet continued like there'd been no interruption.

"I know this is awkward for you both. I'm sorry for that. And I'm sorry I hurt you. I won't keep saying I never meant to. I don't want to fight."

Del inclined her head.

"I only came to you because no one'll help me."

Lola watched, but there was no reaction from Del.

"I'm in danger." Janet's eyes filled with tears. "Del, I need you."

Del reached out and held Lola's hand on the table. Lola could feel in the tension of her fingers, hear in the too-even timbre of her voice, her effort to maintain calm.

Lola pretended it didn't hurt when Del's hand squeezed hers too tightly. She watched Del's face get red. Lola's breath grew shallower and quicker and she tried to slow it down.

Del's words marched out, soldiers in a line. "Go. To. The. Police."

"You have to help me!" Janet shrieked, and she lowered her voice. "I did before I came to you. They look at me like I'm making it up! I'm gonna turn up dead, and it'll look like an accident or a suicide or something. You're the only person who can protect me. I need you, can't you see that? I know you think I'm exaggerating. Don't you think I can tell? But I'm not, baby, I swear."

Her eyes were wild, and Lola watched Del's face. It reflected nothing. This was like watching a game of chess, one in which she didn't know the rules or the pieces. Del's hand tightened further on hers, and Lola stifled a gasp and took a slow, deep breath, trying not to draw anyone's attention.

"So." Del's voice was slow and deliberate. She extricated her hand carefully from Lola's. "You're in danger. Bad people are trying to kill you. That's your story. Right?"

Lola's eyes shot a warning to Janet, who ignored her and nodded. Couldn't she tell this was a trap?

"So what you thought you would do..." Del paused, crackling with rage. "Is come to my house. Park your ridiculous car in front of my fucking house. Manipulate Lola into letting you in—"

She raised her voice a fraction as Janet started to protest, waited until Janet's voice trailed off. Lola chewed her lip, made herself stop.

Del tilted her head to the side and lowered her voice again. "Don't."

Lola shook her head, unaware until her hair swung into her line of vision that she was doing so.

"You came here when I was gone. You knew Lola would let you in if you looked pathetic enough, right?" Anger ebbed into Del's words, and she started again, slowly and carefully. "So you came here and got her to let you in. And if there really are bad, terrible, dangerous people after you, you led them straight to my home, to the woman I love."

Lola held her breath and stayed very still.

"You hid out here, and you left your car there. Who else would drive something like that? Don't think I didn't recognize it. It was a fantasy, Janet. Not something a real person drives."

"I *am* a real person." Janet's voice was low.

"The hell you are." Del's was low too and ice cold.

Del and Janet held each other's gazes, unfaltering, for a good minute. Lola knew they had both forgotten her presence.

Del struck, her voice barely audible. "You're nothing."

Janet's eyes filled and black mascara puddled and ran down Janet's perfect face.

Del sat back. "Poor you, always the victim, right?"

Janet shook her head.

"Let's pretend for a minute I believe you. Say these bad guys follow you to my house. They find a petite brunette. What do they do, Janet? Do they walk away? 'Sorry for the misunderstanding, we're not going to hurt you at all, little lady.' Is that what they do?"

Her voice was loud now, and Lola stifled the impulse to cover her ears, to hide under the table, to run away.

"Oh, no. Del, I never, I swear, I didn't think of it." Janet looked at Lola finally, as if seeing her for the first time. "I didn't mean to put her in danger, I swear. Oh, my God, baby, I didn't even think about it. I was just so scared." She sat back, shaking her head. "I just didn't think."

"That's not good enough."

"Del, I'm sorry. Lisa, I'm really, really sorry."

"You get why I'm pissed, right? Because you fucked me over. And now you think you have a right to come here and play games with us. And, Janet, her name is Lola. Do not get it wrong again."

Janet shook her hair back and glared at Del. "You act like I did something wrong! Dammit, Del, I'm a journalist!"

"A *journalist?*" Del's mocking voice seemed to fill the small kitchen, and Lola flinched against the back of the chair. "Bull. Shit. You fuck people for their secrets, then you screw them over in public and ruin their lives. Remember how we met? You got paid to seduce the first dyke cop you could find and get her to spill on the department, right? Lucky for you I was stupid enough to fall for it."

"That's not—"

Del stood, and her finger jabbed the air in front of Janet's face. "You're a spoiled, selfish, lying little bitch."

Lola couldn't take her eyes off of Del's finger. Beyond it, Janet's face was a blur.

"Right, I'm the bad guy. Yeah. Right." Janet stormed out of the kitchen.

Del followed, and Lola sat frozen. She listened to their voices overlapping in a discordant duet as they stomped, Del's boots thumping

and Janet's socked feet whispering, to the front hallway. Del's voice
was a low, undulating murmur. A stringed bass, perhaps? Janet's was a
trumpet, shrill, piercing and impossible to ignore.

"No, you're absolutely right, Del, I shouldn't have come to you. I
thought you were a cop, not a pouting, adolescent, self-righteous ass."

Del said something, and Lola shuddered at her tone, almost glad
she couldn't make out the words. Then Janet's voice cut through the
wall again.

"No, you're right. I get it, Del. I'm just a little too much for you
to handle. A little too complicated. I actually have a life besides kissing
your ass and washing your dishes, and you just can't deal with that, can
you? What you want is a little wifey to follow you around and sit bitch
on your fucking bike."

Del's voice dropped to a low, indistinct rumble that ended in
an angry question. Lola pushed her palms into the tabletop so she
wouldn't put them over her ears.

"No, forget it, go back to wifey. She doesn't mind you being such
a fucking bully. She'll kiss your ass all day long. And you love it. You're
the big, bad cop on top, right?"

Del said something low and sharp, but Janet's words flowed over
the top of Del's.

"She's your perfect woman, a pathetic little doormat you can walk
all over. Well, fuck her and fuck you too. I'll find somebody to help
me or I'll get killed. Who really gives a shit? Obviously not you, baby."

The door slammed.

Lola sat frozen at the table. Del came in and stood next to her.
They were silent for several minutes, and Lola felt Del pulling her.
She wanted to resist though she couldn't have said why. Still she let
Del pull her up and into a tight embrace. She forced herself to rest
her head against Del's shoulder. She felt Del's body shaking and she
swallowed hard. There were things they needed to address, but Lola
couldn't make herself talk about any of them.

"Why did I let her in?" Lola asked this over and over, not realizing
that she did so aloud until she saw her breath blow a strand of her hair.
She looked up at Del's blank expression and had to look away. Del was
unaware of her existence, let alone her words.

CHAPTER FIVE

The hard part was staying focused on running. Del tried to stop her mind and body from racing but failed at both. She was sprinting faster and faster, pulling a pace that would hamstring her in about two more blocks if she didn't slow down.

"Cool it, cool it, cool it," she whispered. She forced her legs to slow to a more manageable speed, a racehorse reined in by an internal jockey. "Cool it, cool it." The evening air was cool and damp on her overheated skin, and she felt the power of her legs, the strength and health of her body.

Finally, she hit her stride and was able to let her mind go blank. Unknown minutes and miles later, she was at the moment she loved best when running: the strange, intoxicating point at which the body no longer exists. She was flying, and there was nothing and no one in the world but herself and the air bending around her and the last of the day's light retreating before her.

She was an animal, running for pure joy, and she was free. *I am the wolf*, she thought. *I am the deer, I am the flying bird, I am the wind herself. I am all things wild and free.* She pushed her thoughts and feelings away with each thrusting foot forward and was emptied out and made whole again by the clean, sharp air.

As she walked the last several blocks home to cool down, Del went over the evening in her mind. She swung her arms, trying to warm them as her body cooled. What did Janet really want? Was she really in danger? Del couldn't be sure.

She loped into the house and headed straight to the shower, scrubbing down with practiced efficiency. Clean, warm and cursing herself for being a coward, Del rubbed her limbs with one of the new towels. Lola had at some point asked if she could donate the scratchy gray ones Del had used for nearly twenty years. She'd replaced them with soft, fluffy ones in shades of blue. Lola had taken all the hard parts, all the sharp corners and rough textures, out of Del's life and replaced them with comforting softness. Never without asking first. Which had seemed like simple courtesy until now. Now it felt like maybe Lola had been afraid of pissing her off.

Del slung the towel over the hook and ambled into the bedroom, unsure what she'd encounter. The unwelcome arrival of an ex was likely to inspire one of two reactions from a woman: a screaming fit or a weeping bid for reassurance. With Lola, it was hard to know. Del took in Lola's unreadable gaze and the way she hid under the embroidered comforter, another gift from Lola, given only after permission had been obtained. Lola's hand reached out and Del responded with urgent, rising need.

We should talk, she wanted to say, but Lola's lips were parted just a little, and her eyes were shadowed in the dim light. Suddenly, Lola's lightly scented skin, hidden, was a drug Del had to take. She barely noticed the towel dropping from her own body as she reached down to pull the covers off of Lola's. They were both naked, and Del was startled into laughter. Usually Lola had to be coaxed out of her clothes.

"What have we here?" Del was still smiling a remnant of her laugh. It shrank when Lola's mouth tightened into a scared, phony smile.

"Is this for me?"

Lola nodded. Her eyes were wide and dark, her skin pale and goose fleshed.

Del's breath caught, and her stomach fluttered. She let her fingers trail along Lola's arm. Desire coursed through her, and she leaned forward. As her lips grazed Lola's, she hesitated. She wanted to talk to Lola, not sleep with her. She knew Lola's little surprise was not about enticing Del but about distracting her and making her forget about Janet—a pathetic ruse, one she should call Lola on. If Lola felt so insecure, they should talk about it. Del had never let a woman use sex to keep her, a thing that would degrade them both. Del shrugged and kissed Lola again.

"I want you."

Lola started to say something, but Del shook her head. What was there to say? Lola would want to talk about how much she loved Del, about how she knew it must have been hard to see Janet. She would want to be reassured and petted and told she was the most important woman in Del's life. It was too much, all of a sudden. It was exhausting.

"Don't talk."

Lola's eyes widened, but she obeyed, of course. She would always obey, wouldn't she? Because she still believed that Del might turn out to be a monster.

"I don't want you to say anything." She held Lola's gaze until Lola nodded and looked away.

Even after all these months, Del always made sure to hold back, to be gentle and patient. The first time she'd reached for Lola, she'd seen Lola steel herself to not pull away. She had known Lola would be self-conscious and nervous, but she hadn't expected her pale, wide-eyed terror. She'd thought Lola's fearfulness that first time might be partly because of James, because of the trauma of his violence, so fresh that bruises still covered her body.

It had made sense that the first time would be difficult for Lola, especially after her difficult childhood and marriage and the sexual violence Del figured had been a component of both. It would also be scary, Del had reminded herself back then, being with a woman the first time. None of that was hard to understand, at the beginning. Lola would, Del had assumed, learn to trust Del, to feel safe and comfortable and enjoy their lovemaking. But this never happened. Instead her terror barely lessened as the days and weeks and months slid by.

It was becoming increasingly clear that Lola's fear was not a temporary thing. Del was shocked by the way Lola still watched her with wary eyes, the way she seemed to think Del might at any second turn into a violent animal. Whatever desire she felt for Del was still subsumed by her fears, and Del still wasn't sure how to deal with that.

"I'm damned tired of trying to figure it out."

Lola's eyes looked a question and Del shook her head.

"I told you I don't want to have a conversation right now." She stroked Lola's hair, reveling in the luxurious length and thickness of it. Like the towels, like the comforter, like everything Lola brought with her, her hair was an excess of sumptuousness.

"Mine," Del whispered. She slid down next to Lola and smiled at her. Lola started to murmur something, and Del shushed her with a kiss that deepened before she meant for it to do so. She felt Lola startle but ignored that.

"I've been babying you," she whispered into Lola's ear. Del kissed her again and again, her lips and fingers dancing lightly over Lola's skin. She waited for Lola to press against her, but that didn't happen. When Lola tried to cover her body with her hands, Del pushed them away and tried to hold her gaze. Lola looked away and said nothing.

She would never say anything, would she? Even aside from the fact that Del had shushed her, Lola was a passive recipient of Del's passion, not a partner. She would never be a true lover. She would never say no, even if she wanted to. Nor would she ever say yes. She would never reach for Del, the way Janet always had. And probably still would, if Del encouraged her. Irrational rage burned in Del's gut.

She pushed it aside. She felt Lola shiver and ran a trail of kisses down the side of Lola's throat. She pressed her lips against the point where Lola's pulse beat a ragged rhythm. She was so fragile, wasn't she? One nip of a tooth, and this skin would tear like paper, that artery would give way and yield Lola's life. This thought was disturbing and a distraction, and this too Del pushed aside.

When Lola again started to put her hands in front of her, Del grabbed her wrists and held them. Lola gasped but didn't resist. Her pupils were dilated, more from fear than from desire. But Del didn't want to see Lola curl her arms around her body the way she always did, to hide. To protect herself from Del. She let go of Lola's wrists.

"Don't. I already told you not to, didn't I?"

Lola nodded, but Del ignored her. She would do it again, even if she tried not to. She wouldn't be able to help herself. Del pulled her gaze from Lola's face. There was a small scar, a cigarette burn? It lay just under her left breast, an asterisk on her ribcage. Del rubbed her finger on the puckered circle, feeling Lola tense. This was an older one. Faded now. She kissed it. Lola's breathing went shallow, and her arm started to ease forward, as if by instinct.

"No." Del shook her head.

Lola's eyes were black, the pupils huge. Was there any desire mixed in with the fear?

"Maybe, maybe not. Hard to tell. Not sure how much it matters, really. Same effect, either way. I'm the bad guy, right? For wanting to make love to my lover?"

Lola looked away again when Del ran her fingers down her hip. She would always look away, wouldn't she?

"Pretend, then, if that's all you can do. Show me you want me."

Lola gaped at her, clearly unable to guess how to do that.

Del coughed out a barking laugh and pushed Lola into what might have been a come-hither pose. It was like positioning a mannequin.

"Or a corpse."

No response. Lola's eyes were closed, her mouth a thin line. Her nostrils were flared, and she was breathing in quick, shallow puffs. Del registered this, understood what it meant and shook her head.

Lola would never slip naked into the shower with her, never jump into her arms, never demand sex from her. Lying naked under a blanket was the very limit of her boldness, wasn't it? Not even boldness really. She'd undressed and decided to entice Del into bed, a childish attempt to keep Del from leaving her for Janet.

A long scar, a horizontal parenthesis, ran across Lola, almost hip to hip. It was an unusually large scar for a hysterectomy—and those, from what Del had seen, were usually vertical—and a strange shape, according to what Del had read. It was bumpy, thick. Like a rope laid across her in a smiley mouth shape. What had he used, a butter knife? From what she'd been able to dig up, Beckett had done the surgery himself. Had he felt like God, opening up the young girl, playing with her organs, holding her life in his hands? Del hadn't shared with Lola her speculation that the operation had been unnecessary. Had it occurred to Lola?

Del ran her finger along the scar, and Lola shuddered. There was no ambiguity this time. That was fear or shame or revulsion, absent any possibility of desire. But Del ran her finger back the other way. There was a hesitation mark just above one edge of the scar, a dot less than a centimeter in diameter. Had Beckett hesitated because he wasn't a surgeon? Had he even questioned whether it was wrong to mutilate the girl, little more than a child? Maybe he'd worried about getting caught.

Del had always assumed the old bastard just didn't like the possibility that his young victim might get pregnant or have a period or something inconvenient like that. Maybe she really had been suffering from a medical problem. Maybe Beckett saved the kid's life. Maybe back then he actually cared about Lola and was afraid of making a mistake and killing her. Del wished, not for the first time, that she could really know what had happened in Beckett's mind and what had happened between him and Lola. Had Lola loved him? If so, for how long? Did she leave him, or did he leave her? Maybe he just got tired of her when she wasn't a young girl anymore. Del sighed heavily.

"Why can't we just talk about it? Why can't you just tell me?" She didn't bother to look at Lola's face. There was no point, was there?

All Del would see there, all she would ever see there, were pain and shame and fear.

"That's all he left behind, right?"

Running from the juncture of Lola's left hip and thigh all the way up to the rib cage was a thin line of vivid pink that looked many years newer. It was too long to be surgical, too fine to be anything else. Del traced the bright, delicate-looking scar, trying to figure out what had caused it. She'd studied wounds and scars over the years, wanting to be able to look at a body and know what had happened without waiting for the medical examiner's report. She'd become better at decoding the scars over the years. But this scar didn't match up with any in her internal database.

"What's this from, huh? Why won't you tell me? It's not as big and bumpy as the old one, is it?"

Del ran her thumb over the long vertical scar again. She'd noticed it before, of course, but she'd pretended not to. Lola wanted her to pretend not to see the scars. There were so many of them! But this was the one she'd wondered about. The others, she could figure out. Gashes and slashes and bites and burns. Careless marks mostly. From spontaneous, misdirected rage or accidental excess or some sick rendition of lust. No real pattern or purpose other than to inflict pain, arouse sexual excitement or exert control. Some were old enough to have been from before Beckett, from the bastards in the foster homes. Some were only a few years old. Some overlapped each other.

"It's like I'm an archaeologist. This was from the Paleolithic Era. This from the Neolithic. These two crisscross but they're from two different times. This one's really old, but that one's only maybe ten or fifteen years old. Beckett. A corner of a table or desk, maybe? He pushed you? Punched you, maybe, and you fell against the table. Did he sew you up himself? I bet he did. No ER visits for you, right? Somebody might start asking why Dr. Beckett's pretty young wife had so many broken bones and black eyes and split lips, and he couldn't have that, could he? How many times did he break your nose? How many concussions? Why are you crying? I'm not the one who hurt you. I would never hurt you. Not that you'll ever believe that."

Del turned her attention back to the long, thin vivid scar, the one that was different from the others. It was like a line of pink paint drawn by a shaky hand. Had the old bastard been palsied?

"No," Del said aloud. "You were scared. Shaking."

Like she was shaking now.

"Not like paint," Del whispered. "Like a pen. A marker."

He *marked* her. He made her his property.

Lola covered her mouth but a sob exploded through her hands, and Del realized she was crying because of what Del was doing—it was obvious, suddenly. Del forced herself to stop looking at the scars. She sat up and leaned over to peer into Lola's eyes.

"I'm sorry. I—I'll stop."

The answer was a blubbering sob, an incoherent utterance that may have been a word but wasn't.

"I didn't mean to—whatever we are, it's me and pieces of you. That's all. I'll never get to see you, because you got broken into little splinters a long time ago. Didn't you?"

Lola nodded.

"All I want is to just once go to bed with you without feeling like I'm trying to lure you away from the damned cliff. Is that really so wrong?"

Lola shook her head as if in slow motion.

"But this is all you'll ever be, isn't it?"

There was a long delay, but finally Lola nodded.

"And I'm supposed to just accept that."

But Del was talking to herself. Lola was gone gomer, and all she'd left behind was her body. Del watched the empty shell on the bed.

"It's just me," she repeated tonelessly, "and the pieces of you he left behind."

CHAPTER SIX

The tension has been eating away at the lining of my stomach again, and I know it's time to move forward. There's risk involved in the testing process. I always have to meet the candidate face-to-face several times and often in front of others. What if some nosy friend or neighbor, ignorant of the value of my mission, interferes? What if the authorities take me away from my work? Who will save my angels, if I can't?

I take the medicine from the blue container, the one I can let people see. The other one, the red one arranged by my friend, that's the one that matters, the one I already took today. My friend showed me that movie with Keanu Reeves, and the pills are like that, illusion versus reality. For the hundredth time, I am struck by the extent to which my friend has been instrumental in helping me face the truth, even when I didn't know that's what she was doing. Maybe she didn't know that either. Maybe she's an instrument as much as I am.

In the red case rest the capsules my friend counts out carefully and cautions me against taking too many of. I have done that, once or twice, and lost a chunk of time. I know my friend is right, that losing time like that takes away from my mission. Still, I have enough recollection of the feeling of euphoria and relaxation from those lost hours and minutes to dream of recapturing those feelings now and then. Surely I've earned that? But my friend is right. It is the mission that matters, and I must not become too selfish to focus on my work.

I used to lose focus a lot, before that first time in the hospital. And I fought taking any kind of pill for a long time. They made me sleepy and foggy. At least that's what I thought before I realized that is how most people, normal people, think and feel all the time. It's necessary that I know how normal people operate. How else can I assess which candidates are true lost girls? How else will I winnow out the chaff from my angels?

Every time I begin the assessment process, I have to balance my hope that this lost girl is the one true angel who will free me with the need to focus on the girl herself. If I allow hope to blind me, I will end my work before it is done.

The doctors, the medicine, the therapy groups and meditation sessions and my own mind...all of these conspire to muddy my thoughts, and I must struggle every waking moment—and my moments are nearly all waking ones, even with the pills—to keep my mind clear. I can never be sure. I can never feel confident that my thinking is still pure and untainted by emotion and social norms and personal influences. Maintaining the façade I have chosen can color my thinking too, as it did to my friend. She was stained by the very evil she was attempting to eradicate! Again, as happens so often, despair tugs at me and makes me bow my head. I eye the red pills. One at a time, they keep me on task. A small handful would be enough to kill me. I could end the pain and fear and doubt and guilt. I could just stop. After all, I could save a thousand lost girls, and there would still be millions left, suffering and miserable. I am a tiny broom trying to sweep clean a very large and dirty world.

Ah, I have indulged my self-pity and doubt too long. My work continues, and I plot and plan as deviously as any villain. I am the instrument of good, I remind myself, no matter how dark my thoughts may be. I stand at the dock and watch my vessel bob up and down in the lapping waves. My angel awaits and I must not tarry.

CHAPTER SEVEN

"Lola!" Marco's rich, warm voice filled Lola's ear. "How's my best girl?"

"Looking for a date."

He laughed. "I talked you into it?"

"If you still want to go with me. I need to learn how to be part of things."

There was a long pause, and Lola worried her friend and neighbor might have changed his mind about going to the Meetup get-together.

"You know how to be gay, honey. You're doing it right now." He snickered. "Well, hopefully, not *right* now."

"Marco!" Why did it always feel good to talk to him? What was it about his company that made her feel like she wasn't defective or deficient?

"'Cause I'm not sure why you'd call in the middle of—"

"I'm so glad you're my friend," Lola blurted. "I feel like a real person with you."

"O—kay," he responded. "Come on, stop being such a tease and say you'll definitely go with me!"

"Okay. But if you back out, I'm not going without you."

"Deal. Wear something blue."

"You always say that."

"Sooo, take the hint."

Lola hung on to her courage until after she'd hung up the phone. What was she doing? She was actually going to meet a group of strangers, on purpose? At least she didn't have to go by herself. It would, she told herself, be fine.

"Right?" She could have sworn the word actually echoed in the empty house, and no voice piped up to reassure her. It was nighttime, and the house was bathed in twilight. How had she let the whole day slip by? It was like the old days, the bad days with Orrin, when hours would go past without Lola's realizing, and then Orrin would be almost home and she'd have to hurry, hurry, hurry to finish her chores before he came home and got mad.

"I went away last night," Lola announced to the empty house. It had been a long time since she'd gone away, since Christopher James came and scared her and hurt her and she was afraid he would hurt Del. "Maybe that's why I'm sleepy today." Going away, sliding down into the dark, safe hole in her mind where no one and nothing could hurt her had always left her drained. What did it mean, her going away like that? "Just, I'm a big baby, that's all. Del's right. I've been a big, stupid baby too long." The evening slipped by as quickly and senselessly as had the day, and Lola got ready for bed with relief.

By the time Del came home from work, Lola was asleep. Well, close enough to asleep that it would have been silly to turn over and greet Del. *I'm not lying*, Lola told herself, keeping her breathing slow and even. *I'm not avoiding her.* She felt moisture leak from her eyes and swallowed hard. Del muttered a soft something, and Lola held herself quiet and still. *I'm tired*, she argued with herself. Besides, what do I have to talk about with her? *Nothing. Tomorrow night, I'll have something to talk to her about. I'll tell her about going to the Meetup thing, and she'll know I'm trying to get better.* The night was endless, and Lola held herself still for hours, ignoring the way her neck and shoulders hurt. Every time she started to relax, she was startled back into frozen rigidity when Del muttered in her sleep or turned over or brushed against her. By the time the sun came up, Lola was shaking with exhaustion and wanted to cancel the outing. Then she got three texts from Marco, reminding her to wear blue, and she knew she couldn't let him down.

Marco pointed out various landmarks and attractions on their way to Pier 39, which relieved Lola of the need to make conversation, and it wasn't until they were striding toward the group that he grabbed her hand and squeezed it.

"They're gonna love you."

She shook her head. "No, they're gonna love you. I'm just planning to ride your coattails."

Marco's belly laugh turned a few heads, most of them male. Not one of the women who looked seemed to even see Lola. There were almost forty people in the group, nearly half of them women, and she didn't see a friendly face among them.

Is it really that they're unfriendly? Or is it that I don't know how to talk to people? I never have. Her stomach hurt, all of a sudden, and she fought a wave of nausea. She was sweaty too.

"Maybe I'm sick," she croaked. "I think I'm sick."

Marco shook his head but didn't look at her. "Smile, sweetheart. You're beautiful when you smile."

"I can't!"

"You're not sick. You're scared. Just ignore that and pretend they already like you."

"Okay." She tried to do that, she really did. But her smile felt fake, and her greeting sounded phony, which didn't much matter since no one seemed to notice her.

Marco spent the first several minutes of the walking tour trying to facilitate for her. Everyone was polite, everyone responded appropriately, and not one person wanted to talk with her. Lola felt exactly the way she'd always felt in groups, overwhelmed and distressed by acute self-consciousness. She knew no one was really paying any attention to her but still felt inspected and rejected.

The crowd splintered into smaller groups as they walked. Marco kept Lola involved in his interactions, but she knew she was being unfair. He wanted to make friends too, and she was getting in the way.

"Go," she whispered, when the majority of the group wanted to go in the wax museum. "I think it's creepy. Go, mama hen, I'll be fine, I promise. You're just holding me back."

Marco grinned at her silliness. "Meet at the restaurant at one?"

"Go on, have fun looking at your creepy candle people."

She trailed along after the diminished remains of the group but didn't try to engage anyone. By this time, she was staying only so that she wouldn't upset Marco or draw attention to herself by leaving early. She looked around. If she didn't talk to anyone, Marco would feel bad. She zeroed in on the least intimidating woman in the group, a petite blonde in a velour sweat suit.

"Hi, I'm Lola. What's your name?"

The woman didn't respond, so Lola spoke in a more forceful voice that, she realized belatedly, was still barely audible.

"Have, have you been here before?"

The woman's head slowly swiveled, and she eyed Lola coolly. "Are you talking to me?"

Lola nodded, blushing.

The woman made a face. "Of course. Haven't you?"

"Well, actually no. It's lovely here."

"Yes, it's very nice. Listen, have fun, okay? I need to catch up with my friends." The woman sped up. Apparently the conversation was over, but that was okay. Now Lola could tell Marco she'd talked to somebody. She let herself fall behind the group a bit more, wishing for the thousandth time that she knew how to talk to people and make friends and, just once, be a part of things.

"What a gorgeous day!" An elderly woman trilled this to her companion as she walked past Lola. And it was. The whole scene looked like a postcard for some fake Hollywood version of the normally gray, misty city. The sun was bright and warm, the sky a rich, brilliant blue. The water in the bay seemed to dance with light and color and rhythm. There were hundreds of people walking, skating and cycling around the stores, vendor stalls and street performers. Lola stopped to watch acrobats and jugglers, and she peered at elaborate window displays, and it was all beautiful. She stopped dead in her tracks when she saw dozens of pretty sailboats and excursion vessels crowded around the wharf. By the time she realized it was one already, she was a hundred yards or more from the group. She saw Marco looking around and waved broadly, hurrying toward him.

His face was such a welcome sight that she almost hugged him, but she didn't want to embarrass him.

"How was the creepy museum?"

"You know, it *was* a little creepy," he admitted. "You should have come, though. We could have made fun of it all together."

Someone called Marco's name, and he dragged Lola along, rejoining the group.

"You look like somebody stole your ice cream cone," he said through his teeth as they rushed along. "Didn't the other little girls play nice with you?"

"I talked to a lady," she crowed.

"Yes." Marco nodded with a wide, sardonic smile. "I can see you made a new bestie, and she's right here, isn't she? She's two inches tall and has wings and a magic wand, and if you shake her dust on you, you can fly!"

"I did!"

"What you mean is, you talked to someone for five seconds so you could tell me you talked to someone?"

"Oh." Lola pursed her lips. "It's that obvious?"

"Ye-es. Are they all meanies?"

"They're not the problem."

"Don't say that, honey." He linked arms with her. "Come play with the boys. We'll have fun, I promise."

While they waited for their tables, Marco introduced her to his new friends. He tried to draw her into the conversation a few times, but everyone was talking about places she'd never been and people she'd never met. Lola tuned them out and eased away from the crowd.

She stood with her hands wrapped around the guardrail and watched a woman in a bright red sweater bring in an old-fashioned fishing boat, slipping it gracefully through the narrow channels left by other boats and tying it up at the dock. Her short, dark hair, whipped by the wind, looked playful, but her movements were crisp, efficient, focused. Lola smiled.

"It looks like a commercial."

Marco eyed her. "For what? L.L. Bean?"

"Tampons."

Marco laughed loudly, and Lola flushed. "You don't have to babysit me. Go play with your friends."

"Oh, God, not yet. Maybe after a glass of wine. Or three." He inhaled slowly, and she mirrored him unconsciously.

"What's wrong? Everyone seems to love you. Which," she added, "is easy to understand."

Marco stood beside Lola, gazing out at the water. "I have less patience with it all these days."

"With what all?"

"I don't know. The posturing, the little digs. I used to love it, playing the game, knowing everything about everyone and using it to push myself up the ladder. But now, I just want to stay home and paint. The whole social thing seems like a lot of work anymore."

"So why did you want to come?"

Marco turned to smile at her. "Same reason you did. I want to have some kind of life outside my marriage."

Lola made a face. "At least you're good at faking it."

"I'm not sure that's a good thing."

"Trust me, it is."

Marco narrowed his eyes, then tilted his head. "Can I paint you?"

She waggled an imaginary cigar. "I don't know, sonny, can you?"

He swatted at her arm. "Come on, I'm serious. Can I?"

She frowned, considering. "May I think about it?"

"No worries, my sweet."

She nodded. "Nice change of subject, my sweet."

"Thank you." He gave her his most charming smile. "I'm what they call smooth."

"So why do really you want a break from your new friends?"

"I don't know. New people are a lot to take in."

"Yeah." Lola took his hand and smiled. "They really, really are."

They ended up sitting apart at lunch, because the organizer insisted on splitting up the women and men. Lola couldn't seem to engage anyone. Soon, she gave up and ate in silence, eavesdropping on the various conversations around her. She thought maybe she'd be able to learn what she was doing wrong, but it felt strange to just sit and listen to other people talk. Then several people shifted chairs, and she ended up with a new neighbor, with whom she was at least able to make fleeting eye contact and exchange a polite nod.

"I hate these things, don't you?" The stranger frowned at the chatting crowd around them, and Lola answered without thinking.

"Then why did you come?"

"Oh, damn, that's a good question."

Lola raised an eyebrow.

"Uuhhh." The woman laughed. She was pretty, maybe around forty, with black hair, dark eyes and a wide smile. She gave Lola a pointed look.

"Sorry." Lola grimaced. "I didn't mean to be rude."

"No, it's okay. I just feel weird answering when I don't even know your name."

"Oh, I'm sorry. Lola."

"I'm Sterling." Her handshake was firm, her hand strong and heavily calloused.

"So, why did you come?" Lola flushed. "Sorry, I should let you off the hook. Never mind."

"No, it's a fair question." Sterling laughed, and the sound made Lola smile. "People always hang out with the same groups. And they never want to let anyone into their exclusive little cliques."

Lola tried not to agree too enthusiastically.

"Not to mention, everybody's slept with everybody else. This one is that one's ex, and that one's and that one's, and it's all one big, incestuous family. Don't you think?"

Stung anew at the reminder of Janet, Lola nodded.

"So, who here is an ex of yours?"

Lola scrunched her nose. "Nobody."

Sterling boggled at her comically, and Lola faked a smile. She really didn't want to have to explain herself to Sterling or anyone, but she wasn't sure how to get out of it.

"What about you, Sterling? Who here is an ex of yours?"

The waiter interrupted them, and when he left Sterling went to the restroom. Maybe, Lola thought, she escaped because she didn't want to have to explain herself, either.

They were seated in front of a large window overlooking the marina, and Lola was enchanted by the scene laid out before her. Birds, seals, boats, bikes, people walking and talking and flying kites—the whole area was alive with movement and color, but from inside the restaurant, it was noiseless. It was like looking at a painting.

"All it needs is a little white leg sticking out of the water," she whispered to herself. "Poor Icarus! Poor Breughel, for that matter. Auden, too."

Lola saw a flash of light and turned sharply to her left.

"I—should I have said 'cheese'?" she mumbled.

Sterling pulled the camera away and offered a rueful grin. "You just looked so beautiful and sad! Are you mad? Do you hate me forever?"

Lola wasn't sure what to say, but she didn't want to be cold to the one person who'd talked with her. She hated having her picture taken, *really* hated it. And had done, ever since she was a little girl. She pushed that away. This woman, Sterling, had startled her, and she probably should have asked before taking Lola's picture. But, Lola wondered, was that true? Maybe people just take each other's pictures. Maybe it wasn't a big deal. People put pictures of themselves and each other online all the time, didn't they? Maybe she was being overly sensitive. Probably she was. She tried to shake off her discomfort and forced a small smile. It hurt her face, making that fake smile. Did it look as insincere as it felt? She shook her head, still smiling.

"It's okay, I guess."

"I'm a photographer," Sterling put her camera away. "That's why I come to these things. I should be using this time to hand everyone my card. That's pretty much my whole marketing plan."

"Oh." Lola nodded. She didn't know what to say. Should she ask about photography? Ask for Sterling's card? She had no idea. She was getting nervous, but Sterling was still fussing with her camera bag. She pulled out a red sweater, and Lola gasped and pointed.

"You're the woman from the boat," she blurted.

Sterling's eyes widened, and she flushed for a moment. She looked away, and Lola tensed, worried that she'd said something wrong. But when Sterling looked at Lola again, her smile was relaxed, and her eyes twinkled.

"Well, I am a woman, and I do sail. But I think I'd remember sailing with you."

"No." Lola made a face. "I'm sorry. I meant, I saw you parking a boat at the marina a little while ago." She peered out and pointed. "That one, I think."

"Wow, how can you be sure that's the one?"

"I don't know. Maybe it's not."

"I'm glad I wasn't stealing it."

Lola's laugh was an awkward giggle, but Sterling smiled easily.

The rest of lunch, Lola chatted with Sterling, and the meal was over before she knew it.

"So, there I was," Sterling was saying, when Marco walked up to their table and eyed Lola expectantly. "Now, remember, it was hot as anything, and we were hiding from the weirdo. And—"

"Introduce me to your friend," Marco interrupted, and Lola stared at him.

"I'm Sterling. And you are?"

Marco raised an eyebrow. "Marco. Nice to meet you. I hate to interrupt, but I need to get going and we drove together. Do you mind, Lola?"

She rose quickly, embarrassed at having kept him waiting. Sterling stood with her, putting a hand on Lola's arm.

"Wait, hold on. I'd like to show you the photo I took. Here's my card. Call me in the next few days, and I'll have the photo. Don't forget—I'll be waiting for your call!"

"Okay." Lola watched Sterling stroll away. She felt good about maybe making a friend, until she saw Marco's face.

"What?"

"*What?*" He signaled the server. "You're driving back. It'll take at least one more glass of mediocre chardonnay for me to play teacher. You're buying my lunch, I just decided. Oh, and unless I'm mistaken, you're paying for 'Sterling's' lunch, too." He pointed at the bill, left unheeded on the table.

"Oh." Lola fumbled for her wallet. "It's okay. I'm sure she just forgot."

"Yeah," Marco mumbled, shaking his head. "I'll just bet. Listen up, my darling Innocenta, we need to talk."

"What? Why? Marco, what's wrong?" Lola flushed. "Are you mad? I'm sorry for keeping you waiting." Her alarm was rising exponentially, and she heard her voice rise in pitch and volume.

Marco gestured at her to sit down.

"Sorry," she mumbled, embarrassed and flustered.

"No, don't be." Marco sighed heavily. "I'm not mad at you. I'm just a little concerned, is all."

"Why?"

"Well, darling, you just flirted hardcore with another woman. And, lest you've forgotten, you already have a girlfriend. You remember her, don't you? Blonde, about yae tall, carries a gun? Bit of a temper?"

"I wasn't flirting. I wouldn't! And I would never cheat on Del, I swear! I told Sterling I have a girlfriend." Lola shook her head. "I just, she was nice to me, and all the other women hated me." Lola's eyes widened. "Oh, God. I did. I totally flirted with another woman. What am I going to do?"

Marco took Sterling's card and put it on the table, and they both eyed the cardstock like it was repulsive and potentially dangerous.

"Nothing. I'm taking this. If you still love Del, I'll carry this thing around in my wallet until I get to be a senile old man and forget why I have it. If you girls break up someday, then ask me for it back. Okay?"

Lola nodded, red-faced. It would be rude, not calling Sterling. But it would be worse to call her. She could only imagine how hurt Del would be, if she thought Lola was flirting with another woman! Lola offered Marco a weak smile.

"Okay. That's a good plan. Thanks so much for calling me on my ridiculous behavior! Marco, please don't worry. Del and I are together forever. I love her, truly."

Marco waited until he'd been served his wine to acknowledge her words. He eyed her before he drained the glass in a single, noisy gulp. Then he picked up Sterling's card and ran his finger over the raised lettering before tucking it into his wallet.

"Okay, Innocenta. But you know what's funny? I thought you'd tell me to just leave this on the table."

CHAPTER EIGHT

"Asshole," Del muttered, and Phan raised his eyebrows, taking a labored, indelicate slurp and eying her with exaggerated innocence. His left arm was slung carelessly out over the steering wheel of their department-issued car.

"Okay." She rolled her eyes. "I'm sorry I said you take too long to drink your coffee. Just—come on! How long could it possibly take to suck down twenty ounces of shitty slop?"

"Mmmm." He smiled, drawling. "That is goooood caffeinated beverage. I am going to sa-vor this. Yes, I certainly am. Because life is meant to be savored, isn't it, partner, dear?"

Del looked away. Her foot started tapping and she stilled it. The more impatience she showed the longer he would take. Finally after an agonizing thirty seconds they pulled into traffic. They rode in silence for a few minutes while Phan concentrated on the heavy traffic. They were usually spared this kind of work, but a recent sharp rise in the number of missing women in the city meant even homicide detectives were being recruited to interview a family member of yet another of the disappeared.

They finally got through the Tenderloin traffic snarl and to a notoriously raunchy hotel that functioned as an SRO—single-residence occupancy, the city's code for a pay-by-the-week motel. Phan and Del took one look at the scattering scumbags who'd seen them coming. The pair had been to this particular SRO more than a few times. It housed the recently paroled, the newly homeless, the mentally ill, drug addicts, sexual predators, the variously impaired and other fringe folk. Some were on one end of the predator-victim spectrum, some on the other. Some were on both.

"Mrs. Wilson?" It was Del who'd made the call to the woman they were to interview. "Would you be willing to meet us at the sandwich shop down the street from your place? We'd be happy to buy you a cup of coffee, lunch, whatever you'd—"

"Good thinking." The breathy voice had dropped to a barely audible volume. "In case they're watching, right? I'll be in disguise."

Del relayed the earlier conversation to Phan while they waited halfway between the SRO and the deli. The sidewalk's denizens inched away until there was a thirty-yard perimeter around the two police detectives.

"She wasn't kidding about the disguise," muttered Phan, when a walking tower of layered, filthy clothes lunged out of the SRO and waddled over to them. The dingy affair was topped by a face-and-head covering comprised of what looked like four or five layers of aluminum foil, broken up only by narrow slits for eyes and a ragged gap for a mouth.

"My family called it aluminium," Del noted to Phan, who grinned reflexively.

The complainant, a Mrs. Wilson, responded to Phan's smile with one of her own, barely visible through the food-encrusted tinfoil on her face. The partners breathed through their mouths and greeted her. They bought her a turkey club and watched her cram tiny bits of it into her tinfoil-encased maw and forced themselves to listen for the parts of her story that might actually translate into something they needed to know. For the first ten minutes, they endured a rambling monologue about the various dangers of being a private citizen in a government-controlled dystopia.

Suddenly, the odiferous interviewee set down the remains of her sandwich and shot a glare at Del. "You look at me like I'm nothing."

Del was startled and sputtered a protest, but the woman held up a grimy hand.

"Listen. You're right. I am nothing. I always had trouble with just getting by. My head doesn't work so good, I know that. But my Paula, she was something special. *Is* something special. I wasn't exactly

Mother of the Year, you know? She had to pretty much raise herself. But I love her, and I have to make sure she's okay. If she's alive, that is. She was not a hooker, just so you know. She worked, she *works* at a shoe store."

"And she just didn't show up for work one day?"

"Five weeks now. Not a word. And she's not one of these girls that just ups and goes. She's responsible. Tries to get me to go to the doctor's, take the pills, all that. She's a sheep, but she's a good girl. She wouldn't worry me like this."

"Was she seeing anyone before she went missing?"

Wilson slammed her hand on the table. "It's not like that! I told you, it's not just some random crime. I know how you cops are, all of you. You think the victim deserved what she got. That's what they did to me, back when she was forced into me by that bastard doctor."

"Mrs. Wilson—" Phan tried to interject but was cut off.

"Listen to me, the past doesn't matter. I know, lots of women disappear, I see it more than you. Lots of people down here got no kind of papers, nobody knows 'em or wants to. They go poof and nobody even notices, nobody who'll go to the cops, anyhow. You might have a dozen or more folks just gone like nothing and there's not even a peep. But now girls like my daughter are disappearing too. And what are you doing about it? Nothing, that's what! It took seventeen phone calls and me threatening to park my ass in City Hall before you two showed up. Tell me you care, please. Tell me you give a shit about some crazy loon's nobody of a girl."

Del pursed her lips, thinking. "It's true."

Phan, used to Del's maneuvering, sat back, but Mrs. Wilson sputtered with rage. Del waited her out for a full minute before holding up her hand.

"You're absolutely right. If you were rich or famous or something, there would have been a news bulletin and a task force. But you're nobody, status wise, and neither is your daughter. But we know that's wrong. I just don't know how to fix the whole system. What I can do, what we can do, is work our tails off to find your daughter and either bring her back or at least tell you what happened to her. And we're gonna do everything we can to find her."

"Or at least shut me up with a bunch of promises."

"You won't know how we'll do until we do it, Mrs. Wilson. I'd like to share this much. Women do go missing all the time, and lots we don't even know about. And you're right, a lot more women than usual have gone missing the last several months. We don't know why. Do you have some idea?"

Del's question elicited a twelve-minute dissertation on a conspiracy that involved the CIA, the FBI, the White House and the Senate. Through it, Del and Phan each waited for a signal from the other to cut off the increasingly distraught complainant and neither gave it. The woman was clearly mentally ill, but she was just as clearly truly scared for her only child. Finally, Mrs. Wilson wound herself down and abruptly rose, disturbing a cloud of stink that wafted over the detectives.

"You don't have time for chatting. Stop sitting around here like a couple old ladies and get to work. One more thing. If you aren't just humoring me or playing along with the conspiracy, if you truly care about finding my girl, then you are in danger too. Please be careful, will you?"

The partners nodded, twin bobbleheads, and watched the woman stagger out of the deli in front of them. Exchanging a glance, they trudged in silence back to the car.

"Eight bucks for a lousy cheese sandwich?"

"It was worth not having to walk past all the parole violations." Del gestured at the SRO.

"Not to mention having to refrain from shooting the pedophiles."

Del shook her head when Phan headed for the driver's side. "Nuh-uh, bud."

"What?" Phan was red-faced.

"My turn. You drove here, remember?"

He shrugged but seemed peeved, which surprised Del. She took the wheel without trying to make conversation, wanting to see where his head was.

"Fuckin' call should have been handled by Missing Persons."

"Yeah, she's a nut job, but remember the meeting this morning? It's true, we have seen a lot more missing women than usual. You have to wonder, what happens to all of them? Wilson's daughter is a legit missing person. She's been gone over a month. She didn't imagine that."

"Jesus Christ, Mason. Are you lecturing me?"

Usually Phan was annoyingly patient and understanding, and Del was rattled by his short temper.

"You okay?"

"Worried I'm cracking up?"

"You're batshit crazy. It's why I keep you around, for entertainment." Del eyed her partner. "But usually you're a softhearted little girl and today you're acting like this is your very first period."

Phan shrugged but his eyes were doing a nervous dance. Del waited him out.

"It's stupid," he warned.

"That much I figured."

"Dammit, I can't believe I'm freaking out about this when I practically flunked out of school every year."

Del nodded, her eyes on the traffic. Phan blew out a gust of air that smelled like coffee and sour stomach. Another first. Phan was a scrupulous mint popper. He'd even gotten Del in the habit over the last several months. Sneaking a glance, she noticed his hair was too long. Usually he kept it surfer-boy shaggy, but it was edging toward homeless-guy ragged, and Del was surprised she'd failed to notice the hair plus the fact that he was wearing a tie. He usually only wore one when he had to make an appearance in court. She'd been neglecting him, too, hadn't she? Just like Lola and the house and everything else. She tuned back in when Phan cleared his throat, ready, finally, to spit it out.

"Okay." He cleared his throat again. "Well, Kaylee's getting a C in history."

"Oh, no!" Del made a horrified face. "Now how will the pathetic loser ever get into Harvard, Yale and Stanford all at once and with full-ride scholarships?"

"Shut up. It matters, Mason."

"Yeah, I know." Del hid a smile. Phan's big crisis was his kid getting a mediocre grade? "What's the problem?"

"Teacher's mean, mom's mean, I'm mean. Nothing's her fault. And she knows we both feel guilty about the divorce." He shrugged again. "The thing is, she aced the final but didn't do any of the homework. Honestly, I wish the teacher had flunked her. Maybe she'd have learned her lesson."

"So, she's super smart but lazy?" Del surveyed the group of bite-sized gangsters loitering on the street corner as the unmarked sedan eased slowly past them. "Could be worse. Dumb and lazy would definitely be worse."

He ignored that.

"Listen, I don't know shit about kids. But my guess is, Kaylee's a good one, especially compared to most of 'em."

She nodded in the direction of the baby thugs, who eyeballed the car at her gesture. She and Phan held the kids' eyes until some unseen adult wrangler signaled his gophers. The youngsters dispersed, working hard to look casual. It was almost heartening, Del thought.

They were still lousy at being criminals. Give 'em a couple more years, though, and they'd be slicker than spit and harder than the cement their overpriced sneakers scraped. She nodded again at the retreating kids.

"Prime examples, right there. Most of them are around Kaylee's age, some even younger. They're screwed to the wall, have been their whole lives. She's not perfect, okay, but she's nothing like them. She'll get her shit together. Don't you think?"

"Well, she better," he said, too loudly for inside the car. "She's not having any fun with her friends or watching TV until she does. No soda either. Or candy!"

"Meanie." Del stuck her tongue out and smiled when Phan flipped her off. She'd have to keep a closer eye on him. How long had he been quietly falling apart without her noticing? *I'm a detective*, she thought, almost shaking her head. *But apparently I'm blind and deaf when it comes to the people around me.*

"Your turn."

"Me? I flunked history a long time ago."

Phan made a face. "There's obviously something on your mind."

As much as she hated to talk about Janet, Del needed a fresh perspective on things, and Phan was the only person she trusted.

"Well, you remember the reporter? That whole Hahn mess?"

Phan nodded, once, and Del kept her eyes on the road.

"Showed up at my house, said somebody was after her."

Phan again nodded and said nothing.

"Sweet-talked Lola into letting her in. I lost my cool, and she took off. She's full of shit ninety percent of the time, I know that, but what if this time she's not?"

Del parked and wished she hadn't said anything. Phan stayed silent until she turned off the engine and looked at him.

"Well?"

"Did she say who's after her?"

"Yeah, well, I was pissed, okay? I didn't really hear her out. Come on, she lies for a living."

"Sorta like us, sometimes."

"Phan—"

"Yeah, I know." Phan shrugged. "But if she's not lying, you'd feel like shit if something happened to her."

"Yeah."

"Seems to me, you talk to her alone, we go together or I talk to her."

"You'd do that?"

"She's hot, right?"

Del gave him the requisite sneer but couldn't meet his eyes while she considered his offer. Now it was Phan's turn to be impatient. She caught him tapping his foot.

"Earth to Mason?"

"Sorry." She sighed heavily. "Tempting as it is to try to pass the buck, I think I'll go see her tonight. If her story holds water, I'll let you know. Maybe we could talk it over tomorrow?"

"Call me if you change your mind. I'm the dumb shit who can't watch TV because his daughter's grounded." He rolled his eyes.

"Hey, what's our plan for Wilson's daughter?"

"I'd like to go over the file, see what we can dig up. With any luck, she's still alive."

"You and I, hell, even her mom knows she'd dead." Del cut her eyes at Phan. "I can feel it, can't you? Something bad's been brewing for a while now. Something dark."

"Come on, Mason. Let's not get carried away."

"Look at it like this. We got a good twenty percent jump over last year. Twenty percent, Phan. That's seventy women. I been looking at the stats across the state. Figure some left town because of the economy, 'cause women always get hit harder when the jobs go away. Say an extra twenty or thirty went home to Texas or Minnesota or wherever. Maybe another ten or twenty went back to Mexico because their economy is better compared to ours. I'm just guessing but say that's about right. That leaves twenty, maybe more. Say an extra dozen, with the shitty economy, went into hiding at domestic violence shelters. That still leaves maybe ten or more unaccounted for. Maybe they're related. What're the odds ten extra women get snatched or murdered by ten random guys in the same year? No, they're more likely to be connected. And maybe Wilson's daughter is one of them."

"Your logic is damned shaky and you know it."

"But you agree with me." Del eyed Phan, who ducked her gaze.

He waggled his head. "You're not the only one whose gut is talking."

"So let's get to it."

"Tomorrow."

Phan was leaving early to pick up Kaylee, and that meant Del could run Janet's address, her real address, and swing by on the way home. Lola wouldn't even have to know about it.

CHAPTER NINE

Lola ran blindly through the dark forest, twigs and rocks cutting her feet. The cold air burned her lungs and throat, and tears blurred the dim images of trees and boulders. She fell, smashing her knee into something hard and damp. She stifled a gasp and curled into a ball, tucking her legs up under her. Her knee was on fire, and she bit her lip to stifle a moan of pain.

The dark figure of her pursuer passed her at first, and Lola made the mistake of exhaling when she thought it was safe to do so. The figure paused, and Lola held her breath. As the figure advanced, it blocked out what little light the waning moon had offered, and Lola screamed. She awoke and felt the scream die in her mouth.

The last brightness of the early evening lit up a glowing rectangle at the top of the wall across the room. She watched it slide across the ceiling and dim until it was gone. Who or what was the figure? What was she running from? Was it a warning? Was she supposed to avoid something? Or was she reading too much into the whole thing? It was just a dream, after all. But hadn't she learned to trust her dreams? How many times had she dreamed something and figured out later that she would have been better off if she had discerned and paid attention to the message of the dream? Lola examined each detail of her nightmare, dissecting and attempting to decode it, to no avail.

"I don't know what it means," Lola finally muttered, shrugging. "So I can't use it to learn anything."

She sat in encroaching darkness and wished she'd slept through the end of the dream. What good did it do to have these dreams and wake up in the middle of them? Exactly none. She picked up the phone.

"Marco?"

"What's up, sweetness?"

"I was thinking about the Meetup, and I wanted to apologize for my ridiculous behavior."

Marco's rich laughter filled Lola's ear. "Honey, you didn't really do anything. You flirted a little. So what? I was thinking, I know why you did it."

"Because I'm an idiot?"

"No, silly, because—and I may be wrong on this, okay, but—I figure you got married when you were barely legal and, my darling lesbian, to a man, right? Who sounds like he was not exactly Romeo. Then, you were single about five minutes before Del scooped you up. By the way, I don't blame her. You're delicious."

"Oh, Marco, I do love you."

"Anyway, most people would need to sow some wild oats after a lifetime of sexual frustration, and a little smidge of flirting is the closest a choir girl like you'll come to wild oats."

"Hmm. Interesting theory and a generous one. But I'll take it. Anything that lets me off the hook sounds good."

"Gotta run, love, Phil's taking me out to dinner."

"Delfina's, again?"

Marco's groan was the only reply, and Lola hung up, giggling. Maybe he was right. Maybe flirting with that woman was just a minor lapse in judgment and not a major sign of moral laxity. She would have to think about it some more. Maybe not. She'd probably already spent too much time worrying about it. She let out a slow breath and shook her shoulders. It was time to let it go. She had more important things to focus on, didn't she? Like her relationship with Del and the book she'd been revising for, what, a year? There were three different versions of the stupid thing and she couldn't get any one of them finished. She groaned. Writing was either wonderful or terrible, never in between.

"Like love." Was that, she wondered, too adolescent?

"Well, adolescent or not, it's how I feel. Loving Del feels wonderful or terrible, depending, and it's never in between."

Was that a good sign or a bad one? Lola closed her eyes and sighed, not sure she was ready to consider the question.

CHAPTER TEN

I may have found her. I know it is ridiculously early to even consider the possibility, but my hopes soar nonetheless. There's something about her, some spiritual light I think I see. Of course there's every possibility that I'm wrong. I have been before, like with my friend. She has been a greater source of solace and guidance, though, so maybe this new candidate will be the one, or maybe she will be something else to me. Frustration, that old enemy, makes my stomach hurt and my vision blur. I remind myself that God's gifts sometimes come into our lives in ways we cannot understand or appreciate.

I regulate my breathing, allowing the sand to dig into the skin of my back, my arms, my legs. My calves and buttocks and shoulders have it the worst, and I concentrate on the pain. I have taken two of the red pills tonight, a breach of the promise I made to my friend, but they will allow me to pay the price for my uncertainty and self-absorption. This penance is a gift, and I must treasure it as such. I have failed and I must atone. I push aside the thought. It's wasted energy unless it inspires better future decisions. So I focus on the future and fulfilling my mission.

The latest candidate is obviously a lost girl, at the very least. Prototypical. A pleaser. Codependent and uncertain and timid. Easily manipulated. Passive aggressive. Unable to form healthy relationships, lonely in every crowd. Always and unconsciously driven by fear and insecurity. The lost girls are too easy to spot, after my years of study, and I recognize them everywhere. Why I approach this woman instead of that one is never truly clear to me. I simply follow the invisible hand that guides me.

Sometimes I wonder if recent immigrants feel as I do, if they hear an accent or see a piece of clothing or a gesture that tells them a stranger across a restaurant or store is from the same old country. Do they feel the tug, as I always do, the urge to connect with their brothers and sisters?

Of course, I have not rescued any brothers yet, an omission over which I had recently begun to fret. There are certainly men who need help, male angels who want saving. But there must be someone else for them, I keep telling myself. There are far more women, and I alone cannot be expected to save all of the floundering members of the human family. There is, I realize suddenly, a larger puzzle, of which I'm only one small piece. I am, after all, only human. Grandiosity, my therapist would call it, and I am both pleased at recognizing it and appalled at the length of time it has taken me to see it clearly. Surely I was a fool, thinking I was alone in my work.

I feel inadequate so often, too filled with desire and pain and fury and loneliness and doubt. My ego interferes, my pain interferes and I am not enough, ever. I weep as I lie in the bed of my sins, knowing even as I shake with pain and self-loathing that this self-pity is yet another denigration of my sacred work. I am alone and not alone. I am blessed with my friend and with my mission, and I will falter but continue. I will save as many as I can and redeem myself.

The tingling in my head turns to buzzing, and my mouth is dry. I need to pee. I imagine my bladder as a bulging sack, and I imagine letting go. It would be such a relief, allowing my piss to spread below me and soften the sand. I clench my sinner and keep the dirty water inside me where it belongs, and the pressure in my belly builds. It is pleasurable, the way my body's demands complement the pain in the skin and muscles along my back, my buttocks, my legs. My heels are on fire. I allow myself few such pleasures these days, subsuming my desires in my work, and I speed up my breathing. That will increase the pain to an almost intolerable level, and it will excite me sexually, and my bladder will pulse and ache and the agony will be exquisite.

I imagine the lost girl lying on me, wrapped in the salty womb of our mother the sea, sacred in her newly reclaimed purity, and the weight becomes real. I sink into the sand so far that I can feel the damp of the concrete beneath pushing up against me. I take her on, as I have taken on all of them, my precious burdens, my soul sisters, the dear gift bestowed upon me in grace and generosity, and I shiver and press my lips together. A deep, guttural prayer borne of pain and pleasure vibrates my mouth and tickles me.

I come with a start, and my mouth pops open and my bladder lets go at the same time. I feel my body buck and shake. I weep aloud at the beauty of my purpose.

CHAPTER ELEVEN

Janet bunked in a ridiculously overpriced loft on the top floor of a four-story "boutique"—this, according to the sign out front—condo complex wedged between two business towers in the Financial District. Del eyed the place with dismay and climbed the stairs. She didn't quite trust the elevator. In fancy little places like this, good looks tended to matter more than structural integrity and sound design principle. At Janet's door, she hesitated.

Should I even be here? What am I doing?

She almost turned around and walked away. She wasn't in the habit of using department resources to track down people who weren't suspects. How could she explain just showing up at an address Janet had never given her? She probably wouldn't have to. After all, Janet knew she was a police officer, didn't she?

It would probably be best to just go home. What if Janet had seen her, though? Fancy place like this, they probably had a camera on every door. Whether it worked or not, that was a different question. But it might. It would look weird if she walked away, might even give Janet an excuse to show up again, tell Lola that Del had been on her doorstep. Would Janet think she was still interested? She imagined Janet running to her, kissing her. Del sighed.

That's what she used to do. She'd throw herself at me, like she couldn't live another second without me.

Janet talked Del into parasailing in San Diego and scuba diving in Mexico, into a ride on a hot air balloon in Napa. She seduced Del in public restrooms, in cars and motel rooms and anywhere else she could think of. Lola would never want to do any of those things. A part of Del bucked at this disloyalty.

So what? She also wouldn't lie to me or use me or betray me. Janet fucked me over and walked away like it was nothing. Lola would never do that.

She pushed the image of Lola's smiling face to the front of her mind and hammered on Janet's door. It swung open with a crash.

"Oh, my God!" Janet flung herself into Del's arms, so like the way Del had imagined only seconds earlier that she was taken aback.

"Baby, I'm so glad you're here!" Janet covered Del's face and neck with kisses. She was like a puppy, panting and excited and slobbery.

Del caught her breath and eased backward. "Cool it."

"Oh, right." Janet pouted and slid down Del like she was a fire pole, setting her feet down at the last second. "Wifey."

"Janet—"

"Sorry." She didn't sound sorry. She pulled Del into the room with a confident smile. She was babbling on about how sad she was that they'd argued. How she felt about it.

Figures. It's all about her, right? Del nodded and pretended to listen to Janet's long story of a short conversation. The loft was huge, with weird, all-white furniture and spooky, oversized paintings hung from the ceiling on long wires.

The couch was a low, wide circle covered in what looked like white fur. Janet sat, pulling Del down next to her. She was wearing a simple white shift that complemented her dark hair and glowing, golden skin. Her face was artfully made up to look as though it were free of makeup but impossibly beautiful. She was braless, as always. Probably panty-less, as well. Her feet, clad in white ballet slippers, barely reached the floor, and she looked more like a teenager than a woman in her thirties. She was the picture of youthful innocence and guileless beauty, and somehow this rubbed Del the wrong way. Was this all staged? Del nearly snorted aloud. Of course it was. Everything Janet did or said was a performance, always.

The suspended paintings were actually photographs or meant to look like photos, Del realized. She looked at the three portraits facing her and was struck by the fact that each subject appeared to be in agony. One was Janet, her mouth twisted in a scream. Another was of a blonde—no, it was Janet in a blonde wig. She looked dead. A drowning victim, hands pulled behind her back as though bound. It was hard to look at, and Del let her gaze drift as though casually away from that to the third picture, farther away. The third was a child, no, Janet was dressed like a child and crying. Del swallowed hard. The pose was deliberately erotic, and the face was clearly that of an exploited, genderless little kid. All three images were disturbing, but that last, most of all. Del ripped her gaze away from them, aware of the intensity with which Janet watched her look at the portraits. She searched Janet's eyes. Was there some message in these pictures? They'd been chosen deliberately, no doubt. Anyone who sat on the couch, the only real seating in the large room, would be confronted by three tormented faces of Janet. Was this a cry for help? Or was it a naked attempt at manipulation? As usual, where Janet was concerned, Del felt lost and uncertain and a little angry.

Janet was still holding her hand, rubbing Del's palm with one finger, scratching lightly with a recently polished nail—one of those manicures designed to stop her nail biting. Del found it touching, as she always had, that Janet had this childish, nervous habit. Del had forgotten how physically affectionate Janet was, how she made a point of touching Del all the time, rubbing and kissing her and holding her hand. Lola wasn't like that. She was affectionate, maybe, in her own way, but she rarely initiated physical contact with Del. She was too hesitant, still, and maybe would always be too hesitant. Del needed physical affection, but she didn't feel like she could ask Lola for something she wasn't able to give. It wouldn't be fair. *Yeah*, she reminded herself. *And was the other night* fair?

Del realized that she'd been sitting next to Janet for a full minute, just looking at her beautiful face and saying nothing. Janet was leaning into Del's side. Her skin was soft, silky, lightly scented. Everything about her was appealing.

I need to get away from her. Del stood abruptly and strode over to one of the many large windows that made the room look like it was floating in midair. The sun was just about to sink behind the tall commercial building across the street and was shining directly into Del's eyes. She squinted and turned around. She'd hate living in a place like this. Every inch of the overpriced loft was completely exposed. Janet hadn't even put up curtains. Anybody could see in here, anytime. It was ridiculous. Exhibitionist. Janet had no limits. That was part of what was gross about her. And, Del had to admit, part of what was exciting about her.

There was only one hanging picture with its front side visible from this angle, and, Del realized, from outside. In it, Janet stood, artfully posed in a seductive posture, completely naked. In the light, the wires from which all the canvases were suspended were not visible, and this image appeared less like a photo or painting than a real person. The background of the painting was the wall behind it, so it looked like Janet stood there in the middle of the living room, nude. From the outside, it would look even more convincing. Janet must have been younger, even thinner, when the photo was taken. She looked like a kid, too skinny even for the ridiculous standards of fashion. Emaciated. Ribs and clavicles and hipbones stuck out. It was in no way sexy, Del thought. But maybe there were people who found starvation erotic. What little Del knew about beauty magazines seemed to suggest this was the case. Maybe, she reflected, it was less the skinniness and more the childlike nature of the very thin girl. A very thin girl looks preadolescent, and clearly there were many, men especially, who found that particular look highly appealing. Del grimaced in disgust.

"Baby?" Janet's voice was low, seductive. She spoke softly, as she always did when she wanted someone to lean in to her. When Del didn't respond, Janet dipped slightly forward. Her expensively full breasts strained against the light fabric of her dress, and Del stared across the room at her. Janet stared back.

"Just tell me what's going on, Janet." Her voice was shaky. Janet's flimsy excuse for a dress was practically see-through and damned distracting.

Janet shrugged, sat up straight. She was the obedient schoolgirl now, ready to turn naughty the minute she thought it would get the reaction she wanted.

"Okay." She took a deep breath. "I'm doing a story about predatory sexual behavior, specifically photography. You know, upskirting, taking pictures in locker rooms, hidden cameras in bathrooms, stuff like that. The victims often don't even know they're victims, and the ones who do figure it out don't get much justice. Nobody seems to think it's much of a crime if somebody gets stalked or spied on or any of it. The cops don't care, or they can't do anything, and you know women underreport crimes in general, especially sexual ones."

She seemed to be waiting for some kind of response, so Del nodded agreement. It was truer than she cared to acknowledge, and she recalled the overwhelming despair she'd faced daily, and especially nightly, when she'd done her stint in sex crimes.

"Even aside from the generalized misogyny of your profession, my darling Del, people generally still think women with overt sexuality deserve sexual violence. Not to mention, our system rewards criminals instead of defending the innocent. Well, I don't have to tell you that, do I?"

She projected earnest innocence with every syllable. Del hated to admit it, but she almost believed her. And the reality was that Janet was right. How many women had faith in the system? And how wise were those who did believe that society cared about protecting them?

"Sit with me." Janet stroked the couch next to her. "Please, baby? I just want to talk to you. I'm sorry I said mean things about that girl. I didn't realize you'd saved her life. I can see why you feel responsible for the poor thing. She seems nice, very nice. I didn't mean to make you mad. Please, forgive me? I want us to reach some kind of—"

Del shook her head, planted her feet more firmly. "That's not why I'm here."

"Isn't it?"

Del was in agony. It would be so easy to take Janet in her arms. She would want Del with the same kind of hunger Del felt. She would be wild and willing and daring. Del drew in a shaky breath and let it out slowly.

"No, it's not."

"You still want me, baby. I can tell. You didn't have to come here. You could have called me. You wanted an excuse to see me. And that's okay. I understand that. There's always been a connection between us, and there always will be. I think we could make it work this time."

"Janet, stop."

"Baby, I messed up, and I regret it more than I can say. I hurt you, and I'd give anything to take that back. But can't we move past it? Can't we start over and just love each other again?"

For a moment, it seemed possible. After all, Del's career had recovered, mostly. Janet wouldn't do the same story twice. Del could come home every night to this beautiful wildcat, who'd rub against her and purr and scratch and demand sex every single day and pout when Del was late. She'd never be afraid of Del, never flinch away from her touch. She'd never have to be babied or soothed or reassured that she was safe. She'd never wake screaming and crying in the middle of the night. She'd be affectionate and confident and exciting and fun.

Life was an adventure with her, and it would never be like that with Lola. Janet had made Del feel alive in a way she never had before and still missed. Maybe Janet was right and they could just start over. Maybe they could put the past away and start fresh. Maybe it *could* work.

Janet seemed to see Del's hesitation. She came and stood in front of Del, only an inch or two away. One delicate strap was slipping down off her shoulder, exposing nearly all of a perfect, surgically enhanced breast. She licked her lips and smiled the sure smile of a woman who's won. The dress slipped a smidge more, and Del reached down to hitch it back up, annoyed by Janet's smug self-assurance.

The feel of her skin, where the back of Del's hand grazed it, changed things. That little brush of skin started a flood of memories, and Del groaned aloud, wishing she could stop the tide. The first time they kissed. The first time they made love. The first time Janet said she loved Del and cried when she said it.

"I don't love you," Del barked. "And you don't love me."

But it didn't matter, right at that moment. Del's brain was screaming at her to stop, but her body wasn't listening. She was kissing Janet, and she didn't want to do that, did she? Or to run her hands down Janet's sides or wrap her arms around Janet and pull her close, right?

Janet's body pressed against Del's and ignited the old hunger, and Del made a sound that was half growling, half laughter. She grabbed Janet's legs and hitched her up. Janet straddled her, laughed against her mouth, squealed with pleasure.

It felt like coming home, bearing Janet's surprisingly substantial weight, feeling her breath against Del's mouth, hearing her little giggles. Her hair tickled Del's arms, her breasts pressed against Del's. Her strong legs gripped Del's hips, and Del was breathless. She nipped little kisses at Janet's open, searching mouth and felt Janet's desire and pleasure. Del groaned. She walked them over to the couch, and Janet laughed again when Del yanked at the little dress she wore.

"Tear it," Janet whispered, and it was just like the first time.

Del refused to think. She yanked at the hem and felt it shred like paper. She shook her head.

"I hate you," she said. "I fucking hate you."

Before Janet could reply, Del was kissing her again. Janet leaned back, forcing Del to lower them both onto the couch.

"Show me how much you hate me."

Del dove into her, kissing her neck, her breasts, the hollow between her collarbones, her tiny hands and her tiny fingernails, painted scarlet to keep her from gnawing on them and bare at the tips where she'd been at work chewing the paint off. Janet squirmed and wiggled and made the little sounds that Del had always liked, moans and giggles and murmurs of pleasure and excitement.

"Love me," Janet whispered, her glittering eyes boring into Del's.

Del hesitated. This was wrong. It was a lie. But Janet lunged up at her, grabbed and kissed her, and Del groaned. She bit Janet's shoulder, and Janet gasped and squealed. Del kissed her, almost whimpering at the pleasure of Janet's hungry kiss, the way she wanted to devour Del's mouth with her own. She stroked Janet's hip as though absently, and Janet responded as she always had to Del's teasing caresses. She twisted around until Del's hand fell, as if of its own volition, between Janet's legs.

"Come on, baby, please?" Janet was panting into her neck, pressing her heat against Del's unmoving hand, begging for her touch. Del kept her waiting for a few seconds, laughing at Janet's groan of impatience. But she was as frustrated as Janet and gave in. She stroked and petted Janet, who whimpered and screamed and begged for more. It was like the old days, when Del felt like the whole world was reduced to her body and Janet's tangled up together in blissful, easy pleasure. Janet's throaty sex laugh, low and intimate, filled Del's ears and made her shaky with lust. Janet pushed against Del's hand and seemed to pull Del closer and closer with a power belied by her tiny frame.

Del was dizzy, breathless. Her body was responding, but something was wrong. Some part of her was withdrawing. Lola's face appeared in Del's mind—her warm eyes, her shy smile, her guileless gaze steady on Del's, because she would never lie, would never use anyone, would never play games to get her way. Del closed her eyes. She remembered pushing Lola, bossing her, telling her she was nothing but broken pieces.

"Oh, no." Del closed her eyes. "That's what I was doing. Trying to make her act like you."

She pushed away, retreating again to the wall of windows. "Sorry. I can't."

"Sure you can, baby," Janet whispered. She followed Del, smiling coyly.

"This isn't a game."

Janet smiled. "I like games, and so do you. You want me." She sashayed toward where Del stood and ran her hands down her body, over her torn excuse for a dress.

"No," Del mouthed. "I don't."

"I know you do. And I want you. We belong together, don't you see that? You want to tell me what to do?" Her eyes brightened. "That sounds like fun, baby. Tell me what to do, come on, let's play. Then you can punish me for being a bad girl."

Del shook her head, unable to speak.

"I'm yours, baby. Just come *on* and take what's yours."

Del turned around, swallowing hard. "That's not what's happening here. I don't want you anymore. I love Lola. I'm only here because you said you were in danger."

Janet held out her hand. "If that's true, then why did you kiss me? Why did you touch me? Why did you make me want you all over again?"

"I shouldn't have done that. I'm sorry. It was completely over the line and inappropriate."

Janet's face ran with huge, mascara-stained tears, and Del felt like a monster. *Why do I always feel like a monster? Maybe I am a monster, after all.*

"I'm sorry," she repeated. She tried to turn away, but Janet grabbed her arm.

"Baby, why can't you even look at me? It's because you still want me. You still feel something for me. And you feel guilty about that, right? You think you owe something to that poor woman. You think you have to be loyal to her. But it's not fair to stay with her when you still love me." Her voice was honeyed, soft.

"Stop this." Del shook her head but couldn't pull her gaze away from Janet's wide, lovely, and, it seemed, totally earnest eyes.

"She can't give you what I can, baby. She's all sugar and no spice, and that's not enough for you. End it, my darling Del. Let her go. She'll find some nice, boring accountant and be happier without you, because she'll never be enough, not for you." Janet ran her hand down to Del's and squeezed it, pressed against Del, licked her lips. "Tell me you can live with that fat, pathetic doormat and be happy, and I'll walk away. But you can't, can you?" Her tears were gone. They had been an act, like everything she did.

"You don't know anything about me and Lola."

"I know you've been lying to yourself. I know you're not happy. She's not enough for you. If she was, you wouldn't be here, hungry for love and affection. She doesn't give you what you need. She can't, and it's better to be honest about that and stop stringing her along. Face the truth now, before she gets hurt even worse."

Del narrowed her eyes and snorted. "You're lecturing me about the truth?"

Janet peered up at her with wide, wide eyes and twirled a lock of hair around a finger. Now she was a what? Penitent, heart-of-gold, naughty schoolgirl slut?

"Being dishonest cost me the most important thing in my life, baby, you. See how mad you are? If you didn't still love me, you wouldn't still be so mad."

"So you made up a story to get my attention, right? It's okay." Del softened her voice and her expression. "I understand. We do crazy things for love sometimes. I won't be mad, I just want to know."

Janet shook her head, and her dark hair fell into her face. "I didn't, baby. I promise! I want you back, sure. But that's separate. Someone's trying to kill me! You—"

Suddenly, the window behind Del exploded with a giant crash. Janet screamed, and Del pulled her down. She kept herself between Janet and the window, and they duck-waddled over a sea of broken glass. What happened? She tried to clear her head. Rock? Earthquake? Bomb? Gunshot? They headed for the front door and into the hallway. Del shut the door behind her and sat against the wall. She was getting lightheaded, and her arm was numb and wet all the way down to her fingers.

She looked Janet over. She had some minor cuts and was pale and wide-eyed, but she didn't seem to be seriously injured.

"Janet, look at me. Are you okay?"

"I'm fine, baby, I'm fine—but you! Oh, my God! You're bleeding so much! Oh, God! Help, somebody help us!"

Janet was hysterical, and Del ignored her. She had Janet snag the cell phone from Del's pocket and hand it to her. First she called dispatch, then Phan. He was brisk, businesslike, efficient. *Thank God.*

She forced herself to make the next call. This was the hard one, and she shushed Janet before dialing. Del took a deep breath. There was no pain yet, not in her body.

"Hello?" Lola's voice made Del want to cry, though she couldn't have said why. Janet crawled back toward the door, and Del didn't stop her. Get yourself shot, she wanted to say. Go ahead. She had a moment of clarity, wondering if Janet was trying to distract her. Or did she already know that it was safe? She tried to pursue that thought, but Lola said hello again.

"Sweetheart, listen, I'm fine, so I don't want you to worry." She heard Lola's breathing turn loud and fast, and she debated how to continue. "I'm totally fine. I got hurt a little, but it's just a flesh wound, no big deal. There's hardly any blood," she offered. "Anyway, I'm going to the hospital in a minute."

"What hospital?"

"General, I think."

"On Potrero?"

"Yeah."

"Did you get shot, were you shot? With a gun?"

"Sort of. It's not serious. Don't get upset and then try to drive, okay? I'm fine."

"You promise?" Lola's voice was shaky. "You promise you're okay? It's just a—" A strangled sob turned into a rising, hysterical laugh. "A *little* gunshot wound?"

"Seriously, it probably won't even leave a scar. I promise." She lowered her voice. "I'm sorry. I promise, it's okay."

"I'll be there in ten minutes. I love you." And she hung up.

"I love you too." Del whispered into the empty phone, wincing as her arm began to hurt. Janet came back, wearing another little white dress and holding a large towel. She wrapped it around Del's arm.

"I'm so sorry, Del. I shouldn't have come to you. I can't believe they shot you. I never wanted you to get hurt! I'm sorry, my darling. What if they'd killed you? I wouldn't be able to live without you, baby. Never, never."

Del gritted her teeth as the fabric squeezed her arm, but she ignored Janet. How was she going to tell Lola where she was when she got shot? Guilt flooded through her. She'd done a lot more than knock on Janet's door, hadn't she?

She pictured trying to explain how she loved Lola, but then her ex-girlfriend was standing there practically naked, and it was just a little too tempting. How sex with Lola wasn't quite enough to satisfy her. How Janet was so amazing that Del couldn't resist her. Explaining any version of the truth, no matter how sanitized, was more than Del could face.

Janet was saying something, but Del couldn't focus on the words. Her arm started to hurt in the burning way that she remembered from the time she'd been sliced by that drug dealer's girlfriend, what, ten years back? She could almost see that moment when the teenaged girlfriend, a tiny, blank-eyed junkie, practically tripped over her own newborn.

The baby was what distracted Del, she remembered. The junkie girlfriend was shuffling through an inches-thick layer of garbage on the floor. She bumped something, a bundle of rags, it looked like, with her foot. The bundle twitched and started crying, and Del was startled to realize it was a baby. She edged forward. The baby couldn't have been more than a day or two old. The cord had been tied off with a rubber tourniquet, which, like the baby, was covered with feces and urine and vomit and snot. The smell was suffocating, close up. Del eyeballed bruises on the baby's arms, torso, face. Blank, black eyes darted wildly out of the baby's—his, her, whichever—battered, gaunt, filthy face. Had every second of that newborn's life been a nightmare of hunger and cold and pain and aloneness and fear? It certainly looked like it, and Del goggled at the child, frozen in mute, agonized horror.

Del had encountered a lot of disturbing things in her years on the force, but the sight of that baby shocked her, more than it should have. Terri Laughlin, that was the name of the junkie girlfriend, Del remembered now. She was vaguely aware that she was no longer on patrol and in the junkie's house and staring at a terrorized infant. But at that moment, Del felt more like she was that patrol officer, unable to do anything but gawk. She watched as Terri Laughlin lunged at Del with a knife, got her in the thigh. It took a few minutes for it to hurt, just like this. Del lost a lot of blood back then, more than now, and she passed out. She only remembered the baby, later, in the hospital, and it took a team of four over an hour to find the baby in the piles of junk food wrappers and dirty clothes and unopened mail that littered the floor.

"It was dead," she said to Janet, who looked at her in confusion and alarm.

"What, baby?"

Del nodded, but that made her dizzy, so she stopped. "Poor kid never had a chance."

"I don't understand." Janet was getting wavy.

"Donaldson, that was my partner back then, he said the kid would've been doomed, anyway." Del tried to laugh but couldn't summon the energy. It turned into a sob. "Maybe he was right. A lotta kids, it's like their whole life is a tidal wave that just pushes them along. They don't ever really have a choice. We think they do, but they don't. Everything they know tells them to go a certain way. I dunno, maybe. But shouldn't the kid have had a chance? Shouldn't everyone get a chance to make the right choices, at least once?"

"Del, I don't know who you're talking about. Are you okay?"

Del shook her head. "Sorry. I don't know, maybe it doesn't matter. Maybe I just don't know anything." She swallowed. "I'm thirsty. Donaldson wouldn't take the dealer outside like I wanted. Like procedure dictated. Left me in an impossible position, you know? We should have taken him outside, the girlfriend, too, but Donaldson liked to hit suspects. Did I tell you that? That's why we had to stay in the shitbox house and couldn't get control of the situation. Donaldson was a shitty cop. Hated me. Hated women in general. Hated gays even more. His two favorite words were *bitches* and *fags*. Waited half an hour to call for a bus. Beat the shit outta the dealer while I bled in the piles of garbage on the floor. Probably five, six feet away from the baby. Baby mighta made it if Donaldson had bothered to try to save it. Laughlin was just a kid. Maybe sixteen, seventeen. Just had a baby—funny, I can't remember now, if it was a girl or a boy. Not that it matters, but still. Laughlin, she killed herself two years later. Pregnant again. Took a whole shitload of pills. That baby was a boy. Lived four months in an incubator, suffered like crazy until his body gave out. His name was Ronald. Ronald Aaron Laughlin. First baby, I don't know. Used to, can't remember. Aw, fuck it."

"How can I help you? I think you're going into shock."

"It's getting dark," Del thought she must have spoken aloud, but she couldn't be sure. It was hard to remember if she was on the floor in the middle of the drug dealer's rented house on West 91st in LA or in the hallway outside Janet's million-dollar loft in San Francisco.

"Oh, my God. Oh, my God!" Janet's voice was far away.

Del could see Janet clearly for a moment, and she almost smiled. Janet's face was red and splotchy.

"Is this what you look like when you actually feel something?"

"Del? I—"

"I love Lola. I love her."

"Maybe you do. But you love me, too, and I love you. I always have and I always will."

Del tried to say something, but it came out as a groan.

"I'm right here for you. Whatever you need." She was reaching for Del, but everything was getting wavy again and dark, and Janet's arm looked like a long noodle stretching out in front of her.

"Like one of your crazy-ass pictures."

"Baby? Del, what are you talking about? Del? Del?"

Del closed her eyes and leaned her head against the wall. That was a bad idea. Nausea pushed her thoughts away, and she could only swallow hard and try not to vomit. Her arm burned more now, and the burning seemed to spread all through her. A thought kept flickering at the edge of her mind and escaping. What was it? She followed it into blackness and knew no more.

CHAPTER TWELVE

Lola's heart hammered while she waited for an answer from the nurse at the front desk. She clutched her keys so tightly they hurt her fingers, but she couldn't loosen her grip. Those keys were keeping her grounded so she could stand here and wait to find out where Del was. Finally the nurse flicked her gaze in Lola's direction.

"Okay, now, let's see—Mason?"

"Yes, she's a cop. Inspector Adele Mason. SFPD."

"Right. Hold on a minute."

The nurse seemed almost as casual as she was distracted. She was answering the phone, tapping on her keyboard, nodding as she blithely responded to at least three people who were talking to and yelling at her from Lola's side of the counter.

Come on, come on, Lola's mind screamed, and she fought to keep a pleasant, patient expression on her face. At about the moment she'd decided to jump over the high counter, Del's partner Tom Phan appeared to Lola's right. She clutched his arm.

"How is she?"

"Fine. Passed out, up now. Lost some blood, but she's okay. They're gonna give her some antibiotics, some pain pills, stuff like that. It's a flesh wound, left arm, missed the bone, missed the artery, she's too damn stubborn to get really hurt. Couple of cuts from a broken window, nothing major. She's okay, I promise."

"Thanks, Tom, I really appreciate it. Can I see her now?" She tried to move him faster by speeding up herself, but Tom wouldn't be hurried.

"Can I get you anything? Coffee?"

Lola shook her head. "No, thank you. Were you there? Did you get the person who shot her?"

He shook his head. "I wasn't there. She, uh, she'll tell you about it."

"I don't mean to be rude, but where is she? Why are we going so slowly? What aren't you telling me?"

"We'll be there in a sec. Listen, take a minute to catch your breath." He looked over her shoulder at someone and gave a hard look.

Curious, Lola turned around to see Janet.

"You?" She had never been so blindly angry in her life. "She was with you?" Janet looked up at her, her face blank, but Lola could swear her eyes were twinkling. She was wearing a white minidress—with no underwear—and was covered in blood, Del's blood.

Lola forced herself to stop. Several cops, in and out of uniform, were watching her closely. She wouldn't embarrass Del by falling apart. She forced herself to sail past Janet as though unaware of her. She hadn't fooled anyone, of course, but at least she hadn't made a scene.

Then Tom opened a door and there was Del, perched on a gurney. Lola's anger vanished, Janet vanished, everything was gone but Del. Lola rushed forward with a cry and gently hugged her, examining her with careful attention. Her left arm was swathed in bandages, and she was covered in blood. Her eyes were sunken in her pale face. Blood was smeared where she'd rubbed her mouth, pushed her hair back from her forehead.

Lola pasted on a smile, and Del offered a weak shadow of a grin in return.

She reached out her hand, wanting to warm Del's colorless cheek. "Are you all right? Are you in a lot of pain? Do you need anything?"

Janet sidled into the room, and Lola turned slowly to face her, ducking eye contact with Del.

"I know," Janet sulked, her voice low, "nobody wants me here. But, baby, I wanted to see for myself if you were okay. I never meant for you to get hurt. I love you! I always have and I always will."

Del didn't respond, and Janet smiled sadly.

"I'll be here when you're ready to come back to me, no matter how long it takes. I love you so much. I'm so sorry! I should never have put you in danger, my darling. I'd give anything to keep you safe."

She slipped back out of the room like a wraith, and Del mumbled something.

"What was that?" Lola frowned. "What did you say?"

"I'm sorry she came here. I told her not to."

Lola felt an ache drop like an anchor deep inside her chest. She should respond to Del's words, she knew, but what could she say? What did it mean that Janet and Del had been together? Had they been together at other times? Would Lola know they had been together if Del hadn't been shot? Who shot Del? Why? Did it have something to do with Janet? Were they lovers? Lola recalled the night she decided to seduce Del. That strange, terrible night happened after Janet's return. Had Del turned to Janet for the kind of sex she wanted because Lola was a terrible lover? Lola hoped Del would say something that would somehow make it all better, but she didn't.

They stayed quiet until a doctor came in to examine Del. Then another doctor, then a third. It took almost two hours before they made the decision to keep her overnight and another hour before Del and Lola were alone in a private room.

Lola waited until Del was settled in and they were alone to ask, "What happened?"

Del picked at the sheet. "I went to Janet's."

Lola couldn't respond. She couldn't compete with Janet. She was not young or beautiful or exciting or bold. She was boring. She was too quiet and too shy and too insecure and too frumpy. Fat too. Old. Unbeautiful. Unglamorous. A nothing and a nobody, compared to a beauty like Janet. Who wouldn't pick Janet? Janet, who was unbroken. Janet, who wasn't a weak, stupid, worthless, pathetic, broken coward. The ache in Lola's chest sharpened and she bit the inside of her cheek to keep from crying.

Finally she could speak and asked, "Why?"

"Figured she was probably lying, but I needed to be sure. A lot of women have gone missing, dozens more than usual—yes, I know how fucked up it is that there's a usual number of missing women every year. Anyway there's been an uptick. I needed to know if her bullshit story was really bullshit or if maybe it was real. She's done stories before, I found them after—she's done some on trends in crime, stuff like that, it's right up her alley. I figured it was possible she might actually be in trouble if she knew something about the missing women. I figured, if there's any chance, I had to check and she wouldn't talk to Phan."

Lola waited.

"She lives in this big loft. Big windows. No drapes. Giant pictures everywhere, all her. All weird. She was stonewalling me. Playing games. Then I got hit, through the window, I guess."

"Do you know who shot you?"

Del shook her head.

"Were they trying to shoot you or her?"

"I don't know. Yet."

"Did it have anything to do with the missing women?"

"I really have no idea."

There was a long pause while Lola tried to decide what questions to ask. Maybe she should wait and talk to Tom, rather than keep haranguing Del.

"I'm sorry."

"For getting shot, or for going to see Janet, or for going to see Janet and not telling me about it?"

"Yes." Del made a face, obviously trying to lighten the moment.

Lola's composure collapsed. A sob burst out of her, and she pressed her lips together to stifle it.

"Sweetheart?"

"You're not funny, Del. You could have been killed. And for what?"

Del shook her head.

"Do you still love her?"

"Honey, no, I don't. I love you." Del's voice was strangled.

"But you still feel something for her, right? Don't answer right away. Think before you say anything. Just, please, don't lie to me. I can handle anything, as long as you're honest with me." Lola held her breath.

"I don't love her. I—it's hard to explain. I was so hurt, and I never got a chance to just tell her to fuck off. I never asked her why she did it, or if she ever really loved me, or whatever. I thought I didn't care, but she showed up, and I was pissed."

Lola watched her, trying to gauge what her words really meant. "And?"

"I guess I still feel connected to her in a way. I think it's because she was the first person I actually fell in love with. I don't know. But I don't love her anymore. I love you, not her. She's just someone from the past, someone I hate."

"You may hate her, but you're still attracted to her."

"I swear I'm not."

"I saw the way you looked at her. My God, she's perfect! And she's sexy, she can walk in a room and make everyone want her, including you. Especially you."

Del shook her head, and Lola fought to control her hectic breathing.

"She's a better lover than me, right? She loves sex, she never gets scared."

Looking at Del's guilt-stricken face, Lola knew she was right. She shook her head, hugged her middle. "She can have anyone she wants, and she wants you."

"It doesn't matter what she wants. I'm with you." Del's voice was strained.

"Why would you want me when you can have her?" Lola was breathless. The ache in her chest was expanding, and she tried to fight it. If she could only breathe!

"You're the one I love. You're the one I want. I don't want her."

Del's face was pale and drawn, and Lola relented, worried that the stress of arguing would delay her recovery. Now was not the time to get into this. If Del did still love Janet, it wasn't something she'd chosen but something that had happened to her. Berating her for it wasn't going to do any good, and it wasn't fair.

"Stay away from her, Del. Please? She wants you back, and you still want her. Of course you do. But I love you, and I want you to stay away from her."

Her voice was low, and she hated how pathetic she sounded. The ache in her chest filled her. She could almost imagine it circling around her lungs like a cat and settling in for a nice, long nap. She eased in small sips of air, afraid to disturb the pain and make it worse.

"I don't want her. I want you. I'm not going anywhere near her, I swear." Del's face was gray. Her voice was barely audible. "Okay?"

"Just get better. I can't think about anything else until you're better."

"I promise, I promise I'll make this up to you."

"Yes." Lola looked out the window at millions of lights from cars and houses and stores. She couldn't see any stars at all. "Okay."

"I have something to tell you."

"Whatever it is, just tell me." Lola braced herself.

"I want my Giants sweatshirt."

"Huh?" Lola frowned.

Del made a face. "Would it be a real pain to get it now? It's pretty cold in here, and I'd be more comfortable wearing my own clothes. Plus, I'd really like some chocolate chip cookies."

Lola stared at her. "Are you serious?"

"If it's too much trouble—"

Lola went home, got the sweatshirt, and drove around until she found a twenty-four-hour grocery store for the cookies. She wandered the aisles listlessly, in no hurry to get back to the hospital and unsure of the reason. *She's okay*, Lola told herself. *Shouldn't I feel more grateful for that?*

She watched a handsome young man smile at a beautiful young woman, who blushed and returned the smile.

It's not Del's fault she finds Janet attractive. Who wouldn't? She's ten times prettier than that girl, and that girl is ten times prettier than I am. Or ever was, even before I was a broken-down, worn-out old cow.

She waited for Orrin's voice to chime in. Instead, she was awash in classical music floating down from the store's speakers and surrounded by the sounds of shopping carts and low voices and someone talking to Jesus a few rows over. Lola stood for a moment, lost and alone in a supermarket somewhere in the city, fighting an urge to simply walk away.

I could just leave the car I hardly ever drive. Leave the house I don't even live in. Leave Del and start all over in a new place by myself. She'd done it once, though of course she'd left no one and nothing behind, before. Would she really leave Del to recover on her own? No, of course not. Not really.

"I'm stuck," Lola whispered to herself. And she felt like her feet were cemented to the floor. She tried to take a step and could not. *Okay*, she thought. *I'll stay here. That's okay. It's as good a place as any, right?*

She didn't even realize she was crying until a trio of heavily tattooed teens with outrageously colored hair came up and asked her if she was okay.

"What? Oh, yes, thank you."

The tallest kid, a girl, maybe, shrugged. "You need help?"

"No, thank you. I'm just wasting time. You ever want to not go where you're supposed to go?"

At this, the trio broke into stuttering laughter.

"We're in high school," croaked the one with the most piercings. "We get it."

They looked like comic book characters and were dressed more appropriately for an apocalyptic battle than a trip to the grocery store. That seemed right, somehow. They were heroic, weren't they? What more heroic act could there be than continuing to try after the world has exploded? These kids had been born into a reality that was already dying, but they kept getting up out of bed every day and taking the time to put in their various piercings and make their hair stand upright and arrange to meet each other. They were clearly heroic, simply for bothering to try—absurdist survivors on parade!

And to check on a crying stranger in a grocery store in the middle of the night? They were teenagers. They were supposed to be sullen and selfish and surly. But they were heartrendingly, disarmingly sweet. Lola was absurdly grateful for their simple kindness. It let her move her feet and come back to life.

She nodded and thanked the teens for their concern, then made her robotic way to the register and car and finally back to the hospital. She dropped off an extra bag of cookies for the nurses on her way back to the room, where she found Del fast asleep.

Lola put Del's cookies in the cupboard provided to patients for personal items and the sweatshirt on the chair. She rubbed her face and stretched out on the chair and drifted off. When in a chaotic dream Janet came flying out of the darkness at her, Lola snapped awake and went to get a cup of coffee.

She spent a long time reviewing all of the choices she'd made in the two years since Orrin's death. On paper, she'd done pretty well, striking out on her own and finding success personally, financially and professionally. She'd come out as a lesbian, become a published author and a homeowner, joined a book club, fallen in love for the first time in her life, survived Christopher James and even managed to make a friend in Marco.

"Not too bad, really," she murmured to herself.

But there were things she'd do differently if she could, weren't there? She looked over at Del, restless in the grip of some vivid and, if her frown was an indication, distressing dream. What if making those choices differently meant she and Del were apart instead of together? Suddenly restless, Lola abruptly jerked up out of the reclining chair and started stalking the hallways that wound around the floor. There was a middle-aged woman roaming the halls at a slower pace than Lola, and they passed each other four or five times before Lola got more than an absent nod from the woman. The IV pole the woman was leaning on started to tip as the woman rounded a corner, and Lola was luckily close enough to snag it and keep it upright.

"Thank you," the woman said. And that was all. Lola and the stranger in the robe and hospital gown and gray fuzzy socks saw each other twice more before Lola had the hallways to herself, but she kept thinking about that moment as she paced.

"I'm healthy," she muttered to herself, startling a nurse who was coming out of a patient's darkened room. "There's not a thing wrong with me."

"Ma'am?" The nurse was a pretty, petite woman with a warm smile.

"Nothing, sorry," Lola said. "Just thinking out loud."

The nurse nodded. "Happens a lot on the night shift."

That idea stuck with Lola too. There was something there, some story in the cooker about being whole and about the way we talk in the dark more freely than in the light. What was it? A new story, a story about a woman. She was named Olivia, maybe. Before she knew it, Lola was down the elevator and striding down the street. The drugstore was open until midnight, she was sure, and there were things she wanted.

A short time later, she was settled in her chair in Del's room, using her knees as a desk for the notebook she'd purchased. Olivia's world was building itself, and Lola lost herself in the threads of a story whose design she could only dimly perceive. She forgot Del, forgot herself, forgot she was in the hospital in the middle of the night. She wandered in the invisible web of a story whose world only revealed itself to her one tiny strand at a time.

Lola wrote until her hand cramped. She flexed her fingers and picked up the pen again, but it was too late. The story was gone, at least for now. She glanced at her watch and saw that she'd been writing for over three hours. No wonder her hand was tired. She couldn't believe she'd lost the thread of Olivia's story so suddenly. She tried for a long time but couldn't make the story come back. She was eventually too frustrated to continue and she sat back, watching Del sleep.

What am I going to do? How am I going to make things right between us? The answer never came and neither did sleep.

CHAPTER THIRTEEN

I wanted to be a good person, somebody who helped people. I wanted to be worth something. An ache she'd long forgotten rose in Del, and she pressed her mouth shut to keep from crying out. How long had it been since Del had been an innocent? *Mrs. Wendell. What would she think of me now?*

Fourteen-year-old Del was a lanky loner, hiding behind a bushy blonde cloud of curls and sporting the awkward gait of a kid grown seven inches in as many months. She earned money by mowing lawns and doing minor repairs for people in the almost-middle-class housing development a mile or so from the trailer park.

She knocked on doors, asking people if they had any work that needed doing and getting thirty refusals for every yes. For nearly every yes, though, she got a regular customer. She worked hard and charged less than the boys and men competing for day labor jobs, and she always cleaned up after herself.

The money was good, for a kid Del's age, and it gave her peeks into lives very different from her own. Del's favorite customer, a youngish widow named Mrs. Wendell, had her come over two or three times a week. One day the job was refinishing the dining room table, another it was mowing the lawn, another, cutting back the blackberry bushes that threatened to overtake the yard. She always paid Del a fair rate, and she always offered Del a glass of lemonade after the work was done. She was nice to Del, which was a rare and wondrous thing to the awkward, gangly, lonely teen. Soon Del was stopping by Mrs. Wendell's every day, and every day Mrs. Wendell had some job for her.

School, the trailer park, the city of Fresno—sometimes the whole world felt like a foreign landscape. Everywhere Del looked, things were gray and dingy and worn. All the faces seemed hard and cold. She felt like she'd been dropped into the middle of a world that didn't want her. Like somebody had made a mistake and put her on the wrong planet. She was a careful alien, making her face a blameless blank, skulking around the edges of everything.

But she could relax at Mrs. Wendell's, where it didn't seem like there was anything wrong with her. She wasn't in the way or too awkward or a freak. And the world was nicer there. At Mrs. Wendell's house, everything was clean and quiet and bright. Mrs. Wendell always had several windows open, and the smells of fresh flowers and cut grass and fruit trees wafted in from the garden. Large, ancient trees guarded the house from the brutal central valley sun and sheltered a world of cool and quiet and green. Del could almost feel the dust of the world drifting away from her as soon as she stepped through the gate that led to Mrs. Wendell's front walk. Mrs. Wendell always had a radio playing in the kitchen, and the tiny house and yard were filled with whatever station Mrs. Wendell had chosen for the day. Sometimes it was country, sometimes rock, sometimes jazz or blues or classical music, but every time Del locked the front gate behind her she stepped into a world framed by Mrs. Wendell's flowers, her smile and her music.

Every day, Mrs. Wendell sewed while Del worked outside. She loved watching Mrs. Wendell frown in concentration, her brow furrowed, her mouth pressed into a tight line. Sometimes her long, thin braid would fall over her shoulder, and her pale, slender neck would be exposed.

Something about that neck, its fragility and nakedness, hypnotized Del. She wanted to press her hot lips against that cool, soft, skin and feel the knobby bones underneath. They would feel the way a bird's wings would if you could touch them, Del was sure. A few wispy hairs always escaped from the braid and danced in the light breeze from the fan, and Del imagined that they would tickle her skin when she kissed Mrs. Wendell's cool, white neck.

Del was reckless with desire and put all of her love into her work. She built a shed for Mrs. Wendell's yard things. She cleaned out the garage. She learned about cars so she could fix Mrs. Wendell's ancient Chevelle when it broke down. She cut down a willow tree whose roots threatened to pull up the walkway and planted a chaste tree bought with her own money, blushing as she told Mrs. Wendell what it was and that it was a gift. Mrs. Wendell gave her a thank-you card the next day. Del tucked it into her pocket and sauntered toward home, waiting until she was in the privacy of the bathroom to wash her hands before unsheathing the creamy white paper. The words were simple, penned in Mrs. Wendell's neat, even hand. Del smelled the paper. Did the words smell faintly of the lemony soap Mrs. Wendell savored? Maybe it was only imagination, but Del drew in the possibility of the scent until she was dizzy with love. Carefully encasing the note in the crisp envelope, Del put it with the money she kept hidden from her parents, tucked into a cloth sack behind her dresser.

After that, the first thing Del did every morning was glance at the battered bureau, painted a faded gray and covered with the remains of stickers from a series of bands she'd never heard of and places she'd never seen. Behind the castoff junk furniture lay her neatly folded jeans and tees, and behind those lay the money and Mrs. Wendell's note. The secret presence of what Del came to think of as a love note carried Del through the endless hours of school, where no one knew or wanted to know her, and on to Mrs. Wendell's home, where Del offered her gifts of labor with the ardent fervor of a courtier.

At six, Mrs. Wendell would call her in to sit at the table in the cool kitchen, and Del would race in and scrub her hands, worried about dirtying one of Mrs. Wendell's pretty white towels. She'd perch carefully on the chair that had become hers, sitting up straight and hoping that she didn't smell of sweat. Mrs. Wendell would sit opposite Del, and they would eat fruit and cookies and drink lemonade, and Mrs. Wendell would ask Del how school had been, and what the kids were like, and other questions. What kind of person did Del think she was? Did Del believe in God? Did she believe in reincarnation? What did Del think was her purpose in life? What kind of books did Del like? Music? Movies? Del worried about giving the wrong answer or being laughed at or sent away.

Eventually, though, she went from shy and awkward to almost eloquent under the easy acceptance of Mrs. Wendell, who always seemed interested in what Del had to say. She treated Del like a person, not like a kid or a hindrance or competition or an oddity, and Del's gratitude filled her and made her more generous with everyone around her, even her parents.

Day after day, she watched Mrs. Wendell's graceful movements, the shine in her eyes when she grew enthused about something, the way her hair was plaited so perfectly. There would be waves in that hair at night when she took it out, Del knew. The moonlight would shine on those wheat-colored waves. They would hang down her slender neck and back and drape over her knobby shoulders and down over her barely-rounded breasts. Del wanted more than anything to see those waves caress that soft skin. To touch those waves and that soft skin.

She longed to find out what Mrs. Wendell's lips would feel like, taste like. That longing became a hunger that nothing could fill. What had filled her up somehow made her even emptier inside, as the months drew on and Mrs. Wendell remained the same pleasant employer and acquaintance. Del was unable to think about anything but Mrs. Wendell. Food turned to sand in her mouth, other girls looked ugly to her, and she glared at her reflection in the bathroom mirror.

"Why would she love you?" she barked at her reflection. "Why would you think you're good enough for her to love you back?"

One day, Del sat down at the table after her work was done, and Mrs. Wendell turned around and gasped, dropping both glasses on the floor. Del jumped up and started picking up the pieces of broken glass and mopping up the lemonade with paper towels. She looked up to see Mrs. Wendell's gaze fixed on Del's face.

"What's wrong?"

Had Mrs. Wendell seen that Del loved her? Was she disgusted? Del's face flushed with shame. She finished clearing up. Then she sat and waited with her gaze fixed on the table. *I'll lie*, Del decided. *I'll tell her I have a crush on a boy at school and just thought about him right then.*

"Adele, what in the world happened to your eye?"

Del's relief was a physical thing. "No, it's nothing. I fell. We have these wooden steps, you know, and they aren't real sturdy. I fell, that's all."

Mrs. Wendell shook her head. "Please, please, don't lie to me. Aren't we friends now? I want to know the truth. Please." Her watery eyes held Del's.

The truth? Del thought, her mind wild, *the truth is that I love you. The truth is that I think about you every minute of every day, and I want to kiss you and live here with you. I want to touch you all over and smell your hair.* That's *the truth.* But she knew what Mrs. Wendell meant.

"It's nothing, I just walked into a fight. No biggie."

"At school? Don't the teachers keep order?"

"Uh, no, not at school. My folks were just having it out, and I wasn't paying attention. It was my own fault."

"Tell me exactly what happened." Mrs. Wendell's eyes were fixed on Del's.

"Well, I walked in when they were arguing, and I accidently got bumped. No biggie."

"You are lying to me, Adele. I'm sorry to say that, but you are. That injury is no bump."

"It's no big deal." Del was starting to feel weird. The way Mrs. Wendell was looking at her made her mad, for some reason. "Like I said."

Mrs. Wendell's eyes filled with tears, and she grabbed Del's hand. "No, Adele, it is a big deal. It is. You're a child, sweetheart, a little girl. Your parents should love you and protect you and take care of you. Honey, they should never, ever hurt you."

Del pulled her hands away from Mrs. Wendell's bony fingers. "You don't need to get all worked up, Mrs. Wendell. It's nothing." She was getting madder and madder and didn't know how to make this stop. Mrs. Wendell had actually touched her, but it was all wrong!

Mrs. Wendell shook her head and left the room, and Del sat back, defeated. Grief and impotent anger made her eyes sting with unshed tears. She would get sent home now and not asked back, ever. But Mrs. Wendell came back with her purse over her arm and a pad and pencil in her hand.

"Adele, I need you to write down your address for me," she said, her hand shaking as she held out the pad. Del hesitated.

"What for?"

"I'm going to confront your abusive parents and call the police." Mrs. Wendell's cheeks were a hectic pink, and her eyes flashed. Del wanted to sink through the floor. She finally got a rise out of Mrs. Wendell, and it was for all the wrong reasons. She wished she'd realized Mrs. Wendell would get all upset about a stupid black eye. She'd have stayed away until it got better.

Stupid! She punched her thighs with both fists. *Stupid, stupid, stupid!* Now everything was ruined.

Del begged Mrs. Wendell not to go to the trailer park, partly because she knew it wouldn't do any good and partly because she didn't want Mrs. Wendell to see where she lived. They talked for hours and finally agreed that Mrs. Wendell would not go, but only if Del would agree to move in with her temporarily until they figured out a more permanent solution.

"Will your parents worry? Will they call the police?" Mrs. Wendell asked Del, and Del reassured her that it would be fine, they didn't care, they probably wouldn't even notice she was gone.

When Mrs. Wendell made her call home, Del did so, knowing that the phone had been cut off weeks earlier. She read the script Mrs. Wendell prepared, speaking over and into the recorded disconnected-number message, explaining to no one that she was taking an after-school job at a private residence in exchange for room and board. She waited a minute or so and then gave the phone number and address to no one and hung up with a grim nod.

"There, Adele, isn't that better?" Mrs. Wendell pressed a cool hand to Del's hot cheek. "You've been very responsible, sweetheart."

I'll take care of her, Del thought. *I'll protect her. A single woman alone at night, I bet she gets real scared.* An idea came to her: Mrs. Wendell might have been hoping Del would move in with her and take care of her, and Del's shiner was just a good excuse.

On the third night, when Mrs. Wendell came in to the little guest room off the kitchen to say goodnight, Del asked her to sit and talk for a while. After a few minutes, Del surprised both of them by leaning over and kissing Mrs. Wendell's cheek. She hadn't planned to do this, and she blushed furiously.

Mrs. Wendell regarded her with wide eyes. "You need to understand—"

Del knew what was coming and didn't wait to hear it. She kissed Mrs. Wendell lightly on the lips. It was Del's first kiss and she shook with nerves. Mrs. Wendell smelled faintly of sweat and baby powder and lemon, and her dry lips tasted like toothpaste. Finally Del stopped and looked at Mrs. Wendell's face. She didn't seem repulsed. She didn't seem anything. She looked like a soft statue. Mrs. Wendell had turned off the radio before coming in, and the house seemed strange without the tinny sound of blues or rock or honky-tonk. The light was blue with evening and the air was cool, too. The world had become a strange, new place, and Del and Mrs. Wendell were strange and new in it.

Del took hold of Mrs. Wendell's braid, undoing the rubber band, loosening the long, delicate strands of hair. She combed through the silky threads with her fingers as carefully as she could. Mrs. Wendell did not resist. She sighed lightly, her eyes closed. Her hair fell in the loose waves that Del had always imagined. And oh! Had there ever been anything so soft? Del's hands trembled and she could hardly catch her breath. The silence made the moment seem sacred.

Del kissed Mrs. Wendell's hair. Her cheeks. Then she went back to kissing her soft, dry lips. When she didn't resist, Del kissed her again and again. Mrs. Wendell didn't kiss her back, not really, but she didn't move away either. Del kissed her harder, wanting to taste her mouth. She pulled Mrs. Wendell's trembling body closer to her own, her hand resting on the small of Mrs. Wendell's back, and felt her small breasts press into Del's. She ran her shaking hand down Mrs. Wendell's soft, lean arm down to the work-roughened ends of her fingers. Those calluses were hard, compared to the rest of her skin, and Del pulled Mrs. Wendell's hand up to kiss her fingertips, one by one.

Mrs. Wendell finally started responding, kissing Del back and stroking Del's face with her cool, calloused, gentle hands. Del's heart hammered when Mrs. Wendell placed her palm over it. She kissed Del on her forehead, her cheek. She reached up and caressed Del's lips with a leathery fingertip. Del's stomach fluttered and her breath came out as a small moan. Mrs. Wendell smiled at her but looked sad. When Del leaned in to kiss her again, Mrs. Wendell shook her head and frowned.

"No, Adele, stop. No, no, we can't do this. Honey, stop. Dear God, what have I done? Honey, I mean it. I—stop that right now. Get off the bed. Go on now. I mean it, sweetheart. Right now."

Del froze. She pulled away and sank in an awkward bundle of limbs on the floor and didn't realize that she was crying until Mrs. Wendell reached over and used her yellow nylon nightgown to blot Del's tears. Del couldn't look at anything but the floor. She didn't even know what she felt, only that she hurt everywhere.

Mrs. Wendell whispered, "I'm sorry. Oh, what's wrong with me? I never meant to do anything like this. It's wrong. It's so wrong! You are still very much a child, my dearest, darling girl. Please understand I have to do what's best for you, sweetheart, even though it may hurt your feelings. It's the only way. I never meant for this to happen. I need you to leave right now and never, ever come back. It's not a punishment, darling. Never think that. It's to protect you. Please go. Go now."

Del went cold all over. She begged, she remembered that, but didn't remember anything about the rest of that night or the following days.

Now, nearly thirty years later, Del felt the same mix of confusion and shame and regret and fear. She felt cold. She felt empty. She looked around the hospital room and saw that Lola was gone, thank goodness. Stalking the halls again or off getting more coffee.

Am I really this person? This liar? This cheat? Like Daddy? Momma was always accusing him of cheating, and Del knew that he was probably guilty of it, maybe dozens of times over. Was his cheating the reason they were so unhappy? Was his guilt the reason he was so ornery and mean?

Del closed her eyes and saw Daddy standing over Momma, his hands fisted, his face twisted with blind rage.

Is that who I am? Is that how I end up? I ran as far and as fast away from them as I could and they followed me here. They were always here inside me. Their poison is my poison. Their weakness is my weakness. All I ever wanted was not to be like them, and now, here I am, and it's just like Daddy in that trailer all those years ago.

She felt the bile rising in her throat and vomited all over herself, helpless to stop the poison from staining the white sheets and white blanket and white hospital gown.

CHAPTER FOURTEEN

"Vicodin! I want Vicodin! I neeeeed it! God damn you, I'll fucking kill you! Give me my Vicodin, you lazy bitches! Vicodin! Stat, motherfuckers!"

It was a young patient several rooms down the hall, and her screeching broke the pre-dawn stillness. The chain reaction was fast and widespread. Lights went on, televisions started blatting and the nurses' station was emptied. No one came to see Del, though, and she slept through the disturbance, as the screamer went on and on, demanding the drug and cursing. Lola shook Del's shoulder, but she didn't react.

"Hey, wake up. Del, come on, wake up!"

Someone in a white coat came in and asked if there was a problem. Lola waved her arm around to indicate the bedlam and then pointed at Del's sleeping form.

"Shouldn't this wake her up?"

The doctor took one look and pressed the back of her hand to Del's forehead. She frowned and repeated the action, and Lola shook her head. She wanted to ask a question, but her voice wouldn't work. She tried on what she thought might be Olivia's voice. It was slightly patrician but still warm and approachable.

"Years of training and millions of dollars' worth of technology and you're feeling her forehead?"

Olivia has a good sense of humor and she calls on it in what may be a crisis—this is what Lola was thinking. She wasn't focused on Del at all, she realized after a moment. She was still lost in the world of Olivia, a nicer place by far than the real world in which Del was asleep and maybe really, really sick and wouldn't wake up.

It was when the doctor ignored her and hit a button on the wall, muttering rapid-fire instructions at some invisible listener that Lola snapped back into reality.

"What's wrong?"

The doctor asked, "Any other symptoms you've noticed?"

"She threw up," Lola stammered. "That was a few hours ago. She didn't have a fever then, so the nurse wasn't too worried about it."

They kicked her out, and it was hours later that a different doctor came out to the waiting area and explained that Del's blood was infected. He explained this at length, but Lola couldn't process what he was saying. Del was in danger, she understood that much. The blood in her own body whooshed through her ears, stopping them up with pressure and thumping. All she could think was that she'd been sitting there checked out and thinking about herself and her silly story instead of really watching Del.

"I should have realized," she whispered at the doctor's back when he finally stopped talking at her and walked away. "I should have been paying attention."

For most of the next several days, Lola sat immobilized in a plastic chair. Tom came and went. Other cops came, too. Marco and Phil, Tess and Lin, Rachel and Lee. Other people Lola didn't know or didn't remember. She remembered none of it with any clarity.

"Del's going to die," she heard herself say. "She's going to die, and the last thing she'll remember is that I was so lazy I didn't want to go get her a sweatshirt. Why didn't I wonder why she was so cold? She never gets cold."

Someone held her hand and told her Del would be all right, and Lola pulled her hand away.

"She just has to live. She can stop loving me. She can go back to Janet. I don't care. I just want her to live."

Lola found herself saying thank you over and over. A doctor updated her. A nurse stopped by to see how Del was doing. Someone wished Del a speedy recovery. Someone sent flowers. Someone brought her coffee, food, a toothbrush, clean clothes. Someone took notes when she asked questions of the doctors and asked questions when she couldn't think of what to ask.

"Thank you," she said.

"Thank you so much."

"You're very kind, thank you."

Did she sound sincere? She barely knew whom she was thanking or what she was thanking them for. It didn't matter, really, did it? It was all a carefully choreographed set of interactions, a kind of script one had to follow. She began to think of it as a play of manners. Someone goes in the hospital, and everyone has to say nice things and bring coffee and flowers and offer kind wishes, and the sick person or her representative says thank you, thank you so much. Like every play of manners, it began to feel meaningless after too many repetitions.

Lola was only allowed to see Del for a few minutes at a time and only a few times a day. This too became a choreographed dance. Lola would kiss Del on the forehead and ask the same question every time.

"How are you feeling?"

"Okay," Del answered every time. They followed their script like good little actors. Did Del even see Lola? It didn't seem like it. There were doors closed inside Del now, inside Lola too. They were very far apart where it mattered, and Lola felt her heart clawing up, trying to get air, drowning in grief and fear and uncertainty. *Do you love me?* That's what she wanted to ask and couldn't. Or wouldn't, maybe. There was a very real possibility Del's answer would be a gentle, regretful, carefully couched no. Worse, it would be a lie that they both knew was untrue.

Every day, Lola would finish the act by offering to go get Del whatever she needed. She would try to talk about how much she loved Del, would try to fluff her pillow or adjust her blankets, and Del would get irritated and say she was tired.

"I love you," Lola would say in a bright voice, with what she hoped was a warm smile, and Del would nod and repeat it back. It was strange, the way she felt so close to Del when in the waiting room and so far away from her when they were together. Did Del feel that? Did it matter to her?

After some days, Lola wasn't sure exactly how many, Del was released. Marco drove them home and Lola couldn't stop worrying. She was supposed to take Del home and care for her and keep her happy. During the car ride, Lola tried not to chatter at Del, but the uneasy silence between them made her edgy and scared. She blathered on and on about nothing, not even listening to her own words. Marco finally put his hand on her arm and shook his head, and she shut up.

He drove on and she sat watching the traffic as they wove through the crowded streets. How did people go on living? It was such a terrible business, living—tiring and confusing and painful and scary.

By the time Del had been home for a week, Lola was too tired and brittle to think clearly. She hadn't managed more than an hour or two of sleep since that first night and felt like her brain was disconnected from the rest of her. She stood a few feet away from Del, who lounged on the couch and goggled at the blaring television.

"Want a sandwich?"

Del shook her head.

"What would you like? You have to eat something to take the next pill."

Del shrugged.

"Del, I'm sorry to pester you, but—"

Del finally pulled her gaze from the blatting screen and glared at Lola. "You don't have to treat me like an idiot."

"I'm sorry, I didn't mean to do that. I just want to help you."

Del shrugged again and looked back at the TV. "Hmm."

It was Lola's turn to shrug. For the last week, she'd been tiptoeing around Del's moods, and she was exhausted. When the phone shrilled a few seconds later, Lola almost fell over her feet trying to answer before its ringing annoyed Del.

"Hello?"

"Grab your purse and put on your coat," Tess's voice came through like a beacon in a storm, strong and clear and sweet. "You and Lin are going shopping, and I'm babysitting the world's worst patient. Two minutes." And she was gone.

Lola stood staring at the phone.

"Hello?" She knew Tess had hung up, but her brain was stuck.

Tess was true to her word. Two minutes on the dot, and she was hollering from the front porch.

"Helloooo! Come out with your hands up. We've got the place surrounded!"

Lola rushed to yank open the door, cheered in an instant by the sight of Tess's bright, dark eyes and warm smile. She was the picture of health and goodwill and vitality, and Lola let herself soak that in for a moment before stepping back. She mouthed a soundless thank you, and Tess winked and nodded before whistling at Del.

"Still sitting around in your jammies, you big baby?" Tess's voice seemed to rouse Del, who turned her head and frowned.

"What do you want?" But Del was excited to see Tess, Lola could tell, and she took in the way Del's smile won over her mock severity in an instant.

Why can't I cheer her up like that? She shook the thought aside.

"My girl wants to go shoe shopping and I'm not up for that, so I'm having her kidnap Lola. Plus, I figured you'd be too damn rude to invite me for a visit, so I had to invite myself. Also, in case you forgot, you haven't been to my book club or my basketball practices in months. So, you suck. I'm gonna punish you. I haven't decided how yet. Maybe I'll sing to you."

Del's gaze bounced to Lola's face, but she seemed to see nothing suspicious. A grudging smile stole across her pale, haggard face. "Well, if you're gonna barge in, you could at least shut the door."

"Yeah, yeah," Tess set down a six-pack of non-alcoholic beer and a mountain of snacks on the coffee table. "You're not paying to heat the sidewalk. I know, cheapskate. Blow your girl a kiss and turn on the game. Nice furniture, by the way. I assume Lola picked it out. Your old couch was an ugly-ass piece of shit."

"Go to hell." Del actually smiled, and Lola tried to catch her eye.

But Del ignored her, so she sketched a wave and slipped out to where Lin waited in her SUV. Tess would tease and joke with Del and keep her spirits up, and she was, as an RN, better qualified to take care of Del than Lola, anyway.

"Oh, Lin!" Lola was breathless with excitement. "Thank you, both of you, so much! What made you think of it?"

Lin zipped along, shaking her head and laughing. "Are you kidding? I've known Del half my life! I know how grouchy she gets when she's sick, and I figured you might want a break from getting your head bitten off every two seconds."

Lola echoed Lin's lighthearted laughter, though Del's moodiness was anything but amusing to her. Why couldn't she just laugh off Del's grousing like everyone else did? Why was she such a big baby? Maybe Del wasn't the problem at all. Maybe Lola was the problem.

She feigned interest in Lin's chatter over dinner at a cute Italian bistro near the marina, and she forced herself to show enthusiasm when Lin suggested they window-shop for a while. They strolled down a crowded section of Union Street, and Lola managed to keep Lin talking about her job and Tess and her vacation plans long enough to keep her from asking about Del. She was glad to get a break but too tired to enjoy the outing.

"Thanks again for thinking of this," she murmured to Lin, who smiled and shook her arm.

"You make Del happy," Lin chirped. "I don't want her to scare you off."

Lola laughed, trying not to sound like she was agreeing and detecting a distinct note of hysteria.

"Listen." Lin stopped her, staring into her eyes. "She loves you. She's an amazing woman and she's incredible in a thousand ways." She shrugged. "But she's a lousy patient."

"Well, I guess it's hard being helpless when you're so used to being independent. Anyway you're a lifesaver." She eased Lin back into the flow of foot traffic, distracting her by asking about how she and Tess had met. The story was considerably more detailed than the one Del had told Lola months before, and it was easy to show surprise and interest.

Lin squealed in protest when a light mist started following, and Lola steered her under an awning. They stood in silence for a few minutes before Lola noticed that Lin had stopped talking and was watching her.

"Sorry. Woolgathering is a bad habit of mine."

"Are you ready to kill her?"

"Well, it's not her fault." Lola didn't want to say too much. "She's been in a lot of pain."

Lin searched her eyes. "She loves you, you know."

Lola nodded. "I love her."

"But she's wearing you down."

Lola shook her head. "No, I can't take it personally. She's in pain and she's frustrated. I understand."

"Uh-huh."

"I promise not to smother her in her sleep."

Lin's laughter was hearty and made Lola smile.

"Come on," Lin said. "You need a pick-me-up. Let's go in and look around. We can find you a new purse." They were in front of an upscale boutique, and Lin beamed at the array of colorful purses, scarves and sunglasses displayed in the window.

"I'll be happy to keep you company until it dries up a little out here, but I'm too much of a cheapskate for a place like that."

"Listen, I don't mean to be rude, Lola, but that," she pointed, "is the ugliest bag I've ever seen. Let's just take a look, okay?" Lin eyed Lola cautiously, clearly worried that she'd given offense.

Lola didn't have to feign agreement. "To be honest, I've always hated it."

Lin made a face. "Should I ask why you're still using it?"

Lola shrugged. "I don't know. I just never got a new one. It's definitely time, but I'm more of a thrift store girl."

"Don't you use your purse every single day?"

Lola waggled her head. "Still."

Lin looked at the purse like it was a hideous ghoul. "I think you should reconsider. If you see something you like, you can either buy it or look for something like it at a discount store later. As far as this monstrosity is concerned, maybe we should burn it. Have a ceremony."

Lola tried to laugh but couldn't. "Yeah, maybe."

"I've hurt your feelings."

"No, not at all."

Lin shook her head. "I have and I'm sorry." She put her hand on Lola's arm. "I didn't mean to be obnoxious, honestly."

It was Lola's turn to shake her head. "No, you're not obnoxious." She exhaled, trying to shake her dark mood. "It's just that I'm upset with myself. I feel like I don't know how to do anything right, not even replace a stupid purse. I can't figure out anything. I can't make Del feel better; I can't make her happy for even one minute. I can't do anything right." She chewed her lip. "I'm sorry. I didn't mean to turn mopey on you like that. Maybe we should just go home."

Lin pulled her into the boutique. "Come on, you. There's no point in getting away from your problems if you don't get to vent a little. Now let's get you a pretty new purse and grab some coffee. As I recall, you're as much of a caffeine and sugar addict as I am."

For a second, Lola felt like a normal person, a real person, out with a friend for dinner and shopping and chatting. But the minute they were inside, she looked around and felt like an imposter and an intruder all over again. Everyone in the store was wearing designer clothes and a lot of makeup and fancy purses. Lola clutched her ugly old bag tighter. She was a mess in jeans and a sweatshirt, with her hair in a sloppy ponytail. She wasn't even wearing lipstick. She fought the urge to run right out of the store. She hadn't noticed until then how stylishly Lin was dressed, in high heels and a beautiful coat and suit and full makeup.

Suddenly, Lola realized someone was looking at her, a saleswoman, and she forced a smile onto her face, working to meet the stranger's eyes. The saleswoman offered a warm greeting to a woman behind Lola. Lola turned and saw a blonde vision in a lovely cashmere dress. The salesclerk hadn't been smiling at her. Why would she bother? Lola was clearly out of place in a fancy shop like this one.

"I should have changed," Lola muttered lamely.

"What? You're fine," Lin reassured her. "You've been stuck taking care of Oscar the Grouch. You look great."

Lola rolled her eyes. "I look homeless."

"Lola, the only thing you need to change is that ugly purse." Lin whispered. "Don't you think you deserve a nice bag at least as much as these snobby bitches?"

Laughter burst from Lola. "You're crazy!"

"No," Lin averred, suddenly serious. "Your bag tells people who you are, how they should treat you. *Your* bag says, kick me, I'm a doormat with low self-esteem."

Lola giggled helplessly. "Lin!"

Lin continued in a low voice. "I mean it. You need a bag that says you deserve to be treated with respect."

"Is there something I can do for you?" The saleswoman's tone suggested that calling security to have Lola removed would be her preferred course of action.

"My friend needs a day bag. I'm thinking maybe a satchel. Something functional rather than decorative." Lin smiled sweetly at the saleslady. "She's very practical, so think Chloe, not Fendi."

The saleswoman—her nametag read "Cookee"—defrosted only slightly. "Any specific features?"

"A single flat strap—she's narrow in the shoulders. Zippered top, not a flap. She's impatient. No clutches, no crossovers. Oh! And no distinctive patterns or ornamentation. Updated, classic. She's in desperate need of a signature bag, and I'm thinking clean lines, but not too geometric. What else? Definitely a short drop, no beading or bangles and nothing too formal."

Cookee cocked an eyebrow and gave Lin a speculative look. Lola was completely lost. She had no idea what Lin had said or why it was the right thing, but it clearly was. Soon, Lin and Cookee were chattering away about designers whose names Lola had never heard and stores she'd never seen, and they used at least five different names for purses, none of which was purse or bag. Outside, the mist seemed to have cleared a bit, but Lin was obviously having a good time, and Lola wasn't especially anxious to get back to Del's house.

Not home. *I didn't call it "home," but "Del's house."* She frowned.

"Something neutral or a bold splash of color?" Cookee ran her manicured fingernail down the strap of a fuchsia clutch with giant green sparkles on it. She seemed to want some kind of response.

Lola suppressed a shudder.

"Neutral," she answered in a firm tone, and Cookee and Lin shared a laugh. They started grabbing one purse after another, debating the merits of each. Lola wandered away and tried to imagine carrying any of the bags she passed, but they seemed both showy and impractical. She peeked at a price tag hidden deep inside a particularly gaudy tote and saw four digits before the decimal. She carefully backed away from the animal-print bag and sighed.

Overwhelmed, she was headed back toward Lin when her arm brushed something soft. Lola turned to see what seemed like a normal-looking purse with a few pockets for keys and phone and the like. She tried it on, feeling the smooth leather against her arm. She saw herself in the mirror and smiled. The purse was both practical and beautiful. She eyed the tag and closed her eyes. Wasn't that an awful lot of money? The price was lower than most she'd seen but higher than she'd have liked, but she held her breath.

I have a credit card. I've never even used it. I could use it now and buy this purse, and it would be my *purse and not the one Orrin gave me.*

I'll use it every day, she told herself. I'll use it until I die. It's the only purse I'll ever need. I'll take good care of it. She looked in the mirror again, and she thought maybe she looked a little less like an outcast and a little more like a person. *You have to start somewhere,* she told herself.

"This is the one I want," she murmured.

Lin turned and grinned.

"Good choice," said Cookee. "A little safe, maybe, but versatile, classic. Nice."

"It's lovely," Lin crooned, and Lola nodded and returned the smile with real feeling. She would never have come in this store in a million years if Lin hadn't dragged her in.

"I'd like to use it right away." She started pulling out her wallet and things and laying them on the counter. "I can't stand the old one another minute."

Cookee used a wooden hanger to scrape Lola's old purse off the counter and directly into the trash, and Lola felt better when she couldn't see it anymore.

"Good riddance," Lin muttered, grimacing.

Lola started to feel more emotional about the whole thing than a mere handbag seemed to warrant. She tried to explain it to Lin as they strolled to the coffee shop. She faltered to a stop after a few minutes of what sounded even to her like incoherent rambling.

"Your purse defines you," Lin said, shrugging. "It tells people who you are." She said it as though it was an obvious truth and Lola grinned.

"Exactly," she agreed. "I don't know how Del lives without one. Or Tess for that matter."

Lin smiled. "You know how they are. Purses are for femmes." She rolled her eyes. "Whatever. Just don't let Del get in the habit of making you carry her stuff. I end up carrying all of Tess's junk wherever we go."

"Lin?" Lola looked away. "I'm not sure Del would understand why I spent so much on this. It's my own money but maybe she'd think it was stupid."

She's mad at me all the time. I don't want to give her another excuse to be mad at me. I'm a stupid, weak baby who can't handle it when someone's mad at her.

"Oh, honey, I get it." Lin smiled and hugged her. "It'll be just between us."

By the time they got home it was late evening, and Lola was relaxed and refreshed. She tried to thank Lin, who shook off her words.

"You're a sweetheart and I like you. Besides that, you're important to Del and she's important to me. To both of us."

Del was dozing on the couch when they returned, and Lin pulled Lola into the kitchen.

"Go to bed," she whispered. "Tess'll give her whatever she needs and get her up the stairs. You need to catch up on your sleep."

Lola's eyes welled up. "Thank you," was all she could say. She didn't even argue. She just tiptoed up the stairs and went to sleep, too tired to do anything else.

CHAPTER FIFTEEN

I have been dreaming about the angels. Watching my soul sisters transform from lost girls as they disappear into the dark water leaves the rest to my imagination. Are they at all the same after baptism? In my dreams, they are again pure, untouched by sin and pain and shame. They are only the seeds of their best selves, the kernels of soul stripped of the secular and the gross. They are happy and laughing and joyful. I wake with a smile on my lips and lightness in my heart that sustains me through the darkness.

It is faith alone that carries me, and I battle to sustain it. What if I am wrong? What if I am not God's messenger or servant or vessel but instead a misguided tool of Satan? It is possible that I am deluding myself. It wouldn't be the first time. I have always understood that. But my mission has brought me such joy that it can't be a lie. It just can't. The alternative is too nightmarish too consider. Still, it returns to my shattered mind. I am low on red pills. My friend has been distracted, distant. She is impatient with me and wants me to act more quickly than is prudent.

"Expedience is the realm of the uninspired," I tell her and she is surprised by my vehemence. "My mission is sacred and I will not be rushed."

She has agreed to bring me more red pills, which is good. I now need to take three every day in order to maintain clarity, and I am actually able to sleep sometimes now. It's a strange thing to wake in the morning and realize that it's been hours since I was last awake. The red pills bring not only the peace of truth but the peace of rest as well.

As I prepare I am filled with doubt in a way I have never before experienced. I am in the desert, assailed by uncertainty and lonelier than I have ever been. I will fast and meditate and do penance until I am again steadfast in my convictions. I am the servant of good. I am true goodness made manifest in this foul and soulless world, and I am here to do right. I will prevail. Good will prevail, regardless of the cost to me, to anyone.

Tears cool my fevered cheeks as I lie on the rocky shore listening to the surf and wind. I shake, unnerved by the flashes of feeling that push through the doubt and invigorate me. I believe I have met the lost girl who is the one true angel. I am more and more sure she is the one, though there is no reason. She just is. I see her soul shining out of her despite everything and it calls out to me. I must save her, she who does not even know she is the one and will not unless I show her.

"I'm coming," I whisper. The wind carries my words away and I can almost see them flying toward the one I've sought my whole life. I must redeem her soul that she may save us all.

CHAPTER SIXTEEN

Del snapped off the radio with a loud sigh and watched Lola avert her eyes. Somehow, there weren't any stations playing anything she wanted to hear. It was all annoying. The music now was hardly music at all, just repetitive, unimaginative blaring and thumping. There was no feeling in it. Del rolled her neck gingerly. Every part of her body was sore and tired and sick of sitting still and too weak to do anything else. She'd never been incapacitated before and it was making her irritable with herself and everything else.

Lola got quieter and more careful and more tentative every day. She wouldn't snap back at Del, wouldn't call her on her bad behavior, wouldn't tell her to fuck off. Things would be so much easier if she would just get pissed. Then they could have a big, loud fight and make up with wild sex. That was how things would have gone if Lola were Janet.

Would Janet stick around to take care of Del if she needed it? Del shook her head. Probably not. Not like this. For a day or so maybe. But then the tedium of laundry and cooking and dishes and picking up medicine, all of that would get to Janet and she'd pick a fight with Del so she could storm out.

Was that fair? Maybe not. Maybe Janet would do whatever Del needed her to do. Maybe she would break her back trying to keep Del happy even when it was impossible. Lola was certainly more than willing to drive herself into the ground.

How had they gotten to this? Del couldn't believe they were playing this stupid, destructive game. She was nearly recovered, for the most part. Her visible wounds had healed quickly, once the infection cleared up. But sometimes her shoulder hurt. The bullet had just grazed her upper arm, hadn't done any real damage.

She should be a hundred percent by now, she figured, but every once in a while her whole shoulder felt like it was about to pop off. Not often enough to worry about but often enough to be annoying. It was stress, she decided, and she lied, told the doctor she wasn't in any significant pain. No sense making a big stink about it. As it was, they were pestering her to go to physical therapy.

"Forget it," she croaked when Lola offered to make the appointment. "I'll do it myself."

But she didn't. What would they do at physical therapy? Tell her to lift weights and stretch, something like that, and she didn't feel like doing either. She was worn out and starting to wonder if she would ever feel like herself again.

"I actually feel worse than after Janet—"

She looked up at the ceiling. Lola couldn't hear her, right?

"So who am I talking to?"

Her phone buzzed as she headed into the kitchen to grab a beer, and she read the text:

Baby, I'm SO worried! SO sorry you got hurt. Plz txt me! Del eased onto the couch, beer in one hand and phone in the other. Janet had been texting every day. At first, Del had been annoyed. She certainly hadn't responded.

But it might not be such a bad thing to bury the hatchet. After all, somebody had actually taken a shot at Janet's place.

"She wouldn't have hired someone to shoot at herself. Or at me." Del waggled her head. "She did care about me in her own way. Still does, I guess."

"Did you need something?" Lola was at the top of the stairs. She didn't look enthused about coming down.

"No, thanks." Del tried to smile. It must've seemed more like she was baring her teeth, if the look on Lola's face was any indication.

Lola nodded and melted into the darkness of the upper landing. Del had just dropped her gaze back down to Janet's text when she heard Lola's voice.

"Why are you really mad at me?"

Del looked up. Lola was standing there, arms crossed, her face a locked vault.

"I'm not mad at you."

"Is it because of sex?"

"What?"

"Because I'm bad at it?"

"No—what?"

"You want Janet instead of me because she's sexier, right?"

"Lola." Del looked straight at her for the first time. "I want you. I always have. But you don't want me, not really."

"Yes, I do."

"You're scared of me! You act like I'm trying to hurt you or something. I'm not a monster. I'm not a rapist. I don't want to hurt you. I've been pretty patient, you know? But you still act like I'm attacking you. How am I supposed to feel about that? How am I supposed to keep wanting you?"

Lola nodded, her face blank. She looked like someone who's finally gotten the cancer diagnosis she'd been expecting, and Del wished she could take back her words.

"I didn't really mean that," she said lamely. "I'm just in a lousy mood like always lately. I'm sorry."

"No." Lola's voice was barely audible. "The truth is best. And you're right. You have been patient. I'm sorry. For everything."

She again faded into the darkness of the upper hallway. Del knew she should go after Lola, but what could she say? That her words had been a lie? They hadn't. She remembered the way Janet had run at her, rubbed against her, begged for her touch. She remembered the last time she and Lola had tried to make love.

"If you can call it that," she muttered aloud. Lola in some kind of fugue state while Del examined the scars that covered her body? That was not an attempt at making love. It was something darker, angrier, emptier. Del hugged her middle.

"What the hell is wrong with me?"

She rubbed her face with her hands and peered through her fingers.

"Oh, and I cheated. Can't forget that, can I? I used Janet too."

She let her hands drop. A scared, emotionally overwrought victim came to her for help. Regardless of their history, she had no right to take advantage of Janet.

"I should get Phan to work her."

It was a good plan. She knew that, knew she should follow it, but she texted Janet back, anyway:

I'm ok. U safe?

The response was immediate. Janet again declared her love and apologized for putting Del in danger. She reassured Del that she was safe, thanked her for caring, expressed her regret over causing so much trouble and asserted that she'd only gotten snippy with Del because she was jealous of Lisa.

Del didn't bother to correct her. She was too busy texting her back. It was over an hour later that Del noticed that her phone was almost out of battery and signed off. She trooped upstairs, passing Lola—on the computer in the second bedroom as usual—without a word and lay down, smiling at a joke Janet had made in one of her last texts. *I forgot how funny she is*, Del thought, as she drifted off.

It was only the next day that she realized that she'd lost her marbles and needed to get back to living in the world of sanity. When her phone next did its shaking dance across the nightstand, Del checked to make sure of the texter's identity and put it back down. No more nonsense, she vowed to herself. She looked over at Lola's side of the bed and saw that, once again, Lola had stayed up all night to write.

"Or," she wondered aloud, "was it to avoid me?" She plucked at the corner of Lola's pillow.

"I used to think it was weird, the way you're always talking to yourself." She laughed. "Now I'm doing it."

It was probably from being home alone so much. From the time she was a teenager, Del had worked, often two jobs. Sitting around doing nothing was not only boring but also depressing. It was time to get back to being a productive human being again. Del stretched, careful not to wrench her left arm.

She went downstairs to find coffee made, muffins cooling on a rack and the newly wrinkle-free and refolded load of laundry on the dining room table. Lola had even folded things the way Del had, with the shirts in thirds instead of halves, the pants rolled.

"So I wouldn't yell at her for redoing it after I fucked it up. Because I'm such an asshole." She shook her head. All she could see was Lola in their bed that night, her face a map of tears, her body limp and empty and resigned.

"Lola?"

But Del was alone.

The kitchen smelled homey, like coffee and cinnamon and vanilla. Del got coffee and a moist, sweet muffin, sat at the kitchen table and couldn't choke down a bite.

Where was Lola? She was probably out at the grocery store or the dry cleaners or something. Doing something useful. Doing something for Del. Or trying to stay out of her way.

Del curled her arms into a nest on the table, ignoring the pull in her left shoulder, and rested her heavy head, wondering if she'd come to her senses just a few hours too late. What if Lola was gone for good?

She decided to behave as though the last several days had never happened. By the time Lola came back from the pharmacy with Del's last round of refills, Del was dressed and sorting the mail. She ignored the way Lola eyed her with caution, ignored the way Lola tried to take the temperature of the room before she asked the formulaic question.

"How are you?"

Del forced a grin, crinkling her eyes. "Great. Thanks for baking."

Lola froze, clearly looking for the hidden barb. "You're welcome."

Del ignored the pang that followed Lola's wariness. "I called in, and I can go back to work as soon as the doc clears me."

Lola nodded. "Okay."

"So I'm going in Monday, and I should be able to go back to work Tuesday."

"What time's your appointment?"

"Nine."

"What time do you want to leave here?"

"I'll take the bike."

"Is that—" She stopped.

Del kept her face blank, but it didn't make a difference. She saw Lola reconsider second-guessing Del's choice.

"Okay." And she nodded in that new, efficient way she'd developed. Like a servant showing deference to her overbearing master, a nurse reassuring a touchy patient, a parent placating a recalcitrant child.

Del faked a small smile. It hurt, seeing that nod. How much did it hurt Lola to feel she had to act like that? And how long would it take before she knew she could relax and be herself again?

"I didn't mean what I said," Del offered. "You know, before."

"You had every right to feel that way." Lola wouldn't look at her directly. "It's okay. I've made you feel bad, and I didn't mean to do that. I am truly sorry."

"No, it's not your fault," Del insisted.

"Yes, it is." Lola started backing away. "I'm sorry. I'm trying but it's not working. You deserve better. Besides, how could someone like me ever compete with someone like Janet?"

Del only hesitated a second, but it was enough. By the time she formed the right reassuring response, Lola was gone from the room.

Del sat for a while longer, then heaved herself up and started unloading the dishwasher. Her phone vibrated across the table, and she held it still for a moment before looking. Janet again, expressing her love and concern. Was Del okay? Why wasn't she answering?

Del typed in her response: *I love LOLA. Shouldn't have texted you.*

After the dishwasher, she started cleaning out the junk drawer, and when the phone started dancing again she wrapped it in a towel and put it on top of the fridge.

"Out of sight, out of mind, right?"

Del tried several more times to talk to Lola, but it was impossible. Finally she decided to just give it time. She didn't try to kiss or hug Lola and she certainly didn't approach her for more than that. Nor did Lola approach her.

Making it all the way to Tuesday morning without exchanging anything but pleasantries with Lola was like crab-walking a marathon, and Del entered the station with a relieved sigh. She was going to have to resolve things before Lola died from sleep deprivation. Her side of the bed practically had cobwebs on it.

Phan plunked a cup of coffee on her desk a few minutes later and Del hid a smile.

"Thanks, sugar. What's the pie today?"

Phan rolled his eyes. "How come you never get me coffee?"

"You take too long to drink it."

They scowled at each other for a minute.

"Anything moving?"

Phan tilted his head. "I can't read Hahn for shit. She's slippery. We dumped her phone."

It was part accusation, part face-saving opportunity. If she told him, it was better for both of them.

"Yeah. She's been texting me."

"Uh-huh."

"But I haven't been able to get anything useful out of her."

"Ah."

Del examined Phan's posture, his expression. "What aren't you telling me?"

"Hahn's place burned down. The whole building has been condemned."

Del gaped. "When? Was anyone hurt?"

"Couple nights back. Arson investigator is saying it was accidental, just some random thing. You know, 'cause there's no way it could be connected to the fact that you got shot in there right before the fire. I don't know who you pissed off, partner."

Del shook her head. "Who didn't I piss off? Hahn and me together, that's a sore subject after her muckraking article came out. They'd rather pretend it's some weird lesbian shit. Not that they'll come right out and say so."

"Hmm. Anyway, no one was hurt, because no one but Hahn lived in the building and she was gone. She owned it. She—I don't get her game. She never told you about the fire?"

"No. She didn't tell me, and you didn't."

"I wanted to know if she would tell you."

"And if I would tell you." Del sat back. "Yeah. Okay."

"It's just—"

Del waved Phan's words away. "No, I get it. I didn't know. She didn't tell me. Obviously, the apartment was staged. Right? I mean, why else keep the building empty?"

"I agree it's a possibility. But she could have just bought the place and not hired a property manager. She could just like her space. Who knows? She's unpredictable at best. The real question is whether the shooting was staged."

Del nodded. "Yeah. I want to say no, but it's hard to dismiss the possibility. I keep going back and forth about how much I trust her and how dangerous I think she could be. How can I possibly be objective about her?"

"Think about it. We'll see where your head is after a day or two. If she did stage the shooting, we have to consider the possibility that she's dangerous to you, to Lola."

"Yeah, I know. Where is she?"

"Don't know. She's not taking my calls."

"I don't know if it's a good idea for me to keep trying to reach out to her."

"Oh." Phan's eyes searched Del's downcast face. "Got it. You better get to it, time for the third degree."

Before she could return to active duty, Del had to undergo an evaluation, face two rounds of videotaped questioning and dance around the question of whether she was the officer who'd been tapped for Janet's exposé the previous year. No one asked that directly, but it colored every question, every follow-up and the attitudes of the investigators. Del felt more like a suspect than a victim and wondered if all victims felt this way.

"You're probably back on," the head of the committee finally grudged. "Provisionally. We may have more questions."

She was on the outside again and worried it would taint Phan. She tried to talk to him about it but he waved away her concerns.

"You know, this game is getting old."

She turned, startled. "What?"

"You're the best partner I've ever had, darling, now go away."

"Right. Yeah." She shrugged. "I just don't want you to get painted with the shithead brush along with me."

"Too late. I had my own mess, remember?"

"How could I forget?" Phan's old partner had been a corrupt jackass, and he'd tried very hard to ruin Phan's reputation in order to save his own. Del remembered Phan being ostracized by most of the department nearly as clearly as she remembered when she was the scapegoat.

"Why do you think we got paired up? We're the two losers nobody wants to work with."

"Stop with the flattery already."

They spent a few hours catching up on the seemingly endless follow-up and research of tracking the missing women. There were dozens, and each had to be painstakingly run down so they could look for patterns.

"Are we just chasing our tails? I mean, there's gotta be somebody who does this for a living, right? Some profiler or whatever? We don't have the manpower or the expertise to handle such a huge thing."

Phan waggled his head. "If there was budget for it, if the missing women were rich or famous or whatever, blah, blah, blah. Why agonize over it? It is what it is. We're duplicating the same work a dozen other folks are doing, but it has to be done. Maybe we'll hit something."

"Maybe." Del rolled her head on her neck, forgetting to be careful, and heard a series of pops. Something in her upper arm made a hot, searing jab and she stilled. Whatever that was, she didn't want to do it again.

It was mostly quiet in the station, and Del was glad of the chance to focus on something other than Janet and Lola and all the ways she'd fucked up things with both of them. It's pretty bad, she thought, when running in circles on missing women is the highlight of your day. She started getting hungry at some point but didn't want to stop working. She heard Phan's stomach growl then her own as if in response. She looked up and saw Phan grinning at her. He dropped his pen.

"Let's go out to lunch."

"What, out, out? Like to the taqueria?"

"How about I surprise you?"

She frowned at him. His face was wide open, cartoonish in its portrayal of innocence.

"Okay."

It wasn't until Phan's wheezing truck was hugging the coast on Highway 1 that Del shook her head and laughed.

"I give. Where the hell are we going?"

"What's down here, Mason? You've lived in the city for how many years?"

"A lot. Daly City? No, Pacifica."

"There you go."

"Why do you want to talk to me in private?"

He smiled. "Gold star for my partner. After we eat."

He handed her his phone. "Ready to go. Hit it and order two Godfathers."

Del scowled but did as he asked. As they wound down into the valley that hid the small burg of Pacifica in a nearly permanent bank of fog, she started to get edgy.

"Any hints?"

"Use two napkins."

"Phan—"

He smirked. "We'll get our food and park at the beach."

Del looked around, seeing only a shroud of fog. "What beach? I don't want to get frostbite."

"Haven't you ever been here?" He laughed. "Just wait."

Godfathers turned out to be giant, fragrant sandwiches from an Italian deli, and Del gave Phan a look as they carried their booty to the truck.

"Not exactly health food."

"Yeah, well, you look like you're down around twenty pounds, so it's okay."

Del considered as he got back on the highway and headed south. It was true. She'd had to use a screwdriver to make an extra hole in her belt.

"What about you, fatty?"

He laughed. "Alana likes big boys." His girlfriend was a tiny thing, small and thin enough to make a skeleton look puffy.

"Not *too* big, I'm guessing."

He laughed again. "She's making dinner tonight. All vegetarian all the time with her. I need some meat for lunch or I'm gonna die."

"Fair enough."

Phan cleared his throat. "Wilson."

Del eyed her partner. "Penn. Dunlop. Gamma. Prince."

He made a face. "No, tinfoil hat from the SRO. Remember her? Her missing daughter is still on my desk. Can you take it over?"

"Thought you were doing it."

"I was, until she turned out not to be Mrs. Mary Wilson, but an alias."

"How does that change anything?"

Phan batted his scrawny eyelashes at Del. "Y'all are ever so brilliant at tracking down those mystery characters, dahlin'."

"In other words, you're senior partner, so I get stuck with the shit."

"She liked you. She trusted you. And it may be nothing, but it's the weirdest note in the stack of files we've got."

Del considered this. Whether that was Phan's motivation or not, it was true. "She made it sound like a doctor raped her. Don't know if it's true or not. I could look into allegations of rape by psych patients around here. Tinfoil got knocked up in eighty-five, so that's a place to start."

"If they did the paperwork. If she reported it. If she's telling the truth."

"That's a lot of unknowns."

"Aren't there always? We have all these missing women and no thread to pull."

"Theories?"

"God, you know it could be anything. Trafficking, drug mules. They're all over the map, profile-wise. Hookers, homeless and housewives, you know? I don't have time to track it all down, find a pattern, pull it apart and chase Tinfoil."

"Ah, shit. I'll take it."

"Come on," Phan teased. "Lucy in Records has the hots for you. She'll track down Tinfoil Wilson for you. And she'll probably help you find a pattern if you're sweet."

"Yeah," Del responded. "And all I have to do is lead on the poor girl. Unspoken promises of sexual rewards and whatnot."

"She'll survive, Mason. Word is, she's currently screwing every woman and half the men in the department."

"Ah, don't tell me you fall for that shit. She got promoted to sergeant. That's all she had to do to get labeled a slut who's sleeping her way to the middle."

Phan held up eyebrows as if in surrender. "I know, I know. But she does like you and she will help if you ask."

"Yeah, I guess."

It wasn't until they were parked yards from a public beach in a small, sunny bay a few miles south that Del spoke again. "Same town? It's like a whole different place."

Phan nodded sagely and took a huge bite of his overloaded sandwich, muscling it down before answering.

"Right?"

It wasn't hot, but the sun was bright, the sky was clear, and the ocean tumbled over the sand like in a movie about a tropical paradise. The beach was mostly deserted, except for a group of women trudging up and down the beach in matching fuchsia shirts that proclaimed their intention to "Live life to the fullest" in glittery gold script. Just beyond them, a young couple walked three golden retrievers. It felt like a different planet from the station and Del was touched. This was a gift.

"Not bad, I guess."

They ate in silence for a while, then Phan belched loudly.

"Ah," he moaned, holding his stomach. "Tell me that's not the best sandwich you ever ate."

"It's actually pretty good."

Phan clutched his chest. "Is that a compliment?"

Del rolled her eyes. Her partner was distracted now. Thinking over what he wanted to say, she guessed.

"Spit it out."

"Okay." He rubbed his chin for a few seconds. "I want to tell you what I've put together on Janet Hahn. But first I'm gonna tell you why and I need you to just listen."

She pretended to lock her mouth and throw away the key.

"There's no one in her life. No family, no one who's been around for any length of time. There's a pattern. She gets intensely interactive with a crowd of people for a while and then drops them. No one's reported her missing, but I'm not sure there's anyone who would. She didn't die in the fire, so she's out there somewhere in the wind and no one's missing her."

Del nodded, not trusting herself to speak.

"I went back a couple years. Checked her phone, her financials, all that. She's crazy rich, inherited millions from her tech-rich computer whiz daddy and pretty little trophy-wife mommy, did you know?" Phan didn't wait for her nod, didn't look at her. "Talked to her agent. She's a freelancer. You know that, I guess. About a year ago, the agent, a Robby Shaw, talked to Janet about a story on photography and filming as sex crimes. Janet put together a whole thing. Brilliant, according to the agent. The lens as phallus."

"Guys filming the ladies' room toilet, landlords filming their tenants, upskirting, all that?"

"Right."

"She focuses on the effects. Interviews psychologists, victims, the people in their lives, the family and friends of the voyeurs and the vics. Not a quickie. Not a fluff piece."

Del nodded, filing away Phan's insistence on this.

"So Shaw gets the first few weekly updates, and it seems like she might be just starting to get somewhere. Then radio silence. He calls, texts, emails—nothing. She's off planet for a few days, then he gets a text saying she's fine, had the flu, sorry."

"But—"

"Another few days and she sends an email. She tells him she's taking a break, wants to write a book."

"Her computer?"

"One of the few things we took before the fire. Wiped clean. Jones is on it."

"Good."

"Says somebody did a pretty thorough job of cleaning off the hard drive. It may take him a while to get data back."

"Okay."

"I think you should file a missing persons report, Mason. Give us the leash to work this. Maybe she's off doing her thing, maybe she's playing a game, okay, but maybe she's in trouble. Maybe she's part of the pattern of missing women and maybe not."

Del watched the couple with the retrievers throw tennis balls across the beach. Their dogs leapt joyfully and bounded across the sand to retrieve them. One of them wagged his tail so hard it nearly toppled him. Del smiled. She loved dogs. Why hadn't she ever had one? As a kid, she'd probably spent more time with stray critters than people. As an adult, she'd been busy, going to college and the academy and working the lousy shifts of a rookie. But she had a house now. A dog could live there. It was one of the reasons she'd wanted a house so much. Maybe it was finally time to get that dog. Or two. Why not? Lola was a softie. She'd love a nice, playful pup or two. Del's smile died. Janet wouldn't like the shedding or the drooling or the attention a dog would pull from her.

"I don't really know much about Janet," Del murmured, watching the game. "I wonder if she ever had a dog. I wonder where she went to college. I don't know anything about her family. I don't know her friends, her anything. How can you have a six-month relationship with a person and not know anything about her?"

Phan glanced at Del. "I can fill in some details if you want."

Del considered this and couldn't decide if it was sadder that her partner needed to fill in the blanks or that she desperately wanted him to do so. Finally she nodded.

"Filthy rich, you know that. Parents and sister died a long time ago, accident. All the money went to our girl, who was away in her senior year at some exclusive rich, bright and badly behaved kid boarding school in Europe. For the last decade-and-a-half she's been bouncing around the world, mostly Europe and the US. Some college, good schools, never quite finished any real degree. Donates to art and gay rights and women's groups and whatnot. Doesn't really fit in with the rich folks, doesn't really work, doesn't really live in one place. Boyfriends, girlfriends, some drugs, a couple of half-assed suicide attempts, a few short stints in expensive private mental hospitals and rehabs. Lots of shopping and moving and flipping real estate. She'd be in jail if she didn't have truckloads of money. She's fired several lawyers, doctors, financial managers, housekeepers. The only person she's stayed in touch with longer than a few months is you. Nobody but you is likely to report her missing."

Del pressed her lips together, unsure whether or how she wanted to respond to all of that. Was she really the only person who might have noticed Janet was missing? "Okay."

They watched as the couple on the sand kept up the game for a while and gave the tennis balls a good workout. The wind took one of them and it soared toward the highway. All three dogs focused on that one and dashed toward the racing traffic, while the couple chased after them. Del hopped out of the truck and dashed across the parking lot, snagging the tennis ball and hurling it away from the freeway and toward the surf, glad she had one arm that worked.

The couple waved their thanks, and Del stood for a moment before heading back to the truck. The air was cold and salty and clean. She could have stood there sucking up the freshness for an hour. She turned to look back. Phan was waiting for her in the real world, where Janet was missing and maybe in trouble and maybe a bad guy. Del gave the bounding sea a last long look and trudged back to the truck.

CHAPTER SEVENTEEN

"What she really has, the thing that sets her apart, is her finesse." Lola had overhead a stranger say this in a grocery store. She means it, Lola thought at the time. She truly admires whoever it is.

Olivia, that character who'd suddenly appeared—she had finesse, didn't she? Lola could picture Olivia, smiling, confidently steering a classic convertible on a winding highway in the Italian countryside in late spring. Olivia was wearing a beautiful, colorful scarf over her long, smooth, honey-colored hair. And a hat, a wide-brimmed hat with a low profile. Where was she going? Was she meeting a friend for a picnic? A lover for a tryst? A contact for the handoff of some important secret technology? She certainly wasn't going to the pharmacy for multivitamins or deodorant. She wasn't wearing sweatpants or eating crackers out of the paper sleeve or slurping tepid coffee out of a chipped mug. Lola sighed.

Olivia wasn't a schlumpy, awkward slob who could barely make eye contact with people and went around looking like a panhandler. Olivia wore beautiful designer clothes with casual aplomb and sported discreetly expensive shoes. She was well read and cultured and sophisticated. She treated everyone with respect, and people were both thawed and a little awed by her simple elegance. She had a wonderful smile, one that made everyone's heart lift, and her mellifluous laugh drew amused, admiring chuckles from all who heard its gentle sound. She enchanted Lola.

She was an orphan but not a foster home kind of orphan like Lola. Olivia had some romantic beginning plus great resourcefulness and imagination, and somehow she ended up traveling and learning and becoming increasingly chic and wise. How, exactly, Lola would figure out later.

She'd have an adventure—Lola wasn't sure what that would be— and it would change her life forever. Worlds would open up to her and she would learn to be the elegant lady Lola imagined. She would save someone, employing great cleverness and creativity, and this would be life changing. She would fall in love with a woman who was married to a man and the woman would break her heart. She would retreat from her wonderful life, unable to bear the pain of seeing her beloved with the loutish husband. Olivia would take random lovers in her travels, unwilling to bare her heart again. But she would meet someone, a woman with a tender, gentle spirit, someone so kind and honest that Olivia would begin to wonder if maybe, just maybe, she should open her heart one more time.

Lola's stomach rumbled, and she clucked in irritation until she glanced at the clock.

"Three o'clock?" Olivia had sucked up six hours like they were nothing. Lola should shut down the computer and figure out what to do, pronto. Olivia wouldn't just sit there lollygagging in a fantasy. Olivia would make a plan.

Only, as a child, she would be called "Liv." There would be an older, distant relative. No, a neighbor. She would teach Olivia to command respect without having to demand it. Lola looked up, trying to imagine how the woman—Mrs. Sutton—would say it. She and Olivia would be outside on a bright, cool day, and Mrs. Sutton would stop and inhale the intoxicating sweetness of a flower—a peony, maybe—and point out how the flower kept its perfume curled within its petals like a secret.

Like the flower, a lady would only reveal hints of her beauty, Mrs. Sutton would advise, and only to those who dared come close enough and proved themselves worthy. Lola stopped to picture the scene, trying to get the details just right, and noticed that it was dark out.

She looked at her watch: eight o'clock? She checked her cell phone, but there were no calls. And she'd spent the day playing with Olivia's story instead of in the real world dealing with the mess of her life. Things between her and Del were worse than ever and she was clueless as to how to make them better. What would Mrs. Sutton tell Olivia in the same situation? The sound of Del's approaching motorcycle made the question suddenly urgent.

"Blankets warm, but they also smother. They lie still and wait to be used. Is that really what you want to be?" It was Mrs. Sutton's voice, and Lola made a face.

"Mrs. Sutton might be imaginary, but she gives good advice." Lola nodded at her own words. "Don't rush down there like a puppy."

Mrs. Sutton nodded her approval. "Earn her respect," she counseled. "Have some dignity, dear."

Mrs. Sutton was right. Lola waited until Del had been home several minutes before heading downstairs. She fought every impulse. She didn't ask Del where she'd been or if she was okay. She didn't offer to make dinner or apologize for not having done so already.

When Del said she was going back out again, Lola masked her feelings and said, "Be careful. Good night."

"Well done, dear," whispered Mrs. Sutton.

Whether Del noticed Lola's reserve or not, she gave no sign of it, and Lola felt a surge of disappointment. What had she imagined, that Del would rush to her side and ask her what was wrong? As Del dashed out to roar away on her bike again, Lola closed her eyes. Mrs. Sutton's approval felt hollow.

"Okay. I kept my dignity. I kept my self-respect. I didn't smother her or baby her or demand attention and reassurance from her. That's good, right?"

But Mrs. Sutton had retreated into the world of fiction, and Lola was alone and feeling empty. She dozed in front of the TV for hours, unable to sleep and unable to decide whether keeping her dignity and self-respect would mean losing Del. If it wasn't already too late. She knew she'd messed things up by being a bad lover, but it was hard to believe that this was the only problem or even the biggest one. The real problem, maybe, was that Del had never stopped loving Janet.

But was it that simple? Del was going through something, obviously. Being shot was traumatic. Combine that with Janet's showing up after hurting Del so badly, Janet's appealing to Del's desire to protect innocent people from harm and Lola's dimwitted attempts at caretaking her—it was no wonder poor Del was troubled. If she needed a little space, then so be it. Lola turned things over in her mind until she drifted into an uneasy sleep just after dawn. It was nearly nine when she awoke with a start from a frightening dream and dragged herself to the shower. Determined to avoid the trap of Olivia's world, Lola forced herself to run an errand.

"Leave the house," she commanded herself. She trudged to the farmers' market and wandered around, unable to choose anything. She wasn't even sure why she'd bothered walking all the way over here, except that it gave her something to do besides wallowing in self-pity and self-loathing and writing. She made her desultory way around the stalls of produce and breads and jams, unable to appreciate even the simple beauty of the lovely foods around her. She'd just decided to give up and go home, thinking vaguely about how she could land Olivia in a farmers' market and see what would happen there, when she heard someone call her name.

"Lola Bannon, how dare you show your face? I'm so mad at you! You didn't call me!" The voice came from behind her.

Lola whirled around to see a woman, a stranger with dark hair and wide, dark eyes, staring at her in what seemed to be mock outrage.

"You don't remember me, do you?"

Lola flushed. "I'm sorry."

"Wow, that hurts the ego!"

"I'm sorry." Lola didn't know what to say. Suddenly, she recognized the woman from the Meetup. "Sterling?"

"Ding, ding, ding. Give the lady a prize!" Sterling was laughing again, even louder, and Lola was embarrassed. Several people were sending curious glances their way and Lola flushed. She'd had a horror of public spectacles for as long as she could remember, and having someone hollering at her across asphalt at the top of her lungs was definitely in the category of public spectacle, as far as Lola was concerned.

"Hi, hello. I'm sorry I didn't recognize you at first."

"Well, hi, hello to you too. But I'm really hurt. You not only didn't recognize me, you didn't call me!"

"I'm sorry." Lola started edging away.

"Seriously." Sterling leaned close. "Why didn't you call me?"

"I just felt kind of funny about it."

"But why?"

"I don't know,"

Sterling was staring at her, and Lola scrambled for an answer. "I just thought my girlfriend might not like it."

"The jealous type, huh?" Sterling smiled suddenly. "Is there some reason for her to be jealous?"

"No!" Lola was embarrassed. "Of course not."

"Because you think I'm unattractive." Sterling seemed hurt by this, and Lola rushed to erase the hurt in her eyes.

"No, but—"

"That's good."

"Well." Lola was flustered and unsure how to proceed. "But it doesn't matter."

"I think it does." Sterling leaned in again, far too close, and Lola took a step back. "Don't be scared, kitten. I'm no big, bad wolf."

"I don't mean to be rude, but I have to get going."

Sterling grabbed her arm. "Hey, I'm just kidding around. I don't want to make you mad. I just moved here and I don't know a lot of people. I kind of feel like the cliques are closed to me, you know?"

Lola nodded. "It's hard to go to a new place and make new friends."

"I feel kind of shy, actually."

Lola nodded, though Sterling didn't seem especially shy to her.

"Sometimes when I'm nervous I say things, and I don't mean them the way people think."

Lola considered this. "I've put my foot in my mouth more than once."

"Can I show you the picture I took?"

"I don't really have time right now, I'm sorry."

"Please? It won't take long and I'd really like to know what you think. I'm starting my career over and it's so hard." She seemed to be fighting tears.

"I'm sorry."

"I've always wanted to be a professional photographer, but it's more about sales than about shooting pictures, and I really, really need some help to make sure I'm going in the right direction. Please?"

"I guess I could look, but honestly I can't really help you. I don't know anything about photography or marketing or anything. And I wasn't exactly Miss Popular at that thing either."

"I just want a second set of eyes, you know, two minds are better than one, that kind of thing. Please? I could really use a friend right now."

Lola wasn't sure how to get out of this. "I guess," she finally muttered.

"Great!" Sterling grinned easily at her. "Why don't we meet for coffee sometime and you can see the picture and we can talk. Okay?"

"Okay. But no promises, Sterling. I really don't know what I could possibly—"

"Could it be tonight? I'm pretty anxious to get started."

"Well, I—"

"You're the only friendly face I've seen in weeks," Sterling proclaimed. "I'm not asking you to be an expert. I'm just two seconds from running back to New Mexico and giving up on my dream, and I need a tiny bit of support from somebody, please?"

Lola gave a reluctant nod. They set up the time and place and Sterling smiled broadly.

"I really appreciate this, Lola. See you tonight!"

Lola finally got free and could go home. She gave up on her resolve and decided to write about Olivia and forget about Del and about Janet and Sterling and about everything. Olivia was twenty-six and was studying art. Lola stopped and looked over what she'd already written. It was well over two hundred pages, and she'd already given Olivia her challenging, enriching childhood, her turbulent adolescence and the beginnings of her fascinating adulthood. But it all felt pointless.

"Where is this going, Olivia? Why are you here? What are you all about?"

After a minute of silence Lola laughed aloud. Of all the voices in her head, the one she really wanted to hear was absolutely silent.

CHAPTER EIGHTEEN

"But they already basically cleared me yesterday!"

Phan's shrug was nearly audible over the phone. "One more round today, they said."

"Did they say why?"

"Listen, you know they're just covering ass. Answer the questions, jump through the hoops. No biggie."

Del rolled her eyes. "Yeah, okay."

Nothing had changed since the day before. So what was going on? Was this the department taking the opportunity to fuck her over? It was hard to know. Sometimes she felt like part of the department, one of the family. Sometimes it was like she was only there because they couldn't find a way to get rid of her. Was that paranoid? She couldn't be sure. Dealing with the SFPD often felt like dealing with Janet. Del never quite knew what the real rules were. It was murky in her head when it came to both. She was always wondering what was really happening, what she was missing. She remembered going to meet Janet at Steinhart Aquarium, right after it reopened. It had been one of their first dates, and Del had been thrown by Janet's suggesting it. Janet definitely seemed more like a nightclub, rock concert, fancy restaurant kind of gal. But Del was already head over heels and secretly delighted that there seemed to be more to Janet than met the eye.

Del waited by the entrance to the first exhibit, keeping an eye on the time as Janet was ten minutes late, then twenty. By the end of the half hour, several families had asked her for directions to bathrooms and elevators, three parents had complained to her about a creepy guy near the swamp exhibit, whom Del scared off with a prolonged glare, and one youngster had asked to see her gun. Is it that obvious, she wondered, that I'm either a cop or security guard? A second kid sauntered over and peered up at her with narrowed eyes.

"Who're you here to bust, lady?"

"Sorry, bud." Del hid a smile. "I'm just here to see the fish."

The boy scowled, clearly disgusted by her seeming lie, and stalked away. Del had to smile. Maybe cops really were born and not made.

"Making friends, I see."

Del slid her gaze toward the voice. Janet was dressed like a runway model in what appeared to be bridal lingerie paired with red, five-inch fuck-me heels. She looked like an incredibly expensive hooker posing as an angel. Del raised an eyebrow and grinned. Appropriate or not, the look was definitely alluring.

"I'd like to make friends with you."

Janet batted her eyelashes. "I sincerely hope you and I are more than friends."

Del grinned again, nodding.

Janet sashayed past her and stood watching a mosaic of colorful fish in a large tank. Some darted, some meandered, some circled, but Del didn't see anything fascinating in their movements. She tried to make eye contact with Janet, to no avail.

"I'm glad to see you, Janet."

Janet nodded absently.

"Are you glad to see me?" Del was shocked to hear the question come out of her own mouth. She sounded pathetic! Usually, femmes were all over Del, plying her with compliments and begging for their own in return. She'd played with them, teased them, made them come to her for so long that it was disarming to have a girl just stand there and expect to be catered to. Where the impulse to do so came from, Del couldn't imagine. Still, there it was. She wanted this girl like none other, and she'd do whatever it took to get her.

"Ever wonder," Janet asked in a barely audible voice, "how much they think?"

"The fish?"

"Yes, my darling, the fish."

"Yeah, no."

Janet laughed. "Nobody—it's like they're just—nobody wonders. You see a pretty fish, and you think that's nice. I'm glad they put that pretty thing in a tank so I can see it. Then you see another fish and another and another. And you forget about each of them two seconds after you've seen it. So what was the point? What if that fish there or that one," she pointed, "had a great destiny somewhere else?"

"Janet?"

"What if," Janet continued as though she hadn't heard Del's voice, "it was in love with another fish somewhere, but it got taken away? What if it's miserable? But all you see is the pretty fish, and it never occurs to you that it might have feelings or thoughts or hopes. You just think it's there for you."

A little girl standing near Janet burst into tears. "Mommy," she wailed. "The fish are sad. They want to go home!"

The mother glared at Del, who shrugged an apology.

"I guess you're right. I never thought about it. What made you think of it? Is everything all right?"

Janet smiled and linked arms with Del. "Oh, I'm just being silly. Take me to the jellyfish, sexy. They look like pretty girls with their skirts blown up. The Marilyn Monroes of the marine scene."

Del had laughed at the image and now wished she'd taken the time to follow up on that fish thing. What had Janet been trying to tell her? Maybe the only way Janet could share pieces of herself was indirectly. If so, Del had missed the point, at least at the aquarium that day. How many other clues had Del missed? How many times had Janet tried to reveal her true nature to Del, only to be let down by her obtuseness? Del shook her head, trying to focus on the present.

"No." Del had answered the same question six times, varying her sentence pattern enough each time to sound, she hoped, authentic. "I was not investigating a crime. I was visiting an old friend. Then out of nowhere I got shot. Then the building burned down, and now my friend is missing. I don't know more than that."

There was another hour of the same after that, and Del was sent to wait on a bench in the hallway like a kid in trouble waiting for the principal to see her. She hummed inside her head, wondering what kind of music Janet liked. What kind Lola liked. The silence Lola seemed to crave made Del crazy. Who wouldn't want to listen to music? It was like enjoying water as soup. Maybe Lola just hadn't had the chance to learn about music, to appreciate it. Beckett had probably hated music. It sounded too happy.

Del finally got called in and was told in a terse two minutes that she was off the hook. None of the five members of the panel really believed her, but they weren't willing to go on record with their doubts, so she was cleared. The case was out of her hands completely. Not that it had ever been in them, Del reminded herself. The theory seemed to be that Janet had stumbled onto the cover-up of something and had been coerced into silence. That meant it had nothing to do with Del. The department would, Del guessed, end up deciding to bring in the feds and turn it all over to them. Janet's connection to the department and to Del made things hinky, and her vast fortune would mean the Missing Persons report Del needed to file would get flagged as indicative of a possible kidnapping. As soon as there was a kidnapping, the feds loved to rush in and play big shot. They also would want control of the task force that Captain Bradley, long known to his underlings as Captain Wonderbread, had assembled as a result of the department-wide boxfuls of reports on the dramatic uptick in missing women in the city.

"This is great news," Phan insisted as they waited on another bench in another hallway for the last signatures. Del felt like she'd been sent to the principal's office. Again. She cracked her knuckles.

"Yeah. Great."

"You could have been suspended. Not only are you not in trouble, they're pointing the investigation straight in the opposite direction." He rubbed his chin. "You have the opportunity to walk away from this clean. And this is the only chance for that. You've made sure that everyone who should knows Hahn is missing. We file the Missing Persons report and you're clean."

Del made a face. "You're right."

There was a long pause, and Del peered at the pattern of water damage in the ceiling. She heard Phan rub his chin.

"But," Phan spoke quietly, "you feel responsible for her. You can't just pretend it has nothing to do with you."

"It's not that I still care about her."

"Uh-huh."

"Not more than I should."

"Uh-huh."

She shrugged and smiled when he mirrored her.

"She came to you for help so you want to help her."

"Yeah." She dropped her head into her hands, and Phan clapped her on the back. Del tried not to wince at that. He'd barely grazed her shoulder, but it stung like hell.

"Hey, I was wondering where you stood on the 'Hahn as villain, Hahn as victim' question."

Del waggled her head. "I'd like to play it out both ways. Victim first."

Whatever Phan thought about that, he nodded. "Let's figure out who she could be running from."

"A lover? A partner? Investigator?" Del sat back. "I wonder."

"A partner who turned on her, maybe?"

"Let's run it out. Who could it be? Would she have met the partner during the investigation, you think? Or is it someone she's worked with before?"

Del tuned out through the next several minutes of Phan's speculation. He didn't really need her input anyway. He was just running through possibilities out loud the way Del liked to run through them in writing. Eventually Phan wound down, and the partners worked on the missing women files. Del tried to track down who exactly Mary Wilson really was and the day stretched until long after dark. They ran in circles, only occasionally exchanging a glance or muttered comment. Finally Phan slammed a case file shut and shook his head.

"I'm out. I've been looking at the same report for an hour and still couldn't tell you what it says. I'm going home and you should too."

Del rode home in a daze. Were they really doing this? Would she be able to find out who was scaring Janet, who had shot at her? Would she be able to find Janet herself? Del should still be on leave, and she knew it. After an OIS—an officer-involved shooting—the officer involved was placed on administrative leave. But Del's admin leave had taken its course during her recovery, and now, after only a brief reprieve and two hoop-jumping sessions, she was back in the fray. Back to endless hours, fathomless frustration and no personal life.

Del slapped her helmet. She'd missed dinner again and she'd again forgotten to call Lola. After everything else she'd done and failed to do, it hardly seemed important, this one omission. But Del knew it was getting to be a problem, one she could hardly afford to continue ignoring. She resolved to make up for all the things she'd done wrong. She'd romance Lola, give her the reassurance and affection and tenderness she deserved. She parked the Suzuki outside, thinking Lola might like a ride, and took a minute to plan how she'd approach her.

Del clapped her hands together as she headed inside. She'd make a fresh start with Lola, do things the right way this time. She'd never make Lola feel like nothing again. She felt the weight in her stomach lighten. She'd been carrying around her guilt and self-loathing, hadn't she? She couldn't force Lola to face the truth about her cheating without hurting her. But she could give Lola what she wanted and deserved. It was past time to either start treating Lola like the love of her life or to let her go so someone else could.

But Lola wasn't home. Her new purse and keys were gone, her car, too. Del fought panic. Maybe she went to the store. Maybe she went to dinner with Marco. In the kitchen, she found a note:

Dinner's in the fridge. Hope you had a good day. Out late. Love you!

Del fought what she knew was irrational outrage. *I work hard, all day, every day, and she can't even bother to be here when I get home?* She yanked open the fridge and saw a foil-wrapped plate adorned with a heart drawn in marker. Del stood looking at it for a full minute before easing the refrigerator door closed.

She was numb, unable to process her thoughts or feelings, and she sleepwalked up the stairs and eased to a sitting position on Lola's side of the bed.

"Feels like my bones are made of peanut brittle," she said, an echo of what Nana used to say years ago, when the barometric pressure dropped and her arthritis flared up.

"Nana loved peanut brittle," she confided to Lola's pillow. "Even after she lost most of her teeth she still loved it. She'd suck it, rot the teeth she had left." Del only realized that she was crying when a tear spoiled the perfect surface of the pillowcase, and she rubbed it with her thumb, trying to dry it.

"She woulda liked you. She was kinda big and loud and ornery, but she always liked quiet people. She'd draw 'em out, get 'em to talk to her." Del blotted her eyes with uncharacteristic gentleness, still feeling fragile. "She hated liars. Did I tell you that already?"

No, she'd hardly told Lola anything about her family. Why was that? She'd told Janet. Not everything, but enough for Janet to taunt her about it when she was mad. How had Del never realized Janet wasn't reciprocating with her own stories? How had she never realized Janet was just storing up what Del shared with her as an arsenal?

"I opened my heart to the wrong person."

Del nodded at her own words. "You're the one I should have met first. You're the one I should have fallen in love with first." She hugged herself. "But maybe if it hadn't been for Janet I wouldn't have been ready to love you."

Knowing it wasn't productive or helpful, she ran over the previous days and weeks, examining each time she'd been dismissive or demanding or caustic. She started small and worked up from the minor offenses to the bigger ones. She shook her head, not wanting to examine these memories, but she pushed past her own resistance and probed. She watched Lola's face fall over and over, watched Lola mask her hurt feelings and disappointment and loneliness. She watched Lola grow exhausted physically and emotionally. She watched Lola grow cautious. She watched Lola retreat further and further and wanted to stop there.

"Don't be a coward now." Del shook her head again.

"You ain't got to the worst of it and you know it." She sank onto the bed, curling up on Lola's side, making sure she didn't sully the pillow any more than she already had. "Get to it, girl." She played the movie in her head and watched herself cheat on Lola with Janet.

"Every single minute since then has been a lie. And I been taking my guilt out on you."

But the even bigger sin she couldn't face. She knew Lola went gomer when she was scared. It was how she'd learned to survive, obviously. The explanation for Lola's going gomer was easy; what was harder was explaining how that bad night between them had happened.

How could Del begin to explain even to herself that she'd simply lost patience with Lola's inhibitions and reticence? How could she explain that she'd gotten sick of the way Lola was too traumatized by having been a victim for too long and in too many ways?

What kind of person does that? What kind of person says, hey, I'm sorry you were hurt and traumatized, but I'd really like to just fuck you without thinking about that?

"I made you go gomer," she whispered, rubbing her thumb against the embroidered edge of Lola's pillow. "I treated you like Beckett did. Like it was him I was hurting by being so mean. Like it made you mine instead of his." She covered her face with her hands. "Doesn't that make me just as bad as him? I blamed you for being fucked up by him and I punished you for what he did." She covered her mouth with her hands, mumbling through her fingers. "Sometimes it's hard to be around you. I can't stand to look at you."

"I didn't fuck you." Del heard the petulance in her own voice and flushed. "But I made you feel like nothing. That's just as bad. Maybe worse."

Del rubbed her face until her skin burned. She felt like the last person on the planet. Lola was a million miles away because Del had pushed her there. Had she pushed Janet into disappearing too?

"If you both love me so much, why am I always alone?"

* * *

After Del's nearly sleepless night, she and Phan spent another fruitless day tracking down worthless leads, splitting their time between the missing women and Janet. No one seemed to have known Janet for more than six months or a year, and the further back they went into Janet's life the more clearly emerged the pattern Phan had identified. She was a vagabond, flitting among major metro hubs and making dear, dear, beloved friends who disappeared from her life after a few short months without leaving behind more than a picture or series of comments on Facebook.

"Listen," Phan had finally said, "you have as much history with her as anyone we've found. I think I should keep tracking everyone else and you should write down everything you remember about your relationship with her."

"But what's the point? It's not like anything happened while we were together that could lead to her being missing now."

"Maybe not, but I still think it's worth your time."

Unconvinced but unsure how else to proceed, Del sat down to her homework and listed all the places she and Janet had been to together, along with the dates and times. Too restless to keep writing, she decided to visit each place in the city, though she couldn't have said why she was doing this. She'd go to them in order and that meant starting at the bar where they met, if she wanted to be technical. But there was no tug at the memory.

"We were still strangers then. It's where we met, but it doesn't matter."

What did matter was the Amazon Motel, and Del headed south. She forced herself to take her time going down Mission Street, knowing Lola was unlikely to go that route from the grocery store or wherever she was. Del needed to tell her Janet was missing, needed to deal with all of it. Right now, though, Del was lost in nostalgia, remembering that first dazzling night with Janet. She was yanked out of the past when she saw Lola's creaky old Buick wheezing along.

"Where the hell are you going?"

Del pushed away the question of where the hell she herself was going for the moment. There was a woman in the car with Lola, and she was leaning in, playing with a strand of Lola's hair. Del was tempted to follow Lola, but the Buick turned left on Cesar Chavez Street and the Amazon was waiting.

Of course, the Amazon wasn't going anywhere, was it? But Del felt pulled to the little motel as if by some invisible hand. This was not, she assured herself, the result of any reluctance to consider the possibility that Lola might turn out to be someone other than the sweet, loving innocent Del had fallen in love with.

She sat on her parked bike, looking at the low-budget, nondescript motel and trying to catch her breath. Seeing the place was like falling through a hole in time and landing back in the Amazon the first night, and Del let herself pretend she was following Janet up those stairs, her whole body shaking with desire when Janet looked back at her and winked. She saw herself pushing open the door, propelling both of them onto the tired bed, frantic with the need to see and feel and taste every inch of this bold, outrageous stranger. She could see Janet's body straining up to meet hers, hear Janet's moans and squeals and low chuckle. Suddenly, it all seemed ridiculously crass, a tacky scene in a low-budget skin flick. Del detached herself from the past.

"Do you still love Janet?"

Had someone asked that question or had Del imagined it? She wasn't sure. But sitting in front of the Amazon Motel, Del could almost see the question hanging in the air. She felt compelled to answer it.

Del shook her head. What she meant to say was no. But a different word slipped out of her mouth. The word was like a masked thief escaping a bank vault, loot in hand. She couldn't believe the sound of the word for a moment until she heard herself repeat it.

"Yes."

CHAPTER NINETEEN

Lola replayed the evening in her mind, going over every detail in exhausting clarity, trying to understand what had happened. It didn't make sense, any of it, and she ran through the mental playback again.

I got to the coffee shop five minutes early. I walked in, and right away, Sterling jumped up and started yelling.

"You came to me! Lola, hey, Lo-la! Over here!"

Lola blushed as she walked through the maze of tables to where Sterling stood, waving wildly.

"Hi."

Sterling grabbed her in a too-tight, cologne-saturated embrace for just a few moments too long. "Lola, lovely Lola!"

"Can't breathe," Lola finally gasped with a nervous laugh.

Sterling wore a crisp white shirt, purple dinner jacket, and black trousers, and Lola felt frumpy in comparison, wearing old jeans and a pill-covered sweater.

"I was worried you wouldn't come."

"I said I would."

"Yeah, but I have no way of knowing how honest you are."

This was said with such a self-conscious air of frankness that Lola knew she had to produce a smile, even though it felt like she'd been insulted.

"I guess that's true." Lola hesitated, standing behind a chair with her hand on it. "I came because I wanted to talk with you about something."

"Because you feel guilty?" Sterling leaned too close again.

"What?"

"Well, you told me you have a girlfriend. But you're attracted to me, right?"

Lola looked away, unsure how to respond.

"Come on," Sterling yanked the chair sideways, pulling it out of Lola's hands, and gestured at the seat. "There's no law against thinking someone's attractive. It's not cheating to look, is it?"

"I guess not, but—"

Though she didn't really want to she didn't know how to explain why not, so Lola sat.

Sterling patted Lola's shoulder, let her hand linger. "You feel like you're being disloyal."

That was exactly how it felt. Lola nodded, watching Sterling as she plunked down into the other seat.

"I love Del."

"That's great."

Sterling beamed, and Lola hid her annoyance at what seemed like flippancy.

"Let's get you a—hot chocolate? Herbal tea? Triple shot mocha latte? What's your poison? I can tell you're high maintenance, but how high maintenance are you?"

"High maintenance? I don't know why you'd say that." Lola shook her head. "I don't know what I'm doing here."

"Hey, this is a coffee shop, not a swingers' party. Wait, are you into that? I bet you are, aren't you?"

Lola frowned and shook her head, but Sterling was already talking again.

"Never mind, I'm kidding! Hey, I get it. You're not here to hook up. Well, you *think* you're not. We'll see, won't we? No problem. Now, I'll get your coffee. I take care of my women."

"No," Lola protested, but Sterling was pulling her by the arm.

"Are you kidding? This is a business meeting. I'm writing this off." She sailed off, dragging Lola along with her. But it turned out that she'd forgotten her wallet, so Lola ended up buying their coffees and a pastry for Sterling.

After several minutes of wide-ranging small talk, Lola found her discomfort increasing but couldn't determine why. Sterling seemed harmless, but there was something about her that made Lola uncomfortable.

Is it just because I am attracted to her? Is it because I've been frustrated with Del? Maybe there's nothing wrong with Sterling at all, and I'm really just upset with Del.

"Hey"—Sterling was waving her hand in front of Lola's face—"Earth to Lola, come in, Lola."

Lola grimaced. "Sorry about that."

"Thinking about me?"

"Hmm. So, is it okay if we talk about your business? You were going to tell me about your marketing plan, I think."

But Sterling gave her a sly smile. "You weren't thinking about that. You were thinking about me and you and your girlfriend, weren't you?"

Lola looked over her cup at Sterling's smirking face. She was starting to feel like she was dealing with a terribly bright, terribly bratty, precocious child. It was hard to read Sterling. She seemed to swing from one mood to another with almost no warning. Could she be on drugs? Or was she a perfectly normal woman and Lola was just terrible at reading people? That seemed entirely possible, given how lousy Lola had always been at meeting people and making friends.

"I guess you could say that."

"Wow, you dirty girl!"

Lola frowned. "What?"

"Hey, I'm not into threesomes, myself, but I could be talked into it if you're very sweet to me. I could see it, you know? You and me and some other chick—I like the way you think."

Lola shook her head. "No, that's not—"

"Relax!" Sterling laughed and shook her head. "Kidding! I'm kidding. I thought we were maybe pals, you and me. Aren't we?"

"Well, I guess so." Though they weren't, really, Lola reflected.

"Then what's the big deal? Can't you take a joke?"

"Sorry." Lola wished she hadn't come to the coffee shop. She stared down at her cup, wishing it were smaller. How quickly could she get out of here without being rude? She'd met Sterling three times, and she'd been a different person each time. How could one person have three different personalities?

"You're way too serious. Don't you ever lighten up and just have fun?"

"Of course." *But really*, Lola wondered, *do I?* "Not much, I guess."

"Well, that settles it." Sterling grabbed her hand. "As your newest friend, I consider it my sacred duty to teach you how to have fun. Are you ready?"

"Ready for what, exactly?"

Sterling laughed, but she seemed irritated. "God, you're so intense about everything. What's the big deal? Are you a drama queen or something?"

"What do you mean?"

"Come on, I don't see why you're acting like this. It's making me uncomfortable."

"Acting like what?"

"Forget it." Sterling stood abruptly, banging into the table. "I'm really not too happy with being here right now. Can we go, please?"

Lola wasn't sure how to react to this.

"I thought you—"

"Come on, you're being weird, let's go."

"How am I being weird?"

"If you don't know, I can't explain it."

Lola gave up and stood. "Maybe we should just call it a night." She tried to hide the hope in her voice, but she flushed with guilt and saw Sterling notice this.

"Don't run off, okay? Please? Don't abandon me. Everybody abandons me."

Lola swallowed hard. "Where do you want to go?"

"I don't care. You decide." Sterling pulled her through the tables and to the door. When they got outside, Sterling seemed to relax.

"Are you okay?" Lola cast about for a way to end the evening.

"I don't know why, but I was feeling kind of anxious in there. You ever feel anxious like that?"

Lola nodded slowly. "Sometimes."

"Thanks for coming with me. Can we drive around a little?"

"I kind of need to get going. Besides, I thought you wanted to show me that picture."

"God, is that all you care about?" Sterling glared at her and Lola bit her lip.

"I don't—isn't that why you asked me to come here?"

"Maybe I just wanted too much. I really like you and I thought you liked me, but I'm not sure you know what you want. I'm not sure you're an honest person. Are you playing a game with me?"

Lola shook her head. "I've been very clear with you."

"You love your girlfriend, right? But you're attracted to me too. So where does that leave me?"

Lola wasn't sure how to respond to that. "Sterling, what do you want?"

"Just let me walk you to your car. I need to see if I'm right about something."

"I don't think—"

"Please?"

"I don't—"

"I promise, I just want us to be friends and have a few laughs."

Lola shrugged and started walking to her car, too exhausted and confused to decide how to respond. Sterling strode beside her, whistling. When Lola reached the car, she stood for a moment.

"Well, good night."

Sterling shivered. "Hey, can we talk for a minute?"

"Sterling, I—"

"Come on, have a little decency. I'm freezing. Please? Would you really leave me out here like I'm nothing?"

Lola was quiet until they were both sitting in the car. "I don't understand what you want from me."

Sterling shivered again. "Could you give me a ride to BART? It's not far, but I'm really cold."

"Okay." Was that what this was all about, Sterling wanting a ride to the train station? It was a little chilly out but hardly cold enough to warrant all the dramatics. Lola started up the car and tried to analyze what was happening, to no avail. She was clearly out of her depths. Sterling played with the radio dials, opened and closed the glove compartment, looked in the backseat. She reached into the little storage drawer under the car's radio and pulled something out.

"What's this?"

Lola almost grabbed Sterling's hand but couldn't let go of the steering wheel.

"It's a music box." It was the music box Orrin had given her, back when he was her friend Dr. Beckett and she was still free and young and hopeful. Why she kept it in the car, she couldn't say. It didn't belong in Del's house, for some reason. It contained the only mementos of her childhood self, and she certainly didn't want this stranger, this weird and sort of scary woman, pawing carelessly through it.

"Huh." Sterling poked around and pulled out the rings. "Yours?"

"Yes." Lola swallowed hard. The last thing she wanted to do was discuss Orrin with this woman. She waited until they were at a light to take the music box back and put it in her lap.

"Geez, fine. You think I'm a thief or something?"

She pulled up in front of a fast-food restaurant across from the train station, but Sterling didn't move and Lola didn't know how to get her out.

I'll ignore her, she thought. She pretended to have forgotten Sterling's presence and watched two colorfully clad women scream at each other outside the burger joint. Lola gasped, horrified, when one of the women grabbed the other by the hair and smashed her face into a wall. Sterling laughed out loud and cheered when the woman with the now bleeding face punched her attacker. The brawling pair went into the restaurant, shouting obscenities at each other, and Lola looked around. She couldn't leave Sterling here, as much as she wanted to be rid of her.

"It seems kind of dangerous here."

"You should see the station on Sixteenth. That one really sucks."

"So, do you want me to leave you here or take you somewhere else?" Lola braced herself.

Sure enough, Sterling was angry. She huffed and glared at Lola. "So, I guess you don't care if I get robbed or murdered?"

Lola sat for a moment, trying to think of a way out of this situation and unable to do so. Finally she gave in.

"Sterling, do you want a ride home?"

Sterling pointed at a man berating a teenager wearing a halter-top and short shorts. "That's a pimp, you know. The kid's one of his bitches."

Lola frowned. "Sterling?"

"If you want to, I guess you can give me a ride home."

Sterling sat back and took a deep breath. She was relaxed, clearly, and Lola fought a flash of annoyance. Maybe Sterling was broke and she couldn't afford a car. It would be humiliating, having to beg rides from strangers. So, Lola wondered, was that her boat, that first day? Or had Sterling borrowed it from someone? Or was this all some elaborate game? Maybe Sterling had been in a terrible accident and was unable to drive because of the trauma. Maybe—Lola shook her head slightly.

I'll drive her home and never have to see this woman again.

Seemingly oblivious to Lola's discomfort, Sterling chattered about the places they passed. She directed Lola toward the Bernal Heights neighborhood, and Lola fought the impulse to ask Sterling what was going on. She didn't want Sterling to get angry again, so she followed her directions up and up the steep hill. Finally they were in front of a pretty bungalow. If Sterling could afford such a nice house and a boat and her nice wardrobe, why didn't she have a car?

"Here you go." Lola didn't plan to stay, but Sterling just sat there for a full minute, and finally Lola shut off the engine.

"Thanks for the ride." Sterling seemed shy now, and Lola fought impatience.

I'm tired. And very annoyed and confused by you and a little scared of you. But Lola didn't know how to say those things. Instead, she fell back on a strategy she'd developed as a child, counting. It helped her stay calm when anxious, and she got to three hundred and seven before Sterling broke the silence.

"Was it really so awful, driving a couple of miles up here?" Sterling sounded like she was crying, and Lola felt two things in equal measure, guilt over being unfriendly and annoyance at being manipulated.

"No, of course not. I just—"

"You think I'm pathetic."

"No!"

"You're blaming me because you want me."

"No, Sterling." Lola shook her head. "I don't understand what's happening here. I thought you wanted my advice about your business. I thought you wanted to show me the picture you took. I don't understand any of what you say or do."

"Have you been thinking about me?"

Sterling was leaning close again, and Lola eased toward her door.

"No, I haven't."

"Liar, liar," Sterling crooned. "Are your pants on fire?" She reached down as if to grab Lola's leg but pulled her hand away when Lola flinched.

"Whoa, skittish much? God, I didn't even touch you. Don't you dare say I touched you. I didn't lay a hand on you. Don't you fucking make up lies about me, bitch, or I swear I'll make you pay."

Lola couldn't speak for the lump in her throat. What was happening? Why was this happening? She couldn't believe she'd let herself get trapped in her own car—Orrin's car—with this crazy woman. No one knew where she was or who she was with. She'd set herself up. Hot tears stung her eyes, and she wished that just once she could feel bad without crying. It was humiliating. She pressed her lips together, unable to say anything or stop the tears that had started leaking out.

"Knock that off, now. Just be a good girl, and you and I can still be friends. I can be very, very charming. You like perversion, don't you? Homosexuality? You do, I know you do. You already showed your sinful nature."

Lola was too stunned to react and gaped at Sterling's too-close face.

"Don't be like that. You can act as prissy as you like, it doesn't do any good. You are lost, and you are filled with pain and anger, aren't you?"

Lola shook her head, unable to voice a more meaningful response.

"I gave you two of the tests, and I already know you're going to fail the third. I hate to put both of us through it, I really do. But I have to be sure, you understand? Sure you do."

Her breath was warm and sour and too close, and Lola turned her head away. Sterling was touching her hair, her arm. She'd undone her seat belt and slid across the bench seat. She pressed up against Lola and undid Lola's seat belt. Lola gasped but kept her face turned away.

"From the first time you saw me, you wanted me. Admit it. You noticed me, didn't you? You liked what you saw, right? You can play ice princess all you want, I know what you are. I know what perversions you turned to when you got too scared to follow the natural path of a woman's life. I understand, really. It's not your fault. You got twisted away from your true purpose by the sickness of bad men. I'm going to free you, sister."

Lola couldn't take a deep breath. Finally she found her voice.

"Stop it, Sterling, that's not happening."

"I think it is." Before Lola could react, Sterling was leaning over her, pressing down on her. Her lips were on Lola's, her hands had pinned Lola's arms, and her weight was crushing Lola and making it hard for her to breathe.

Lola panicked, flailing and crying. She pushed against Sterling, who seemed suddenly larger and stronger and impossibly heavy. Lola tried to squirm free, to no avail. She went limp, thinking this would spoil Sterling's fun, but Sterling didn't seem to notice her resistance or her passivity.

Sterling whispered with hot breath into Lola's ear, but Lola didn't hear the words, just felt the spoiled, wet breath that carried them. Something was pressing into Lola's leg, and she focused on that. What was it? She pretended Sterling wasn't kissing her and touching her and that the thing by her leg was the only thing she could feel. She didn't want to go away, but it was getting hard to stay focused. The too-strong scent of Sterling's cologne was making her gag, and she swallowed hard.

"My music box," she tried to say, but Sterling's mouth and tongue were in the way. Olivia would know what to do in this situation. But Olivia would never let herself get in this situation, would she? She was too smart, too sophisticated. Besides that, in Olivia's world, good was rewarded and bad was punished, and people were who they said they were. If they weren't, Olivia could always tell. She was much smarter than Lola, and she was much better at reading people. Thinking about Olivia made it hard to go away, Lola realized, and she let go of Olivia like releasing a balloon into a breeze. Olivia floated away, her long hair sailing behind her in the moonlit sky, and Lola closed her eyes and waited for the darkness to swallow her and keep her.

"That's right, let the truth out."

Lola heard Sterling's voice as if from far away and ignored it. She was very tired, and the hole yawned beneath her, dark and warm and safe. Soon she would be gone, and then she would come back when it was all over. She sighed, relieved. Sterling kept kissing her, but Lola knew the kissing was far away and not important.

Lola watched Sterling shift into the passenger seat and look around outside the car, watched Sterling reach over and shake Lola's cold, boneless body.

"You're just a lost girl, aren't you? Aren't you?"

Lola watched Sterling regard Lola's still frame for a moment.

Lola watched Sterling look around outside the car again. A man was walking up the hill behind the car, a pair of small dogs on leashes trailing after him. He was maybe four houses away.

Lola watched Sterling wink.

"That's okay, you don't have to answer me. I already have my answer. You failed the last test. I know this was bad for you, but I promise it's okay. You don't have to be scared. I'll take care of everything."

Lola clutched the music box and curled her arms over her body. She scrubbed at her mouth with her sleeve.

Sterling was reaching for Lola again when the sound of an old-fashioned car horn interrupted her movement.

"Whoops! Should have silenced that. Hold on." Sterling pulled out her phone and made a face. "Well, okay. That is not a text I can ignore." She eyed Lola. "I hate to do this to you, I really do. But I have an emergency to take care of. We have to take care of our friends, don't we? You may not understand that. You've never been very good at making friends, have you? It's okay. So sorry, I have to go. Don't mention this to anyone, sweetheart. This has to be our little secret. Think your girlfriend would believe you didn't cheat? She won't.

I know her even better than I know you. See you soon. Actually, it may be a little while, I'm going to be busy, but I will see you again, I promise."

"No! No, you won't." But the door slammed on her first word and muffled those that followed. Lola skidded away, forgetting to release the emergency brake for nearly a mile before she realized why she was going so slowly. She pulled over, put the car in park, and stilled her shaking body.

Nothing really happened, silly. So she kissed you. Big deal. People kiss each other all the time. No biggie.

She put down her music box to release the brake and realized the little wooden case was broken. The lid was cracked and one of the hinges was bent. She put the pieces back in the little drawer under the radio. She moved the gearshift to the place where the little "D" used to be. It had been worn away even before Orrin gave Lola the car twenty years back.

Lola nodded and took a long, slow breath. She drove to Del's house carefully, afraid—though she knew it was a ridiculous fear—that if she didn't maintain constant vigilance, she'd drive right off the surface of the Earth and disappear forever.

CHAPTER TWENTY

I scrub with the steel wool until blood stains the water. I am dirtied by the mission, and I retch until my vision goes spotty and then dark. I am weakened. I should eat. I should sleep. I should take the pills, red and blue. I should call my friend back. I do none of these things. I fall with a crash onto the wet, red-ringed bottom of the tub and weep. The old man took me to see the giant block of sandstone before artisans made it into this vessel for bathing. He loved me at least a little, I think. Back when he was still able to move his body by sheer force of will. He was a vessel too, given to me as a tool to use in my mission. I used to feel guilty, pretending to love the lonely octogenarian. But he was weak, in spirit as well as in body, and he was using me too. He'd pushed away everyone who loved him with his severity and rages, but I was used to severity and rages. I understood, and still do, how this dirty world hurts the soul of the truly loving. It is designed to squeeze our hearts until they turn to stone as hard as the surface of this tub. I run my fingers along the pinked waterline, seeing its history more than feeling it. This piece of earth's lifespan knows more than most people, as do I. That's why I asked the old man for as much stone in his house—our house—as possible. I wanted it to remind me that what we are now, these empty shells we have chosen to become, are just a blip on the radar of humanity's larger story. We are more than mere lemmings, though we have to fight to remember this.

What am I? Despair holds me in its dead hands, squeezing my heart. I cannot raise my body out of the water or my spirits out of the depths.

She finds me. I weep at the memories of the dozens of times she has found me right when I was so overcome with defeat and doubt that I could hardly breathe one more second. And every time she is there. My friend, slight though she is, lifts me out of the tub and eases me onto the sandstone floor the old man chose because he likes consistency. It makes the tub look like it rises out of the center of the huge bathroom like a shrine to my body, he said, shaking with desire in his throne-like wheelchair. But that was back when he could sit up in the thing, before he became the shell that breathes only because the nurses I have hired stand watch two at a time, twenty-four hours each day, monitoring the machines that monitor his body's limited life. When he dies I will inherit millions, maybe billions. I don't know. The lawyers my friend found for me have sewn everything up neatly by handing out many millions of dollars to his so-called family to make them go away forever. I haven't seen his sons or ex-wife in years. I used to mourn for the old man's loneliness but now I appreciate the freedom it offers me. My friend helped me find that appreciation and a use for that freedom.

She cleans the blood off my body with a soft cloth, going lightly where the steel wool has opened the skin. She blots my tears. She lifts my head, and sweet, warm tea soothes my throat. She is talking to me, her voice honeyed and barely audible. I don't hear her words, not really, but the spirit of them fills me with ease. I am quieted in my heart and mind. She puts pills in my mouth and gives me more tea to wash them down. I fall asleep, dreaming two things at once. My friend and I are dancing in the Promised Land with the other angels, lighthearted and giggling and free. At the same time, the very same time, I am slipping down, down into darkness deeper than any ocean and my friend slides down after me, screaming silently in horror and terror. I cannot know which dream is the truth but it no longer matters, not really. I know that wherever this path leads, I am on it and will be until I am done.

CHAPTER TWENTY-ONE

Janet's fingernails must be a mess. Del almost smiled at the thought. She wondered, not for the first time, what would have happened if she hadn't broken up with Janet. Sure, her feelings had been hurt and she'd been humiliated. She'd felt betrayed and let down and used. But what if she was wrong? What if Janet wasn't the manipulative, lying user Del thought she was? What if Del used the article Janet wrote as an excuse to break up with her? Stuck, it seemed, in front of the Amazon Motel, Del found it hard to imagine Janet had never felt anything for her.

Del looked over at the Suzuki, thinking about how she'd bought it without even asking Lola what she thought about that. Del had talked to the salesman about how she wanted a two-seater, but in the two months since she'd bought the Boulevard, she hadn't asked Lola once if she wanted a ride and Lola hadn't brought it up, either. Had Del really bought the bigger bike so she could take Lola? Or was it just a matter of wanting a new bike and using Lola as an excuse? Had she thought about Lola at all, really, since Janet had shown up? Lola was undemanding, that was for sure. Was that part of what Del liked about her, like Janet suggested? Certainly, Lola never asked more of Del than Del offered. And Del had never realized just how little she offered.

"You're afraid of intimacy," one girlfriend had claimed. Who was it? Tamara? Elise? Joan? It was hard to remember, which was a disconcerting thought. At the time, Del remembered, she'd laughed at the girl, whoever she was. Now, she had to consider the possibilities. She wanted closeness, craved it. It wasn't only a desire for sex that had sent her out night after night whenever a relationship ended—whenever Del ended a relationship—seeking a new lover. It was more than that. She wanted to touch souls. She wanted to feel completely enclosed within a circle of love and trust. She felt a shudder rip through her at the mental image. That circle looked a lot like a cage, didn't it?

She loved Janet. As soon as she'd realized that, Del had felt a spurt of guilt. Because she loved Lola too. How could a person love two women at the same time? It seemed impossible. It sounded like a stupid countrified ballad sung by a mediocre hack in a tacky love flick. But it was the truth. Del loved Janet's wildness and humor and spontaneity and free-spirited, reckless, over-the-top love as much as she loved Lola's gentleness and empathy and intelligence and kindness and vulnerability and deep, abiding, forever-and-always love. It was maybe like choosing between a cat and a dog. But was that fair? Was she really seeing the two women she loved clearly, or was she only seeing the parts of them she wanted to see? Del shook her head.

What am I supposed to do? How do I figure this out? There was no one to ask, and no one answered. Del closed her eyes. Where were Janet and Lola right this minute, when Del was lost and lonely and confused? For a full minute, Del sat and waited. Who was that woman Lola was in the car with? And was Janet really in love with Del or was this all a game?

Del barely noticed she had left the bike parked and was heading toward the tiny office of the Amazon. She registered under a fake name and used most of the cash in her wallet to pay for the room. It wasn't until she was sitting on the bed and looking at nothing that she wondered what exactly she was doing.

"I just need a quiet place to think," she whispered. "I just need a break, that's all."

Out on the sidewalk, a burst of raucous laughter sounded, and a crowd of nighttime revelers chattered as it migrated down the street. Del nodded. "Yeah, you're right. It is laughable. 'Cause I'm not 'taking a break,' I'm running away. I'm a damn coward, after all. Wouldn't Daddy be proud?"

CHAPTER TWENTY-TWO

"Where were you last night?"

There was a long silence, during which Lola held her breath. Should she ask Del if she was okay? Why had her first question not been if Del was hurt? Should she ask how Janet was? Or was that completely paranoid? It probably was. It certainly was. But did Del really care if Lola was okay? Because, if she'd asked right then, Lola would have answered in the negative. She would have said she wasn't okay and asked Del to come home and hold her and tell her she loved her.

"I had to work. And I'm still working. Bye."

"Del?"

Lola waited, pressing the phone to her ear, but Del was gone.

The phone vibrated in her hand, and she looked down, thinking maybe it was Del, but it was a text from Sterling: *Get ready*.

Lola went to the office, grabbing the phone and dialing Lauren's number. She'd forgotten the area code and had to dial again. It was nearly an hour before Lauren returned her call, and by then Lola was limp with exhaustion.

"Lola?"

"I'm sorry to bother you—"

"No, I'm glad to hear from you. Where are you? Are you okay?"

Lola didn't know how to answer that. "I guess so. Yes."

"That's not exactly convincing, Lola. Are you alone? Are you safe?"

Lola nodded. "Yes, fine. I'm fine. Sorry for worrying you. Listen, I live in San Francisco now. I was hoping you could refer me to a therapist who's closer to the city. Can you do that, please?"

"Sure, of course." There was a moment of silence. "Do you need more immediate help? Are you able to wait for an appointment?"

"I'm okay." She cleared her throat.

"We can talk over the phone, if you like."

"I appreciate that, but I think I need to set up something regular here."

"Sure thing. Just give me a moment."

Lola heard her typing on a keyboard. She could picture the little computer Lauren always had in her lap, typing with the lid partway up and partway down, covering her hands. She'd always maintained eye contact with Lola and typed only occasionally, but Lola had often found herself listening for the little tapping sounds that meant Lauren wanted to record her impressions. She felt for a second like she was in Lauren's cheerful office and hadn't already made a thousand mistakes in what was supposed to have been her new and better life.

"What? I'm sorry, I didn't hear you."

"You sure you're okay, Lola?" Lauren's voice brought Lola all the way into the present.

"Yes, sorry. What was that?"

"I have a couple of names for you."

Lola wrote them down and assured Lauren that she was fine, and she knew she'd probably never talk to Lauren again. It was too hard. It made her feel helpless and lost, and she couldn't afford that.

She called the first therapist on the list, making an appointment for the next day. It was only after she'd hung up that she wondered how Lauren had selected the particular therapists she had. People who specialized in patients who were too weak and too broken and too pathetic to get along without some kind of emotional crutch?

"Turn off that record," Lola told herself. But it didn't stop playing in her head.

Del had been gone since the previous morning and wouldn't be home until, at the earliest, the next night. There was nothing Lola could think of to do until she could go to the new therapist's office. She printed out the directions, cleaned the house, sat at the computer and wrote, what, she didn't know. The cell phone, which she'd brought with her, buzzed now and then, and Lola checked it each time. Sterling, every time.

"What should I do?"

She asked the phone, but it sat, useless, in her hand. She didn't read the texts until long after she'd gone to bed and listened to it buzz across the top of the nightstand five times. She counted.

"Thirty-four?"

Sterling had texted her thirty-four times since that morning? Lola shook her head and skimmed the first several, slowing down when the tone changed from friendly to pleading to raging. By midafternoon, Sterling had cycled back to friendly. By bedtime, she'd gotten back to outraged again. Lola felt like the phone had become an enemy, and she put it in a drawer in her dresser, unsure what to do. She couldn't sleep now, and she sat on the side of the bed, unable to think. She listened to the phone buzzing in the dresser drawer and watched the clock, counting down the minutes and hours until her nine o'clock appointment.

She got to the new therapist's office nearly an hour early. The waiting room was a study in beige and muted blues. It was soothing, Lola thought. Like the beach, maybe. Not that she'd ever been to the beach.

"Lola?"

She startled awake and looked up. A slight woman with curly red hair was smiling at her.

"Yes, hi. Sorry."

"I'm Margaret. Are you ready to come in?"

Her office was small. Lola looked around while the therapist asked her a few questions. Everything was white and ivory and very light beige. There was a tall white vase on the table near Margaret's white chair, and the flowers were white. The stems were green, but faintly, almost apologetically so. It could have been a cold room, medicinal looking, but it wasn't. It was more like what Lola imagined a spa would look like, not that Lola had ever been to one. This was a running theme, wasn't it? *Lola's Litany of Lost Living.* Lola realized that Margaret was watching her.

"Sorry. I like your office."

"Thank you." Margaret crossed her legs. "Did you hear me ask you why you called?"

"No, uh, I'm just—" Lola shrugged. "I don't know."

"Okay." Margaret had close-set, dark brown eyes, and she wore square tortoiseshell glasses. She looked over them at Lola expectantly, clearly awaiting a real answer.

"A couple of things are kind of out of control. Lauren McMillan was my therapist back in Sacramento, and she recommended you."

"What things?"

"My girlfriend has been kind of weird lately. I think maybe she's still in love with her ex. Plus, I met this other woman, I told her I have a girlfriend, but she's texting me a lot, and I think she might be kind of disturbed. It's freaking me out. I'm not sure what to do."

"When you say you met another woman, do you mean that you're also dating her? Or want to?"

"No, no, I told her I'm not. And she, I don't really—anyway, it's my girlfriend I'm worried about. I mean, about us. I want to talk about that, please."

"Okay. Lola, it would be very helpful if we could talk in general terms for a bit about you and what's going on with you on—"

"I'm sorry, could we please really focus on what I want?"

"Okay. What do you want to focus on specifically?"

"Her ex."

"What makes you think your girlfriend—what's her name?"

"Del."

"Why do you think Del is maybe still in love with her ex?"

"She went over to Janet's house—the ex. She got shot." She took in Margaret's widened eyes. "No, she's fine now. She's a cop, did I say that? And Janet told her someone was after her, but Del didn't believe it, but then she got shot over there. I think she's trying to help Janet, but she's not telling me anything! Maybe she's just annoyed with me. I'm pretty annoying, I guess. Anyway, I think maybe she still loves Janet. Maybe."

"Have you asked Del about it?"

"No, no, of course not."

"Because?"

Lola searched for an answer. "It's hard to—I mean—"

Margaret just kept looking over her glasses at her, and Lola shrugged. The silence stretched out for a long minute, and Lola tried again.

"What if she says yes?"

Margaret took off her glasses. "Well, what happens if she says yes?"

"I need to let her go back to Janet. Even though I love her."

Margaret watched her, and Lola felt cold tears slide down her face. "Because I love her."

They talked for a while longer, but that was the moment that stayed with Lola as she drove home. She heard herself saying those four words over and over—*because I love her*—as she put into action the plan she'd formulated in the moments after they came out of her mouth.

By dinnertime, it was done. Lola looked around one last time before leaving her letter stuck to the refrigerator. Del's insistence that nothing should mar the plain surface of that appliance meant anything on it would be noticeable.

"This is the right thing," she told the empty rooms. "This is better for both of us. I need to give her the chance to decide what she wants." She looked around, hoping to find some reassurance, somehow, but there was none to be found. Finally, she locked the door behind her and started over to her house.

"Hey, sweetie, what's up?"

"Hi, Marco." Lola tried to sound more enthusiastic than she felt, but his face told her she'd failed.

"What's going on with you?" He crossed over before she could decide how to get away gracefully.

She looked around. "Come over, if you want."

He turned toward Del's house. When Lola dipped her head the other way, he frowned and followed her.

"Did something happen? Is Del okay?"

"Oh, yes, sorry. Del's fine. I'll tell you everything in a minute, okay?"

He nodded, and they went inside without a word.

"Coffee?"

"Please."

She'd put on a pot on her last trip over, and she watched him take in the fresh fruit on the counter, her purse on the doorknob where she'd hung it when she'd lived here before.

"You broke up?"

"Maybe. I'm not sure. I hope not."

Marco watched her doctor his coffee and then her own. "I don't even know what to ask."

Lola took a deep breath. "Okay. Well, long story short, I think we moved in together for the wrong reasons. We've never even been on a date, never even gone out to dinner. It's like, from the very first minute, we've been acting like an old married couple. I've never been on a date in my life."

Marco watched her over the rim of his cup. "Does Del know you moved out?"

"I left a letter for her." When he made a face, Lola shrugged. "I'm not strong enough to talk to her. Not that I know when she'll be home, anyway."

"You love her."

"I always will. And I hope that she gives me a chance to prove it. But I'm not sure it even matters. I don't know how to make things right."

"It couldn't have been easy."

Lola shook her head, fighting sudden tears. "No, it wasn't. But, Marco, it was the right thing." She met his eyes. "I do think, I really hope, it was the right thing."

"Okay."

She raised her eyebrows.

"Hey." Marco spread his hands out. "You love Del, and you're doing what you think is right. So, okay."

"Can we talk about something else?"

"Actually, there's something I've been wanting to talk to you about."

"That sounds ominous. Are you okay?"

"I'm fine." He seemed to be searching for words. "The Meetup, Pier 39?"

"What about it?"

"Sterling. I was wondering if that, if she, had anything to do with this move."

Marco's face was carefully blank, and Lola read consternation in that.

"No."

"Just, no?"

"I can't—Marco, listen to me." She tried to think of a way to explain it. "I don't want to say more than Del would want me to." She waggled her head. "This is just between us, okay?" She waited for Marco to nod vigorously. "I think maybe Del still has feelings for Janet. I think she's gone so much because she doesn't want to be around me. She wants to be around Janet."

"I don't get what that has to do with—"

"I think she's looking for a reason to end things with me. If I tell her about Sterling, she'll have a reason."

Marco's jaw dropped. "Oh."

"Not because—it's just, Sterling, I think she's maybe not such a nice person."

"Explain."

"I just, she just, she keeps texting me and being weird. I met her for coffee—not a date, I didn't even want to go. She was weird and it was weird, and now she's, like, texting me weird stuff."

"Like what? Can I see?"

Lola handed over her phone and watched Marco read the dozens of texts. His face was blank, but his hands gripped the phone tighter as he read.

"You need to tell Del. This woman is a lunatic."

"It's too big a risk."

"The risk is letting this freak think she can harass you like this."

"If she actually threatens me, or if I think she's following me or anything like that, I'll tell Del. But, please, don't interfere, please?"

"I don't know." Marco eyed her. "What if—"

"Just wait for a week or two, okay? Then, if you're still worried, we can talk."

He shook his head. "One week, and I mean it."

"How's Phil?"

"God, Lola!" Marco laughed. "That's the least subtle change of subject ever!"

She grimaced. "Sorry. I just want to be as good a friend to you as you are to me."

"You are far too easily pleased."

"I feel so stupid. I must have led her on without realizing it."

"I doubt that." He grabbed her hand. "Listen, honey, crazy people don't need to be led on. They do all the leading. Don't blame yourself. Okay?"

She shrugged, unable to speak.

"Hey." Marco's voice was soft, and his eyes searched hers. "Don't you know, I think of you as the little sister I never had? I don't want anything bad to happen to you."

Lola was embarrassed to find that she was crying again. "Oh, Marco, what did I ever do to deserve you?"

"You got lucky."

"Yes, I did." Lola shrugged again.

"Honey, call me any time, okay? If things get worse."

"I keep hoping she'll just get bored and go away."

"You and me both, sis."

CHAPTER TWENTY-THREE

Del was still in a fog when she walked into the kitchen. She couldn't stop thinking about the woman she'd seen riding with Lola the night before. This was absurd, obviously. She'd spent the night hoping to recapture some sense of her relationship with Janet, maybe hoping Janet would just show up there at the motel. She should have followed Lola. Or at least called her to check in either last night or sometime over the course of the long day. Or actually talked to Lola when she called. Something. Because this too-little-too-late curiosity was frustrating and scary and made her stomach hurt. Who was Lola with? Why was she with someone else? Was she cheating?

That last one made her stop short. She looked at the clock. It was ten at night, but Lola's new purse—the purse she'd bought on the sly, keeping the receipt out of the monthly budget file—wasn't on the hook by the door. Del bounded up the stairs. No one was home. The closet door was ajar, and Del held her breath as she eased it open further. Del's dress uniform hung in its plastic dry cleaner's sheath. Del's other clothes were arranged on wooden hangers. Lola had replaced the plastic ones months before, after asking permission, of course. Del didn't have an extravagant wardrobe, just the essentials, but she still had more clothes than Lola owned. All were Del's now.

The other side was empty. In the back sat the camping gear and gun safe. Nothing of Lola's. The top of the dresser held nothing of Lola's. Del waited until she'd gone through every drawer in the dresser, the bathroom, the office. Lola's stuff was all gone.

Several hours later, Del was sitting at the kitchen table, a mug of vodka in front of her. She'd finally noticed the envelope stuck to the fridge with a magnet, ripped it open, read Lola's letter. She couldn't do more than sit and breathe for a long time. She examined the letter again, but she couldn't remember what the words meant. She tried a third time to understand. Still nothing. She pushed the letter away.

"What do you need?" Del glared at her wavy reflection in the chrome-plated toaster. Lola had replaced the battered yellow one, the one that used to smoke and burn the toast every time, no matter how closely Del watched it. It had never occurred to Del to replace it, had it? And of course Lola had asked permission. Just like always. She'd been a guest, hadn't she?

Del spent her second consecutive sleepless night walking around the house and noting the ways Lola had made it a home with her thoughtful little gifts. She'd knitted the beautiful red throw tossed over the back of the couch, put plants in all the rooms. She'd been careful, always checking to make sure it was okay to do any little thing. But she'd kept at it, turning the cold, lifeless rooms into homey dens of warmth and comfort and companionship. And Del had never thanked her, never told her how much she appreciated Lola's efforts. She'd never told her how happy she was Lola was in her life. She'd taken her for granted. Why? Because she wasn't a nymphomaniac, like Janet? Del peered out her living room window at Lola's house up the street, wondering what Lola was feeling right now, if Lola still loved her, the way her letter insisted she did.

Del eyed herself in the window's gray reflection. "She left. She can claim to feel whatever she wants, it's what she did that matters. She met somebody else while you were off thinking about humping your ex, and it's your own damn fault."

She talked to herself in the shower while the sun came up. "You didn't deserve her anyway," she told herself, almost choking on the stream of water. "She was too good for you all along, you just didn't want to see it."

It was a relief to go to work. Del sat at her desk, ignoring her hangover and wishing she had a clear enough head to actually figure out where Janet was. Dozens of missing women in the city, Janet missing and maybe in trouble, and Del was sitting here like a lump and completely useless. Looking at Phan, Del saw him watching her.

"What?"

"You've been doing that a lot lately."

"What?"

"Rubbing your arm."

Del looked down. "Yeah, it's a little sore. No biggie."

Phan frowned. "Any tissue damage?"

Del shrugged. "I doubt it."

"What does the doc say?"

Del colored. "I didn't actually tell him it hurts."

"Mason—"

"I know." She waved away the subject. "Listen, it's nothing."

He shook his head. "Listen yourself, macho Mason. I don't plan to get shot because your ego won't let you make sure you have two working arms. Go to the doc, or I go to Wonderbread and get you put on desk duty."

He waited for her reluctant nod.

"We're done here. The storm is getting lousy, and I want to be home when Kaylee gets there." As if to underscore his words, sheets of rain slapped the windows with sudden, increased force.

Del nodded and rose to pull on her jacket, unable to hide a grimace of pain. Phan raised his eyebrow as he pulled on his own jacket, and Del diverted his attention.

"How's she doing?"

He shrugged. "I'll let you know tomorrow. Haven't seen her for a week."

"How come?"

Another shrug. "Says she wants to stay with her mom."

"And you're letting her get away with that?"

Phan's laugh was dry and humorless. "I can't wait till you become a parent, Mason. It's a lot harder than it looks."

"It looks pretty damn hard from here."

Phan's laugh had warmed her until she'd gotten home. She had to strip down in the garage and drape her rain-soaked clothes over the utility sink Lola had asked her to install but which wasn't yet hooked up to the plumbing. Shivering, Del raced upstairs to the shower and stood under the pounding waterfall, letting the heat and pressure warm her and loosen the muscles in her neck and shoulders.

"You're being wasteful," she told herself after several minutes. But she didn't want to leave the shower. It wasn't until the water started to cool that she shut it off and grabbed a towel. She dressed as quickly as she could, telling herself the chill she felt was from the weather, but turning up the heater didn't make a difference. Before too long, she was busy telling herself she'd pulled on a buttoned shirt because she liked it better, not because it hurt her shoulder to put on a pullover.

Del leaned over and rested her cheek against Lola's pillow, closing her aching eyes. She breathed in Lola's scent or the memory of it—she wasn't sure which it was—and felt a sob shudder through her. Hadn't she already done this? Hadn't she already cried like a baby on Lola's pillow? She shook her head.

"No more of that." She stripped the bed and bundled the sheets and pillowcases into the washing machine, using only her right arm. "That's enough." The cycle started, and Del turned away from the rocking appliance.

She was able to keep busy for almost three hours, cleaning the house, doing laundry, paying bills. She managed to do all of this without using her left arm, and she managed to ignore that fact, for the most part. She gnawed on a microwaveable burrito while standing over the sink and noted the burrito was nearly the last edible thing in the house. How could that be? It wasn't like Lola had been gone for long. Still, there it was.

"She used to buy the food," Del told no one.

"She used to be here, and she would cook for me and write me little notes and leave them all over the house. She made this place feel—"

Del dropped the rest of her burrito into the trash, giving in and trudging upstairs and to bed. The sheets smelled clean and untouched, and she wished she'd put off washing them one more day.

"She left me," Del whispered, rubbing her left arm. "She left me."

By the end of the week, she was ready to give in and get her arm checked out. Phan insisted on driving her, going in with her.

"Are there particular motions or activities that cause the discomfort?"

A shrug from Del. At Phan's glare, she waggled her head. "It feels weird if I try to sleep on my left side. It hurts a little, not where I got shot. Up here." She pointed at her shoulder. "Uh, putting on a shirt. Picking things up. Reaching for things. Carrying pretty much anything. It feels like the top of my shoulder's gonna pop right off. Like it's already popped off, only you can't see it from the outside."

She had to go back the next day for an X-ray and an MRI, and it was nearly a week before she got a call from the nurse practitioner. She was at her desk, ignoring Phan's intent stare, and hung up the phone with a grimace.

"You off the streets?"

Del picked up the phone to slam it down again, but the plastic receiver just tapped against the plastic base, and she glared at the thing in disgust. "Remember the old phones? Weighed thirty pounds? If you slammed the phone, it sounded like it?"

Phan rolled his eyes. "Talk to me?"

Del made a face. "Okay. The shoulder is wrecked. I didn't really get the technical explanation. I was supposed to go see some doctor after I got released to set up physical therapy—"

"You didn't."

"No."

"So now you're pulled."

"Sorry. I don't even get to sit behind a desk. I'm completely off work for a week, at least, then desk duty and physical therapy, no lifting, no anything. They won't say for how long. Shit, Phan, I'm sorry."

"It might not be such a bad thing."

"I can work the Hahn case."

"Exactly."

"It'd be nice if I had a plan."

"Well," Phan stood and grabbed his jacket. "Now you have time to come up with one. See you tomorrow. No, scratch that, I'll talk to you tomorrow."

The next morning, Del went over her extensive notes on Janet for the first time in several days. She sat at the kitchen table, organizing the limited and disparate pieces of information on note cards, the way she used to years ago. It felt strange, going back to the old way of looking at things, the way Halloran, her training partner back when she was a rookie, showed her. He'd known she'd make detective someday, long before she'd even thought about it.

"Think like a scientist," he'd said. "Look at the data without any emotional bias."

His advice had been invaluable, and it had shaped her both as a cop and as a person in general. It had also dovetailed with his other big advice, "Cool it, kid."

"Wish you were here now," she muttered aloud. "Sure could use your thoughts on this shit." She tried to imagine Halloran was sitting in front of her, taking her in with his calm gaze, assessing and guiding her. She hadn't thought about Halloran in a long time, and it was strange to realize he was dead, had been for years.

Her father might be dead too, for all she knew, Momma too. Daddy would know what to do, she realized. Daddy and Halloran seemed very different on the surface, but they were both smart and tough and strong. They were also the most important influences on her, the two people she'd most admired and wanted to emulate. Would they be proud of her? Would they think she was a good person, a good cop? Del thought about herself as a kid, so determined to grow up to get away from her lousy parents and to be a good person. What would that kid think of Del now?

"Oh, Daddy," Del heard herself whisper. "Why did everything have to change?"

Janet and Daddy had that in common—they did everything right until they were sure Del loved them, and then they turned on her and broke her heart. Funny, hadn't she thought just a few weeks ago that Janet was like Momma? Maybe she was like both. Selfish, slippery, volatile, often drunk and unreliable—it was like Janet had been designed specifically to act just like both of Del's parents.

"No wonder I fell in love with her. It was like coming home."

CHAPTER TWENTY-FOUR

"Let me get this straight." The bored man on the other side of the table scratched at a patch of eczema on his hand. "You met a woman. You went out with her. You gave her your number, and she texted you. Right?"

"Yes. Several dozen times a day."

"She hasn't threatened you."

Lola hesitated. "Not directly, no."

"She hasn't shown up at your house or your job or whatever."

"No, but—"

"You asked her not to contact you."

"Yes. If you would just read—"

"There's not a lot we can do." He turned away from her and started stabbing at the keyboard of his computer. "We fill out this harassment complaint. It's a misdemeanor. Goes in the computer, and you can update it every time she bugs you. Okay?" His drooping brown eyes pleaded with her to just nod, and she gave up and did so. Five minutes later, Lola was outside and looking around. She was on her own.

Her phone buzzed again, and she knew she should ignore it. She managed to do so until she'd taken two different buses—six more buzzes—and gotten home. She checked all the windows and doors and turned on the alarm. She was by this time fighting tears.

"Why is this happening to me?" It was familiar, the feeling of being hunted, and she hated the familiarity of it and the accompanying self-pity almost as much as the hunted feeling itself. She waited until she was in her bathroom with the door locked to read the texts that had come since she'd gone to the police station.

The police can't help you.
I'm the only one who can.
You need saving but not from me.
You were lost but now you are found.

Lola put the phone on the counter and turned to the mirror. She'd dressed carefully that morning, wanting to look respectable and credible so that the police would help her. But it hadn't worked. Or it hadn't made any difference. Why had she imagined it would?

She logged in and checked the wording on the report. It read: "Complainant dated a lesbian named Starla and terminated the relationship. Starla is texting the complainant."

"This isn't what I said at all!" Lola shook her head. "You didn't even spell her name right. You didn't care, did you? Nobody does. I didn't explain it right."

The phone buzzed again, and Lola went back to her bathroom.

"You can't do anything right, can you?"

It was Orrin, and Lola shook her head.

"Apparently not." The phone buzzed again. Her gaze flicked to her red-eyed reflection before she forced her gaze away to check the name on the screen: Sterling.

"I shouldn't read them," she explained to her mirror self. "But I feel like I have to know too." Her reflection seemed dubious, so she continued. "What if she says, 'hey, I'm coming to your house to kill you'? Don't I need to know that?"

Her reflection stared back at her with clear disdain. Then it flew away as she pulled open the medicine cabinet and put her cell phone on the bottom shelf inside. She eased the door shut. It was maybe three minutes before the phone buzzed again. Lola watched, but the door held.

"The battery'll die eventually," she told her right-handed self. "I don't have to do anything now. I went to the police, and I put the phone away, and now I don't have to do anything."

The doorbell rang, and she jumped. Lola raced downstairs but hung back, checking the peephole before yanking the door open.

"Del?" She looked terrible. Her hair was overgrown, her eyes, bloodshot. Lola gestured at Del's sweater, which was spattered with some unidentifiable crud that looked like a few meals' worth of drippings.

"I have a shirt that would fit you," she blurted out. "Clean. If you want it."

"What?" Del scowled. "A shirt? I'm not here for a shirt."

"I—would you like to come in?" As she led the way to the kitchen, Lola tried to catch her breath.

We haven't talked in over a week. You've been acting like I dumped you, but I didn't. I said that in my letter, very clearly.

What she said, though, was, "Can I get you some coffee? Something to eat?"

She turned to see Del shaking her head no.

"I can make my own coffee. I'm here because of Marco."

"Marco? Is he okay?"

"He says you have a stalker."

"Oh." Lola poured Del a cup of coffee and handed it to her, stalling for time. "No, it's nothing. I already took care of it."

Why did I say that? I need her help. I need someone's help, don't I? But she didn't know what to say.

"Okay." Del put the mug on the counter as though it were made of kryptonite. "If you took care of it, you took care of it." She stalked back toward the front door, and Lola trailed after her.

"I've called you every day."

"I know."

"You never answer me. You never call me back."

Del rolled her eyes. "Do you need my help or not?"

Lola hesitated, shook her head. "Thanks for coming by."

"I did it for Marco. He was worried."

"Will you talk to me, please?"

Del turned around so suddenly that Lola took a step backward. "About what? How you snuck out on me like a coward? How you up and left me without a word?"

Lola shook her head. "I didn't—that's not what happened."

Del's face was a mask of rage. "The hell it's not!"

"That's not fair. Did you even read my letter?"

Del whipped the envelope out of her back pocket and shoved it in Lola's face, nearly hitting her in the eye with a frayed edge. "I read it."

"I told you, Del, don't you understand? I love you! I want to be with you. I just want—"

"I don't give a shit what you want. You gave up the right to tell me what you want when you left me."

"That's not—"

"You. Left. What you tell yourself to make it okay has nothing to do with me. I loved you. I would never have left you like that. But you did, so, okay, I guess we're different. Fine, there's nothing left to talk about." And she was gone, slamming the door shut behind her.

"I didn't leave you. I moved back into my own house. So we could start over and do things the right way. Because I love you. But it doesn't really matter, does it? You still love Janet, and you and I were over the minute she showed up on *your* doorstep."

She stood staring at the door, as though it would open and admit Del, who would somehow have heard what she'd said and understood it and want to work things out.

"She's not coming back," hissed Orrin.

Lola focused on breathing. Why was it so hard to breathe?

"I said, she's not—"

"I heard you," Lola snapped. "She's not coming back. She doesn't love me. No one loves me. I get it."

Orrin was silent.

"Moving out of her house was the right thing," Lola asserted. "She may have hurt feelings over the way I moved out, but it didn't matter. She stopped loving me weeks ago. If she ever really loved me at all."

She was tired, all of a sudden. Her gaze wandered up to the ceiling, and she tried to imagine a way to make things right and couldn't.

"I do everything wrong," she whispered. The kitchen phone rang, and Lola went to tell the woman on the other end that no, she didn't want to win a trip to Lake Tahoe or receive valuable information about an exciting investment opportunity available only to a select few. She put the phone down.

"It was Janet. She just showed up and played Del like a harp."

Orrin snorted. "How do you know they weren't together before that? For all you know, your godless man hater was whoring around with that Oriental slut the entire time you were living in sin with her."

"Ignore him. He's a racist, sexist, homophobic monster. Everything's fine," Lola told herself. "Fine."

She looked around the kitchen, and it was somehow filled with the smell of Christopher James. There was no home here. It was only the wreckage of her home. It was all tainted with that day, and his hands and his mouth and his knife and his gun, his pants, his skin, his blood. Lola leaned over the sink to vomit, but there was only retching and noisy, useless emptiness.

Had Sterling smelled it on her—the fact that Lola was spoiled and rotten inside? Was that why she'd been so strange? Maybe that was why Del turned to Janet for something clean and unspoiled. Maybe she was too wrecked to ever be anything but a lightning rod for violence. Maybe that was why Orrin turned into a monster. Maybe that was why they all turned into monsters. Maybe it had always been Lola, all along, since the day she was born. Maybe that's why her parents gave her up. They could smell the rotten inside her.

"It's all my fault. It was always my fault. I was always the problem."

CHAPTER TWENTY-FIVE

Sitting in the stone castle the old man has built to please me, I try to convince myself I am worthy of my mission. How can I be? But maybe the unworthiest vessel is made worthy by her mission. This is what I tell myself when my doubts and despair overcome me.

I am more than what I have experienced, after all. Still, I am drawn back into the scenes of my life against my will and surrender to the wallowing with guilt. I remember my life in a series of snapshots, like still photos from a movie I saw a long time ago, drunk or high or whatever.

Scene: a malnourished, silent, hollow-eyed toddler, huddled in a closet, covered in urine and feces and bruises, shrinks against the rat-infested back wall of the closet when the door is yanked open.

Scene: a kindergartener with a black eye and a broken arm—in that spot halfway between elbow and shoulder where abused kids always seem to sport a broken bone—pretends not to know how to read. Being smart draws adult attention, and if there is one thing this kid understands it is that adult attention is a bad thing.

Scene: a gaunt, blank-eyed twelve-year-old, pregnant with her father's child, closes her eyes while the cash-only, no-insurance doctor with a suspended license performs the first abortion to the sounds of pop music. The girl will forever hate Madonna, Sinead O'Connor, Mariah Carey and especially Vanilla Ice.

The scenes get blurrier after that. No more furtive reading, a thing she had forgotten doing. No more daydreaming of a better future once she is able to get away from her father. No more hope. The girl, thirteen, is drunk and letting her youth pastor pull down her panties, mostly because he reminds her all the time of how smart she is and how pretty and how nice. At least he is willing to talk sweetly to her, and he even gives her a little money and a beer and some Xanax. The girl, fifteen, is on her knees in front of her father, smiling up at him through the haze left behind by the fat marijuana cigarette they have shared, ready to earn her keep the way she always has, first on her knees and then on her back, because Daddy is greedy and wants it all. The girl, sixteen now, is living in her boyfriend's car, kicked out by her father when she turns up pregnant for the fourth time and he doesn't want to pay for an abortion for a kid who could be anybody's. She feels the baby kick and squirm inside her and smiles, wishing she didn't have to get an abortion this time. Maybe her boyfriend will help her. Maybe they can raise the baby together and give her a good home. The baby's a girl, the kid's sister-daughter, and she's healthy, according to the nurse practitioner at the clinic. There's a squeal as the boyfriend yanks open the car door and pulls the girl out of the car. He's drunk, angry, and starts hitting her. Everything goes dark.

She next remembers earning money on her knees in the manager's office of a bar she has sneaked into. The girl, finally almost eighteen and unaware of it because she's hooked on the little pills her new boyfriend—she refuses to think of him as her pimp—has used to keep her docile and needy and working the street. She gets beaten by a particularly brutal john and nearly dies. In the hospital, they abort yet another baby, and she realizes she cannot keep track of how many babies she has had sucked out of her. The next day is the first time she tries to kill herself.

Then it is a blur of social workers and doctors and nurses and orderlies and telling people what they want to hear and blowing some and letting some fuck her and lying and stealing and pretending to listen to people who are less intelligent than she. She is bipolar, she is schizophrenic, she is narcissistic, she has borderline personality disorder, she has post-traumatic stress disorder, she is faking mental illness as part of her drug-seeking behavior. She is anti-social, has religious mania, is unipolar with depressive features and schizoaffective presentation with dissociative features and a bunch of crap she doesn't even remember anymore. She is whatever she needs to be in order to get out of whatever legal hold they place her under, and she has a dozen different diagnoses. It doesn't matter. They put her in the hospital, they let her out. They take away her drugs, they give her other drugs. They fuck her mind and they fuck her body. None of it matters.

Then she starts reading again, mostly because she is clean and sober for a few days and not yet doped up from the new meds cocktail and is bored in the game room of whatever hospital she's in for another ten-day hold. And the reading saves her. She starts to feel things again, which is scary, but she holds on long enough to get herself let out and to find a library and a menial job and a studio apartment to sleep in.

There's a slow blur as she flounders through the next decade or so, trying to build something like a normal life. She tries on jobs and colleges and churches and men. She tries on different personalities, never quite feeling authentic in any of them. After several wearying years she is ready to give up on authenticity and focuses on being able to pretend well enough to get people to buy the act. She learns to talk the right way and dress the right way and read the right books and listen to the right music, and people start to treat her the way she always wanted them to. One day a nice old man comes along and wants to take care of her, and she marries him. It's strange, kind of hating him and kind of liking the way he loves her. When she's well, she can do what she wants as long as she comes home to him. When she's sick, he makes sure there's someone to take her to the hospital. He never makes her feel anything but safe and free, and she figures maybe this is the closest to love she can feel. But then she meets her friend, and her friend helps her find her mission, and she knows there is real love, and it is the love she feels for her lost girls.

I blink and the movie ends and I am here. I have my mission, whether it comes from God, as I sometimes think, or from some other unknowable source inside or around me, as I often believe. It will redeem me. I have murdered my own children and my own soul, and I am perhaps beyond all hope. But I don't really believe this, not inside of me. I can save the souls of other girls, the ones who cannot save themselves, and this'll have to be enough penance, because it's all I can do. I have come to believe that one of these girls is my savior, as I have been—with the help of my dear friend—the savior of so many others. All I can do is save the lost girls one at a time and hope one of them will save me.

CHAPTER TWENTY-SIX

Del glanced at the clock with surprise. How had half the day slipped by? She headed for physical therapy with a sense of relief. It would, she thought, be nice to focus on something not related to Janet. The therapist, a young woman with dark blue hair and what looked like several dozen tattoos, made it easy to forget about Janet. Nicole was calm, encouraging and the toughest taskmaster Del had ever encountered.

"A Marine, huh?" Del pointed at the bulldog on Nicole's well-toned arm.

Nicole's dark eyes twinkled. "If you're surprised, I'm not working you hard enough."

Del let go a shaky laugh, too tired to respond further.

"I know it sucks, but this is the only way to rehab that arm and shoulder."

Del nodded, not wanting to waste breath on words. By the time Nicole released her, Del was barely able to stand, and she slumped in a plastic chair in the reception area and took a breather. Ignoring the glare of an older woman across the waiting room, Del pulled out her cell and called Phan.

"What's up?"

"You ever find out about Wilson? She need a psych intervention, or what?"

"Oh, no, she's not paranoid, Mason. She's just more insightful than the rest of us. Remember?"

"Ha-ha. We need to close the open question of who the mother is, Phan. If we don't they'll round file the missing daughter, you know that, and I'm not able to sign it off now."

"Why's that, partner?" Phan let the silence develop for a moment. "Oh, yeah, because you were too goddamn stubborn to take care of business with your injury. Yes, now I remember."

"I'm sorry, Phan, I really am. I just—no excuses, okay? I should have taken care of it, and I didn't. I fucked up, and that means extra work for you. I'm sorry."

"Just take care of it now."

"I am. I just had PT, which, by the way, sucks balls."

Phan chuckled. "Serves you right. What have you gotten done on the missing women? On Hahn?"

"*Nada.* I spent the first half of the day trying to get somewhere, and there was nothing, nothing I could see. Oh, shit, I gotta get a car. I'm not supposed to ride the bike for a while, 'cause of my shoulder."

"Renting or buying?"

"Buying."

"Sucks."

"It's about time, I guess. The Boulevard's bigger than the Rebel, but it's still not exactly a passenger vehicle. Lola—anyway, I'll call you after."

Two hours later, she was several thousand dollars lighter and piloting a battered white Ford Ranger. It was nearly twenty years old, but the engine seemed sound enough. The tires were pretty new, and the brakes were good. She'd settled for an automatic transmission, and it was strange, steering with her right hand after twenty years as a cop had trained her to steer with her left. But her left arm and shoulder, burning after her first round of physical therapy, needed the rest.

Del tried to tell herself buying the truck had nothing to do with getting prepared to dodge a possible tail but gave up the pretense after trading in her cell phone for a newer one. The Droid was, according to the saleswoman, a computer and a GPS and an address book and God only knew what else. It didn't matter, really. She used the new phone to call her partner, after looking up his number in her notebook.

"Come over for dinner. I want to see your truck. Plus, Kaylee can program your phone for you."

Del was touched. She hadn't told Phan that she was lonely and freaked, but he'd obviously figured it out. Then she smirked. Maybe he just wanted a buffer between him and Kaylee. "Want me to bring a pizza or something?"

"I got it. Bring whatever you want to drink. Come by at seven, yeah?"

"See you then."

By nine, the extra large pepperoni was demolished, Phan had nearly given up trying to prove his truck's superiority to Del's and Kaylee had programmed Del's phone and typed up a set of instructions on how to use it. The tween, still baby-faced and in her school uniform, grabbed the sheet from the printer and handed it to Del.

"Thanks," Del said, flashing Kaylee a smile.

"No sweat." Kaylee picked at her fingernails and shrugged. She'd been quiet the whole evening, and Del had the feeling that she wanted a break from her dad.

"Hey, take her for a spin." Del tossed her keys at Phan as he came out of the kitchen. "Drive my baby and tell me she doesn't kick your ugly little toy in the teeth."

Phan was quick, she had to give him that. He dropped a nod and a wry smile.

"Back in a minute." He gave a wicked grin. "Unless your piece of crap dies on me."

Once he'd left, Kaylee's tension visibly lessened.

"Good riddance."

Del raised an eyebrow.

"Sorry." Kaylee peered at her from under her lashes. "He kind of irritates me, you know?"

Del considered. "Sometimes he irritates me too." She blew out a breath and shrugged. "Not as much as most people."

Kaylee rolled her eyes. "He just wants to control everything I do, and—why am I even telling you this? Whatever."

Del made a face. "At least your dad gives a shit. My dad was a drunken asshole."

Kaylee's eyes widened at Del's deliberately inserted profanity. She looked so much like her dad! Del fought a smile.

"Seriously?"

"Big-time. Didn't much care what I did, long as I stayed out of his way."

"Doesn't sound so bad."

"Wasn't, mostly, but I knew if I needed anything I was on my own."

Kaylee narrowed her eyes again. "Everybody's always on their own."

Del waggled her head. "I guess, at the end of the day. But if I needed something, your dad would help me. Has helped me. He'd do the same for you—and a lot more."

Kaylee shrugged and turned away. "Whatever."

"Maybe it's just part of becoming an adult," Del offered. "Being annoyed by your parents. Otherwise, maybe you'd never leave home. Stay with them until you're my age."

Kaylee smirked. "God, that's pathetic. What about college?"

Del laughed. "Not everybody goes to college."

"Only if they suck at school."

Del shrugged this away. "What college are you going to?"

"I don't know. Maybe Caltech, if I can get in. Or Cal. I'm not sure."

"Cal, I know. That's UC Berkeley, right? Tell me about Caltech. Where's that? What do you like about it?"

Del listened as Kaylee detailed the various attributes of the apparently amazing southern California college, hiding her astonishment that a supposedly apathetic middle schooler was so highly focused and goal oriented. She didn't sound like a kid who'd lost her way but a kid who knew exactly what she wanted and how to get it. Del refrained from saying this, sensing adult approval would only annoy the girl. Delight overcame Del as she heard Kaylee's exhaustive rundown of the various merits of Caltech, and she wondered at the source of the feeling. Whatever discontent and unhappiness the girl was experiencing, she had the hopefulness and confidence of the safe and well loved. Thinking back on her own childhood and adolescence, recalling the hundreds of children and teens she'd seen on the job, Del could only wish everyone had lived Kaylee's life. Imagine what the world would be, Del thought, if every kid had this girl's upbringing!

Phan's footsteps pounded up the stairs and Kaylee interrupted herself and drifted away. "Call me if you need help with your phone, Del. I programmed my number for you."

"Thanks for your help with that, Kaylee. And for telling me about Caltech."

"Whatever." But she was smiling as she headed for her room.

CHAPTER TWENTY-SEVEN

"Why did we do this again?"

"Because I have to make an appearance, and Phil wouldn't come, and I need you," Marco replied, his wide, fake smile covering what she knew to be a bad headache.

"Sorry. It's just that you don't seem to be enjoying yourself. Is everything okay?"

He gave her a look. "Listen, sweetie, this is as much a part of my job as painting."

"I'm not complaining. I'm worried about you. You look like you're in pain."

"You don't exactly look like you're ready to do somersaults yourself."

"Ouch," Lola raised an eyebrow.

"I know, I'm sorry. But you and Del both look like hell, and—"

"Thanks a lot."

"But your bag," Marco ran a finger down the strap of her new purse.

"Isn't it lovely?"

"It really is. I've been meaning to mention it. Did you actually spring for an honest-to-goodness designer handbag from a real, live retail establishment?" He faked a heart attack, and she laughed. "Good for you. Now we just need to get you a wardrobe to go with it."

Lola rolled her eyes. "This was scary enough."

"Scary, how?"

Suddenly, Lola was fighting tears.

"I'm sorry." She turned away. "Never mind. It doesn't matter."

Marco shook his head. "Talk to me. Please?"

"I hid the receipt." Lola rolled her eyes and wiped at them with her sleeves. "I didn't want Del to find out how much I spent. Who does that?"

"Oh, God, honey, everybody!"

"That's not true, is it? That can't be healthy."

Someone came up and hugged Marco, ignoring Lola, and she waited until he'd managed to extricate himself. She was going to have to do a better job of masking her loneliness and worry over Sterling and Del and Janet and everything. If she let him see how anxious she was, he'd probably go to Del and start that whole business up all over again. She couldn't let that happen. Why had she told him about the purse? She was ashamed, and she could still feel the receipt, tucked deep into her wallet so Del wouldn't find it. She felt like a sneaky child, hiding the wrapper from a stolen piece of candy.

"What's wrong with me?"

Did I say that out loud? Lola reddened again. She felt like she was held together by the thinnest veneer of good manners and that, underneath, she was a crumpled mess of wet paper, too ruined to be worth anything.

"What on earth are you thinking about? You have the strangest look on your face."

"I'm just proud of you!" She beamed at him. "Painting isn't the hard part. This is, isn't it? You're a people person, but this is torture for you anyway. You do it because you have to."

"Well, you know." Marco shrugged. "We all do things we don't want to. It's not that I don't like seeing everyone. It's just—"

They were interrupted again, this time by a man who wanted to show Marco a particular painting. Marco shot her an apologetic glance, which she mirrored, unwilling to tag along as the dealer dragged Marco through the throng crowding the gallery. Lola searched mindlessly for the fire code bulletin, the sign specifying how many people could safely occupy the gallery. Whatever that number was, she thought, scanning the crowd, this bunch was easily twice that.

Everyone around Lola was making smart-sounding comments about a suite of off-putting paintings that looked to Lola more like the product of a demented kindergarten back-to-school night than art. Lola was the only person not wearing black, not wearing expensive shoes and not sporting a carefully casual hairstyle. Marco seemed to know everyone, and everyone seemed to know him. In the ninety-plus minutes since they'd arrived, Lola had been ignored by dozens of people who'd hugged, kissed and fussed over Marco. She looked over and saw him rubbing his temple with an absent hand while a petite, effusive woman laughed loudly in his face and her companion, a wildly gesticulating man in a black fedora, talked at him with an excess of enthusiasm and a mouthful of what looked like cream cheese and red peppers.

"I know what you're thinking, girlie. What a bunch of ridiculous, self-important art scene phonies!"

The voice came from behind Lola, and she turned to see whose it was. A muscular man with a shaved head and large-framed eyeglasses waved his champagne glass at Lola.

"Am I wrong?"

Lola shrugged.

"You don't have to answer, your face already did. I get it. To an outsider it all looks very fake. But it's no different than making deals on the golf course or at a titty bar. Can you see a difference?"

"I don't know enough about business or the art world to say."

"Cop-out." The man narrowed his eyes. "I guess you're just another phony, you're just not very good at it."

Lola wasn't sure how to respond to that either. She turned and tried to make eye contact with Marco, but he was being hugged by yet another overdressed matron in a very revealing, very little black dress.

"Can you think of a single reason why this idiot has a show and Marco doesn't?"

"What?"

"Can you?"

"I don't know." Lola wasn't sure what to say to this polished stranger, whose too-wide brown eyes were now fixed on her face. He was shiny with sweat and fairly vibrating with tension. His body odor hit her, and she fought the urge to cover her nose. It was strange, that bad smell coming from someone in such clearly expensive clothes. His designer suit was obviously custom-tailored, and he wore a watch that probably cost six figures.

"Oh, come on, look at this garbage!" The man waved his glass again, at what was labeled a landscape. All she could see was a pink and yellow blob in a field of gray spatters. "What do you see? Huh?"

"Well," Lola started to speak but was interrupted.

"That thing's a nightmare! Jordon's an idiot, but at least he knows how to play the game. Kiss the right asses, say the right things. Anyone with any sense gets it. But not your friend and mine—yes, I saw you come in with him. I thought maybe he'd grown a head on his shoulders, coming here. Thought maybe he was ready to play nice. But no, he's still the same old Marco, thinks he gets to do whatever he wants. Ignores me. Me!" The man's voice carried, and he'd dribbled some of his champagne on Lola's arm.

"Uh. Please excuse me, I need some air."

But the man grabbed her arm. His reddened eyes searched hers, and Lola was startled to realize that he'd pulled her up onto her toes and close enough that she could feel his body heat. He was a good six or seven inches taller than she, and she was looking up into his face. She was frozen with surprise and discomfort. She tried to ease away, but the man's grip on her arm tightened.

"Marco's my friend," she blurted.

"Tell your friend he's a fool. This could have been his night. *Could* have been, you understand? But he fucked with Ray Stowe, and I don't take that shit from anybody. This is the price he pays until he's ready to crawl on his fucking hands and knees like my goddamn prodigal son. Got it?"

Lola nodded. She swallowed bile and kept nodding until he nodded back. He released her so suddenly Lola almost lost her balance, and she rubbed her arm where his fingers had dug into her skin.

Ray Stowe stalked off into the crowd, and Lola searched for Marco. He wasn't in any of the knots of people, and she eyeballed the various anterooms and exits.

"Tag, you're it," Lola said, when she finally found him in the stairwell that led to the fire exit. He sat with his head hanging between his knees, and she tucked in next to him, rubbing his head gently. "I don't think I much like your friend, Marco, and I'm not sure he's really your friend, but he asked me to give you a message."

"What friend, what message?"

"He said this could have been your night, except you made him mad, something like that. His name was Ray, Ray Stowe."

"Oh, God." Marco grabbed her arm, the same one the other man had. He hauled her to her feet and hustled her down the stairs. "Come on. Now!"

"What's wrong?"

"Later. Hurry, come on," he sprinted toward the back exit, dragging her along with him. "We have to go!"

Marco was really running now, and Lola had no choice but to keep up with him as he half-led, half-dragged her down an alley. Their footsteps seemed to echo in the relative quiet here, away from the music and the laughter and the voices getting farther and farther behind them. It was getting darker, and the alley seemed to be narrowing, when suddenly they were out of the dark alley and on what seemed to be a side street. Marco didn't slow down, though. He seemed to know where he was going, and Lola simply followed him, trying not to fall and trying not too breathe too loudly.

"In here," Marco ducked into a doorway and pulled her in with him, shoving her against a metal security door and leaning against her. He was sideways, they both were, and he was watching the street. She couldn't see anything over his shoulders, and the metal of the gate was digging into her hip and shoulder, but she said nothing. *He's trying to protect me, even though he's scared*, she thought, and she finally let out the silent tears that had been building in her since the strange man had grabbed her arm. Marco was shaking, and she tried to somehow reassure him, but he seemed too keyed up to notice her.

They'd been in the doorway only a minute when someone trotted past them. After another endless minute, Marco eased forward. He gestured at her to be quiet and ducked his head out. He grabbed her hand again and pulled her along the quiet street, keeping near the buildings and watching, it seemed to Lola, in every direction at once. After several minutes, they started seeing more cars and more people and lights, and Lola felt Marco tense up again. They were near Market Street, and Marco quickened his pace as they got closer to it. A bus was just pulling up near the intersection, and Marco pulled her into the line.

She didn't ask any questions until they had been on the bus for a few minutes. They'd been able to get seats together, near the back, and she leaned in close. Marco's eyes darted around, trying to see every pedestrian.

"We're going the wrong way."

"I know. We'll get off soon."

"Who—"

"Not here." He eyed the other passengers as though they might be spies or something, and Lola bit her lip. He seemed fragile, suddenly, and Lola shivered with a chill born of unease.

She remembered a family of paper dolls she made for herself when she was a child, too young for school. She was able to hide them from everyone because they were so small, and she dreamed up dozens of adventures for them. One day, she thought they could have an adventure in a boat, and she made a little paper boat for them. Of course, they sank into the murky water of a mud puddle immediately. She pulled them out and smoothed them. The paper children survived the initial bath, but neither parent. It was important for reasons she didn't understand to save those children, but only one survived. Lola held onto that little paper doll for days, trying to think of ways to save the tiny, sodden scrap.

She experimented with squares of paper, wetting them and then trying various methods of strengthening the fibers. Nothing she did worked. One day she took the paper doll and laid her on the sidewalk. The paper was wavy and curled. It was discolored and twisted. The paper doll was grotesque, a mockery of itself. Lola let the wind take the now useless thing and carry it away.

"Once they get wet, they're never the same. When bad things happen to us, they change us. Maybe we can never get changed back. Maybe we're just ruined." Her voice sounded strange. She imagined a paper throat, curled up and unable to make a proper sound. She absently stroked the side of her neck, then caught herself and dropped her hand. Marco grabbed her wrist and pulled, and they were off the bus and into a taxi before Lola could catch her breath.

"Here?"

Marco shook his head and sat back. He seemed more tired than Lola had ever seen him. By the time they were on Eighteenth, Lola was shaking with adrenaline and cold. She started to head over to Marco's, but he shook his head. His face was still grim and set, and Lola let him lead her to her own house with some apprehension. Whatever he was going to tell her, it was bad, and she wasn't sure how much more bad she could handle.

It was ten minutes later that they sat on the living room couch not sipping coffee and not nibbling cookies.

"Lola, I'm so sorry."

"No—"

"I should have told you about Ray."

She was silent, afraid to say anything that would make him even more hesitant than he already was.

"Oh, God." He put down his cup and hugged himself. "Okay." He grimaced. "It's stupid. I feel so incredibly stupid. It's humiliating."

She took his hand and squeezed it. Again, she had the feeling that saying anything at all would stop the trickle of words, maybe forever.

"I met Ray about three years ago. Phil—you know how he is—he'll go to openings and shows and parties if I beg him to, but after twenty minutes, he's ready to leave. Well, I don't have that option, not if I want to make the right contacts."

Lola nodded.

"I meet Ray at a reception at my friend Becky's very fancy place in Hillsborough, down on the peninsula. I have to go by myself, of course. Anyway, this guy comes up to me, seems nice. I don't know how I was so stupid. I thought he was a really nice guy. He's really rich, knows a lot of influential folks in the art world, all of that. But I didn't know all that. I just thought he was a nice friend of Becky's. We started talking about tennis, Becky told him I was looking for a singles partner, and we set it up. We play, he's pretty good for such a big guy, and all is well. We don't really hang out, you know, we just play. One day he asks me to score some coke for him. I don't know why he thought I was the person to ask about drugs, but he gets pissed when I tell him I'm not that guy. He starts hollering about how he can make or break my career, he's a huge big shot in the art world, all this stuff. Well, by this time, I knew he was all that, but I didn't have any coke, and I wasn't about to go trolling for it for this freak."

"But he didn't believe you?"

"I don't know what he believed, honestly. Maybe he thought I was holding out on him, maybe he was worried I'd tell people about it and embarrass him."

"Weird."

"He kept telling me how important he is, how he can make or break me, and I'm like, 'Yes, okay, wow,' you know? 'That's great, but I still don't have any blow.' What else should I say? He gets pissed, shoves me, screams at me, says he'll ruin me."

"Crazy," Lola replied without thinking. "Scary."

Marco nodded. "The thing is, I used coke a couple times when I was young, maybe Ray heard about it, and I was too embarrassed to tell Phil that part. Anyway, pretty soon, Ray's texting me, emailing me, calling me, and it's getting weird, and I don't know what to do. Del comes up to me one day—God, I love that woman—and she asks me what the hell is wrong with me. Just like that. I knew Del a little. I mean, we're neighbors. Yeah, we'd met, waved, said hi. Then she just walks up to me and demands an answer, just like that."

Lola smiled. "That does sound like Del."

"I told her about Ray. I didn't plan to, it just came out." Marco shrugged. "I don't know what she did, exactly, but she said if he ever showed up or texted me or whatever, call her right then. I only saw Ray once after that, at a party, and he started to walk over, but I pulled out my phone. He's, like, bulldozing through the mob right at me, and I pull out my phone, and he walks away, just like that."

"Until tonight."

"I'm sorry you got pulled into this."

"He was scary. He said you made him mad, and that's why you couldn't have a show. Is he really powerful enough to sabotage your career?"

Marco shrugged. "Who knows?"

"I'm so sorry this happened to you."

"I'm going to tell Del and she may want to talk to you about it. Is that okay?"

Lola nodded but all the blood drained from her face. She felt it. Her body was cold and stiff.

"What happened between you two?"

She shrugged, tried to speak, couldn't. She shrugged again.

"Never mind," Marco said, his voice low and thick. "I know what happened."

She looked at him through tears.

"Janet."

Lola hesitated. What she should say was that it wasn't Janet. It was some fundamental misunderstanding or imbalance of power or miscommunication. It was because they moved in together before they were even a couple. It was Lola's never managing to work through her sexual hang-ups. It was a thousand things wrong before Janet returned, all of which centered on Lola's fundamental defectiveness. But she didn't say any of those things.

Marco nodded. "What a horrible day this turned out to be. I was so excited. I never get to see you anymore. I never get to go out anymore. I don't mind Phil being a little on the quiet side. I always figured it was good that we balanced each other out. But he's getting harder and harder to talk to, and he never wants to do anything."

"I'm sorry, Marco. He loves you and you love him. That's something, anyway."

He pursed his lips. "I don't mean to complain. Phil's wonderful. And Del is too."

"Oh, please, I don't want to think about that right now, okay?"

"If you say so, love. Listen, I think we gave you a pretty decent bottle of wine for Christmas. I must not have known back then that you don't drink. I don't suppose you still have that?"

"Oh, sure. It's in here somewhere." Lola rummaged around the cupboards while Marco pulled out two juice glasses. She finally found the bottle and held it out. "Ah, here we are."

She handed it to him. "Sorry I don't have the right kind of glasses."

"Doesn't matter. Got a corkscrew?"

"A corkscrew?" She turned the word over and over in her mind, unable to form an image.

Marco laughed.

"What?"

"Honey, when you say you don't drink you ain't kidding, huh?"

"Sorry," she mumbled, embarrassed.

"We're going to my house. Don't mention Ray, okay? But I have glasses and a corkscrew, and Phil can either join us or go pout in his office." He plunked the bottle of wine on the counter.

"Don't you want to take that with?"

"Let's leave it here for an emergency. I have an open bottle at home."

"Aren't you telling Phil about Ray?"

"Wine first, then talk."

She faked the laugh he expected and received an equally fake smile in return.

Phil wasn't home when they got there, and this seemed to make Marco even more upset. "Can you believe this? He didn't want to go. He said he wanted to stay home and relax when he finished work. But he isn't even here!"

Lola didn't know what to say. She watched helplessly as Marco stormed around the kitchen and put together a tray of wine, fruit, cheeses and crackers. When he started to pour a glass for her she shook her head.

"Have you really never drunk wine?"

She shook her head. "Once, a bit, a long time ago. I didn't like it."

"People's tastes change as they grow up, Lola. Try it. If you don't like it, fine. But don't you think it's time to at least know if you like it?"

She shrugged. "I think you need it more than I do."

It was over an hour later that they heard Phil's car pull into the garage, and by then Marco was fuming. He shook his head when Lola asked if she should leave.

"Please stay. I need someone who actually cares about me."

"You know he cares about you! Are you really sure you want to stay mad at him without even hearing what he has to say?"

Marco shrugged. "I do a lot for him. I go to these stupid dinners where nobody talks to me. I clean up after him, I cook ninety percent of our meals, I eat at Delfina's two, three times a week because it's the only restaurant he likes, and I sit home night after night and watch TV because he doesn't like it when I go out. I hardly ever ask him to do anything with me, because he'll make it miserable even if he does actually say yes. But I asked him to this because it was important, and I thought he could maybe, just once, do one thing for me. But it was too much to ask. You didn't even hesitate, Lola. You didn't want to go, but you came to support me. He's my husband. He should want to support me!" Marco's control broke, and he pulled away to rub at his face. "God, I'm not going to cry. If I cry he thinks I'm an idiot."

"I could never think you were an idiot." Phil's voice was soft, but it carried from the hallway. "But I sure felt like one when I got to the gallery."

Marco stared at him. "You went?"

"It seemed important to you. I just wasn't sure I could get out of the meeting in time. But you weren't there." Phil's face was tense and he seemed wary. Lola eased toward the front door, glad that she'd stuck her keys in her pocket instead of lugging over her purse.

"I was there." Marco looked like a child whose parents have remembered his birthday a day too late.

"I—"

"We," Marco croaked, waving his arm in Lola's direction. "We were there."

"But you left." Phil peered at Marco. "Everybody said you just disappeared all of a sudden."

"He was there." Marco's words were hollow, and Lola chewed her lip and eased closer to the door, trying not to draw attention to her exit.

"Who?"

"Ray Stowe."

Phil's face fell. "Lola, thanks for going with Marco. Can you get home okay?"

She nodded and backed toward the door as Phil took Marco in his arms and whispered something. Sudden tears clouded Lola's vision, and she stopped spying to fumble her way outside and sprint across the street. She got home before the sobs broke through and left her curled up on the couch she'd had delivered—to replace the one destroyed by Christopher James—ragged and breathless from crying. Her body ached. She missed Del with a longing that she hadn't allowed herself to acknowledge until just this moment.

She was glad, wasn't she, that Marco had Phil? She was glad that when Marco was scared and hurt Phil immediately wanted to comfort him.

"I'm glad Marco has that love and support. I'm not jealous." She laughed. "Not much."

She hugged herself, looking around her empty house.

"But I would give anything to have someone who loves me—someone who'd wrap her arms around me when I'm sad or scared. But I don't get that, do I?"

Orrin's low chuckle and its echo, Tami's shrill cackling, filled Lola's head. *Oh, good, now Orrin's girlfriend is chiming in*, thought Lola, *that's all I need.*

"Because you're right. You were right all along, Orrin. I was always the girl nobody could love."

CHAPTER TWENTY-EIGHT

The pain had become a thing separate from her, an enemy that struck over and over without mercy. She could see it, a large, gray beast with tendrils. It was smoky and sneaky, evil and insidious. It woke her up when she tried to sleep, pulled her concentration from her and made her feel weak and helpless and angry. Most of all, angry. Del wondered sometimes if she would ever again experience a moment free of bitterness, anger and regret. She watched the last dim rays of the sun disappear into the darkness of night and despair washed over her. She felt completely alone and lost.

The doorbell rang, and she peered out to see a drawn-looking Phil tapping his fingers on the doorframe.

She yanked the door open. "What's wrong?"

"Ray."

"Here, now?"

He shook his head.

"Give me ten minutes."

Del washed up, trying to regain some of her professional demeanor. She hadn't really looked in the mirror in days and was surprised to see how much weight she'd lost. Her face looked ten years older. She showered, brushing her teeth at the same time.

By the time she was locking her front door, she felt almost like herself again. She had on her duty weapon, a button-down and jeans. She'd had to use the old belt from her patrol uniform to keep her jeans up, and she felt a little like a kid wearing a grown-up's clothes. But she had her fancy new phone and her weapon, and what she had would have to be enough.

Phil let her in with a nod of thanks, and Del was again struck by the stress etched on his face. Marco looked even worse. He was sitting in a corner of the couch, curled up under a blanket. His eyes were ringed with dark circles.

"Tell me," Del ordered, her voice low and, she hoped, warm.

"Oh, Del," Marco's voice was a hoarse croak. "I should have called you days ago."

Del masked her worry. "Tell me what's happened."

"I went to a gallery show, Lola came with me. Ray was there. He went up to Lola, told her to give me a message. Something about how I couldn't have a show because I pissed him off."

"Did you talk to him?"

"No. We left right away and I haven't seen him since."

"When was this?"

"A week ago. He's been emailing, calling, leaving me messages, texting every day since then."

"Saying what?"

"I'm what's wrong with the art world. I'm going to hell because I'm a bad, queer liar."

"Just like before." Del stood up. "Call me, text me, whatever, anytime you hear from him. Forward every email to me. If you see him, call or text me right away. I'll check it out. I'll get back to you with anything I find. He has a record in two other states and may have racked up more charges in the meantime."

"Why isn't he in jail?"

Del made a face. "Listen, I know it sucks. But he's smart enough to know what's a misdemeanor and what's a felony, and the reality is that misdemeanors just don't get prosecuted unless the DA has something to gain by pursuing it. Or something to lose by not doing so. He's got friends in high places. He's a deacon in some fancy church, and he's ridiculously rich." She sighed. "I'll see what I can do to make this right."

"We both know there's nothing anyone can really do."

"It feels like that but listen to me." Del grabbed his foot and tugged it playfully. "I will always protect you, okay?"

Marco smiled. "I appreciate that, but—"

"But nothing."

Phil's voice was a low rumble. "If you're going to protect people maybe you should include Lola."

Del turned to him in surprise.

"What do you mean?"

Phil gestured, but it was Marco who answered. Del turned around again.

"Remember that woman I told you about? She's still stalking Lola and she's as scary as Ray."

Del shook her head. "Lola said it was taken care of."

Marco's laugh was loud and humorless. "Don't you know anything about women?"

Del crinkled her eyes. "Considering I am one, uh, yeah."

"She was *lying*. You just dumped her for your ex. She wasn't going to ask you for help."

"I didn't dump her. Is that what she said?" Del bristled.

Phil's hand clamped onto her bad shoulder, and she stifled an urge to punch him.

"Shut up and listen," Phil barked. "The point is she's scared."

Del shook off his hand, wincing at the pain this caused. "I'll get back to you about Ray. Thanks for the heads-up on Lola."

When Lola didn't answer the door, Del hesitated only a moment before using her key. She went in to find Lola sprawled on the floor, a wine bottle next to her. Del was so surprised by this that she stood and gaped for a full minute before she could speak.

"You started drinking now?"

"Yes, I did. Not very well, apparently. It tastes disgusting and have you smelled it? Gross." Lola gestured at the bottle, laughed and tried to sit up, with no success.

"Whoa there." Del grabbed her and eased her onto the couch, using her right arm as much as possible. No lifting, the physical therapist had said, but Lola was too wobbly to get up on her own.

Del surveyed the scene. There was a pretty floral hatbox on the floor, overflowing with bits of paper, and she grabbed the one on top. It was a note she'd written to Lola, saying she was going to work. A nothing, a throwaway. But Lola had saved it and, it looked like, every other note Del had ever written her. There were dozens. Del rifled through them, her breath coming quicker with each second.

"Why did you save these?"

"I think I'm going to be sick."

Lola was a noxious green. Del tried to get her to walk up the stairs, but she was too shaky. Finally she picked Lola up and carried her. Del's shoulder felt like someone had shoved a few hot pokers into it, but it held, and she tried to shift as much of Lola's weight to her right as she could.

Lola moaned at the movement.

"You've lost weight," Del murmured. "Dear God, you smell like you're wearing more wine than you drank."

"I drank it once before. When Dr. Beckett took me out to dinner for my birthday." Lola was crying. "I thought he was my friend."

Del laid her on the bed, ignoring her burning shoulder, and turned on the bathroom light.

"Maybe you can just rest for a while. Do you still think you need to throw up?"

"I don't like drinking. It's yucky."

Del shook her head. She went downstairs and made tea. How many times had she carried a drunk Janet to bed? At least a dozen. Of course drunk Janet was usually loud, argumentative, seductive and volatile. Weepy once. And of course there was Momma. Del had been big enough to drag Momma to bed for a few years but had rarely tried. She'd felt guilty about it, of course, but drunk Momma was even more volatile than drunk Janet and a lot less likely to calm down and pass out. Was Lola heading down that road now? Surely Momma hadn't been a drunk her whole life. Maybe she'd been a perfectly nice woman until Daddy fucked her over enough times to turn her into an angry, bitter alcoholic. Maybe Del had turned Lola into an alcoholic too. Del shook her head. *The woman had a little wine, one time, and I think she's a drunk?* She grabbed a couple of aspirin, dry swallowing three of them herself, and snagged a large, deep basin—Nana would have called it a barf bowl—to put by the bed just in case. Lola was out cold and Del covered her, careful not to touch her.

She searched all over and found a cordless phone, but she couldn't find Lola's cell. She called the number but it went straight to voice mail.

"Where's your cell?"

Silence.

"I need to know where your cell phone is. Lola? Honey? Come on, sweetheart." There was a long pause and Del shook Lola's arm through the blanket.

"What?" Lola opened one eye.

"Cell phone."

"Bathroom."

"What? Where in the bathroom? Why is it in there?"

But Lola was out again. Del looked on the counter, in the drawers, on the back of the toilet. Finally she found it in the medicine cabinet. The battery was dead. Del plugged in the charger and got herself a glass of water and a couple more aspirin. Lola had added a small armchair to the sparse furniture in her bedroom, and Del sat in it, grateful for the chance to rest. Her shoulder was on fire, but she ignored it.

She picked up the phone and started scrolling through dozens of texts, many of which were downloading. Apparently several had been sent after the battery had died. Waiting for the messages to download took several minutes, and Del scrolled through the ones from before that. They were clearly menacing. She eyed Lola. After everything she'd been through, meeting the craziest lesbian in the whole city was the last thing Lola needed.

"I know you're tired, sweetheart, but we need to talk about this."

There was no movement from Lola. Her eyes were closed and she appeared to be asleep. Del took a deep breath and closed her eyes.

You can't just go after this creep. Work within the system. That was going to be hard.

"Sterling, huh? I wonder if that's your real name?"

Del should have been tired as midnight struck, but she was getting agitated, picturing Lola scared and thinking she couldn't come to Del for help. She pulled out her own phone and logged in to the department's website. Sure enough, Lola had filed a harassment complaint weeks before. Nothing had happened, but at least the groundwork had been laid. Del started tapping out notes in her phone, struck by the fact that it had replaced her notebook and even her laptop. Hadn't she written on note cards just a day or two before? She sent a copy of her notes and a link to the report in an email to Phan and tried to decide what to do next.

Janet. Del had avoided thinking about her, hadn't she? A spasm of pain cut her breath short. Everyone was having trouble. Janet was in some kind of crisis, though it was hard to know what the details were. A stalker was harassing Marco. A stalker was harassing Lola. Phan's kid was going through something, who knew what? And Del was a wreck over her messed-up shoulder because she snuck off to Janet's to—what? Ostensibly to help her but at least partly to see her again. To get tangled up with her again. Del pictured herself lunging at Janet, kissing and fondling her.

"I'm so sorry," she whispered, not even looking at Lola's sleeping form. "I fucked everything up."

There wasn't any other way to look at it, was there?

"God, I was such an asshole." She buried her face in her hands, feeling a pull in her left shoulder. The pain was almost welcome. It provided a distraction from everything else.

"I keep going over everything I did wrong, but it doesn't make it better. I don't know how to make it right!"

She fell asleep trying to decide whether she should leave or stay. Lola's sudden cry of terror woke Del, and she stumbled to her knees scrambling over to the bed. She managed not to gather Lola in her arms only because her shoulder froze up. She sat next to Lola, stroking her forehead and soothing her with nonsense words. Lola was weeping, begging, terrified.

"I almost forgot how horrible this is," Del whispered.

Lola's eyes fluttered open. "Del?"

"Are you awake?"

Lola nodded.

"You okay?"

"I was drinking wine. Bad idea. I'm sorry, did I call you?" Lola awkwardly pulled herself to a sitting position.

"No, I came because of Marco. Because of Ray, that guy? I let myself in. I hope that's okay."

"Did something happen?" Lola eased past Del to stand. She leaned against the wall to steady herself, and Del followed her sluggish progress down to the kitchen. She had to fight the urge to help Lola, to carry or at least hold her.

She's not mine anymore. I don't have the right to touch her.

"I mean, something else? Is Marco okay?"

"Yeah, no. Nothing else happened. Phone calls, texts, that's it."

"I remember you came here. Sorry for being such a mess. I'm not usually—"

"Yeah, I know."

"Coffee?"

"No. I didn't mean to wake you up. I'll take off."

"No, stay. I feel yucky. I don't think I like drinking." Lola started the coffeemaker and pulled out cookies.

"What made you try it tonight?" Del regretted asking the question as soon as the words had left her mouth, but they were out there.

Lola shrugged. "I don't know."

"Your stalker or Marco's?" Del pretended not to watch Lola. She might shut down if she felt cornered. "Or me? Or—"

"Oh, Del." Lola turned away.

"I've been an asshole and I'm sorry. We need to talk about it. But right now we need to focus on your stalker and Marco's."

"Marco's."

"Yeah." Del watched Lola pour coffee, put together a tray, lead the way to the living room.

"It feels like that time last year, doesn't it? Thanksgiving?"

Lola nodded. "Too much. I didn't think I'd ever feel hunted like that again."

"Yeah. At least Ray Stowe isn't a rogue FBI agent."

"As far as we know."

Del rubbed her forehead. "Anything I should know about Stowe?"

"I don't know." Lola tucked her legs under her and played with her hair. She was wearing Phil's castoff Red Wings jersey, and it hung even more loosely on her shrunken frame than before. She tugged it before it could slip off her shoulder, and Del felt a familiar and unwelcome flash of desire.

"Anything you remember could be helpful."

Lola chewed her lip. "Well, I don't know. He was kind of smelly."

"Smelly, how?"

"Bad breath, body odor. Pretty gross. If he had access to a shower and a toothbrush, he didn't seem to be using them."

"Funny, you noticing how he smelled."

"Well, because of you. Because of when you asked me what the man who attacked me—creepy Christopher James—smelled like." Lola shrugged.

Del smiled. "Are we getting nostalgic about that? Let's not. What else do you remember about Stowe?"

"What else? Expensive, maybe tailored clothes. They looked clean. Very pricey shoes. He really smelled bad. Like sweat and cologne." Lola wrinkled her nose. "He was gross. Other people must have smelled him. He was so odd. Shaved head, but not, like, in a deliberate way. Patchy." She shook her head. "I didn't even notice it at the time or thought I didn't. But he had scruffy bits around his ears and here and there. It looked like he was blurry."

"Was his behavior odd enough for other people to notice?"

"He was loud and most people were speaking in very hushed tones, you know. Some heads turned. It was his eyes—"

"What about them?"

"He had crazy eyes. Intense. You know? Like one of those screaming preachers on street corners? 'The world is ending tomorrow so repent'—those kind of eyes."

"What did he say? Do you remember?"

"He said Marco would never have a show because Ray wouldn't let him. I found Marco and he was really upset. Scared." Lola shuddered. "We snuck out and ran, literally ran, took a bus and then a cab. He was trying to cover our tracks, I guess."

"Okay." Del sobered. "Thanks. I may have more questions later."

"Whatever it takes to make sure Marco is safe."

"Absolutely." Del took a deep breath, noting the way Lola braced herself. "Listen, I have to confess something."

"What?"

"You told me that your stalker or whatever was taken care of, but I get the impression you just didn't feel comfortable talking to me about her. So when you were still kind of awake, I asked you where your phone was."

"Oh."

"I read the first couple hundred texts." Del made a face. "They were still downloading when you woke up. I never would have invaded someone else's privacy like that, and I had no right to invade yours. I'm sorry."

"It's okay. I filed a report. I went to a different station."

"Yeah."

"I—"

Lola was crying, and Del shielded her own eyes with her good hand. "I know. I looked it up."

"Del, I'm sorry for hurting you. I never meant to, I—"

"No." Del shook her head again. "We need to talk about your stalker. The other stuff we'll deal with later. Tell me about Sterling."

Lola sat back, tucking her feet under her, crossed her arms even tighter. If she were a snail, Del thought, she'd be all the way in her shell. This was, Del noted absently to herself, the third or fourth time she'd thought of Lola as being like this animal or that. What did that mean?

"It's okay." Del spoke as softly as Lola had. "Whatever happened, it wasn't your fault. I just need to know."

Del wasn't sure she really meant that. Was Sterling the woman she'd seen in Lola's car, the one playing with her hair? It had seemed a more intimate gesture than Lola was likely to be comfortable with. Had she even been aware of the woman's hand on her hair? Suddenly that seemed possible. How had Del not considered it until now? Then she thought about Lola and the wine. Maybe the innocent was finally ready to sow her long-dormant wild oats. *Too bad*, Del thought with real regret, *I fucked things up before that*.

Lola was frowning. "What do you mean?"

Del had to recall herself to the moment.

"Well, you don't seem too eager to talk about it. Whatever happened, I won't be mad or blame you or whatever. You can trust me."

Lola nodded, but Del had to work to keep her expression bland.

You can trust me? You can trust the woman who cheated on you, lied to you, bullied you, ignored your feelings—yeah, you can trust me. Of course you can.

"I went to Pier 39 with Marco," Lola mumbled, and Del tilted her head. "There was a Meetup group. Do you know what that is?"

Del nodded. It was time to put on the badge again, act like this was just some woman. Not, she reminded herself, that she'd ever done that particularly well where Lola was concerned.

"So I was hoping to make friends." Lola shrugged. "I thought—anyway, this woman was there, she—"

"You thought what?" She shouldn't interrupt, of course. She waited for the answer with badly concealed impatience.

Lola regarded her with hooded eyes. "Does it matter, really?"

Del shrugged.

Lola's words came in a rush then. "I brought nothing to our relationship. You had a life of your own and friends and a real mind of your own. I didn't. I was like an empty shell standing next to you. I was given a second chance to rewrite my life and I didn't. I chickened out. I didn't have any friends of my own. I didn't work, not really. I just hid in your life, in your house. I wanted to do things better. I thought it would be better if I didn't depend on you so much. That we could have a better relationship if I worked on being more independent and less of a helpless baby."

"Okay."

Lola curled up into a tighter ball on the chair, a snail inside a shell inside another shell. Or was she a deer, veering toward a cliff? Or a sea turtle, clambering awkwardly toward the beckoning sea? Del shook away the images.

"We went to lunch, a big group, and no one would talk to me, and this woman Sterling was talking to me. She seemed nice. Then she took my picture."

"Took your picture? Just like that?"

"I know, right? But I—it's stupid, but I honestly didn't realize—she seemed nice."

"So, she took your picture."

"She gave me her card and I gave it to Marco."

Del tilted her head. "Because?"

Lola flushed, shrugged. "Well, I don't know. I—okay." She sat up straight, set her feet on the floor. She cleared her throat. "So Marco said I was flirting with her. Which I'm sorry but I think it may have been true. I didn't mean to and I didn't realize I was doing anything wrong."

Del shrugged, trying and failing to feign nonchalance.

"I told her about us by the way. But maybe Marco was right. I don't know."

Del nodded, unsure what to think of that. "And then you left?"

Lola nodded. "I never expected to see her again."

"But you did."

"Yes. I ran into her shopping, and she was kind of hurt because I didn't call her." Lola started folding up again, and Del forced herself to nod and keep a neutral expression on her face.

"So you felt guilty even though there was no real reason to."

You let her manipulate you just like you let Janet manipulate you. Like you let me manipulate you.

Lola shrugged.

"She acted like you owed her something even though you didn't." Del heard the irritation in her own voice and snapped her mouth shut.

Lola sat back and let her head fall against the back of the chair. She looked like a blow-up doll that had been deflated. Her eyes were dull, her voice flat. She told her story like she was reciting a grocery list. She stumbled to an abrupt stop suddenly, and Del tilted her head.

"So you gave her a ride home? That's it?"

"Yes. But I looked up the address online, and it's not her house. It belongs to a very nice elderly couple who've never heard of her."

Del nodded. "In the car—"

"Nothing. She was weird, you know, like in the coffee shop. Hopping around different subjects. But no biggie. Just weird. It's the texting that freaks me out."

"It's rotten," Del blurted out.

"I know," Lola whispered. "I know. Whatever's wrong with me, it's never going to get better."

Del fought irritation. Lola was obviously holding back. She still didn't trust Del, and it wasn't hard to figure out why, was it? She had reached Lola's limit with her for the night, that was obvious. She offered a small, reassuring smile.

"Listen." Del cleared her throat. "What you said, there's something wrong with you. I—"

"No," Lola interrupted. "I shouldn't have said that."

"You know it's not true, right?"

"Right."

Del laughed. "God, you're a lousy liar."

Lola didn't react to this.

"Hey." Del stood and stretched carefully, babying her shoulder. "I want to talk to you."

"Okay." Lola's face was neutral, careful, wary.

Del had planned to talk about how to handle the stalker. Instead she heard herself saying, "I'm sorry."

"Sorry? What for?"

"For everything. I didn't mean to—I don't know how to tell you." She couldn't seem to stop the flow of words. "I cheated. With Janet. Right before I got shot. Didn't tell you because I'm a coward. A cheater and a coward and a liar. Didn't want to lose you. Felt guilty, took it out on you by being an asshole. My shoulder's fucked up now, just like everything else, because I didn't want to go to the doctor so I didn't. I didn't want to do physical therapy so I didn't. I wanted to be with Janet so I did that. I acted like a selfish ass, and I took what we had and threw it away for nothing. I'd take it back if I could but I can't."

"You—"

"But that's not even the worst thing and you know it, don't you? The worst thing was that night, the last night we even tried to make love. But we didn't. Because I made you feel—I—"

"Please stop, please." Lola's voice was a hoarse whisper.

She stood and turned toward the fireplace. She was still and silent for several minutes, and Del was frozen. Should she leave? Try to explain? She started to feel like she was drowning. Her chest was tight, tighter. She sucked in air and felt something in her shoulder rip. She gasped in pain.

Lola turned around and she was the efficient nurse, the obeisant servant, the placating nanny.

"Are you all right? Do you need anything?"

Del shook her head. "I don't want to upset you. Shouldn't have done this. Not like this. I fucked this up too. Oh, shit."

"Del, do you need to go to the hospital?"

Del shook her head, careful not to move too much.

"Please, tell me what you need. Del?"

"This was pretty lousy timing on my part, and I'm sorry for that. Too. Sorry for that too." She barked a bitter laugh and turned away.

"Del, are you sure you're all right?"

"I'll look into this Sterling chick. I'm gonna need a description, the times and dates, all that. Can I just take your phone, is that okay?"

Lola nodded. "I haven't been using it anyway."

"It's not hard to see why."

Del's face wore the grim, determined look that made her seem more like a soldier off to do battle than a cop, and Lola was reminded of the day she first saw Del.

"You looked like the Faerie Queene," she murmured, and squeezed her lips together. "I didn't mean to say that. Sorry."

Del blinked at her. "Are you gonna go gomer?"

Lola frowned. "Go 'gomer'?"

"Never mind." Del shuffled toward the front door. "Listen, I gotta get started and first I gotta go to physical therapy. Lock the door. Set the alarm, okay? I'll call you tonight and I'll know more by then. Email a timeline. I'll get her card from Marco. I have your phone. I'll talk to the leader of the Meetup group. Hopefully the psycho has priors. Bye."

CHAPTER TWENTY-NINE

"I don't want her to rescue me."

"Okay." Margaret regarded her with an unreadable expression. Lola fought a surge of resentment. She was in therapy specifically because she needed help from someone who could detach and analyze things objectively. So why, she wondered, was she so disappointed that Margaret was detached and analytical and objective? What did it mean that she sort of wanted Margaret to like her, to care about her? Was that normal?

"I don't want to need rescuing. I want to be able to take care of myself."

"Want to?"

"Can. I can take care of myself." Lola covered her face with her hands, then pulled them away. "Sort of."

"But you need help to deal with Sterling." Margaret pushed up her glasses. "Does it have to be Del who helps you? Could another officer do it instead?"

"They don't care." Lola shrugged. "Del's the only one who wants to help."

"How does Del's helping you with Sterling affect your relationship?"

"It makes me dependent on her again. Which I definitely don't want."

Margaret didn't say anything.

"But I am scared."

Again, Margaret only watched her.

"Have you considered maybe there's a part of you that—"

"—wants to feel safe and loved and protected?" Lola sniffled. "It means the world to me that Del cares if I'm safe. Of course! But that's not what I want our relationship to be. I want to be her partner and her lover and her friend, not the damsel in distress she has to rescue."

"Have you told her that?"

"Oh!" Lola shook her head. "Not really." She snuck a glance at her watch and felt a surge of relief.

"Well, I think we're out of time."

Margaret gave her a hard look and Lola smiled in embarrassment. She wasn't sure therapy was such a great idea. Maybe it would be better to work things out on her own. Maybe depending on Margaret was just as bad as depending on anyone else.

"You're a big, fat chicken," she told herself, glancing in the rearview mirror at the red sports car tailgating her. That's when she remembered the boat.

"The first time I saw Sterling wasn't in the restaurant," she told Marco minutes later over the phone. "It was before that. I was looking at the boats and there was a woman in a red sweater, and she was Sterling. I recognized her at lunch, but I forgot."

"I have a thought." Marco sounded almost like his old self, and Lola realized she hadn't heard him sound like that since the night at the gallery. "We could go there, see if we see the boat."

"Oh, I don't know." Lola frowned, staring out the window at the darkening clouds. "I wouldn't know one boat from another, and what are the odds she'd happen to be there right then? Anyway, it's gonna rain."

"No, it's not." There was a pause, and Lola could almost picture Marco looking out the window. "Even if it does, who cares? Oh, come on, wouldn't you just once like to take the upper hand? At least to try?"

Lola surprised both of them by bursting into tears.

"Yes," she blubbered. "I really, really would."

An hour later they were walking arm in arm along the walkway where Lola had first seen Sterling bring in the little sailboat. It wasn't raining, but it was dark and cold and windy enough to drive most people indoors, and they had the area mostly to themselves.

"All of a sudden this doesn't seem like such a great idea."

"Yeah." Lola made a face. "I couldn't begin to tell you which boat it was or which dock. And nobody's sailing today, obviously."

Marco's hand was cold in hers, and Lola let go of it with a regretful smile to tuck her hands inside her pockets.

"I'm sorry," she said, scanning the marina. The sea was choppy and forbidding, and she could understand why only a couple of very large vessels were on the move in the bay. At the rows of docks spread out along the shoreline, the boats—which all looked basically the same to Lola—seemed to be dancing in their moorings. Several banged into their docks over and over and Lola shivered. She couldn't imagine wanting to get into one of those flimsy things to face the icy, forbidding waters of the bay.

"At least we tried." Marco sighed heavily. "I sort of had this fantasy. She'd be here, we'd confront her and it would make things better. Stupid."

"No." Lola bumped him with her elbow. "We have a right to live our lives without being scared. That's not stupid. And okay, so we didn't find Sterling here. So what? Like you said, at least we tried."

There was a flash of light off to her right, and Lola shielded her eyes to check it out. What was that? Was it coming from one of the boats? She searched all over but didn't see anything.

Suddenly, one of the larger boats seemed to break loose from its moorings and start banging around and out of its slip. As though guided there, it went straight toward the opposite side of the narrow channel. The smaller boat in the opposite slip slapped against its moorings as though trying to escape a pursuer.

"Hey, should we do something?"

"I don't know," Marco murmured. "Whoa! Look!"

The big boat smashed into the smaller vessel, which broke apart almost immediately.

"Oh, my God," Marco cried out. "It's crumbling like a cookie!"

Lola murmured in agreement, too stunned to do more. As they watched, the larger boat battered the smaller one into pieces. Then it bounced out and careened wildly around the channel between the rows of slips. Too shocked to do anything but gape at the spectacle, Lola and Marco watched the boat head out into the open water.

"Who do we call? What do we do? Is there someone watching the boats?"

"I don't know!" Lola shook her head. "I don't—do you have your cell?"

"Here!" Marco shoved his phone at her, but she could only stare at it blankly. It was just a dark screen, and she groaned at him helplessly before handing it back.

"How do you make it work? Can you call Del? She'll know what to do." Lola heard the blind confidence in her voice and realized how childish she sounded. But then Marco was dialing the phone, somehow, and she listened while he left a message for Del and one for Phil.

"Tom," she suggested. "Del's partner, Tom Phan. I have his card." She dug it out and handed it to Marco, who was able to reach Tom and explain what was happening.

"He says he'll make sure the right people know," Marco said, holding up his phone to take pictures of the rogue boat as it was tossed on the powerful waves of the open channel. "At least the owner can show the insurance company what happened."

"Take a picture of the empty place," Lola urged, as the runaway boat bobbed in and out of view. "For the owner of the little boat that got smashed up. For their insurance."

"Right. They can identify it by the slip number. Good." Marco took several pictures of the surrounding area, then cursed softly and tucked the phone into a pocket. The rain she'd predicted had finally arrived. As they turned to leave, Lola bumped into a large homeless woman covered by garbage bags.

"Oh, excuse me, are you all right?"

The woman nodded and ducked her foil-covered head, reeling away toward the wharf. Lola and Marco watched her as she staggered first in the direction of the boats and then veered toward Pier 39, where the tourist attractions were centered.

"Funny, it almost looked like she was going toward a boat, didn't it?"

Marco shrugged. "Let's get out of this rain, sis."

"You got it, brother."

They trotted toward the car, heads down, and headed for home with a loudly shared sigh of relief. It wasn't until later, after she'd gotten warm and dry and was sipping a large mug of coffee, that Lola wondered why Tom had answered his phone but Del hadn't. She called Del's phone from the kitchen and left a message.

She did some writing, discovering after a time that she'd managed to incorporate a runaway boat into Olivia's story.

"Oh, silly," she chuckled. "Olivia as a sailor, though, that's kind of interesting."

She could picture Olivia at the helm of a beautiful craft, the wind blowing her lovely hair away from a sun-pinked face. She was tanned and muscular, healthy and lithe, full of confidence and courage. Lola was enthralled with this image of Olivia. Unmoored from conventional ties, Olivia could sail the world as a young woman. But why? What would it mean? How would it work? There was something there, something about the sea as mother or the unconscious or something, and Lola let the story play in possibilities. It was some hours later that she was startled out of Olivia's universe and back into her own. She realized she had given Olivia one of Del's little quirks, her habit of pushing her hair off her forehead when she was stressed.

"How much of fiction is autobiography?"

Orrin guffawed, and Tami's snide, snorting laugh rode behind his. "You think you're a writer? You're a fake, Lolly. You're nothing."

Lola shrugged. "Maybe everyone is, Orrin. You ever think of that?"

She smiled at the silence that met her words. Maybe the truth would set her free, like the gospel said. Only the truth wasn't found in some distorted version of ancient spiritual teachings, maybe. Maybe the truth was found in her own imperfect, confused and confusing, all-too-human self. And maybe writing was the only way she could decipher the truth. She rested her fingers on the keyboard and closed her eyes.

"Okay, I'm ready."

CHAPTER THIRTY

The moment is coming. I can feel it. I must prepare myself. I fast. I pray. I take the blue pills and the red pills and I let my friend soothe me. Her fingers trail lightly over my skin. Her presence is a balm to my overworked mind, and I breathe her in.

"Do you like this?" Her whisper wafts down through the thick fog around me, and I nod.

"I want to help you," she murmurs, and I nod again.

"You do."

"Is she the one?" Her thoughts are a sharp rapping now, no longer on the mission but on herself. "Will you save her?"

"You don't want me to save her. You want me to get her out of your way. I won't help you gain the spoils of your sin, my friend."

She pulls away. "You don't mind the spoils of my sin when it suits you."

I open my eyes, reluctantly forced to deal with the pettiness her ego has wrought. Even the broken branch can be of use, I remind myself. She is like the divining rod and has led me to the healing waters. Her motives are irrelevant, as long as I keep them in mind and anticipate her next moves. I have always been a consummate chess player, and my friend, dear though she is, serves the mission only as well as she can.

"You and I soothe each other. We heal each other's wounds. But it is nothing more than that. You deceive yourself with your foolish fantasies about what a mate is. You play like a child."

She is angry now and gathers her things. She snaps on her clothing, such as it is, and brushes her hair with sharp cracks of the brush. "You idiot. What can a man do that a woman can't?"

I start to say, make babies. But then I think of the babies I have killed, and I drift away on a current of grief and guilt and shame. I was a child, I remind myself. I was ignorant and afraid and merely human. Still, I feel the time slipping back until I am watching the scenes from my movie again and lost in them.

When I am recalled to myself by the chill of evening air on my skin, my friend is gone. Ah, well. She has already served her purpose. It may be that I must save her, after all. Or nudge her toward where she was headed when I met her and let her kill herself. I shrug away the subject. My friend is a distraction now, one I can ill afford. It is time to make the final preparations, and I must focus on the mission.

CHAPTER THIRTY-ONE

"Has it occurred to you that the whole thing—"

"Seems a bit too coincidental? Yeah. But I don't know."

"Okay, let's run it down." Phan ticked items off on his fingers. "One, Janet shows up out of the blue, help me, help me. You go over there and get shot, then Janet's place burns down. She disappears. Two, Lola meets a creepy chick that turns out to be a stalker. Three, Marco's stalker pops up after a long absence. Just like that."

"Yeah." Del blew out a long breath. "It sucks, but I can't see how the three things are connected, really. I mean it's not like Janet's pulling Ray Stowe's strings. I don't really see Janet as a criminal mastermind. Would she lie to get her way? No question. Manipulate and play games? Sure. But she's not violent. Not ever. She's a mess, but she's not some sociopathic criminal. Someone could be pulling her strings, but it doesn't track, her getting involved in violence. Of course, I could be totally kidding myself. As I am well aware."

"I don't have any idea how to break this all down so it makes sense."

"Me either."

"Not to mention the extra dozen or so missing women."

"Or more. We still don't really know how many are extra aside from the shitty economy."

"Time to sleep on it. Maybe we'll get lucky and some clues will come and slap us awake tomorrow."

Del laughed out loud. "Some detectives we are."

"Hey, now." Phan pulled on his jacket and stood up. "Speak for yourself."

"Hey, I got an email about that goofball from the SRO—Wilson."

"Yeah, Lucy sent me the same email. Whatever her real name, Wilson doesn't match up with any outpatient, parolee, sex criminal, vic, newly released psych patient. Nothing. She's nobody."

"Can't you just sign it off? If a complainant—"

"I know the code, Mason. I just think there's something going on there."

Del sat back and regarded her partner. He always listened to her when she had a gut feeling, and she owed him the same courtesy.

"Okay. I trust your gut. What do you want me to do?"

"Let's tag each other out. I'll take a turn following up on Wilson. You focus on Hahn, see if you can figure out who could be putting this all together and why. We'll compare notes tomorrow." Phan grimaced. "Lucky me, back to the SRO I go."

After several hours of fruitless efforts to find Janet or anything useful on her, Del was beyond tired. She gave it up by sunset. By the time she got home, parking the Ranger on the street again because, as she silently noted, she still hadn't cleaned out the garage, Del was exhausted. She was always tired lately, it felt like. Her shoulder hurt and she missed the bike. She missed Lola and couldn't quite believe things were as lousy as they seemed. She paused by the truck, unable to move until the mist lay thick on her shoulders and head and neck, chilling her. She wanted to go straight to her own front door and knew she wouldn't. She hadn't even reached Marco's front steps when the door flew open.

"Anything?" Marco was wearing painting clothes, a bad sign. If he was still working at this time of night, that meant he was freaking out.

Del shook her head. "Got the word out, checked for recent activity, but nothing. Phil keeping the pistol handy?"

"He's not home yet." Marco's eyes roamed the street. "He'll be at work until ten or eleven at least. I can't believe he's not here with me!"

"Come on, come over." Del tried to summon a smile. "I've got beer and pizza. Well," she laughed weakly, "the number to the pizza place, anyway."

"I appreciate it, sweetie, but you look about ten paces past tired, and I'm not quite that helpless. Go home and get some sleep, all right?"

Del smiled in acknowledgment and tried to hide her relief as Marco blew her a kiss and eased the door shut.

She could have gone straight to bed, she was so tired, but it was possible that as the evening wore on Marco might change his mind. She washed her hands and splashed water on her face. She wandered around the kitchen, finding nothing to eat and nothing she wanted to drink. She sat on the couch and stretched out her legs. She could take a quick catnap and still be alert if and when Marco came to her. She felt her eyelids close before she'd finished the thought and sighed in relief.

When the doorbell rang, Del knew it was a dream. She watched her dream self yank the door open without looking, assuming it was Marco. But it was Janet. She stood framed in the mist and the dark, shivering and damp and beautiful. Dream Janet was too thin and wearing designer jeans and an oversized cashmere sweater. Expensive-looking thigh-high leather boots completed the ensemble. Who was she playing today, the spoiled heiress, the misunderstood beauty? She looked out of place on Del's plain, functional porch, like she belonged on the lavishly decorated terrace of some fancy restaurant in some overpriced hotel.

"Come in." Del cleared her throat but couldn't think of what to say next.

She half expected Janet to brush past her in a haughty huff, but the tiny fashionista ducked inside like a refugee seeking sanctuary. She was wide-eyed and pale underneath her heavy makeup, and Del had to once again remind herself that Janet was not her lover and best friend but something else.

What was Janet to Del exactly? Right now she seemed like a victim, maybe, or possibly the enemy. Could she be both? Del gestured toward the kitchen, unable to articulate anything, not even a grunt. She trailed after Janet and watched her pull out the teakettle Del bought because Janet liked tea after a night of hard drinking. There were a lot of nights of hard drinking then for both of them. Del fought a smile. Lola's attempt at hard drinking had barely put a dent in a single bottle of wine, and she'd passed out.

"I guess you're pretty mad at me." Janet's voice was barely audible.

Del got out the tea canister, the one Lola forgot when she left. She was always saying she wanted to cut down on the coffee and drink more tea, but she'd never been able to stick with it. She slept too badly to give up her coffee, didn't she? Her big vice, coffee.

Del shook her head to clear it. Janet watched her, clearly waiting for a response. What had Janet said? She'd asked for reassurance, something like that.

"I'm more confused than anything. I wasn't sure if you were dead or kidnapped or on the run or what."

Janet sighed heavily and watched the kettle, waiting only long enough for it to start gurgling before she yanked it off the burner and snapped off the gas.

Del smiled and saw Janet's confused look.

"You're so impatient," Del explained, still smiling. "I'd forgotten that. It's funny, the things you forget." Her smile died and there was a long silence.

Janet dunked her teabag up and down, and it was a moment before Del realized she was crying.

"Hey," she crooned, rising automatically to go to Janet. She caught herself and sat back down. "Don't cry, okay? You know it messes me up."

Janet tossed the teabag into the sink. Another thing Del had forgotten. How many sticky, dried out, used teabags had she fished out of the sink? A hundred? Maybe more?

"Okay." Janet sat at the table, tucked her hair behind her ears. She cradled her mug in her hands and Del noticed her chewed-up fingernails. The manicure was destroyed. At least that was familiar. This Janet was brittle and distant and too polished to be real, but the real Janet, if there was a real Janet, was still human. She was impatient and a little careless and chewing her fingernails and still loved Del. In some way, whatever that was. Not that it mattered, of course, because Del still loved Lola.

This is a dream, Del reminded herself. But it didn't feel like a dream. Del realized she wasn't watching from the sidelines anymore but was in the dream proper. She heard herself adopt an unfamiliar tone. Did it sound as much like begging as she thought?

"Talk to me, please?"

"I never meant for things to get so lousy. All I ever wanted was you." Janet laughed and it was a joyless sound, more like a sob than a chuckle. She seemed to see that she'd done it wrong and smiled as though apologetically.

"You had me." Del kept her voice low. "But I wasn't enough."

Janet shook her head. "No, you were. That was the whole problem, baby."

"What the fuck, Janet?" Del pushed back her chair, but that hurt her shoulder, and she gasped. "Shit, I keep forgetting. Ah, God."

Janet stood and came around the table. She eased into Del's lap and laid her head on Del's good shoulder. "I'm sorry you got shot. I'm sorry for everything bad, baby."

Del knew she should get up and make Janet get off of her, but she needed Janet to talk to her. If it also felt good to have Janet cuddle up with her like nothing bad had ever happened, that was incidental. She was working Janet, she told herself. She swallowed hard.

This is a dream, she reminded herself again. It was getting increasingly hard to remember that.

"Talk to me, baby, please? I don't know what you're talking about. How am I supposed to know? I don't understand."

"You never gave me a pet name, never called me anything but Janet or baby, and you only called me baby when you were working me. Like you are now."

Del stiffened, but Janet laughed. "No, it's fine. I understand. You're working me, but you still love me too. You told me and I believe you. I think you love her too, that housewife. But I understand that. It makes sense in a way. She and I are so much alike."

Del snorted before she could stop herself, but Janet didn't react to that. She started gnawing on a fingernail, then caught herself and started petting her long hair instead.

"What are you trying to tell me?"

"It's complicated." Janet shrugged, her shoulder digging into Del's breast.

"That hurts."

Janet snuggled in at a different angle, reaching up to stroke Del's cheek.

"It was easy to just love you, you know? From that very moment. But it wasn't you. I know that now. You represented something else. But then I knew you and I loved you for real. That's the crazy thing! Please don't be mad at me. I loved you every minute and I always will."

Del shook her head to push away Janet's hand.

"Stop playing games," she croaked.

Janet turned to lean on the table and started crying, and Del fought impatience as hard as she fought the urge to wrap her arms around Janet and comfort her. Was she telling the truth? Was any part of what she said the truth?

Janet rose and turned. She made a face that reminded Del of the hideous religious paintings Nana developed a passion for at the end of her life. All of them featured a saint or sinner rising above a roiling mass of tortured souls, endlessly engulfed in the hellfire of damnation. Janet's face looked exactly like those of the damned souls, and Del nearly reared back in her chair. She caught herself in time and saw that Janet's face was masked again.

Janet rolled her eyes. Now she was a recalcitrant teenager. "I tried to tell you, Stretch. Lola and I are the same person. Don't you get it? That's why you like her!" She dumped her tea in the sink and snagged a vodka bottle from the freezer. She poured a slug into her mug and offered the bottle to Del.

"No. What does any of this—?"

"Blah, blah, Lola. Blah, blah, blah." Janet had already chugged down the first vodka, and she refilled the mug.

She put the vodka on the counter. "You think I'm bad but I'm not. I'm a lost girl, that's all."

"I don't get it." When Janet held the mug to Del's lips, she drank, telling herself it was to work Janet and knowing it was a lie. "How do I find the person who's after you? How do I protect you? Did you have anything to do with the woman stalking Lola? With the missing women? With any of it?"

"What? No way, baby. You can't pin that shit on me."

"I won't get mad if you did. Maybe you didn't mean to. Maybe— please, tell me who's after you, who's after Lola. How do I protect both of you?"

"You can't," Janet said, pulling the mug away and laughing at the look on Del's face. "Once a monster has you in their sights you're a goner."

Del struggled to think. "No, baby, that's not true. I can save Lola and I can save you. Please talk to me. Tell me who and what and where, please?"

Janet shook her head. She was a little girl now, stubborn and precocious and adorable.

"Nuh-uh." She licked the rim of the mug, a sexy vixen now. "There's something else I'd rather do."

Del shook her head. "You've gotta be shitting me."

The sexy vixen disappeared and was replaced by a morose child. Tears coursed down Janet's face, and she looked suddenly naked and more vulnerable than Del had ever seen her. Was this finally the real Janet?

"Janet, talk to me."

Janet shook her head. "All I can say is good night."

"Tell me what you want."

Janet laughed as she walked away. Del heard her calling out as she headed toward the front door.

"The same thing I've always wanted. You."

Del awoke to find she was crying.

"It was just a dream," she insisted to herself. Feeling ridiculous, she nonetheless remained unconvinced until she'd checked the kitchen. No teabag, no vodka, no mug, no evidence of Janet's presence at all. Del sniffed the air. Was that a remnant of Janet's perfume? She sniffed again. This was silly. She was alone. Still, she checked the rest of the house just in case.

"Knock it off," Del told herself. "She was nothing but a ghost." Restless suddenly, Del started to head for her bike and swung abruptly to dash toward her truck. "Time to get outta here."

She meandered south, hardly knowing where she was going, in a daze and still not entirely sure she was awake. It wasn't until she sat parked for a while that Del felt roused. The sun had long since sunk behind a thick bank of fog over the beach at the south end of Pacifica, but Del still sat with the windows down and soaked in the fresh, crisp, dampening breeze that flowed through the truck. She was starting to love the truck. The camper shell had a little leak in it, but that would be easy to fix. The truck itself felt solid and strong and timeless.

The Ranger was not a macho truck. It was an automatic. It had bucket seats. It had air conditioning and was surprisingly comfortable. But underneath it was still a truck. Driving it made her feel like she was back in Texas with Daddy, and Nana and Momma were back at the old place, and she was still Daddy's best pal, and nothing was wrong, nothing in the whole world, that her daddy couldn't fix.

"Stupid," Del said aloud, but the cold, wet air soaked up the sound, and she still felt good.

"I'll figure it out," she told herself, as she watched the lone straggler on the beach, an older man bundled up in a heavy jacket and wool cap. He had his hands shoved in his pockets, and he trudged along the upper part of the beach, avoiding the jagged wet line that marked the edge of the surf. He looked like a grim traveler driven by force to some terrible destination, and Del had to laugh. The beach was tucked into a little cove and went nowhere. The man had chosen to come to this place in this weather for no apparent reason, yet he wasn't enjoying the walk at all.

"Maybe he is, though," she muttered into the mist-spotted windshield. "Maybe he likes it more than it seems." She pushed her hair off her forehead. "Maybe he likes having something to complain about. Maybe he wants to suffer."

CHAPTER THIRTY-TWO

"She never called me back." Lola froze at her own words, fingers over the keyboard, and felt a rush of panic.

"She always calls me back. Well, almost always unless she's mad. Eventually."

She ran downstairs and fished out Tom's card again.

"Tom?"

"Hey, Lola. You okay?"

"Yes. Is Del okay? Did something happen?"

"No, why? What's up?"

"She didn't call me back."

There was a long silence. "Well, okay. Is it possible that she just hasn't called you back yet?"

Lola made a face. "It's been hours! And why could you answer your phone and she couldn't? That's weird."

"She's off the job for now, because of her shoulder. Maybe she's at physical therapy or something," he offered.

"I don't know," she started. "It just—"

"Tell you what," Tom interrupted. "My daughter programmed Del's new phone. I'll ask her if there's a way to find out where she is, where her phone is."

While she waited for Tom to get back to her, Lola tried to talk herself out of panicking.

"She's a cop," Lola told herself. "She carries a gun. Sometimes two. She's more aware of her surroundings than anyone I've ever known."

She paced around the house for a good twenty minutes, trying to imagine reasons Del wouldn't call her back, ones that didn't involve her being dead, maimed or injured. After a while, she could only think of the worst possibilities. She snapped into action, jogging to Del's house and using her key to get in.

She took the gun Del kept in the drawer in the entry table, hoping she was holding it right. She tried to imagine what Del would do, if their roles were reversed.

Okay, just look around. Be quiet. Hold the gun in front of you. It's a revolver, right? Del explained this, remember? It's got no safety, no hammer. All you have to do is point it and squeeze the trigger if there's a good reason to. No worries. Probably no one's here, anyway. Del maybe went off to a bar or something. Or she's with Janet. Lola went from room to room, seeing nothing and no one out of place. Del's keys and wallet were gone, her boots too. There was a lingering scent of perfume in Del's bedroom, and Lola realized it was probably Janet's.

"Oh."

That was it. Del and Janet were together. After all, Janet was the damsel in distress now.

"That's why she was interested in me before," she told the living room furniture. "She likes to save people. She only liked me because she saved me."

"Now she's saving Janet so she likes Janet," she told the kitchen appliances. "Maybe that's the only way Del can like a woman, if she saves her." That didn't feel like the truth, but Lola was as always unable to trust the accuracy of her perceptions.

Her gaze was caught by something sparkly on top of the fridge.

"It's none of my business."

Even as she told herself this, she was reaching up. It was a tiny bracelet, very fancy, probably Janet's—no one else would wear something so fancy or be able to fit it around her wrist. Lola fingered the string of blue and green gems separated by lovely silver beads with small diamond chips on them. She draped the bracelet over her own wrist. It wouldn't fit Lola, of course.

"Even my wrist is too fat," she muttered. "No wonder Del likes her better."

But why was it here? Was Janet staying over? There hadn't been any tiny, fancy clothes or shoes anywhere. No extra toothbrush, no extra shoes, no makeup anywhere. So why leave only one thing behind, aside from the scent of perfume? Why leave the fancy bracelet on the fridge? Was Janet laying claim to Del's space? Or was that paranoid? Only Del would have put an expensive piece of jewelry atop a refrigerator and forgotten about it.

"Del must have found it in the bedroom or somewhere. And she put it up there so it wouldn't get lost." That made sense, didn't it?

She was about to put the bracelet back on the fridge when her attention was caught by a picture stuck on the fridge. It was an old photo from Del's early days on the force, and she was barely distinguishable from the other gangly youngsters in their stiff new uniforms with their hats pulled low to shield their eyes. The photo caught her eye because Del had objected when Lola wanted to take some photos and put them in magnetic frames on the fridge. Lola couldn't believe that, after making such a stink, Del had allowed this picture on the fridge. Maybe it was because Janet had done it. Maybe there were things she let Janet do that she would never let Lola do.

"You really do love her, don't you?"

Lola couldn't help but wonder where Janet found the photo. Del hated having her picture taken. Lola had almost no photos of her life, and she'd begged to see Del's albums, to no avail.

"Oh, Del." She stood and tried to read the expression on young Del's face, tried to imagine being that scrawny young woman surrounded by all those hard-eyed, broad-shouldered young men.

"You had to be so tough, didn't you? Just to survive." Young Del was stony-faced, flinty-eyed, like the other rookies. She had the same perfect posture, the same wide stance, the same lifted chin as all the boys. The earnest stiffness of all the young cops made them seem somehow younger, like they were trying to prove how grown up they were. A sob escaped Lola's lips.

"Oh, love. Why would you go back to her? After she hurt you so much?"

Suddenly Lola needed to get away from Del's house, Del's picture and the knowledge that she did not belong in Del's life. She fled, almost forgetting in her haste to lock the door. It wasn't until she'd gotten home that she realized she was still carrying Del's gun and Janet's bracelet. She was about to head out to return them when the phone rang.

"Hello?"

"Hey, Lola, it's Phan. Tom. It's a no go on the phone. But I really don't think there's any reason to worry. She's very able to take care of herself."

"Uh-huh." Lola tried to keep the doubt out of her voice.

"Listen, if neither of us can get in touch with her by about ten or so tomorrow morning, then we'll do something, okay?"

"Well, actually, I was just about to call you, Tom. I stopped by Del's—really, I shouldn't have let myself in, but I did—and it looks like maybe Janet was there earlier. So I'm thinking maybe they're together."

There was a short silence, and Lola stifled a nervous laugh.

"Listen, as far as Del's concerned, we're broken up, so there's no drama here. I just wanted to make sure she was okay, and I'm pretty sure Janet didn't overpower her or anything, so it's fine."

"Yeah, okay. Thanks for the update." Tom cleared his throat. "If you do hear from her, no matter how late or early, just give me a call if you can."

"Sure thing, Tom. You too?"

"You bet."

"You sound a little worried." Lola frowned into the phone, wishing she could see Tom's face. "Because she was shot when she was with Janet?"

"Well, yeah." Then she heard him rub his chin. "Listen, she's probably trying to find out who shot her, but we haven't really made any headway on that. I'm sure she's safe."

"Yes, I agree." The doubt in his voice came through loud and clear, and Lola wasn't sure which she was really agreeing with—his words or his concern. Dissatisfied by Tom's response but not sure how exactly she could get a better one, Lola set down the phone harder than was necessary when the call ended.

"I don't want her to be with Janet. Or with anyone who'd hurt her." Lola swallowed hard. "I want her to be with me. But mostly I just want her alive and safe. That's all that really matters."

"And for yourself? What do you want for yourself?" *Who was that? Not Orrin, certainly.* Was it her own voice? Lola wasn't sure.

"What do I want for myself?"

Lola sat on the couch with the gun and bracelet still in her hand. She laughed and put both on the coffee table. They looked so incongruous together that she laughed again.

"Where do I put you two?"

Together, obviously.

When she saw Del, she'd give her both. Looking at Del's gun and Janet's tiny, pretty bracelet made Lola smile. How could she really worry that Janet would be dangerous to Del? It was ridiculous! Not only because Del was clearly stronger and savvier than most people, but also because Janet obviously loved Del. It had been written all over Janet when she'd come by, hadn't it? Lola's smile slid away.

"Dear, I believe I asked you a question."

"What do I want for myself? Good question." Hot pressure built behind her eyes. "I don't remember anymore. If I ever knew."

The silence around her grew oppressive. It was broken, finally, by a sure, confident voice that seemed to taunt her with its dulcet, even tones.

"I want freedom, peace, respect, fun, quiet, comfort, love, support, passion, humor, challenges, achievement, to make a difference and a really great wardrobe."

"Well, Olivia, that's just great." Lola heard the bitterness in her own ugly squawk and made a face. "But, seriously, you can have whatever you want. That's who you are!" She pushed her eyes open and strode over to drop the gun and bracelet into a cloth shopping bag by her purse. "That's why you exist—to have all the things I can't have. I want you to live the life I can't live."

The truth of this hit home only as Lola heard her own words. She reeled, catching herself with a steadying hand on the wall.

"That's why your life is so perfect." She was murmuring now, not entirely sure if she was speaking aloud or not. "But you're not real, are you? You're the heroine in the world's most boring fairy tale. A shiny princess who's perfect and flawless and totally unreal." She covered her mouth with her hand and mumbled to herself. "That's why I can't figure out where your story is going. Because there is no story. You're too perfect to need a story."

She looked around, suddenly aware of her aloneness. There was no Olivia, was there? No Mrs. Sutton either. Was there a Del? Was there, had there ever been, an Orrin? How about Tami? And Sterling? Was she real? Was anyone real? Or was everyone just a figment of someone's imagination?

"No!" She heard the firmness and certainty of her voice and was glad of it.

"I'll fake it, if I have to," she told her reflection in the mirror, as she straightened up and shook back her hair and tried to reassure herself that she was real. "I'll fake being a real person until it comes naturally. No problem." But her voice had lost some of its certainty, and she turned away from her reflection. "I don't know how to fix it."

Her reflection stared blankly back at her and offered no solutions.

"Maybe I just can't fix it." She listened for an answer, wondering who would respond, then braced herself when she heard Mrs. Sutton clear her throat.

"Have you considered the possibility that there is nothing to fix?"

Mrs. Sutton could, Lola thought, be just a bit annoying at times. She was imperious, certainly, and far too free with her unsolicited advice.

"What do you mean?"

"If Miss Mason prefers the company of a woman of Miss Hahn's character, perhaps she is not the woman for you."

Lola considered this. "Maybe you're right."

"Besides," Mrs. Sutton began, and Lola snapped her fingers.

"Enough," she hissed. "I don't need anyone else telling me what to do."

Del was apparently safe. And Marco was fine, at least for now. And she was fine, least for now. There was no imminent crisis, there was no fire, there was no horrible problem with her as a human being.

"I'm not defective," she whispered. "There's nothing wrong with me."

She thought about this for a while. "I'm not perfect, but so what? Being a real person means being imperfect, and I'm not mean or worthless or a bad person. I'm just as bad and just as good as anyone else."

Staring at her reflection, Lola tried to marry her image with what she was feeling inside. Who she was and how she looked didn't match and the dissonance was suddenly unbearable to her. She yanked a pair of scissors out of a drawer and started hacking at her hair.

"I should've planned this haircut," she mumbled into the mirror. But she kept going. There was no plan, no picture of where she was going with this, and there was a secret thrill in that. Lola had been careful—no, more than careful, paralyzed by uncertainty and an inability to choose a particular path—her whole life. She'd dithered and deliberated and tried to anticipate the consequences of every possible choice and minimize the risk and maximize the positive. Where had her efforts gotten her? Mostly nowhere good. Trapped in Orrin's house, for one thing. Afraid and unsure and desperately lonely and disconnected.

"Fuck it," Lola sang out, grinning at herself. She examined her reflection. Her hair was short, shorter than Del's or Marco's, short like Phil's. Her face looked different. Her outside matched her inside, finally, and she couldn't stop staring at her own grin. She'd always thought of herself as a fat, frumpy lump, and the woman beaming back at her was almost entirely average in height, weight, and features. Almost entirely average was a big step up from hideous, repulsive beast, wasn't it?

She went to her appointment with Margaret the next morning, enjoying her therapist's raised eyebrows and slow smile.

"Lola, you look amazing!"

"Thanks. I feel amazing."

Margaret cocked her head to the side a bit. "Accepting a compliment without arguing with it?"

"Can you believe it? I don't know what happened but I feel like a new person."

"Tell me about that."

Lola searched her mind. "It's like, my whole life I thought there was something wrong with me. Nobody loved me, nothing good ever happened—all that self-pitying, self-loathing junk. I didn't deserve parents or to be safe or loved or happy. I didn't deserve friends or fun or anything. I really *believed* I was worthless and unlovable. And if anybody was nice to me I would do anything for them. I couldn't trust for a second that somebody might actually like me for me. Like that was impossible." She shook her head. "I don't know if I'm a hundred percent over that, but I do finally see it's pretty ridiculous. I don't have to kiss anybody's butt. I don't have to accept being treated like I'm second best. I don't have to make somebody feel good to earn my place. I'm worth more than that."

"Yes, you are."

The rest of the session was a blur. Lola drove away thinking about those words.

"I *am* worth more than that."

She parked near Pier 39, arriving there before she'd decided on a plan to do so. She wanted, she realized, to try one more time to find the source of the problem with Sterling.

Why did Sterling pick me? She went over and over her actions that day.

I was too shy. Too self-conscious. Too self-absorbed. Not friendly enough. I went there with a chip on my shoulder, figuring there was no way anyone would like me, and so they didn't. I leaned way too hard on Marco. I acted like it was up to everyone else to reach out to me. I was childish. I couldn't, wouldn't just meet people and get to know them. I thought I had to figure out how to earn my place with them, and I tried too hard and in all the wrong ways. I was never myself.

She stood near where she and Marco had watched two boats crash into each other during the storm. What exactly had they hoped to accomplish? She couldn't even remember now. There was a flash of light somewhere behind her, and Lola whirled around.

"Who's there?"

She searched the darkening area. There were small clusters of tourists around, but none of them were looking at her. They were busy talking to each other and looking around. She tried to imagine what could have caused that flash of light. Hadn't there been a flash like that somewhere before? Then one of the tourists took a picture of his companions, and Lola remembered.

Sterling. The day they met, at that lunch. Lola's gaze darted toward the restaurant. She had been looking out at the sea, and Sterling had taken her picture. That was the flash, wasn't it? It had to be. And another time too, though she couldn't place when or where. Was it Sterling who had taken Lola's photo just now? Or was that paranoid? It was hard to know—maybe Sterling wasn't that crazy. Maybe weird texting was the extent of Sterling's repertoire of creepy actions. Remembering the way Sterling had been so skillful at manipulating her into acquiescing to her requests, Lola was sure Sterling had gotten a lot of practice pushing people in whatever direction she wished. She was too good at it to be anything but seasoned. What else did she do? What other strange and disturbing things would Sterling want to do? Suddenly chilled, Lola hustled to her car. She locked the doors and raced home, whispering to herself.

"What does she want? How do I stop her?"

Standing with her back pressed against the front door, as though doing so would keep out the world and all its ills, Lola shook her head, amazed by the ease with which her little bubble of confidence had popped.

CHAPTER THIRTY-THREE

Something pinged for Del, though she couldn't have said what. She shivered, chilled by the damp, and started up the truck to head back to the city. The phone buzzed just as she was about to back out, and she stopped to answer Phan's call.

"Hey, what's up?" She noticed that there were several missed calls from Phan, from Marco, from Lola's house, and she bit off a panicked question—had something happened? She pulled up her professional voice. "Sorry I missed your calls. Everything okay?"

"Yeah." Phan sounded annoyed, not worried, and Del let out her breath. "But you need to answer your damn phone, Mason."

"Yeah, sorry. Went for a drive. Phone vibrates, but I didn't feel it. I'll turn the ringer back on."

"Listen, just a heads-up—Lola was freaked, thought you were in trouble. She went to your place."

"Yeah, so?"

There was a silence.

"Phan, what's up? I don't care if Lola went to my house. She can go there anytime she wants. What's the big deal?"

Phan scratched his cheek. "Said she saw something that told her Janet had been there, so I just thought you should know."

"What? I—"

"Forget it," he growled. "If you're stupid enough to dump Lola for that freaky little bitch, that's your business. But—never mind. Hahn is a missing person, remember? You couldn't even call me? You're a fucking idiot. Meet me at the coffee shop in an hour." He hung up.

Del eyed the phone and dialed Phan's number, but he didn't pick up. He was really pissed, wasn't he? What was he talking about? She called Lola's house and left a message, called Marco and left a message.

"Well, now it's everybody else's turn—tag, you're it." She headed up the steep hill that led out of the little coastal town and back into the city.

"Janet hasn't been in my house, dammit. And I didn't dump Lola. I love her."

The little voice in the back of her head wanted to remind Del she still loved Janet too. That one she drowned out by blasting a Johnny Cash CD and singing along with the Man in Black. In the thick mist that kept drivers at a pokey crawl along Highway 1 and then the 280, Del felt strangely disconnected from the rest of the world, like her truck was a spaceship that traversed some strange universe comprised mostly of fog. It was a little clearer in the Mission, and she headed gratefully into the coffee shop. It was only when she saw Phan's cool expression that she recalled his irritation with her.

"Hey, Janet hasn't been in my house, Phan. I would've told you, asshole. But I should have answered my phone. I was just taking a little break."

Phan's response was a grunt.

"Lola seemed pretty sure."

"Well, she's wrong. I'm the one who filed a Missing Persons report on her, remember? Do you honestly think I'd see her and not report it? Jesus, Phan, have a little faith."

"Okay, okay. Jeez. Still, answer your damn phone. Who the hell just ignores the phone? You're still on the force, unless I'm mistaken."

"Yes, I'm still on the force, Momma."

"Then answer your phone. Don't leave it up to me to handhold your ex."

Del fought the impulse to retort back and shrugged. "Okay. Sorry. I guess I like being alone."

"Yeah, well, who doesn't?" Phan shook his head. "God, it's great—you can do whatever you want, and you don't have to think about anyone but yourself, and you can be as selfish and arrogant as you want. It's awesome!"

Del rolled her eyes. "Come on, man. You know what I mean."

Phan sat back, thawing only slightly. "Here's what I know. When I was single—the first time—I had a great life. Drove a fucking cherry Viper, lived in a sexy ass condo with a view all the ladies loved. Spent all my money on myself. Partied every night. I drank like a fish, screwed any woman who'd let me and thought I was happy. Never imagined for a second that I'd want anything more."

"I'm not some dippy college kid—"

"But things changed for me. I can't explain it." Phan shrugged. "There's something about having someone who gets you, you know? If you're sick, when you've had a shitty day, you want somebody there who gives a fuck. Do you even know how lucky you are? She loves you, Mason. She's been there for you no matter what. Aw, hell. Maybe you and Lola aren't right for each other, I don't know. So fine. But Janet, she's something else. She'll shit on you the minute you let your guard down."

"Phan—"

"You know this!" Phan stood and paced around the table, startling the woman at the table behind him. "How the fuck can you be so stupid?"

"Excuse me!" The woman glared at Phan until he waved an apology and sat back down.

"Sorry," he muttered, and Del watched him. He was red-faced and agitated, and she realized she'd never seen him so upset.

"Is this tirade really all about Janet? Who, by the way, I haven't seen, remember? Or is something else going on?"

"You make it really hard to give a shit about you sometimes."

Del didn't know how to respond.

"Okay." Phan crossed his arms. "Listen, do your thing, whatever. It's not like we're friends, right?"

"Hey." Del frowned. "You're getting really wound up here. I don't get it. Yeah, I'm an idiot where Janet's concerned, so what? I know she's no good. I know Lola loves me. I get it, okay? But—"

"The heart wants. Yeah, I know."

"So, if you know, why are you so pissed?"

Phan shrugged. "Who knows?"

"I haven't seen Janet, Phan."

"Fine. I just hate to see you fuck up your life. Believe it or not, I happen to think you're a halfway decent human being."

Del faked a heart attack. "Does this mean you're sweet on me?"

"Well, actually," Phan was turning red again, "I owe you. I don't know what you said to Kaylee, but she's only slightly peeved with me, instead of totally hating me."

"I didn't say anything to her. She's just got a short attention span."

Phan's loud laugh startled the woman he'd already annoyed once, and she glared at him.

"Let's get outta here," Del suggested.

"Hey." Phan leaned forward. "Sorry if I was an asshole."

"You weren't. I know you're right. I'm an idiot."

"Shut up. Listen, Lola and Marco went to the wharf. They were trying to find the stalker—her stalker's—boat."

"Sterling has a boat?"

"You didn't know that?" Phan shook his head. "Here's a suggestion: talk to Lola. The only reason I brought it up is that you might want to warn her about playing detective, okay? I'll check with the harbormaster, see if we can get a rundown on the owners who dock by the wharf."

"Yeah, okay." Del checked her watch. "Listen, I'm glad Kaylee's dialed it back to mild disdain, and I appreciate you checking on the boat. I got too much to figure out. Obviously, I want to get Marco's and Lola's stalkers, of course, but whoever's after Janet took a shot at me, and somebody burned her place down, and she is still missing, so I figure that's the priority, at least for now. Not to mention the, like, thirty extra missing women. You know, we'll find them in our spare fuckin' time."

"Sure, yeah." Phan shook his head.

"Seriously, what the fuck?"

Phan waved her toward the door. "No, I get it. You're right."

"But?"

"But there was a time, not so long ago, when you would have put Lola's well-being over anyone else's. Janet shows up, and now, she's the priority. Over Lola, over Marco, over a dozen missing women. You can rationalize it all you want, but that's how it shakes out." And he was gone before she could respond.

"Fucking nosy Phan," Del complained to the dashboard on the short drive home. "Thinks he knows me—I love Lola." She was at a stoplight. "I have to go after the perp who shot me, and I have to find the missing women, but both of those are complex. I mean, that's just simple logic. Lola met a goofball who sends mean texts. I'll take care of it, but how could I justify prioritizing that higher than a missing person and a shooter?"

Del couldn't erase from her mind the image of Lola lying on the floor, drunk on what couldn't have been more than a glass of wine, hiding from the phone. Putting it in the medicine cabinet because she was scared. Not telling Del because she was scared. Marco, pale and shaking and dark-eyed, scared and confused.

Del parked on the street and rested her head against the steering wheel. Her head was swimming with images of the women whose photos she'd been studying for weeks. The petite brunette with freckles, the one whose grown son kept calling the station. The young blonde, Tinfoil Wilson's daughter, whose fathomless eyes bespoke a maturity belied by her birth date. The graying prostitute, the overweight gas station clerk, the dishwater blonde with the oft-broken nose and a graduate degree. All gone without a trace. All dead or suffering or who knew what. And they were all waiting for Del to save them.

"What should I do? What am I supposed to do? I don't know how to protect any of them." She hugged herself. "I'm lost. I'm totally, I'm so lost. How can I find anyone?"

She called Lola.

"Hey, you okay?"

"Yes, are you?" Lola's voice was careful.

"Yeah, yeah. Not sure why I called exactly." Del couldn't have explained why she was smiling, but she couldn't stop. "I'm sorry."

"What for?"

"I took what we had for granted. Took you for granted. I didn't mean to and I'm sorry. That's all." She hung up, not even listening for a reply, not sure she could handle it if Lola cried or was mad or was grateful, absurdly grateful in that way she had sometimes.

"Acts like a starving puppy," Del muttered to herself. "Acts like it's a big damn deal if I do any little thing for her."

The lightness she'd been feeling evaporated as quickly as it had appeared and Del sank onto the steps of her front porch. She watched the sun disappear behind the buildings to the west and wondered what the dark would reveal. The sky turned orange, then fuchsia, then purple before going the blue-black of a rare clear night. The colors were vague at first, then brilliant, then dim as they faded one into the other, and Del soaked in the changing palette with pleasure. Still, whatever joy it offered, the sunset gave her no insight, and she finally gave up, trudging inside and heading for bed. She was back to desk duty in the morning, finally, and it couldn't come soon enough.

She should have felt glad to get back to work, but the next morning Del was nothing but angry. She had no right to be pissed. Del knew that as surely as she knew the day of the week. But knowing she had no right and managing not to be pissed were two different things. She hadn't been in the station more than an hour before she slammed her cup down on her desk too hard, sloshing coffee on her sleeve.

"Fuck."

"Nice." Phan raised an eyebrow. "Rough day already?"

"You don't wanna know."

He shrugged and they worked silently on their paperwork for several hours. It was tedious but oddly calming, and Del felt her tension reducing bit by bit. Finally she looked up to see Phan watching her.

"One of the things I like about you," she drawled, allowing herself a small smile, "is how you don't need to chatter about every little thing."

"Well, darling, here's how it is." Phan's drawl echoed hers. "We both know how utterly charming you can be when you're in a mood. Having the vapors and whatnot."

Laughter gurgled out of Del and she pushed back her chair.

"Okay." Del pulled out her phone. "I have a couple of ideas about something."

"No can do, pardner. Gotta pick up Kaylee. Her mom's got us all going to a counselor. Today's the first session."

"Hmm." Del wasn't sure what to say. "Good luck."

Phan laughed. "Same to you."

Del finished more scutwork back at the station after Phan's departure and managed to make it home without having to talk to anyone. She got her weapons out of the gun safe, visually inspecting each.

"Been too long since I cleaned the old ones," she told herself. "Got to maintain the munitions."

Daddy used to say that. Back in the early days when he was still one of the good guys or seemed like one to Del, Daddy had sat down maybe every few weeks at the kitchen table, a special towel spread out before him. He would pull out his two revolvers, his pistol, his shotgun and his two best rifles and line up his cleaning kit. As he took apart each weapon, he'd explain to a rapt Del how each mechanism worked, why it was designed that way, what each gun was most effective for. She could see them before her as clearly as if Daddy were perched on the chair across from her. She could have cleaned those guns herself, she paid such close attention. The guns had been beautiful to Daddy and thus beautiful to Del, and she'd never lost her admiration for the perfect balance, proportion and symmetry necessary to well-designed firearms.

"Like a surgical kit." She laid out her own tools and supplies on her own special towel on her own kitchen table. She took her time, relishing the precision of the work, the quiet and the smell of the gun oil. It was a smell that she'd always liked, that and the smell of the metal. She could hear Daddy's voice in her head.

"Slow and thorough but not fussy," she repeated the words he'd muttered to himself and to her.

"Who taught you how to clean 'em, Daddy?" She'd never wondered this before. "Was it Nana?" That didn't seem likely. "Your daddy? Who was your daddy? How come I never knew him? Did he stick around when you were a kid?"

Funny, she'd never wondered about her paternal grandfather or either of her maternal grandparents. Her world when she was a child was run by first Nana and Momma and Daddy and then just Momma and Daddy. Daddy, mostly, because he was the center of Del's universe and Momma's, just like he'd been the center of Nana's. And that was just how it was.

"Did you ever wonder what I'd be like as a grown-up? Or did you wonder much about me at all? How come things changed so bad?" She forced away her maudlin musing and focused on her task. It was starting to feel like drudgery now, though she'd barely started. Wanting to recapture the nostalgic feeling, Del decided to clean even the weapons she usually only pulled out a few times a year.

She went to the front hall to get the old .38 she kept in the entry table drawer, but the drawer was empty.

"What the hell?" She stood, mouth agape and one hand in the empty drawer, trying to remember the last time she'd actually seen the revolver. What could have happened? She grabbed her phone.

"Hey, how you been? Ready to join the team again?" Tess's voice sang through the line.

"Hey, my .38 is gone, the old one. Did I take it to the range last time? Do you remember?"

"No, you haven't taken it since last year, maybe even the year before. Where do you keep it?"

"Table by the front door."

"Locked?"

"Drawer, no lock."

"Oh."

"Yeah."

"You don't think maybe Lola took it?"

Del let go a shaky laugh. "Why would she?"

Tess drew in a hissing breath. "Put yourself in her shoes, *mija*. If you moved out of your cop girlfriend's house, and she had a handful of guns and a hair-trigger temper, wouldn't you want a little insurance?"

Del faked a laugh and got Tess off the phone as quickly as she could. She drifted to the backyard and eased carefully into the rickety old lawn chair that was still the only furniture on the back porch. It protested with a groan.

"You think she was scared of me?" She closed her eyes. "You think I have a hair-trigger temper?"

She let the afternoon shadows lengthen for a while before she went back inside to finish cleaning her weapons. Usually it was a good task for thinking, quiet and orderly. The smell of the oil, the satisfying sounds and feel of the metal parts moving smoothly in tandem—these things had always soothed her mind and freed it up from the day-to-day world, allowed her to get clarity. But today, even after she finished and put away her weapons and her kit, she was restless and edgy. When the phone rang, Del was glad to see Lola's number.

"Hey."

"Hi." Lola seemed to be tongue-tied too. There was a long silence.

"Listen," they blurted out at the same time, then laughed and went silent at the same time. There was another long pause.

"Do you have my .38? The one from the front hall?" Del's voice sounded brusque, she knew, but she didn't know how to soften it after the fact.

"Oh, yes, sorry, I just—"

"No, it's cool, whatever. I just wanted to make sure—"

"I can bring it back to you—"

"No, keep it."

Del could hear Lola shaking her head. "I couldn't."

"Seriously, I want you to have a weapon, in case."

Another silence.

What am I doing?

"Del," Lola's voice was hesitant, "I appreciate it, that doesn't seem like the right word. I just don't even know how to shoot it properly. It's very kind of you, but—"

"No, you're right. I just thought, in case you needed it. But you're right."

"Well, thanks, anyway."

"No problem. I'll get it tomorrow if that works for you. Around six?"

"Sure, okay. And, listen, if you wouldn't mind, I do think I'd like to get my cell phone back."

"Yeah." Del knew she should have given it back days ago. Keeping the phone had seemed like a way of protecting Lola, but it hadn't been, not really. "Sure, no problem. Should've done it by now, anyway. I'll bring it by."

"Hostage exchange," Lola quipped, and they both laughed too hard for too long. There was another long silence.

"Well, bye, then."

"Yeah." Del made a face. "This is gonna sound stupid, okay? But I feel like once I have the gun and you have the phone—"

"No!"

Del was startled by the loudness and vehemence of Lola's interruption. She picked at the grout on the kitchen counter.

Lola laughed. "Sorry, I just—hey, let's leave it at, I'll see you tomorrow around six, okay?"

"Okay. Bye."

"Bye." And there was a click. Del stood with the phone in her hand for a long time.

"How did we get here?"

She noticed there was a vodka bottle on the kitchen counter. Del tried to remember getting it out and couldn't. It was still cold. Suddenly, some nice cold vodka sounded like a good idea. She poured herself a generous helping in the mug sitting next to the bottle and tossed it back.

God that was good. She took another slug and took a deep breath. The tightness in her shoulder and back released for the first time in weeks. Had she been this pain-free since the shooting? She couldn't remember. She couldn't quite place how she was feeling. Tired, she guessed. More like, relaxed. Very, very relaxed. She could almost sleep. She let her eyes close or maybe they closed on their own. She wasn't sure.

Am I actually falling—?

Del opened her eyes and couldn't place where she was. There was a stuffed pig next to her, nearly three feet long and two feet tall, black with white markings. There were two baby pigs nearby. They had little snaps on their snouts, and there were corresponding snaps on the big momma pig's belly, like teats. The babies would attach to the momma, Del realized. But there were eight snaps and only two pig babies. Piglets and momma were a nightmare of mutilation. The snaps were about the only parts of any of them that were untouched.

The baby pigs had been burned. They were singed, and there was melted wax all over them. Red candle wax, once upon a time, it looked like, but there was dirt and crud stuck to the darkened sludge that covered much of the synthetic fuzz. What looked to be knife marks, stab wounds, had exposed the little white balls that comprised the baby pigs' innards. They were discolored, some of them, tinged with red and black and dusty gray.

But it was the momma pig that had taken the brunt of someone's rage. There were scars all over the huge stuffed animal. Stab wounds, burns from matches or cigarettes or a lighter, maybe. The face was smashed in, bloodied. Had someone punched the thing until his—or her—knuckles bled? Both eyes were gone, and what had once been a snout was missing, too. There was part of one ear dangling, and a hole where the other had been. The momma pig was stuffed with foam, firmer than the baby pigs. Less give. Del found herself calculating how many times she'd have had to punch the thing to bloody her knuckles. A lot, a whole lot. Hundreds of times at a go. The tail was still attached. Del peered to see that the thread was shiny, newer. So it had been reattached at some point. Back when someone was trying to take care of the piggies.

Momma pig looked old. Maybe twenty or thirty years or more. So, assuming it was a childhood plaything—or voodoo doll, or whatever—the room she was in belonged to someone in maybe his or her thirties or forties. The stuffed animals had occupied Del's attention for several minutes, but now she could take in more than those strangely mutilated toys. She was in a small bedroom, what looked like a child's bedroom, and she was tethered to a narrow bed.

Del tested the wrist restraints that held her. They were leather, lined with soft synthetic fabric over foam, surprisingly comfortable. Good quality, tight enough to keep her secure without leaving bruises. Locked, the straps connected to the bed frame on each side, just below the mattress. The lock and key were probably a brand universal, not that this helped. She didn't have the brand name or the key. The headboard was old-fashioned, solid, too solid for Del to take apart with her bare hands, even if they'd been untethered. The room was mostly bare, save for a night table and bureau, white like the headboard, with long-faded stickers of farm animals in the center of each drawer. The knobs were pink. It was a room meant for a girl, then. Well, Del amended to herself, a woman who thought of herself as a girl. A man who thought of himself as a girl, maybe.

She ran through the possibilities, implications, strategies—after what she guessed was an hour, she grunted in impatience. Enough waiting around, she silently commanded her captor.

Show yourself. This didn't work, so Del went back to analyzing her options.

Del knew what she was doing, intellectualizing in order to keep her cool. Most people, she realized, would panic in a situation like this, handcuffed to a little girl's twin bed in a darkening room. She had no memory of how she'd gotten here, who might have drugged her—this seemed the most likely possibility, given her lack of defensive wounds. She wore her usual knit boxers and a tank top and socks. She did not feel sore, bruised or achy. So she hadn't been here long. Only her shoulder hurt, but no more than had become usual.

The perp could have attached the restraints to the headboard instead of the side rails but hadn't, so her comfort mattered. Or there was some advantage to keeping her hands by her sides, with minimal but not entirely limited mobility of her arms. Did the kidnapper know Del had a shoulder injury and not want to exacerbate it? Was there something the perp wanted her to do?

Her legs were free. Why? Was it a miscalculation? It didn't seem likely. Del had the feeling this whole thing was planned down to the smallest detail. Leaving her legs free meant something. But what? Was the kidnapper overconfident? Or were there multiple armed kidnappers? No gag, either. She'd been awake for some time, but no one had come to check on her. Had she metabolized the drug more quickly than anticipated? She weighed more than she looked like, so maybe. Or she was in a location so isolated that it didn't matter if she hollered. The mirror above the dresser could be a two-way, of course, but she didn't have the sense that this was so. The night table was bare, but if she could reach inside the top drawer—unlikely but worth a try. Maybe there'd be something useful in there. Maybe she could reach a foot over. Del had just started stretching out her leg when she heard a key enter the lock on the other side of the door.

"Hungry?"

It was Janet. Del tried not to give in to the relief that threatened to throw her guard down. It might be little, winsome-looking Janet holding the door open with her foot because both hands were burdened with a tray of food, but that didn't mean this wasn't still dangerous. Pretty little Janet had managed to drug and kidnap Del, tie her to a bed, and keep her from escaping. She was clearly far more dangerous than she looked.

Janet's eyes darkened.

Del eased her leg back away from the night table. She wouldn't have been able to reach it anyway. The restraints limited her movements just enough to ensure that she could move around a little and not enough to do anything.

"I don't blame you for trying. I'd be disappointed if you didn't! You don't really think I'm silly enough to leave anything lying around here, do you? You'd leave before we were done, given half a chance, don't think I'm unaware of that, baby."

"Done with what?"

Janet set the tray on the bureau and turned with a wide smile. "I'm so happy to see you looking rested, my darling. Are you comfortable? Shoulder's not hurting too much, I hope."

Del shook her head. Dozens of possible options raced through her head but left her in a muddle. Was that from the knockout drug or because part of her didn't want to believe Janet had kidnapped her?

"You don't have to do this," Del whispered, surprised to hear how hoarse she was. "I won't leave. I want to be here with you, Janet. I swear."

Janet turned away, hiding her face with her hair while she moved things around on the tray. "Don't lie to me, baby, please? I know it may seem unfair but I really need us to be honest with each other."

Del shook her head. "I'm not lying." After a moment, she realized that she was in fact being at least somewhat truthful. She wasn't exactly thrilled at being tied up, but she genuinely wanted to hear what Janet had to say. She tried to express this, but her dry throat could produce only a raspy squawk.

"Shhh," Janet crooned, nudging in behind Del, propping her head up. She held a straw to Del's lips and Del was absurdly grateful to taste orange juice a moment later.

"There you go, sweetheart, that's it. Poor Del, poor baby."

Del knew about Stockholm Syndrome or whatever the so-called experts were calling it these days. She knew that kidnapping a person and making her dependent on you for food and water and life itself would bind that person to you and make her loyal and all of that. But that didn't stop tears from spilling from her achy, swollen eyes at Janet's soft words and the careful way she held the glass so it wouldn't spill and the way her free hand stroked Del's cheek gently and soothingly. It felt ridiculously good to lean against Janet's body, to feel the way she'd arranged herself to cradle Del.

"Thank you." She slurped up the last of the juice and hiccupped a sob.

"I'm going to take good care of you, I promise."

The glass went away and so did Janet. Del tried to reach for her, but her arms wouldn't move. Why wouldn't they move? She was too tired to pursue the question.

"Lie back down, sweetheart. That's it."

Then Del's eyes were closing. Her body was leaden and her mind was shutting down along with it.

"You drugged the juice," she murmured. "You drugged me again."

"Don't worry, darling." Janet's voice was both close and far away. Her moist lips kissed Del's forehead. "It's only until you're ready."

"Ready for what?" But there was only darkness and silence, and the question echoed over and over in Del's mind until even the darkness and silence were beyond her ken. *Ready for what? Ready for what? Ready for what?*

CHAPTER THIRTY-FOUR

"Nonetheless." Lola tried to keep the impatience out of her voice. "All I need is my phone."

"I see." Janet's voice cooled another few degrees. Another few exchanges, and the frost in her tone would turn the line—Lola imagined a string between two paper cups—into a long trail of ice.

"Janet—"

"I'm sorry for your inconvenience." Janet's words were clipped. "But Del's illness is a higher priority than your cell phone, isn't it? I will arrange for someone to deliver your phone to you. Please do not call again."

"I'm sorry to bother you, really. But please just tell Del—"

The line was dead. Frozen to death, Lola thought. "I hope she feels better," she finished lamely into the nothingness. She hung up and looked around the kitchen. Poor Del!

After a moment, Lola felt a giggle gurgle up out of her. "Poor Janet!"

No wonder she sounded so grouchy! Del was a horrible patient. If Janet was playing nurse, she must be exhausted. Lola sobered. Del was strong and healthy and stubborn. If she was too sick to drive home from Janet's, she had more than the flu. What if she was really ill?

What if she needed help? Lola vacillated between annoyance and worry for the rest of the day.

"Del's made her choice," she told Marco later that evening.

He tipped his wineglass at her. "Tell me you're just making this up."

She laughed, a sour sound, even to her own ears. "Is it really that hard to figure? Come on, Janet's a knockout!" She tried to laugh again, but the sound was more like a sob, and she waved it away with a wry smile.

"You're a knockout, too. Especially with your dyke chic hair." He smiled and raised an eyebrow.

"You like? Thanks. I'm still getting used to it." Lola shrugged. "Anyway, who would you pick, if you were Del? The fat old cow who does your laundry or the hot young sexpot who turns you on? I never had a chance."

"She loves you, Lola. And you're not a fat old cow, silly. You're wearing a size medium according to that little tag sticking out of your collar."

"Oops, thanks for the heads-up. I love her. If I had been stronger, if I'd been, I don't know, better, maybe we'd have had a chance. But I was a placeholder. While the two of them licked their wounds and made their way back to each other."

"She loves you," Marco insisted again. "And she was happy with you. She was never happy with Janet, not even at first. You're ten times better for her than Janet ever was."

"Maybe. But people love who they love, and they don't always love the person who's best for them."

Marco groaned and leaned his head back. "This sucks."

"Yes." Lola made a prim and proper face to get Marco to smile. "This sucks very much indeed."

Later that night, unable to sleep, Lola grabbed a notebook from her nightstand and started writing. At first, it was all a jumble of nonsense about Del, about Olivia, about Marco and about Orrin. But eventually, it became a frightening story about Janet. Lola wrote until her hand cramped, and then she went to her computer.

The story twisted around on itself like a serpent, and Lola had a hard time making sense of where it was going. She worked and reworked the details until it made some kind of sense. She read it over and had to shake her head at her own nonsensical thinking. Surely, this fiction had no relationship with reality! But Lola had the nagging sensation there was some purpose to this story. Maybe it was a message from her subconscious, trying to warn her. The things she'd written were surely not literally true, of course, but symbolically, they might mean something.

"What if I'm right?" Lola rubbed her shorn head. "What if Janet's dangerous? What if she's not who she seems to be at all?"

She felt silly.

"I'm jealous of Janet. That's probably where this is coming from. This is paranoid fantasy."

She sat for a minute, trying not to panic.

"What if it's not?"

She took the time to make coffee, to shower, to dress, before she sat at the computer and stared at the screen.

"It would be impossible to find out much," she told the humming processor. "But I could maybe do a little research and see how close I am on some of this. With any luck, I'll turn out to be totally wrong, and I can let it go."

Her coffee cooled as the sun made its path across the sky and Lola did her digging. One crazy conjecture after another led to digital confirmation, corroboration or correlation. Lola started to feel dizzy as day became night. Her lunatic theory, born as much out of jealousy and resentment as anything else, began to feel almost like reality.

"Okay," she whispered. "Don't jump to conclusions here. Just because you made some guesses that turned out to be right or close to right, that doesn't mean the rest of your guesses are right too. All it means is that you intuited some things about her, things anyone with half a brain could have put together, and stirred them into your crazy imagination."

She glanced at the pale sky of dawn, streaked with pink and peach and violet and promising a clear, cold day. So, she'd worked on this for a full twenty-four hours and was just too sleep deprived to think rationally. Nothing sinister was going on, surely. Del was sick. Janet was cool to Lola because anyone would be in the same situation. And Janet was hardly strong enough to overpower Del and hold her against her will.

The doorbell rang, startling Lola. By the time she'd reached the door, a uniformed messenger holding a clipboard was ringing again.

Lola signed for a large, baggy envelope and waited until she was in the kitchen to open it. Her cell phone tumbled out onto the counter. Lola stared at the now-unfamiliar object for a long moment. Then, hesitating, she picked up the phone. It still had a full battery, thank goodness. Del must have charged it for her before she got sick—or, Lola's fevered imagination put in, been kidnapped.

Lola didn't think, she dialed. He didn't seem exactly thrilled to hear from her, but Tom Phan listened to her rambling for a good five minutes before cutting her off.

"No, I get what you're saying, Lola, but I think you're seeing ghosts."

"I know how it sounds. But hear me out. I—"

"I wish it was different," Tom inserted. "But it's not. She picked Janet. It's damn stupid of her, and Del's hurting herself and anyone who gives a shit about her, but Janet's not some lunatic criminal. She's just a run-of-the-mill, lying, using, manipulative bitch. That's all."

"But—"

"You take care, okay, Lola?" Tom sounded far away. Tired or resigned or something equally distant. "Gotta go."

Lola hung up the phone and shook her head in impatience. "Why did I think he'd listen to me? No one ever does."

She looked at the phone she'd waited so long to get back.

"Why doesn't anyone ever listen to me?"

She tapped out Marco's number.

"Hey, I'm sorry to call when you're painting. I need to talk something through with you. Could I come by this evening?"

"Why wait?"

"Well, I want you to get a chance to work before I interrupt you, and I have some stuff to do too. About five?"

"Can't wait, sis."

Flooded with relief, Lola hung up and made a list of things she wanted to get done before talking to Marco. As she wrote down the last item, Lola realized making the list and crossing off its tasks rendered her upcoming conversation with Marco a mere formality. She shrugged.

"So be it." Flagging after her detailed preparations, Lola barely remembered to take her keys with her before dashing across the street. After a few minutes of chat, she was ready to broach the subject of her thoughts, or so she thought. Faced with the prospect of being ignored or dismissed, Lola felt stifled.

"I want to throw something out there, and I don't want you to tell me it's stupid."

Marco rolled his eyes. "I'm sure it's not. Just tell me."

"So, I was thinking about Janet. And sort of feeling sorry for myself and for Del. Then I started feeling bad for Janet."

"Come on!"

They lay squished together in a large hammock in Marco's backyard, and Lola stared up at the bright sky above through the dark green leaves of the tree under which they lay. Lola had never been in a hammock before, and she was surprised by how relaxing it was. She felt how bony Marco's side was and hid concern. His distress over Ray Stowe was affecting his health, clearly. She made a mental note to bake something special for the guys after the situation with Del was resolved, one way or another. It was pathetic, really. All she had to offer were baked goods.

"Lola, Janet's a truly selfish, destructive, terrible person. She made Del miserable."

"I know. But I also know how it feels to make a mistake. I don't think she's evil, not really."

"Hmm." Marco's tone of doubt was restrained, and Lola squeezed his hand. How had she gotten so lucky, stumbling over such an amazing friend?

They were quiet for a while, listening. Late weekday afternoons in the city were quiet, but the evening brought traffic and noise and music and laughter. In the peaceful backyard, Lola felt insulated from the bustle and bluster of the congested neighborhood.

"I wrote a story about Janet." Lola felt Marco stiffen and try to relax.

"Why?"

"I wanted to see things from her point of view, understand why she's done the things she's done."

"I can tell you exactly why. She's a selfish, immature bitch."

Lola smirked. "I'm so glad Del has you in her life. And that I do too."

He panted and raised his hands as though begging for a treat.

"Har, har." She waited until he dropped his hands. "I just couldn't understand her, you know? So I tried to put myself in her shoes. I wrote a backstory for her. Just made it up."

"And?"

"Well, the thing is, the more I wrote about her, the more I felt I understood her. The more like me she seemed to be."

"Isn't that just the nature of creative work? Sometimes when I paint a subject, I start to feel like them."

"I guess, but maybe it was more than that. After a while, I could almost see things from her point of view."

"That's a scary thought." Marco struggled to get out of the hammock. "Listen, sweetie, I think it's nice that you wanted to empathize with her, okay? But you are nothing like Janet."

"But that's not the whole story." Lola accepted Marco's hand as she made her own escape from the hammock.

"Yes, it is." His tone brooked no argument. "Leave it alone, Lola. She's a fucking monster, but Del picked her, and there's nothing you can do to save someone who's in love with a monster."

CHAPTER THIRTY-FIVE

My friend is doing her job as I do mine. The little fly buzzes around, trying to get free, but she doesn't understand that I am delivering her from the prison of her life. She will, though. That is what makes her special, that she will know the truth of what I am saying and doing in a way the others have not.

I knew that as soon as my friend explained her to me. I studied her, the way one studies a beautiful work of art. I have never gained such insight and clarity on any of the lost girls, and I have only been able to infer who they had become from little snippets of information, from impressions, from my knowledge of behavior patterns. I have used my camera, that most sacred tool, to examine them with the clarity and objectivity necessary to wisdom. I have put my lens to their faces, their bodies, their friends and families and lovers and cars and homes. I have put my lens to their lunches and their shoes and their everything and it has all been for naught. But the angel, my angel, my redeeming light—she knows she's lost. I took so much time, days on end, poking at her to see what she'd do. It was hard on her, letting her stew in fear. I'd never done that before, and I hope to never do it again. I don't think I'll have to. I am up to four red pills a day now and they are working their magic. They help me understand this lost girl is more than just my misplaced hope personified.

Like me, she has failed to find true refuge. She's tried, certainly, but has failed, over and over, to escape the reality that she is spoiled and unhappy in this life and will never find joy on this earth. Her truth has caused her pain, and for this I am both sad and overjoyed. Her pain is the path, like my pain has been the path, and we shall both soon be free. She will be my new sister, my new daughter, my new self, made pure and whole in the peace of freedom from this tainted world. I will save her and that will save me.

CHAPTER THIRTY-SIX

"Are you listening to me?"

Del pretended to be asleep.

"I know you can hear me, baby." Janet's face went away, and Del heard her chewing her fingernails. The sound made Del nostalgic, and for a moment she considered offering to kiss each of Janet's fingers if she would stop biting on them. Del almost smiled. Janet had been thrilled by the offer once upon a time, and Del had been happy to fulfill her sweet obligation, day after day. Of course, Janet never really kept her end of any bargain. Del had ignored the ragged ends of Janet's nails, bestowing an affectionate token without reservation. She would have been delighted to do so again. But they were not lovers, not anymore. Janet had kidnapped Del and was holding her captive.

"How did this happen?" The question slipped out before Del could stop it. She made a face but then realized that Janet hadn't been fooled by her Rip Van Winkle impression anyway.

"Oh, Del." Janet sounded close to tears. She sat on the bed next to Del.

I could use my legs to immobilize her, Del thought. *Pin her, get her down close to my hand.* Del played out the possibilities in her head and decided to wait.

I need to gain her trust. Get her to take off the restraints.

"I honestly don't know."

Del struggled to pay attention to what Janet was saying.

"I know you're angry at me." Janet sounded reproachful.

"Maybe if you explained it to me," Del prompted. She had to be careful. Janet could get worked up and lose her cool. God only knew what weapons she had on hand. Or what help. But she had to get Janet to talk. It was the only way to figure out how to escape.

"The frustrating thing is, you should understand!"

Del suppressed a groan of impatience. "I'm sorry, I don't."

Janet stood and paced. Del watched her go back and forth, her long hair the only part of her visible unless Del craned her neck.

"Oh, let me get you a pillow." Janet made a face and ducked out. She was back in a minute.

Del again had to stifle the impulse to try overpowering Janet. She nodded her thanks and settled back, glad to be able to see Janet more easily.

"Better? Good. Okay." Janet smiled uncertainly at Del, and for a moment she was just a sweet, pretty girl who'd made a few mistakes and wanted another chance. Del fought sudden tears.

She loves me, I know she does. So why didn't I just forgive her and move on? How did we get here?

"Oh, I can't do this!" Janet was crying too, and Del shook her head.

"Janet—"

"Finish your oatmeal, and we'll get you cleaned up." Janet was suddenly all business and Del bit her tongue. She'd been locked in this dark little room for, what, three days, maybe four? Why wasn't anyone looking for her? Phan? Lola? Anyone? She let Janet spoon in the cereal and wipe her mouth.

"Can I take a shower?" She hated the begging tone in her voice but she knew it would work. "I stink. Please?"

"I'm getting a bath ready for you. Remember when I had the flu, and you gave me a bath?"

Del nodded. She was surprised Janet remembered the incident from early in their relationship. She'd been a terrible caregiver as she recalled it, but Janet had been absurdly grateful. Like Lola, now that Del thought about it. Surprised anyone would bother to do any little thing for her.

"It meant a lot to me, the way you took care of me. Now I'm taking care of you. I'm doing a good job, right?"

Del nodded again.

"I'll be back for you in a bit."

They were in a trailer, Del suddenly realized. This made her feel better, though there was no real reason it should. A trailer seemed more permeable, somehow, less imposing a prison. Should she try something when Janet came back for her? It would be hard to do much, she was so stiff and sore from inactivity, but she thought she could maybe get free if a chance presented itself. She might, of course, need to help that opportunity along. After that, she'd need to find a way to connect with civilization. They were remote, clearly. Del hadn't heard a single car, cell phone, airplane, helicopter, siren, anything. But she knew how to track, at least a little, and she would just pick a direction and go until she found people. If they weren't too high up, if it wasn't too cold at night, then maybe she'd survive. She closed her eyes. She was so tired! Maybe it would be good to rest up as much as possible until she made her move. Del woke to find herself bathed.

She drugged me again. She must have used a gurney or something. No, a wheelchair would fit better in a trailer. So, she came prepared. She plans to keep me here for a while. She could smell shampoo, soap, lotion, deodorant. Her mouth tasted clean too. Did Janet have help? This was the question she kept asking herself and needed to find an answer to. Evading more than just Janet or having to escape without knowing if she needed to plan on another potential assailant—both possibilities could complicate things. Del felt for the first time how truly helpless she was.

"I've been kidding myself," she muttered. "I'm stuck here as long as she wants, helpless as a baby."

Though she was ashamed of it, Del cried until she fell back asleep. Hours later, judging by the quality of the darkness—it was darker, somehow—Del awoke and sensed her aloneness.

"Think about this," Del called, unsure whether anyone could actually hear her. "They're going to miss me. Phan. Lola. Marco. Tess. I have a job, neighbors, friends. They're gonna come looking for me. And what then? A shootout? Maybe you think you can talk—or buy— your way out of this. But you can't."

No response. Del needed to pee and she was thirsty and hungry.

"You can't just keep me tied up here forever." She flexed her shoulders, wincing, and jiggled her arms and legs. "I'm getting dehydrated. I'm not getting enough to eat."

She waited another few minutes.

"It hurts," she mumbled. "Leaving me tied up here is hurting me." No response.

"Please?" Her voice was thick. She wouldn't cry, she wouldn't. She'd sworn it to herself. Not again.

"What do you want? What do I have to do?"

Silence was the only answer.

"Janet?" She swallowed the tears that threatened to stifle her words. "Talk to me, please?"

CHAPTER THIRTY-SEVEN

"This is stupid," Orrin hissed.

She didn't respond.

"You're going to get yourself killed," he warned.

Lola shrugged his words away.

"Stop ignoring me!" He roared this when Lola stopped to make a pot of coffee, and she nearly dropped the glass carafe.

"Stop having temper tantrums, you big, dead baby," she snapped. Jabbing at the grind button on the coffeemaker, Lola waited for the screaming roar of the machine to drown out Orrin's phantom presence and the cackling of his spectral sidekick, Tami Holden. She managed to keep their nagging voices away while she made her preparations but felt there was more she needed to say to both of them.

Really, she thought, as she packed the car, *am I sorting through what I want to say to my dead husband and his equally moribund paramour?* By the time her heavy sedan was crawling through mid-morning traffic, Lola was ready to talk with Orrin again.

"I was so scared of you," she told the phantom.

"I know." He sounded smug and Lola tried to ignore her ire at this.

"Did you ever love me, really?"

The question hung in the air for a long time.

"In some way at least?"

No answer.

Lola sighed heavily. "I wish I knew. Not that it matters, I guess. You're dead, and I'm alive and alone and about to get myself killed and maybe get Del killed too."

She checked her rearview mirror, wondering for a second if she was seeing things. Was that Sterling, that woman in the SUV a few cars back? The woman had a baseball cap on and it was hard to see her, but she had Sterling's coloring and bearing. Lola shook her head.

"Paranoia."

She saw herself as if from a short distance and nearly turned the car around.

"This is a fool's errand," she told herself. "Based on nothing at all, I'm going to the home of a total stranger who lives hours away. All because I have some crazy theory that Janet has kidnapped Del and is holding her prisoner in this place she bought under a fake name that no one but me would think Janet might use. Only someone like me would think, oh, anagram, Hannah Jet, sure, that makes sense. This is ridiculous! All based on a made-up story no one but me would think could be true."

Orrin's chuckle in her ear, accompanied by Tami's snorting chortle, was all the derision Lola needed to decide that, fool's errand or not, she was headed upstate to find Del. Some time later, she shucked on her hands-free headset and dialed the phone.

"Talk to me, honey." Marco's voice sounded far away. "Where are you? What's going on?"

Lola considered what to tell him. "I don't want you to tell me I'm nuts, okay?"

"Lola—"

"I have a hunch. It's probably a total waste of time, but I'm going to chase it down."

"I'll come with you."

"No." Thinking her tone too firm, Lola softened the word with a laugh. "Listen, I need to satisfy my curiosity about something, that's all, and I feel kind of silly about it."

"So what? Remember when we went to the wharf? Remember how silly that was? But we did it together."

Lola grimaced, slowing as the Sacramento traffic grew more congested. "I'm already a couple hours out of town."

Marco huffed. "Where exactly? Do you really think I'm going to let you go off and get yourself hurt?"

"You don't *let* me do anything, Marco. I'm a grown woman, got it? And I decide what I do and when, not you." Lola held her breath, shocked at her own pique but not willing to take back the words.

"Honey, I just want to make sure you're okay. That's all."

Lola let out a long breath, slowing even more as the traffic eased to a crawl. "I'm sorry. I'm just worried about Del and not sure what to do. Listen, I have to go, traffic's terrible here. I'm headed up past Sacramento, near Placerville on the 50. I wasn't going to stop for the night in Sac, but the traffic's making me think I'd better. I'll call you tomorrow night by seven or so, all right? If I don't, just tell Tom to look for Hannah Jet in El Dorado County."

"Who's Hannah Jet?"

"Okay, thank you, sweetie. I have to go, bye!" She disconnected the phone and dropped the headset into her purse. She'd hesitated about calling him at all, but it seemed prudent to at least let one person know where she was and what she was doing. Sort of. In the vaguest possible way.

She spent another forty-five minutes dribbling along the highway with thousands of commuters before she started recognizing anything. She laughed when she saw the sign for Rancho Cordova.

"I need to stop for the night," she told her skeptical-looking eyes in the rearview mirror. "And I know how to find it and how to find the freeway in the morning. Plus it's very affordable. And I know where the ice machine is."

Mrs. Sutton huffed in Lola's ear, but it was Orrin whose voice slithered inside her head.

"It's just what you deserve," he hissed.

His voice was cold and hard and Lola shivered. She nearly stayed on the freeway, but Mrs. Sutton's disapproving voice pushed her to take the exit.

"Really, my dear, this is hardly an appropriate choice. I forbid it."

"You should know by now, ma'am," Lola drawled, in unconscious imitation of Del, "I don't much like being told what to do."

There was a new desk clerk staring glassy-eyed at the same old battered television and struggling one-handed with the same old worn-out cash register behind the same old scarred lobby counter. He directed Lola to a ground-floor room, and Lola resisted the urge to request her old room, the one she'd lived in, once upon a time, the one where she'd found out that Orrin was dead, that Tami Holden was dead. The one where she'd thought Orrin was playing a trick on her and was going to show up at any moment and take her by the hair and drag her into the car and make her go back to his house and never let her outside again. It was too easy to imagine that she wasn't Lola Bannon but Lolly Beckett and that the past several months had been a dream.

Lola closed her eyes, hoping to block out the thought, but that only made it worse. The smell of the new room, so like the other, assaulted her and made it hard to remember where she was.

"It wasn't a dream. I'm not her anymore. I won't ever be her again. It's over." She shook her head and felt how light it was.

"No hair." She reached up and felt her head. "Short hair. Lola Bannon has short hair." She opened her eyes and saw her purse, the pretty new purse she bought with Lin when Del was hurt. "None of it was a dream. It was real and I'm real." She touched her purse and felt how soft it was, and she was all right again.

"Back in the here and now," she whispered.

She remembered how her face had felt big back then, swollen and sore. It had been hard to breathe and she'd had a hard time seeing. She'd looked in the mirror and not recognized herself.

She walked now as if in a trance to the smudged, speckled mirror in this other room in the same motel, wondering why she'd chosen to stay in this place of all the hotels and motels—dozens lined Highway 50—she could have selected.

"Maybe I needed to see how much I've changed."

Her reflection gazed coolly back at her. She didn't recognize herself in that reflection for a long time. She had clearly defined features and a bold, androgynous haircut. She didn't look afraid or cowed or invisible.

"I'm in there," Lola whispered, and the sound of her own voice made her reflection somehow shift so that it was old Lola and new Lola all in one. She had the short, chic hair, but it was uncombed and lank from sweat. She had the balanced features, but the skin was sallow, the eyes ringed in dark circles, the mouth drawn close and tight. If she puffed up her cheeks a little she would look like her old self again. She held her breath and stared unblinking until her eyes were watery, and there she was, new Lola.

"Sometimes it was easier to be the old me," she confessed to her image. "No one expected me to know anything or be anything or do anything. I just had to try not to make Orrin mad. Not that it ever worked, but at least I didn't have to think so much."

She turned to the misshapen bed in the center of the dark, mildew-tinged room. This mattress, like the other, sagged in the center. The edge of it, she remembered, had been the only firm part. It had bruised the backs of her thighs when she'd sat on the side on the bed, unable to sleep. She recalled inching towel-wrapped ice toward her face the day Orrin threw her out. Remembered finding out that Tami—what was her last name? Lola's gaze darted around the room.

"Have I really forgotten? Didn't I just know it? I did, didn't I? Holden." That was it, Tami Holden.

"Were those her sunglasses?"

"What do you care?" It was Orrin's voice, the old one, the scary one that meant he was building to an outburst. The one that was a warning to her and a kind of verbal foreplay for him. She'd started, at some point, to think of all of his assaults as sexual in nature. It was all about power, wasn't it? Exerting power over another person and erasing her. Punching her over and over, throwing her against the wall or the table or whatever, screaming and spitting in her face while slamming her into the ground or the kitchen counter or the wall— Orrin been aroused by the violence. How had he learned to associate violence with sexual arousal? Lola hadn't really wondered about that in a long time, but early in the marriage she'd spent endless hours trying to decode the man she'd married, figure out how he'd become a monster. Her thinking had gotten her nowhere, and eventually she'd stopped trying to figure out how he got that way and started focusing on how to survive him. Paying close attention to Orrin was Survival 101, a thing she'd learned from the foster homes, and the first law of the world she lived in was to monitor the dangerous person closely. Look for cues in facial expression, body language, tone of voice, everything. Had she ever stopped doing that? Orrin's face froze at some point, probably because of the Botox injections he thought she didn't know about, but his warning voice was a thing he couldn't hide. It had held a kind of power over her after a while, had acted as a sort of paralytic on her thinking, and it had, she'd come to believe, held a note of glee in it.

"You liked getting mad," she whispered. "You wanted to get mad."

Had he ever had sex with her without getting mad first? Without scaring and bullying and hitting her? She tried to remember.

"It's all such a blur," she said, sitting on the edge of the bed. It cut into her thighs, just like the old bed in the other room.

"It's right there, upstairs and over that way." She pointed.

Why am I here? She tried to remember but couldn't. All she could remember was that Tami Holden was dead, dead, dead.

"And it's all my fault." Lola shook her head. "Enough of this! I can't save Del if I just sit here like a lump."

"You couldn't save yourself. What makes you think you can save Del?" The voice was low and indistinct.

"I don't even know if she needs saving."

"She probably doesn't. You just don't like it that she picked Janet over you even though you knew she was too good for you."

Lola nodded. "I did know she was too good for me. It was just a matter of time before she figured it out."

"Janet is young, hot, sexy—and smarter than you."

Lola nodded again.

"Still," the voice—Lola realized with vague unease that she wasn't sure whose voice it was—continued, "she seems like a bitch."

"I don't know her very well."

"She lied."

"Yes."

"She hurt the cop."

"Yes." Lola gathered herself. "Who am I talking to? Who are you?"

There was a laugh. "Haven't you figured it out, dummy?"

Lola shook her head. "I thought at first you were Mrs. Sutton. Maybe Olivia. But now I'm not sure. This is crazy."

"No crazier than driving past a dozen nice hotels to stay in this dump."

Lola flushed. "I knew the way here. And there was traffic. So I stopped at a place I'm familiar with, that's all."

The voice offered no comment.

"Well," Lola conceded. "I guess there were a few nicer places I passed on the way. It just never occurred to me to stay at one of them. I don't know why."

She looked around the room. It was dirty, even by third-rate motel standards. There was a wad of used tissue under the nightstand and a piece of candy wrapper near the door. The carpet had been vacuumed, albeit carelessly, and the bedding changed, and there was a faintly chemical smell that suggested someone had cleaned the sink and toilet. But Lola had seen how many rooms the housekeepers in this place were expected to clean in a very short time, and there was no way they were actually getting anything clean. They were just making the rooms look clean enough to placate the customers.

Lola looked out the window at a trio of scantily clad young girls loitering by the lobby. Prostitutes? Maybe. There had been a steady parade of men in and out of certain rooms last year. From late morning to early afternoon, usually, then from about four to midnight. Lola had barely noticed them, at first, except for noting with disgust the way they spoke to the girls. They treated the young prostitutes with disdain and a kind of self-righteous disgust even as they haggled for a better price for exploiting the teens. It had made Lola sick, back when she'd lived here, and she'd gotten in the habit of either keeping the curtains closed or turning her back to the view.

"Sartre says we have to decide whether to live or to kill ourselves and that once we decide we have to act."

"Hmm." The voice sounded almost disinterested.

"But I don't think it's that simple. I think we have to decide every day, several times a day, not to kill ourselves."

"Yeah, yeah." Bored, now.

"With everything we have to survive, everything we carry around all the time, it's hard." Lola's voice broke. "It's very hard, sometimes."

"Waaaaah! Life is hard! It's so hard to be alive. Poor Lola, poor baby Lola, has to deal with fucking being alive! Poor, poor you!"

Lola hugged herself. "You're so mean! Why are you being so mean?"

"Oh, come on! Haven't you figured it out? Are you really that stupid?"

At that, Lola closed her eyes. She took a deep, shuddering breath before easing them open. "Tami? Is that who you are?"

There was a long silence.

"I'm sorry," Lola whispered. "I'm so sorry. It's all my fault you died. You were so young, and I'm so sorry."

"You're *sorry?*"

Lola held her breath.

"Is that supposed to make me feel better? Is that supposed to make up for killing me? Huh?"

"No, I can't make that up, I know that. All I can do is say 'I'm sorry.'"

"You murdered me, you coward. And you have the balls to sit there and whine about how hard it is to be alive?"

"I'm sorry."

"Oh, well, fine, then, Killer."

Lola shook her head. "Please don't call me that, Tami."

"Why not, Killer, does it hit a little too close to home? Huh?"

"Please."

"You killed me. You murdered me. I hate you. I will never forgive you because you KILLED me!"

"I didn't kill you."

"What? What did you say?"

"I didn't kill you." Lola stood and shook her head again. "I was a coward and I didn't stop Orrin from hurting me, but I didn't even know about you. I had no way of knowing he wanted to run off with you. I didn't know anything about you or about the money, if he really was embezzling it. I wasn't responsible for what he did. I didn't kill you. I'm sorry you're dead, and I wish I could make it never to have happened but I can't. I did not kill you."

She looked around and waited for the voice to come back, for Tami Holden to argue that it was all Lola's fault. But she didn't. Lola wiped her streaming eyes and blew her nose and looked around one more time.

"I made a lot of mistakes." She picked up her purse, brushing it off as though to clean the memory of this dirty place from its supple surface. "But I didn't kill Tami Holden, and I don't have to spend the rest of my life drowning in guilt over her death. I didn't even know I was doing that, but I was and it's time to stop. Enough."

She was in her car ten minutes later and stopping at the same Starbucks where she got her first coffee that strange, terrible day after Orrin threw her out. It was gratifying to be just another customer, not the pathetic ragamuffin with the battered face she'd once been. She sat at a table, pulling out the laptop and completing her last-minute preparations. What were the people around her doing? Going over their tactical plans? She doubted it. Writing poetry, finishing marketing reports, writing their first or tenth or fiftieth novels or short stories or memoirs. No one looking at Lola would peg her activities now. What would they see, looking at her? Not Orrin's wife, that was for sure. Not a woman on the way to rescuing her beloved. She was wearing all black, it was true, and she was focused and serious. But she could have been planning a birthday party or composing an email to a financial advisor for all anyone knew.

Lola knew she was a different person from the punching bag who'd staggered in here back then and different from the passive recluse she'd allowed herself to become after that. If she survived the night, would she be different again? Or was she kidding herself? Would she always be, underneath, the pathetic excuse for a human being she'd allowed herself to become? As she headed out to the car with her untouched coffee and laptop bag, she felt the cool night air on her scalp. No more shroud of hair to hide behind. No more shroud of hair to hide the world from Lola. She'd been wallowing all that time and hadn't realized it. She'd let her guilt and shame and fear and self-pity build a wall around her, and she was finally ready to kick down that wall. She'd never forget Tami Holden, but she was done hiding behind Tami's death.

"I was carrying her around," Lola told the darkened night as she headed toward Highway 50. "It was making me sick inside, carrying her around like that. It infected me and my relationship with Del and everything. It stained me from the inside out."

"Now I'm ready," she announced to the blurry lane line, as she left the last lights of Folsom and headed up to the foothills. "Now I can save Del."

CHAPTER THIRTY-EIGHT

"Wake up."

Del resisted the urge to open her eyes. It was time to start thinking clearly and get out of here. She needed to know Janet's endgame and her mental state.

"I know you're awake, Addie."

Del's eyes shot open. Her shock over Janet's hard tone was even greater than her shock over Janet's use of Del's old nickname. Was she being deliberately cruel?

"I understand, you know."

Del eyed Janet, whose appearance would have seemed flawless from ten feet away. Up close, her mask was cracking. Her makeup was streaked with tears, her hair frayed, her fingernails bitten down to almost nothing and blood-tinged. The circles under her eyes were deep and dark, and she'd developed the lax skin of a much-older woman. Dehydration? Possibly. Del knew she herself was dehydrated.

"You feel powerless. So you're trying to scope things out. What do I want, how do you get over on me, it's natural to focus on that stuff."

Del tried to look innocent.

"It's not gonna work, Del. I don't begrudge you the attempt, but it's not going to work."

"What do you want?" Del's voice came out a raspy croak.

Janet pulled on a loose strand of hair. "There's a feeling you get when you surrender to the inevitable, my darling."

"What do you want?" Del tried to let her voice harden a bit, but it was again only a croak. Her throat hurt. She really was very thirsty, but there was some stubborn part of her that refused to beg for water. As she watched Janet play with her hair and gaze at her with eerie calm, though, her thirst began to overtake her stubbornness.

"We call it surrender, we think that's a show of weakness, but it's really oddly proactive. It's taking control by surrendering control."

Del regarded Janet blankly.

"I know it's confusing. But it's what has to happen or this'll never work." Janet made it sound so reasonable, as if she were talking about a recipe or car repair.

"What'll never work?"

Janet leaned over to kiss Del's forehead. "I have to save you, my darling. That way we can have a healthy relationship."

"What?" Del started to sputter but regained her composure. "What do you mean, you have to 'save' me?"

A thrill of fear ran through her at her own words. What the hell did Janet have in mind? Del flashed to a scene familiar to every movie-watching child of the late century—bad guy has good guy tied to a table or a railroad track or a board over a pool. There's some imminent threat—table saw or oncoming train or man-eating shark—heading ever closer to the trapped hero. The bad guy calmly explains his rationale for his mad schemes while the good guy seems doomed and helpless. Somehow, though, the hero finds a way out of the trap and saves the day.

I'm not gonna be able to save the day.

Del tried to swallow but couldn't. Her throat was thick and clogged with sobs. I'm so thirsty, she tried to say, not caring anymore about what a hero would do or how craven she sounded, but no sound came out. Not even a croak.

I can't even ask for water. How can I save the day?

"I can only save you if you let me."

Del turned her face to the wall. Her throat was on fire, and she should be trying to work Janet if only to get water, but she couldn't seem to control her emotions. It had been hours, maybe a full day, since Janet had given her a final kiss on the forehead and then left without a word. Now she was back, her face painted with sympathy and kindness and fatigue.

"Darling, please look at me. Sweetie?" Janet's voice was soft, warm, sweet. Janet was, Del figured, most dangerous when she was trying to be sweet.

If I make things too hard for her she might just leave me here again, this time for good.

Back when Del had been a patrol officer and dreamed of moving up to investigation, she'd done a lot of reading. She'd studied weapons, sexuality, finance, sociology, psychology, forensic science, anthropology and more. She had mostly studied death. She'd pored over pictures and descriptions of decomposed and decomposing bodies. She'd haunted the morgue, wanting a firsthand look at the human body after its various experiences. She'd studied what happened to the human body when it was stabbed, beaten, shot, drowned, strangled, raped, smothered, burned, overfed, saturated in drugs and alcohol, exercised or not. She'd also studied abuse of various kinds and read accounts of people who'd survived various tortures, abuse and neglect.

One account had haunted her for years, and she recalled it with disturbing clarity now. It was an interview with a woman who'd survived being locked in an underground cell by a serial rapist. Captured by police, the rapist had for nearly three weeks refused to divulge his victims' locations. He'd wanted, Del recalled, to negotiate for his own freedom in exchange for the lives of the women he'd left underground. Finally, investigators had managed to track down the victims. Del shuddered. She had imagined, reading the account years ago, that she could hear the broken, halting voice of the lone survivor. She could hear it as clearly now.

"The first three or four days without food were bad," the anonymous account related. "I thought it was terrible at the time, of course. I thought it hurt, those first few days."

The interviewer mentioned that the survivor laughed with great mirth and for a long time before continuing.

"It was the fifth day when things truly got terrible. I was cold all the time and my skin hurt. I got all twitchy and my back hurt a lot. I couldn't move very well after the first week or so. Everything hurt. I had a little water and I tried to make it last. Maybe I should have just drunk it all at once."

The interviewer asked if the survivor wished she'd died.

"Oh, gosh. Well, some days. I don't know. I guess not. I was the only one who lived, you know? It seems wrong to wish I died too. I guess."

The survivor had lost much of her hair. Her fingernails had splintered and peeled. She'd been unable to move and had gone into a dream state, drifting in and out of consciousness.

"The funny thing is that I got all flabby. My skin got loose and kind of wrinkly, and my muscles turned to nothing. But I was still flabby. Weird. In fact, I'll tell you, I felt fat—how crazy is that? I'd never felt fat before in my life."

The interviewer noted that the survivor again burst into raucous laughter.

"I kept looking at my stomach. My arms and legs were sticks but I had a flabby gut. I kept thinking how delicious it would be if I could just take one big, juicy bite out of my belly. It looked so good! Like a little pork bun or something. Sometimes I think about that, how I used to wonder what I would taste like. It sounds pretty crazy, I guess, but at the time it seemed perfectly reasonable. Like, it's flesh and fat, right? What's a hamburger? What's a steak? I bet my gut would have tasted pretty good."

Del had been haunted by that particular image for years, and it was alarmingly vivid now. She could clearly see herself in the young woman's place, staring down at her tummy, at the little mound of puff around her belly button. It wasn't hard to imagine seeing that tummy as a thing separate from herself, thinking it would be tasty.

The thing that had to happen was survival. That was all that mattered. Not her pride or her self-image or whatever it was that kept her turning away from Janet and failing to deal with her. Del forced herself to open her eyes and turn around.

"I'm thirsty," she tried to say, but her voice was gone. Janet seemed to understand, though, and she helped Del sit up and gave her what tasted like sweet tea.

"Thank you," Del whispered. She was absurdly grateful not to feel thirsty, but she also suddenly felt very hungry. She eagerly slurped Vietnamese porridge—a favorite from when they were together, Del noted vaguely—as Janet fed it to her with soothing words and loving murmurs.

Del was sleepy after eating, but she didn't feel drugged. Her stomach actually hurt a little from being overfilled, but it felt good.

"Feel better?"

Del nodded.

"I never wanted you to suffer, my darling. Things just took a little longer than I expected. I needed to get things ready for us. You forgive me, don't you, baby?"

Del nodded again. What did that mean, 'get things ready'? Ready for what?

"Now I won't have to leave you alone again, I promise, so you won't have to worry. I would never let anything bad happen to you. I would never let you starve to death."

"How did you know—?"

"You talk in your sleep, lover, at least when you've had a sedative." Janet laughed. "You certainly have a busy little mind, Del. You fascinate me, you always have." She sobered. "But I never meant to scare you."

"You kidnapped me, Janet." Del kept her voice low and her expression neutral. "You drugged me, you tied me up." She lifted her hands and wiggled her arms in the restraints. "You are keeping me here against my will. Maybe you didn't mean to leave me here alone too long. I get it. But this is hurting me. Don't you understand that?"

Janet took a long time to answer and Del held her breath. Had she pushed too hard? When Janet finally spoke, her voice was low and pleasant.

"I can see how this looks from your perspective. I just didn't know how else to help you." She made a face. "I'm not very good at explaining things, obviously."

"Do you really think this was the only way to get me to listen?" Del searched Janet's face.

"Well, kind of." Janet laughed. "You don't really listen, you know? I mean you could probably repeat back every word I've ever said to you. But you don't hear what I'm really saying."

"Try me."

Janet shook her head. "That's the thing. You're entrenched. You— you listen from inside, someplace I can't reach you. Like you're behind this wall of superiority and logic and verbal sparring, where nothing I say matters unless it jibes with what you already think."

"That's not fair, Janet."

"No, what's not fair is that you don't let yourself be influenced by what I say or think or do. You're so sure of yourself, your point of view is the only one that counts."

"No, I—"

"Didn't you do the same thing to Lola?"

Del let her head, which had been straining up without her noticing, fall back against the stale pillow. Had she done that? She closed her eyes. Maybe she had. She certainly had pushed Lola to do things she hadn't wanted to. She'd never meant to bully Lola, but maybe she had. Had she done it to Janet? It was harder to know that. She didn't have as clear a picture of their relationship, just little fragments of memories.

"I never meant to do that."

Janet's voice was gentle. "I know. That's why we're here. I know you can do better and so can I. You and Lola broke up for a reason, Del. She could never stand up to you like this. She doesn't have the strength to force you out of your comfort zone. I have the strength and the determination. We're here to shake things up and start over fresh. It's the only way we'll ever make it. And I want us to make it, lover."

"So do I."

Janet shook her head. "Not really, not right now. Right now, you'd say anything to get over on me. But at least this way we'll have a chance."

"What has to happen before you feel—?"

"Don't try to work me." Janet's voice hardened.

"I'm sorry." Del felt her stomach muscles tighten. Janet had some kind of plan, but what did it involve? How dangerous was she? Her behavior had always been erratic, at best, but Del would never have anticipated this.

"I'm sorry but it's the only way. You need to give up control, Del. And this is the only way I can come up with to help you do that."

Del felt tears leaking down the side of her face and into her hair. "Could I sit up, please?"

"Sure, honey. No problem."

As Janet helped prop her up with an extra pillow, Del felt the full measure of how helpless she truly was, and she fought the panic that ballooned in her stomach and pushed out all the porridge Janet had so carefully fed her.

CHAPTER THIRTY-NINE

The coffee was lukewarm by the time Lola turned off the highway and pulled over on a quiet road just north of Placerville. It was a cute little town full of restaurants and shops, a tourist attraction in the middle of a forest, and Lola thought she'd like to visit it sometime.

"If we survive," she said aloud. She went over her plan once more. She had several miles to drive before she reached Del and Janet, and she could have waited until she was closer to do a final review, but she was too nervous to take any chances. What if Janet had help? What if she had cameras or security people near where she was keeping Del?

There were, as Lola saw it, several scenarios she was likely to encounter. She had a plan for each of those she'd been able to think of, but what if she walked in to find something she hadn't anticipated? What if she blundered in and made things worse for Del? What if she got Del killed?

"Okay, enough," Lola whispered to herself. She checked the gun and made sure for the third time that it was loaded. She felt like a kid in a Halloween costume, and she wished she'd practiced wearing the things she'd found in Del's closet. The thigh holster was clearly adjusted for someone taller than Lola, though she'd jimmied the straps as much as possible. The fanny pack thing fit okay around her waist, but the stun gun and pepper spray were digging into her ribs—Del was obviously longer in the waist than Lola.

"It's fine," Lola told herself. "You'll be standing up, silly."

She was shaking. Was it fear or adrenaline? She couldn't have said. Maybe there wasn't a difference. Maybe the two things were too tied together to tease apart. It didn't matter, anyway. This was the point at which she either went ahead and did what she'd planned or decided not to. She pulled her cell phone out and called Del, hoping against hope she'd answer.

"Last chance," Lola croaked. But there was only ringing and then the voice mail prompt. And she'd known that, hadn't she? She'd known before pulling out the phone that there was no point. It was just a last-ditch effort to avoid what had to be done. Avoiding what had to be done had become Lola's specialty long ago. Pretending she didn't know what she needed to do. She started the car and calculated when she'd need to turn off the headlights. Maybe three miles out, she figured. She'd studied the maps and satellite photos well enough to have a good mental picture of what she could expect to see, at least outside.

"She's still alive. She's waiting for you to save her," Lola muttered, as the car's headlights bored tiny tunnels of light into the dark night. Reluctantly, she turned the headlamps off a few minutes later and turned down the dirt road that led to the back edge of Janet's—Hannah Jet's—property. The one advantage Lola had was surprise, and she wasn't about to squander it by announcing her presence while toodling down the half-mile long driveway. The hilly terrain of the satellite photos had seemed pastoral and safe, but here in the cold and dark of the real world Lola realized how unprepared she really was. The car groaned and squawked and struggled over the rocks and holes and gullies in what was less a dirt road than a long-disused trail. It was easier to imagine gold miners leading overloaded donkeys up this hill than anyone driving a car or even a truck up it.

"Slow down, it's getting worse." The last thing Lola needed was for the car to break down. She heard a clanking sound, insanely loud in the nighttime stillness, coming from under the car. She slowed to a crawl but went down into a low spot that made the car groan before it slammed into a huge bump. The car lurched to the side and stopped with an awkward growl. She sat idling for a moment, unsure what to do. The clanking sound had been much louder in her head than outside the car, surely. But what if she was wrong?

"I should have rented a truck," she muttered. But it was too late for such considerations now, wasn't it? She couldn't take the chance Janet would hear the car's noises, so she turned off the engine. The tiny flashlight Del had insisted on putting on her key ring turned out to be indispensable—Lola was able to do a final equipment check before easing open the car's door with only a low squeal. The dome light had died many years before, and now she was glad.

She headed up the road. It was a steep hill, and her breathing sounded labored within a few steps. She half expected to hear Orrin's derisive commentary at her pathetic lack of fitness and finesse, but he was silent. Maybe, Lola thought, letting go of Tami Holden meant letting go of Orrin too.

It took nearly an hour of trudging uphill before Lola reached the giant stump of a storm-split tree that marked the last short leg of her hike. She tried to ignore what felt like a thousand insects batting her face and body. Suddenly, she felt entirely inadequate to the task she'd set before herself.

She was sweating, and her lungs ached from the cold air and exercise. Her legs were shaking and she hadn't brought any water. She should, she realized, have brought the coffee from the car. But she hadn't, so she tried to collect spit in her mouth by thinking of water, which didn't actually help. Her feet hurt. Sneakers were not, it turned out, the best hiking shoes, especially in the rocky, uneven terrain of the foothills. She'd bruised one heel pretty badly halfway up the hill, landing too hard on a shard of something.

None of it mattered. There was a dim yellow light off to the left where Janet and Del were, and the sight of that yellow light made the cold and thirst and bruised heel and the bugs irrelevant. Lola stood by the stump for a minute or two to quiet her breathing and was reminded of the day she stood by Aunt Margie's front door and waited to quiet her breathing.

Thirty years ago, that was. Lola's throat closed a bit then. Aunt Margie was probably long dead, wasn't she? Along with her beloved Mrs. White. Beautiful and cool and sweet, with her soft hands and pink lips and warm eyes. They'd been in love, she'd eventually realized, but too afraid to be open about their relationship. If they hadn't been stuck in secrecy and shame, would Lola have been able to realize that loving another woman was all right? It was impossible to know.

I hope they were happy. I hope they got to live together somewhere and be happy for a long time.

She and Del had been able to live together, unlike Aunt Margie and Mrs. White. Lola wasn't exactly thrilled at the prospect of getting married again, but she and Del could build a life together if they didn't mess it up. Living in the Castro made things easier, of course, but

Lola was beginning to realize they could live wherever they wanted, do whatever they wanted, and not have to hide or lie or keep to themselves. She was absurdly grateful for this.

What if we'd been born fifty years earlier, or a hundred?

But they hadn't been born earlier. They'd been born at exactly the right time to meet each other and fall in love and build a life together, and the only thing getting in their way was their own thinking. All they had to do was figure out themselves and each other and what they wanted their life together to look like, and then they could build it. It seemed so simple suddenly. Walk toward the little porch lamp. Save Del. Rebuild their life together and do a better job this time. Just like that.

It seemed strangely homey, that soft light and its shroud of winged acolytes. Lola found it unnerving, the way the innocuous porch lamp made the whole place seem guiltless. Inside the trailer, there could be a nice little family, the loving parents just putting the kids to bed and chatting about the day. Or it could be an elderly couple, dozing in front of the blaring television and too stubborn to admit they were sleeping and just go to bed. But the image was a lie. There was no happy little family there, no sweet grandparents either. Del was in there being held against her will. She was either drugged or tied up or both.

All I have to do is rescue her from this madwoman, and then we can start over.

Lola grinned, closing her lips quickly when a large something flew into her front teeth. The bugs up here were monstrous, weren't they? And as the night grew darker, they were getting thicker.

Well, she thought, *what are we waiting for?* She crept along, hiding in the shadows and feeling foolish. Was anyone even looking outside?

By the time she got close enough to really worry about being seen, Lola was supercharged with adrenaline. She had to force herself to stop and crouch behind a low shrub. The trailer was, she knew from tax records, fifty-five feet long and twelve feet wide, about the size of a small apartment. The rooms were small, shotgun-style. Janet had bought the place a year earlier, at around the time Lola met Del. She'd had plenty of time to modify the structure as needed. Lola had imagined possibilities like locks on the doors, restraints, a variety of weapons. She didn't imagine Janet wanting to hurt Del, just control her. But Del's size and strength meant Janet needed to either drug Del or restrain her at all times.

If Lola managed to surprise Janet and subdue her, she still had to get Del out of there and in to town. Lola's car might or might not be operational. Janet's fancy red car was nowhere to be seen. Lola eyed the dark yard. There was something visible just beyond the trailer. A white truck, the one Del had just bought, it looked like. So Lola would need to get the keys to that once she'd subdued Janet. If she managed to do so. She pushed her body up and forward before self-doubt could eat away at her resolve.

She sneaked up to the trailer and peered sideways into the large front window to ensure she couldn't be spotted from inside. There was no one visible in either the kitchen or the living room, which were mostly bare of furnishings. Clearly, Janet didn't envision this as a romantic hideaway but as a training camp. This was the place she'd gotten to break Del. That was the plan, wasn't it? Lola had thought about this for a long time. Orrin broke Lola and it was easy. All he had to do was isolate her, scare her, make her think she was nothing. But Lola was a teenage girl with low self-esteem when Orrin met her. Del was no kid and she had a strong sense of self. She would be hard to break. How long did it take to make someone feel scared and weak and powerless? How long to break Del? If Lola managed to get Del away from Janet, would Del even want to leave?

Lola sidled along the outside of the trailer, eying the living room. She heard a strange hollering that sounded like a child, then a bang, like someone was slammed into a wall, and suddenly all her calm left her. She'd assumed Janet wouldn't physically harm Del. Apparently, she was wrong. Flinging her body toward the trailer's entrance, Lola forgot to be quiet. She yanked open the metal screen door and stopped short when she felt someone close behind her, close enough to tickle Lola's ear with hot, minty breath.

"Sterling?" Lola froze. She twisted her head to take in Sterling's amused, sardonic expression. It didn't matter. Del was here and someone was hurting her. Lola looked down and scrabbled for the gun in her thigh holster. She managed to get it out, but Sterling lunged forward, crushed Lola's fingers in her iron grip and took the gun away. Lola tried to fumble for the pepper spray, the knife, the stun gun, anything, but Sterling swung the pistol at Lola's face.

Lola tried to duck away, but the gun came at her too quickly, and she only managed to avoid some of its force. She was knocked into the sharp doorframe, and she was reminded of Orrin's sharp white doorframe and how she grabbed for it on the day he kicked her out.

How many times had Lola been hit in the face? Her nose was a little crooked from being broken a few times, and she was missing a molar that had been knocked out. It was amazing, Lola thought, trying to recover her sense of time and place, that she had a face left at all. She remembered looking at the mirror in the motel room. It had been hard to see herself in that reflection, hadn't it? Again she had the feeling of being sucked out of the present and into another time, but she fought it.

"Stay here," Lola mumbled, pushing herself into an upright position. She grappled with Sterling, but something was taken from the big belt she wore and then she was being hurt.

"Stud gud," she mushmouthed a few minutes later. Sterling had hit Lola with her own stun gun.

"Datsh nod good."

"Thought you'd play Rambo, huh?"

Sterling's smile, looming over Lola's blinking eyes, was actually friendly looking. That, Lola decided, was really scary. A lot scarier than an angry face. Friendly faces on lunatics were always a bad, bad sign.

"You think so?" Sterling's smile grew broader, and Lola realized she'd been speaking aloud. "Well, I guess you're probably right. Hunh, how about that? You learn something new every day."

"What did you do? Why are you two here?"

At the sound of Janet's voice, Lola twisted her head around and struggled to a sitting position. Sterling used her foot on Lola's chest to push her back onto the floor, and Lola watched Janet and Sterling eye each other. Who was in charge? It was hard to tell. Janet pointed an accusing finger at Sterling.

"You said you were taking her right away."

"Change of plans. I told you she would be the one."

"This messes up everything." Janet let her hands fall lax against her thighs. "I don't know what to do now."

Lola let her gaze wander between the two women. She needed to exploit what seemed to be a power struggle. Del was somewhere inside the little trailer, and the situation was too volatile.

Sterling shook Janet one more time. "Understand one thing. This is my mission, and you are only here as a favor from me. You know this."

Janet nodded.

"Go get your cop."

Janet nodded again and slipped away, and Sterling stood watching Lola for a moment. Lola tried to clear her head and come up with a new game plan. Had Janet arranged for Lola to meet Sterling? How were Janet and Sterling connected? Who was really in charge? Was Janet playing Sterling? Were they playacting for some reason?

"I like to see how your mind tries to put it all together." Sterling's smile was easy. She was relaxed. She clearly thought she was in charge, but was she? "I really do like you. Dark, clever, more resilient than most. But still in need of my redemption. Sometimes I think you're the one, but I'm not sure."

"And you get to decide? You're in charge?" Lola heard the archness in her own tone but didn't soften it with a smile. Maybe strength was all Sterling understood. Could Lola back up her words?

Sterling laughed. She hoisted Lola up and shook her lightly. "I've been playing all three of you for a long time. You don't even know it's a game, do you?"

"What are you playing for?"

Sterling smiled broadly. "I like that. Most people would ask what the game is. But your mind is a dark, twisted place. I wish you had passed the tests, even one. Then you would be free and we could be friends."

"What tests?"

Sterling shook her head. "Not for you to know right now."

Lola frowned. "You never answered my question."

"What does everyone play for?"

Lola considered. "Love. Money. Power. Fun."

"None of the above."

"Please explain it to me. Maybe I can help you."

"*You* help me? Well, maybe. But the fact is that you have demonstrated an appalling lack of ability to take care of yourself, so now I have to take over. You've left me no choice."

"She's ready," Janet called from the edge of the hallway. She had Del in a kind of wheelchair.

"Lola?" Del gaped.

Sterling inclined her head. "If you talk, you get a shot that makes you go nighty-night. Do you want to go nighty-night, cop?"

Del shook her head.

"Good."

Janet cleared her throat. "Sterling, I—"

Sterling shook her head and Janet stilled.

"Everybody freeze for one minute. I have to get something from the truck."

Lola felt a flip in her stomach and swallowed hard. Her face was throbbing, her head swimming. Sterling had hurt her carelessly, casually. She would hurt Del too, with more pleasure because Del was a worthier opponent. Lola waited until Sterling yanked the door open with a metallic screech and slammed it shut behind her. Sterling had left the three of them alone, and Lola wasn't sure why. She eyed Janet.

"I thought you loved her." Lola gestured at Del. "How could you do this?"

Janet shook her head. "I didn't mean to hurt her. I—"

"We don't have time for that. Sterling is nuts. You have to let Del go before Sterling decides she's too much of a threat and kills her."

Janet's eyes welled up. "You think you know her? You think you know me? You don't know anything."

"So tell me. We need to get Del safe. Please help me do that." Lola searched Janet's eyes. Was there a sane person under there?

"She is safe. That's part of the deal."

"Safe? You've tied her up. Obviously you've been starving her. She looks half dead!"

Janet's gaze drifted to Del's drawn face. "It'll be better soon."

"Sterling is crazy. How do you even know her? Why would you let such a dangerous person around Del?" Lola stopped and caught her breath. "We don't have time for this. You have to help me get Del away from that lunatic."

"She's not a lunatic."

Lola's face must have communicated something, because Janet's twisted. "She's a little unstable. But it's okay. I know how she thinks. She'd never hurt Del, and it'll all be okay. I promise." She turned away from Lola and shrugged at Del. "I swear, baby."

"I don't understand why you'd do such a crazy thing, and with someone like this." Del was gazing up into Janet's face, clearly as bewildered as her whispered words suggested.

Janet's eyes filled and she shrugged.

"It's hard to explain, baby. I know it looks bad. But Sterling saved my life. I couldn't handle everything. It was so hard. I was hurting so much, and she saved my life. We were both in the hospital, I had taken too many pills, I guess, and they had all these therapy things, pottery, painting, photography, and Sterling was amazing. She took pictures of everything, and she took pictures of me, and I couldn't believe how clearly she saw me. She used her camera and showed me who I really am. It's hard to explain, Del. She saw through everything to the real me, and I needed that. I needed her lens to be my eyes. I wanted to be my real self with you. I tried, I really did. But I was weak. And now here we are. I needed her help and I'm even able to help her sometimes. She's braver than I am. She's willing to do whatever's necessary, and I'm not always strong enough. You just don't get her. She's not going to hurt anyone. She helps people, baby. She's different, sure, but artists often are. You should know that. Marco, he's an artist. You should understand."

"She's gonna kill Lola. Whatever she told you, however she tricked you into helping her, you tying me up is so she can do whatever she wants to Lola without worrying about me stopping her."

Janet shook her head. "No, it seems like that, but it's not. Things are—complicated."

"So explain them." Del seemed to be trying not to cry.

Lola stepped forward. "I'll go with Sterling, get her to take me somewhere else. Just let Del go after we leave, please?"

Janet reached out as if to touch Lola. "I'm sorry. I can't do that. Things are already past that point."

"No, they're not." Lola struggled to think, ignoring the whanging pain in her face and head. "Let Del go, that's all you have to do. We'll take care of the rest."

"Please, you know this is wrong." Del's fingers flexed, like she was trying to gesture, and all three of them looked at Del's trapped hand.

Janet seemed torn, and Lola held her breath for an interminable moment. *This is it. This is when Del finds out whether Janet loves her enough to do what's best for Del instead of what's best for herself.*

Please let her pick Del's happiness over her own. Please let her show Del she loves her more than her own self. Please let her show Del it was worth loving her so she can stop feeling like a fool.

Janet suddenly lunged toward Del with something shiny in her hand. Lola, fearful for Del's safety, had nearly reached them when she realized Janet was cutting Del's restraints with a pocketknife, and Del was shaking her arms and struggling to stand even as Janet struggled with the ties around her ankles.

"Hold it, almost got it," Janet huffed. She'd gotten all but Del's left foot free when the squeal of the doorknob alerted them to Sterling's return. Janet was still hacking at the last plastic tie when the door swung open with a crash.

CHAPTER FORTY

Del was tangled up in Lola and Janet, who shrank back against her when Sterling came strolling in brandishing a Glock 19. A slightly smaller version of the macho 9mm, another model Del liked too. Del could barely feel her limbs and nearly toppled but felt both Janet and Lola brace her. They weren't cowering away from Sterling and her weapon, they were trying to protect her from Sterling. She felt their love brimming over and spilling out onto her. She could do anything, defeat any enemy—if she could only keep her feet! Del staggered against the two women who struggled to hold her up, but they fell in a heap against the back wall of the trailer.

"Aw, how touching." Sterling didn't seem surprised Janet had released Del. In fact, she seemed almost pleased. She was relaxed, but her grip on the Glock 19 was steady. She held the weapon like someone who knew guns well enough to be confident. Was she an amateur shooter or did she have some professional experience? Had she been the one who shot Del? At the moment, that seemed pretty likely.

"You knew she'd let me go," Del murmured.

Sterling blushed, seeming bashful. "I hoped, but you can never be sure. You know." She looked directly at Del. "You're good at reading people too. That's one of the things I like about you. I was really pulling for you and her." She gestured at Lola.

Del nodded as though she understood what was going on. Obviously, whatever relationship existed between Janet and Sterling, Janet wasn't in on all of it.

"What are you talking about? What's going on?" Janet backed away from Del, and her eyes bounced between Del and Sterling.

"She set you up." Del grimaced. "I don't get the whole game, but—"

"I passed!" Janet screamed this, and Del saw Lola cover her ears. "I passed, you said! You said I passed!"

Sterling ignored Janet and eyed Del. "Take her." She gestured at Lola. "I was hoping she would win."

"This was a test?" Janet was hysterical, screaming, her breath heaving, her body curling in on itself. "You were testing me *again*? How could you do this to me?"

Del nodded at Sterling. "You're just letting me and Lola leave?"

Sterling smiled. "So you'd leave her here?" She pointed the Glock at Janet.

"What are my choices?" Del fought for calm and shrugged. "You shoot me, you hurt Lola or you hurt Janet. I'm not sure what else I can do."

Janet sank into a bundle of limbs on the floor. "No, you're right, go. I never meant, I didn't want to hurt anyone. It's better this way. Sterling, I don't understand all of this. You said we were friends. Said I was special to you. That you wanted to help me. That you wanted my help. Why didn't you just leave me alone? I would have been better off dead. Been able to rest. I'm so tired! Just leave, Del, it's better that way."

"See? There you go, off the hook." Sterling's easy grin seemed to quell the last of Janet's will. Del watched Janet curl into a helpless ball and start chewing a thumbnail. Del also eyed Sterling's weapon hand. It had to be getting tired.

"What're you gonna do with her?" Del noticed her voice sounded disinterested.

"What do you care?"

Del shrugged again. "If I'm leaving her to her death, I'd like to say goodbye. If you're just gonna mindfuck her, whatever."

"I like that, mindfuck. Did you tailor that to me?" Sterling tilted her head. "You're very good at that, figuring out where people are coming from and using that against them."

"So are you," Del admitted. "What's your background? Military? Law enforcement? Some government training, I'd guess."

Sterling laughed so hard her weapon hand dropped a few inches. "You're so transparent! I love that. All cop, all the time. Can you ever turn it off?"

"No, I guess not." Del shook her head, using the gesture to cover a quick survey of the room. What could she use as a weapon? A glint of metal on the floor near Janet's quivering figure caught Del's gaze, and she forced herself to continue her visual sweep without pause.

"I'm not mad," Sterling insisted. "You can't help what you are. We are who we are, and we can't change it. That's why I have to do what I do." She nodded as if agreeing with herself.

"What do you do?"

"Are you taking off or not?"

Del nodded. She pulled Lola close and eased between her and Sterling. "We're going. Janet, I'm sorry. I have to save Lola."

There was no response.

Del shuffled toward the door in tandem with Sterling's progress away from it. It felt like some strange, ritualistic dance, the two women circling around some invisible no-man's land between them, eyes locked, bodies contorted in defensive postures.

"We can't leave her," Lola mumbled this into Del's neck.

"It's okay," Del murmured, not taking her eyes off Sterling's. The Glock wavered only slightly as Sterling completed her semicircular journey.

"No, it's not."

"Lola!"

Lola shrank away at the anger in her tone and Del held her more firmly. She steered them both out the open trailer door and backed down the stairs, not taking her gaze from Sterling's face until the last possible moment. She hustled Lola farther from the trailer, ignoring her slight resistance, and waited until they were a good thirty yards down the hill before letting Lola stop her.

"What are you doing? You can't leave Janet alone with that woman!"

"Shhh. Hey, look at me." She guided Lola's face with gentle hands. "Look at me. I'm going back. I'm not gonna just leave her, of course not. I just wanted to get you safe. We're gonna give it a few minutes, then you're gonna start walking back the way you came. Just keep walking until you hear from me."

"What are you going to do, fight with Sterling? She has a gun and you don't. She's at full strength and you're weak as a kitten. Del, it's not that I don't have faith in you, I just want to understand your plan."

Del's smile was genuine. "I love you," she blurted and gently dabbed away Lola's sudden tears.

"I love you too, and that's why I want to know. I'm not just walking away while you run into the line of fire. You wouldn't let me, would you?"

"Of course not. But I have a plan. Janet is a lot stronger and more resilient than Sterling realizes. You know how she was cutting me free? She's staying close to that little knife, and I bet she's playing possum until I'm there to distract Sterling. I know how to disarm her, and I know exactly how Janet and I can get over on her. All I need is the element of surprise and Janet's got us halfway there."

"You're going to work with Janet to overpower Sterling. Don't you think she's anticipated that?"

Del smiled. "I'm counting on it."

CHAPTER FORTY-ONE

Lola watched Del sneak back up the hill and let out her breath with a sigh. Everything would be all right now. She'd bought enough time to ensure Del and Janet would be safe. She turned and nodded at Sterling, hidden behind the clutch of bushes nearby, then followed her down the rest of the way toward the black SUV that loomed before her far too quickly. It wasn't until they'd jounced along the dirt road for a few minutes that Sterling tossed the handcuffs into the backseat. Lola slid them into place, chilled by the metal against her wrists.

"How long ago did you figure it out?" Sterling sounded amused, disinterested.

"It seemed strange, your leaving us alone with Janet. But I wasn't sure until you started playing with Del. 'You're so good at reading people,' all that stuff."

"But the cop didn't pick up on it."

Lola waved around her shackled hands in a vague gesture. "She's not at her best, you know. Being kidnapped and starved and whatnot, plus Janet and me together in the same place? It's a lot to process."

Sterling nodded. She seemed distracted now, and Lola sat back against the leather upholstery and eyed Sterling's quarter profile. She was sore all over and very tired, and she let herself doze as they headed south on the 50. She figured she had a few hours at the most, and she wanted to be as well rested as possible. It would be easier, she thought as she drifted off, to just relax completely and accept that this was the end, but she knew Del better than that.

"She's going to come and find me," she murmured, only dimly aware that Sterling was listening.

"Try to find you." Sterling's chuckle rang with overconfidence, and Lola frowned as she drifted off.

If Sterling was right, then fine. Del would be traumatized by Lola's death, but Janet would be there, and Tom and Tess and Lin and Marco and Phil. They would all reassure her that she'd done everything she could, that it wasn't her fault. Oh, she'd have a hard night now and then, but Janet would comfort her. She loved Del and Del loved her, and they would be alive to recover from the whole thing together.

There was a nagging doubt at the back of Lola's sleepy mind, and it followed her into sleep: what if she does find me? But she figured Sterling was probably right. How in the world would Del ever figure out they were going to the marina? By the time they reached it, Lola had recovered enough of her strength and awareness to feel every ache in her head and body. She stared at the little boat and made a face.

"Did you name it?"

"Her." Sterling snorted a laugh. "You call a boat a her. And yes, I did."

"The *deus ex machina*? Like in a play?"

Sterling waited until she'd finished fiddling with a rope and some stuff in a cupboard and was seated across from Lola in the stern. "Spoils it all if I have to explain it."

They bounced along the relatively calm waters of the inner bay for a while, and Lola looked up at the dark sky.

"Did you wait for a waning moon because it would be darker?"

"Plus I like the poetry of it."

"Ah." They were far enough from land that Lola could see the lights along the shoreline as a pattern. "It's beautiful."

Sterling followed her gaze and pointed southeast. "See that cluster over there? Pacifica."

Lola craned her neck to look. What was Sterling trying to tell her? She waited until Sterling's voice sounded again. Now it was softer, hesitant.

"From the outside, we were okay, you know? Just another family. Nothing special."

"But?"

"But my life was hell. Every day, every night. You know the details. I know your life. You and I, we survived the same hell. Janet too. That's what binds us."

Lola let that sink in. She had a hundred questions but wanted to let Sterling talk.

"Then you look at the same cluster again, and you know." Sterling pointed. "This one is a nice family, good people. That one is a monster, beats his wife. That one is a sweet old lady. A couple of nice, dotty sisters live in the next one. And the one next to that, the lady will kill herself to make sure she cannot abuse her kids. From here, they look all the same."

"From here, you can pretend they're who you want them to be."

Sterling's smile was wide and warm. It was the smile of a lonely, lonely soul who's finally found a kindred spirit, and Lola found herself crying for the woman whose pain and isolation rendered such small kinship so joyful. "See, I knew. I knew you would understand."

Lola reached out to touch Sterling's hand, and the handcuffs scraped Sterling's knuckle. "Oh, sorry."

Sterling shook off the apology. "I can't take them off. I hope you understand."

Lola nodded. "Would it be okay…? I mean, I accept that I'm dying here, I'm not trying to trick you. I just want to know what's going to happen and why. Is that okay? Would you mind telling me?"

"Oh, I will. I just want to get out a little farther."

"You've done this before, I take it?" Lola fought the deep chill that her own words, uttered so coolly, brought. Seeing her shudder, Sterling snagged a thick jacket and arranged it carefully around Lola's shoulders.

"That better? Good. I do want to you be comfortable, if that doesn't seem strange."

Lola shook her head. "Thank you."

Again, Sterling smiled with relief. "You can't know how long I've waited to hear those words."

"'Thank you?'"

Sterling nodded. "Usually lost girls are scared. They try to negotiate, bargain, plead for their lives. Offer me money, sex, drugs. All kinds of crazy stuff."

"They don't understand what you're giving them."

"Exactly!"

"Didn't understand."

Sterling's smile was truly brilliant this time and Lola grinned in response. "Right. Didn't—understand. Anyway, I've wanted to be done for a long time."

"You're tired."

Sterling's laugh was hysterical. "That can't even begin to cover it. I'm—"

"Weary."

Sterling leaned close. "I know there's every possibility you're playing me. But I've waited my whole life for someone who understands me, and I can't tell you how happy I am that I found you."

"I'm not playing you, Sterling."

"Can you tell me what you think we're doing out here? Then I can fill in the gaps."

"I think you want to save women who've suffered the way we've suffered, you and me and Janet. Women who've been hurt too much, and now we're just not right."

"Spoiled."

"Yes." Lola took a deep breath. "Like my paper dolls that got wet."

Sterling was crying. "They're never the same."

"No, they're not. Only they don't know that. They keep trying. They keep wanting to be real."

"But they're not real, not anymore." Sterling's sobs choked her and Lola whispered her next words softly.

"So you set them free."

"Yes." Sterling rubbed her eyes. "I set them free."

"You see a woman who's like us and you watch her to make sure."

"I don't want to take an innocent by accident."

Lola smiled gently. "I know. You're very careful. You arrange to meet her and you give her tests. Like Janet said."

"Yes."

"She thought she passed, but she didn't."

Sterling mouthed the word "no."

"And I failed them too."

"Yes. Just like the others."

"The others you saved." Lola waited for Sterling's vague nod before continuing. "So you make sure she's one of us. You take her picture. You follow her around and look at her life."

Sterling nodded slowly. "I have to be sure. The patterns are very consistent, you know. The little choices, the big ones, people think their lives are in their own hands. But free will is an illusion, Lola. We make the choices we are forced to make."

"Forced by our genes, our early lives, Fate, whatever." Lola nodded in understanding as she spoke. "We get railroaded and don't even know it. We're puppets." Lola held out her shackled hands as though she were controlling little marionettes.

"I have to make sure, you know. I didn't take as long with you. I have been there nearly every minute with you. When you went to the marina with that guy that night, I almost had to laugh. You'd seen me on the boat, did you remember?"

"Not then. Not until later."

"Remember the homeless woman?" Sterling smirked at Lola's shocked face. "Yup, that was me. Pretty good disguise, huh? I saw you. I thought my friend, I thought Janet was just pointing me at you because she wants the cop back. But I saw you and I knew you were the one. My special angel. Even if you don't realize it yet. I had to be sure. Just like with the others."

"You find them, somehow. And then you bring them here. You figure out a woman is one of us, one of us who's lost, and you watch her and you take her picture. You make sure and then you bring her here. You give her medicine, maybe?"

"So she can relax and not be upset." Sterling's voice was that of a child, wondering and dreamy and relaxed.

"You don't want to scare her or hurt her."

"Of course not."

"And then you baptize her. She goes to sleep and you wash her in the salt water—it's cleansing, isn't it? And then she's clean again."

"And?"

Lola finished. "And then she doesn't have to suffer any more."

"I knew," Sterling crowed. "I knew you were the one."

"Because the one girl you really wanted to save, all that time, was you."

Sterling hugged herself. "But I couldn't."

"Not without saving as many of us as you could first."

"But now I can be done. Now I can rest."

"Yes," Lola said with a loving smile. "Now you can rest."

"I'm a little scared," Sterling admitted. "There's a reason I drugged them. There's a reason. So scary and cold. I don't want to feel anything."

"Neither do I," confessed Lola. "I hope you brought enough medicine for both of us."

"Well, no." Sterling looked embarrassed. "I can't have the medicine. How would I get you overboard? I have to just deal with drowning awake."

Lola looked around the deck of the small craft. Everything was stowed neatly and polished to a high shine. The two women sat in silence for several minutes, and Lola finally shook her head. "I don't think it's right."

"What do you mean?"

"You've been helping your sisters—how many?"

"Nine, not counting you and me."

"Nine sisters have gotten the fresh start they deserve without a moment's fear or suffering. Why don't you deserve the same?"

"Listen, if this is some kind of trick—"

Lola shook her head. "It's not a trick. I just think there's got to be a better way. What are you planning to do, let me do a Sleeping Beauty dive, then follow me into the drink? You have to be cold and scared and alone? No, that's not fair."

Sterling shrugged. "I knew this was how it would end. It took so long, but—"

"We could share it. Each take half the dose. Then we're sleepy and relaxed and you don't have to suffer nearly as much."

"I can't do that, Lola. I have a sacred duty. I can't take the chance that you may suffer needlessly. I'm here for you. Yes, I want to die too, but my first responsibility is to you."

"Are you straight?"

"Maybe. Why did you ask? Does it matter?"

Lola shrugged. "I guess, I was just wondering if you saw this as a sort of Romeo and Juliet kind of thing. You know? Two lovers torn apart by the cruddy world they live in? Death is the only way?"

"Huh." Sterling cocked her head. "I guess I see it more like a bouquet for Ophelia."

"Yeah, okay. Well, Ophelia, I think you deserve more than freezing to death, scared and alone, in the dark."

"It's what I deserve."

"I don't think so, Sterling. I think you suffered just like we did, and I think you've dedicated yourself to saving our sisters and me. That means you should get the peace and release you deserve."

Sterling shook her head vigorously, and Lola frowned at her.

"Why not?"

"I killed them. My babies."

Lola nodded slowly. "But maybe they were better off?"

"Yes." Sterling offered a sad smile. "I'm certain of that. It's the one, I didn't remember, you see."

"I don't see. What one?"

"My daughter. It was too late by the time I knew I was pregnant. They kicked me out because of her. But I was going to keep her. I thought my boyfriend—but he was just like the others. I thought she died when he pulled me out of the car, but she didn't. She didn't die. They took her because I was a minor and my parents signed her away and got me to sign her away or forged my signature or something. I don't remember. I was pretty fucked up all the time then. Only she was alive and they put her in the system. And I didn't even know. I should have known, don't you think? That she was alive, somewhere out there? I should have sensed it."

Lola sat back and let the jacket slip off her shoulders. "But you didn't. How did you find out about her?"

"She died."

"How do you know? How did you find out?"

Sterling shrugged. "I just knew. By then I was clean and I just knew things. Nobody had to tell me."

"So you think you have to pay for her suffering. For not knowing she was alive and not protecting her."

"Doesn't that seem reasonable?"

Lola waggled her head. "You believe in an afterlife, right? Well, doesn't the way you die change who you are? Won't you be reunited with your daughter? Don't you want to meet her in a state of peace and love rather than fear and anger?"

Sterling eyed Lola suspiciously. "Don't demean us both with games, sister."

"I guess I am a little scared. I understand it's got to happen, but I still feel scared. I'm a coward. I just want to go together instead of alone. Is that so bad?" Lola stood slowly on shaking legs and turned to face the open waters of the Pacific Ocean. She didn't dare look at Sterling but kept her gaze on the rising swells that glistened in the faint moonlight.

Sterling stood next to Lola and rubbed her back. "I appreciate you thinking about me, but—"

Lola didn't think about it. She just eased the second, smaller stun gun out of her pants pocket and gripped it tightly in her left hand. She'd practiced using the thing for a long time, worried she might accidentally shock herself, and she ran through the practice and the online instruction manual carefully for a few seconds before pressing the business end of the stun gun into Sterling's hip. She kept it pressed hard against Sterling even as the taller woman convulsed and flopped to the floor—deck, Lola corrected herself—and twitched into unconsciousness.

Standing there in the vast loneliness of the ocean with her kidnapper lying helpless at her feet and the knowledge that nine innocent women were dead somewhere beneath her, Lola considered her options. Even handcuffed, she could get Sterling over the side before she awoke. No one would ask many questions. After all, they could have struggled. There could have been a moment when somehow, as they fought, Lola managed to get a lucky break and shove Sterling. Sterling could have gone overboard that way. She was, after all, a serial killer. No one would question it. Even if they wondered, deep in their hearts, they would never pester Lola about their doubts. Because, they would think, killing a monster was a kind of public service, right?

But that was the thought that kept Lola from actually doing what she was considering. Sterling believed, truly believed, she had saved those women. She thought of herself as their savior. As a doer of public service.

So in the remaining seconds before Sterling could again become a threat, Lola used her restrained hands to truss Sterling using the neatly coiled rope in one of the stow bins under the bench and to find the hypodermic needle and the little glass jar in the small medicine bag and administer the premeasured dosage to keep Sterling asleep. She steered the little boat as close to shore as she dared, then drifted for a while until she could calm down enough to call for help. Someone, she never quite figured out who, talked her through dropping anchor in a safe place.

Waiting for the rescue boat to pick her up, Lola watched Sterling's sleeping face. She was childlike. Round cheeks, dark curls, relaxed mouth. She would go to prison, Lola figured. What would she become there? What would she do to the women in the prison? Lola had always assumed women were usually in prison because they'd killed an abusive husband or boyfriend or father. If that was true, and she wasn't sure it was, were those women more likely to have been abused as children? Would Sterling feel compelled to "save" them too?

"Who could you have been? If your parents hadn't hurt you, would you still have been a monster?" The question haunted Lola. Weeks later, after life had resumed a less hectic pace, Lola would find herself looking in the mirror and wondering why she was herself and Sterling was who she was.

CHAPTER FORTY-TWO

"You okay?"

Lola nodded and smiled, but she was clearly deep inside her own head, as usual these days. All through finding out Lola was still alive, through the arrests and trial preparations and sentencing, Del had been watching Lola, waiting for her to return from the landscape of her thoughts, but it wasn't happening. Thanksgiving and Christmas went by with all the appropriate food and decorations and gifts at both of their homes, and through it all Del felt like she was doing a scene in a play, acting alongside a robot.

"I miss you," she blurted one day.

Lola turned, her face a mask of surprise and confusion. "What? I'm right here."

Del shook her head. "No, you're not. You're out on that boat or somewhere. But you're not here."

Lola smiled and came close, rubbing Del's arms. "I'm a little shaken up, that's all. Does it seem so strange?"

"I guess not." But it was.

Day after day, Del tried everything. She was patient, loving and kind. Attentive but not hovering. Loving but not demanding. It was exhausting and it didn't make a difference. It had been more than a month since Sterling and Janet were sentenced in their separate trials, and Lola was still fathoms deep and unreachable and frustratingly, painfully polite.

Things had more or less returned to normal, though only on the surface. No one was stalking Lola, no one was moving crap around in Del's house, no one was taking pictures of Lola everywhere she went. Even Marco was stalker free, at least for time being. Creepy Ray Stowe had faded into anonymity again, so Del was able to put that worry aside for the moment. Would he show up at some point? Del had a feeling Stowe was like any other bad guy. As long as he was breathing, he was a potential threat. But he did seem easily scared off and easily bored. All Del could do for the moment was wait to see if and when that particular bad penny might turn up again.

If he hadn't happened to go to—or maybe planned to accidentally show up at—the same gallery as Lola and Marco, would Del have even known about Sterling? Or would the lunatic have been able to take Lola and kill her? Del tried not to think too hard about that. How many more women would Sterling have murdered if Lola hadn't stopped her? A dozen? More?

It was still impossible for her to believe Janet had actually done all the things she was supposed to have done: conspired with a serial killer, kidnapped Del and drugged her, deliberately brought Lola to the murderer's attention in hopes of getting rid of her. The Janet Del remembered falling in love with was smart, funny, vulnerable and kind. She was also, Del reminded herself, fully capable of justifying lies, manipulation and game playing whenever they served her best interests. Maybe she was as good at lying to herself as she was at lying to other people. Wasn't that the secret to being a good liar? You had to be able to convince yourself of the lie before you could convince anyone else.

Del couldn't reconcile her Janet with the woman who'd set up Lola to be killed. Or with the pale, gaunt scarecrow she'd watched sit passively in the courtroom, a silent specter who'd simply pleaded guilty and waited for sentencing. Del had almost felt sorry for Janet's overpriced lawyer, whose hands had clearly been tied by his uncooperative client. It had been strange, a little side note of weirdness, feeling bad for a defense lawyer.

Sterling's overpriced attorney had tried an insanity defense, of course, but the prosecutor was good and the public appalled. There was nothing like a female criminal, Phan observed one day, to stir up the community's outrage. Sterling's sugar-daddy husband had died of heart failure the night of her arraignment, and his children spent some of their father's considerable estate providing the press with salacious and unflattering details about the woman who'd managed to enthrall their doddering old dad and cut them out of his life. She'd been convicted not only of the nine kidnappings and murders but also of the attempted murder of a police officer, arson, and attempted murder.

Sterling sure had been a busy girl, and her lawyer had been busy, too. Del still couldn't believe Janet was going to Chowchilla while the murderer was going to Corona. While she was glad they wouldn't be at the same prison, it hardly seemed fair to Del that Janet had to deal with the overcrowded, gang-infested mess of the larger facility while Sterling got special treatment down south. But wasn't that always how it was? If you had a good lawyer, you got a better deal. Justice wasn't so much blind as turning a blind eye. At least Sterling would never get parole.

Del sat at the kitchen table reading an article about the treatment of female offenders on the new tablet Lola had given her for Christmas. When Lola unexpectedly rested her hands on her shoulders and kissed the top of her head, she tried not to react.

"Are you back?"

Lola settled onto Del's lap. "Getting back. I had to dive into Sterling's head, you know? It was a bad place."

"How did you know what to do?"

Lola shrugged. "She and I clicked. I don't know how to explain it. When I met her at that restaurant that day, it was like meeting someone I used to know. Like I recognized her. She was nuts, but she wasn't evil, Del. I feel like she and I and Janet, we had something in common."

Del stared. "You're nothing like either of them. I don't get what you're saying."

Lola shrugged and nestled her head against Del's collarbone, and Del let the subject rest for a moment. Should she press it?

"So...What about her? What did you recognize about Sterling and you and Janet?"

Lola sat up and waggled her head. "I don't know how to say it. I had this whole thing about paper dolls I was thinking of. I don't know."

"Paper dolls?" Del held back judgment. Sometimes Lola got to the right place in a pretty roundabout way.

"When they get wet, they're ruined. You know? Structurally, they're never the same. Like a car with a salvage title. Moth-eaten fabric. Spoiled food." Lola made a face. "Sterling talked about being abused. She—you know this from the trial, Del—she picked women who were 'spoiled' like that, 'cause she figured they could never be happy."

Del frowned. "You think that's true? You think you can never be happy? That anyone who's been abused or a victim of violence is ruined forever? Don't tell me you believe you're 'damaged goods' or some garbage like that."

Lola was silent a moment. "Not exactly. I think maybe some people are more resilient than others. Genetically or because they have a good support system or whatever. But even if you're not that good at recovering, I think you still can. It just takes a lot of courage and a lot of hard work. And maybe that hard work never ends. Maybe your whole life, you have to keep working hard to move past the bad stuff. And it's never easy. It doesn't seem to get easier."

"I don't know what you mean."

"Don't you? You got shot, Del. You got kidnapped. I think you will be dealing with the aftermath of those things for a while. And I get the idea your childhood wasn't exactly Disneyland and lollipops. So there may be some garbage from back then too. Maybe we're both a little banged up, maybe we could work on getting over things together. We could help each other. I want to do that. I want to help you and for you to help me. Can't we do that? Doesn't that seem like it's worth looking at?"

Del shook her head. "I have two choices here: either I sit in the corner rocking and sucking my thumb, or I get my shit together and do my job. You caught a serial killer, Lola, one I couldn't. But the one thing I can do is deal with my garbage like a grown-up. And I intend to do that."

"But isn't the grown-up thing to face things directly?"

"I don't need hours of navel gazing to face what happened. Things got a little fucked up, fine. Now they're better. Done."

"Maybe you are different from me. Maybe it really does all roll off your back like nothing. But I don't think so. I think people find weird ways of dealing with stuff they're not even aware of."

"What's that supposed to mean?" Del couldn't keep the sharpness out of her tone.

Lola stood and walked toward the window, facing out for a full minute before turning to face Del. "Have you considered the possibility that you didn't take care of your shoulder after getting shot because you wanted to punish yourself for cheating?"

Del gaped. "What?" She shook her head. "That's nuts, Lola. No way. What kind of neurotic mess do you think I am?"

Lola shrugged. "Okay, maybe I'm wrong."

"You are."

"Okay."

Del realized she was glaring only when Lola broke eye contact and hugged herself. Del pushed her hair off her forehead.

Nice job, asshole. Bully the woman, why don't you? You were supposed to protect Lola, and all you managed to do was let Janet come and ruin our relationship, let her get almost killed by a lunatic, and then act like she was supposed to be over the whole thing in five minutes. Nice.

She gestured Lola to her and pulled her back into her lap. There was a long silence, and Del savored Lola's safe, comforting presence.

"Maybe you should go see her. The prison's only a few hours away." Lola's voice was muffled by Del's pullover.

"Janet? Hell, no. That bitch can rot in hell for all I care."

"But—"

"End of discussion, Lola. I mean it."

Lola dropped it, of course, but having heard the idea Del couldn't seem to put it away. She tried to picture sitting across the table from Janet. Tried to picture Janet locked up in a prison for the rest of her life. Her fingernails would be ragged, her hair a mess. Was she safe? She was tiny and vulnerable and beautiful, a rough combination in prison. Del shut her eyes tight to block out the images of Janet as a victim, but they returned to her over and over.

"Maybe I will," she announced one morning, breakfasting at Lola's table.

"See Janet?" Lola responded as though the conversation had taken place over the course of a few minutes instead of a few weeks, and Del smiled. Maybe Lola wasn't as out to lunch as she seemed.

"What would you think of that?"

Lola smiled. "You'll never know until you do it."

"What if it's worse than I imagine?"

"What if it's not?"

"My shoulder's gotten a lot better," Del mused. "I could take the bike. Unless you want to come with me. Then we should take the truck."

"Go by yourself but take the truck, it's more comfortable," Lola urged. "Make it a little vacation. Chowchilla's not far from Fresno, right? You could go see if your folks are still there."

Del made a face. "What made you think of that? Why would I want to go see them? That's nuts. If I wanted to know where they were—if they're even alive—I could use the computer."

"I know." Lola's smile was gentle, and it melted Del's bristling.

"I guess I could overnight it. Stay in Fresno after going to the prison. Swing by in the morning, see what's what. Odds are the whole place is an apartment complex or shopping mall or something by now."

"Maybe."

"But maybe I'll just see with my own eyes." Del mused, thinking back to Mrs. Wendell's house and the chaste tree and the lawns she had mowed around that neighborhood. She remembered the little stray animals and kids she was always picking up and trying to take care of. "We lived in an apartment for a while before the trailer. That might still be there."

"Who knows?"

"Yeah." Del nodded. "Maybe I'll do that. Sure you don't want to come with?"

It was Lola's turn to nod. "This is your trip to take, Del. And I'll be here when you get back."

Her tone was final, and Del was surprised to find herself nodding. She'd worried for months about walking all over Lola, who seemed so pliable much of the time. But she had managed to outthink all of them: Janet, Del and Sterling. And there was no way Del would be able to talk Lola into going with her to see Janet. She'd managed to get Del to agree to go see Janet in the first place, a thing Del wouldn't have considered on her own. Maybe Lola was a lot less prey than predator. Del shook off the thought. Lola was finding a little spine, that was all. No biggie.

"What'll you do while I'm gone?" Del asked, and Lola shrugged her shoulders. She seemed to be less wary than before, and Del had to wonder whether that was a matter of Lola's having gained some self-confidence or a matter of her not caring as much about Del.

"Nothing exciting. Write, you know, laundry, paint the laundry room."

"Why do I have the feeling something's going on with you?"

Lola shook her head. "Because you're freaked about being kidnapped, about Sterling, about seeing Janet. Who wouldn't be? You still expect me to be mad and jealous and all that. But I'm not. I love you. I get that you loved Janet, and you still do. That's okay. I don't blame you for it. You need closure with her, Del. And I promise, I will be here when you get back."

Before she knew it, Del was sitting in her truck, waving at Lola through the rearview. She'd caught up on paperwork, explained her trip to Phan, had her awkward little thank-you-for-closure-I'm-sorry-for-your-loss meeting with Mrs. Wilson, gotten approval to use some accrued vacation time and packed her single duffel bag. Somehow, the weeks between Lola's suggestion and the actual trip seemed to take only seconds. Del wasn't even sure she wanted to go anymore, but she no longer felt she had a choice. Lola wanted her to go and she was going. What was that about? What did Lola want her to do? Was this a test? Had Del already failed it by agreeing to go?

Del decided to let it go. She should go see Janet. They never really dealt with anything, did they? And whether Lola really wanted her to go or not, she'd suggested it. So, okay. The more important question was, what did Del want out of the trip? She thought about all the time she'd spent with Janet and all the time she'd spent thinking about Janet. The latter outweighed the former by a lot. What did that mean? What would happen when she saw Janet in prison? Was Janet expecting her? What would Janet read into Del's coming to see her? How much of going to see her was about their relationship as a whole and how much was about being kidnapped by Janet?

Do I still love her?

"I guess I'll know when I see her."

The other part of the trip, the part about maybe going to see her parents, or where they used to live, or maybe going to some cemetery or whatever, that part was a little too big to think about. As was the Lola question. Where were they headed? And were they headed there together? When Del came back, would she see in Lola's eyes the dismissal she half expected? Was she still in love with Del? Would she really still be waiting when Del got back?

Del found a country station on the radio and cranked up some Dwight Yoakam to drown out her thoughts. That worked for a good while. Dwight had some help from Reba, Willie, the Hanks and the Judds. Dolly did her best, and so did Lyle and Roy. But distraction can only do so much, and after a while Del had to work to stay focused on the music. A single question shadowed Del's heartbeat and whatever song was playing on the radio on the long, lonely trip down the interstate.

Will she?

Bella Books, Inc.

Women. Books. Even Better Together.

P.O. Box 10543
Tallahassee, FL 32302

Phone: 800-729-4992
www.bellabooks.com